AMERICAN NEGRO
SHORT STORIES

EDITED BY John Henrik Clarke

AMERICAN CENTURY SERIES
HILL AND WANG • NEW YORK

Manufactured in the United States of America

FIRST EDITION SEPTEMBER 1966
SECOND PRINTING (FIRST AMERICAN CENTURY
   SERIES EDITION) JANUARY 1967
THIRD PRINTING OCTOBER 1967
FOURTH PRINTING MARCH 1968
FIFTH PRINTING JUNE 1968
SIXTH PRINTING SEPTEMBER 1968
SEVENTH PRINTING DECEMBER 1968
EIGHTH PRINTING FEBRUARY 1969

To my daughter, Nzingha Marie

ACKNOWLEDGMENTS

The editor wishes to thank all authors, publishers, agents, and other copyright holders for permission to reprint the stories in this book. Specific acknowledgment for the use of each story is given below.

"On Being Crazy" by W. E. B. Du Bois. Copyright © 1907 by W. E. B. Du Bois. Reprinted by permission of Shirley Graham Du Bois.

"The City of Refuge" by Rudolph Fisher. Copyright © 1924 by Rudolph Fisher. Reprinted by permission of Jane Fisher.

"The Overcoat" by John P. Davis. Copyright © 1928 by John P. Davis. Reprinted by permission of the author.

"Truant" from *Gingertown* by Claude McKay. Copyright © 1932 by Harper & Brothers; renewed 1960 by Hope McKay Virtue. Reprinted by permission of Harper & Row, Publishers.

"A Summer Tragedy" by Arna Bontemps. Copyright © 1933 by Arna Bontemps. Reprinted by permission of the author.

"The Gilded Six-Bits" by Zora Neale Hurston. Copyright © 1933 by *Story Magazine*. Reprinted by permission of *Story Magazine*.

"Bright and Morning Star" by Richard Wright. Copyright © 1938 by Richard Wright. Reprinted by permission of Paul R. Reynolds, Inc., 599 Fifth Avenue, New York 17, N.Y.

"The Boy Who Painted Christ Black" by John Henrik Clarke. Copyright © 1940 by John Henrik Clarke. Reprinted by permission of the author.

1887
1890
1938
1946
1952
1963

CONTENTS

[xi

Contents

INTRODUCTION

The people of the United States, in general, have been reluctant to accept the fact that this is a multi-ethnic nation, and the literature of this nation, when it is honestly seen and understood, reflects this fact. What is called American Negro Literature remains the least understood of that massive body of writings that is called American Literature.

Until recently the contribution of Negro writers to the development of the American short story has been sadly neglected. In view of the evidence of this contribution, extending from the latter part of the nineteenth century to the present day, this neglect is not excusable.

After the initial poetical debut of Jupiter Hammon and Phillis Wheatley in the 1760's, the main literary expression of the Africans who were brought to the United States against their will was the slave narrative. The best known of these slave narratives was written by Frederick Douglass, one of the foremost personalities in the antislavery movement. The first half of the nineteenth century was a period of great pamphleteering on social issues in the United States. The free Negroes in the North and those who had escaped from slavery in the South made their mark on this time and awakened the conscience of the nation. The lack of formal education among these first Negro writers lent their narratives a strong and rough-hewed quality.

It was not until 1887 that a Negro master of the short story form emerged. This writer was Charles W. Chesnutt. Chesnutt, an Ohioan by birth, became a teacher in North Carolina while

still in his middle teens. He studied the traditions and super-
stitions of the Negroes of that state and later used this material
in his best short stories.

Paul Laurence Dunbar, a contemporary of Charles W. Chesnutt, made his reputation as a poet before extending his talent
to the short story field. Both Dunbar and Chesnutt very often
used the same folk material as subject matter for their stories.
Chesnutt and Dunbar in their day reached a larger general
reading audience than any of the Negro writers who came before
them. The period of the slave narrative had passed. Yet, the
Negro writer was still an oddity and a stepchild in the eyes of
most critics. This attitude continued, in a lessening degree,
throughout the richest and most productive period in Negro
writing in the United States—the period called the Negro
Renaissance, which was mainly the years between 1921 and
1931.

The community of Harlem was the center and spiritual god-
father and midwife of this renaissance. The cultural emanci-
pation of the American Negro that began after the First World
War was now in full force. The Negro writer discovered a new
voice within himself and liked the sound of it. The white writers
who had been interpreting Negro life with an air of authority
and a preponderance of error looked at last to the Negro writer
for their next cue. In such short story collections as Jean
Toomer's *Cane* (1923) and Langston Hughes's *The Ways of
White Folks* (1934), the life of the Negro was presented in an
interesting manner that was unreal to some white readers
because it was new and so contrary to the stereotypes that they
had grown accustomed to.

In *Mules and Men* (1935), Zora Neale Hurston presented a
collection of folk tales and sketches that showed the close relationship of humor and tragedy in Negro life.

In the midst of this renaissance, two strong voices from the
West Indies were heard. Claude McKay in *Ginger-Town* (1932)
and *Banana Bottom* (1933) wrote of life in his Jamaican
homeland, debunking the travelogue exoticness usually at-
tributed to the Caribbean area. Before the publication of these
books, Harlem and its inhabitants had already been the subject matter for a group of remarkable short stories by McKay
and the inspiration for *Home to Harlem* (1928), still the most
famous novel ever written about that community.

In 1926, Eric Walrond, a native of British Guiana, explored and presented another side of West Indian life in *Tropic Death*. In these ten naturalistic stories Eric Walrond concerned himself mostly with life in the Panama Canal Zone, where a diversity of people and ways of life meet and clash.

Rudolph Fisher, a doctor and writer, was another bright star of the Harlem Renaissance. The new light touch he brought to his stories of Negro life did not hide his essential seriousness. The message in his comic realism was more profound because he skilfully wove it into the design of his stories without destroying any of their entertainment value.

During this period of a literary flowering, Harlem became the Mecca, the stimulating Holy City, drawing pilgrims from all over the country and from abroad. Four men, W. E. B. Du Bois, James Weldon Johnson, Alain Locke, and Sterling A. Brown, guided the movement without becoming a part of the social-climbing and pseudo-intellectual aspect of it. As editor of the magazine *The Crisis*, W. E. B. Du Bois introduced many new writers and extended his helpful and disciplining hand where it was needed. James Weldon Johnson, as a participant and one of the historians of the Harlem literary movement, helped appraise and preserve the best that came out of it. Alain Locke, then head of the Department of Philosophy at Howard University, fostered and encouraged every meaningful aspect of the movement and became its major interpreter. His anthology *The New Negro* (1925) is a milestone and a guide to Negro thought, literature, and art in the middle twenties. Sterling A. Brown, as teacher and critic, called attention to the values of Negro writing and trained a generation of students to appreciate those values.

Opportunity, then edited by Charles Johnson, and *The Crisis* were the major magazine outlets for new Negro writers. The yearly *Opportunity* short story contest provided a proving ground for such competent young writers as Cecil Blue, John F. Matheus, Eugene Gordon, Marita Bonner, and Rudolph Fisher.

In 1936 "Big Boy Leaves Home," Richard Wright's first short story to receive any appreciable attention, appeared in the anthology *The New Caravan*. "The Ethics of Living Jim Crow: An Autobiographical Sketch" was published in *American Stuff* (Anthology of the Federal Writers' Project) the next year. In 1938 when his first book, *Uncle Tom's Children*, won a five-hundred-dollar prize in a contest conducted by *Story*, his talent received national attention. With the publication of his phenomenally successful novel, *Native Son*, in 1940, a new era in Negro literature had begun. Here, at last, was a Negro writer who wrote considerably better than many of his white contemporaries. As a short story craftsman he was the most accomplished Negro writer since Charles W. Chesnutt.

After the emergence of Richard Wright the double standard for Negro writers was over. Hereafter Negro writers had to stand or fall by the same standards used to evaluate the work of white writers. The era of the patronized and pampered Negro writer had at last come to an end. In the final analysis the closing of this era may be Richard Wright's greatest contribution to the status of Negro writers and to Negro literature.

In the years before and immediately following the emergence of Wright, the pleading tone—prevalent in many short stories by earlier Negro writers—disappeared. Now the tone was insistent and demanding. The first short stories of Ralph Ellison exemplify the new tone and vitality of the Negro short stories of this period. (A contribution from Mr. Ellison is regretfully missing from this anthology solely because I could not obtain permission to use any of his work.)

During the Second World War the short stories of Ann Petry began to appear in *The Crisis* while she was working as a reporter for *The People's Voice*.

The Negro Caravan, edited in 1941 by Sterling Brown, Arthur P. Davis, and Ulysses Lee, the best anthology of Negro literature since Alain Locke's *The New Negro* (1925), appeared with much new material. The collection included work by Chester B. Himes, who turned out a number of remarkable short stories while working in shipyards and war industries in California. In 1944 Himes received a Rosenwald Fellowship to complete his first novel, *If He Hollers Let Him Go*. In 1945 Frank Yerby won an O'Henry Memorial Award for his excellent short story, "Health Card," that had been published in *Harper's*.

A new crop of Negro writers was emerging. In their stories they either treated new aspects of Negro life or brought new insights to the old aspects. Principally, they were good storytellers, even if they did have a message to impart to their readers. The weepy sociological propaganda story (so prevalent during the Depression era) had had its day with Negro and all other writers. There would still be protest stories, but the protest would now have to meet the standards of living literature.

Opportunity and *The Crisis*, once the proving ground for so many new Negro writers, were no longer performing that much needed service. The best of the new writers found acceptance in the general magazines. Richard Wright took up residence in Paris and never returned to the United States to live.

When Richard Wright died in Paris in 1960 a new generation of Negro writers, partly influenced by him, was beginning to explore, as Ralph Ellison said, "the full range of American Negro humanity." In the short stories and novels of such writers as James Baldwin, John O. Killens, Paule Marshall, Mary Elizabeth Vroman, Frank London Brown, Albert Murray, William Melvin Kelley, LeRoi Jones, Martin Hamer, and Ernest J. Gaines, both a new dimension and a new direction in writing is seen. They have questioned and challenged all previous interpretations of American Negro life. In so doing they have created the basis for a new American literature.

JOHN HENRIK CLARKE

May, 1966

AMERICAN NEGRO SHORT STORIES

The Lynching of Jube Benson

PAUL LAURENCE DUNBAR

Gordon Fairfax's library held but three men, but the air was dense with clouds of smoke. The talk had drifted from one topic to another much as the smoke wreaths had puffed, floated, and thinned away. Then Handon Gay, who was an ambitious young reporter, spoke of a lynching story in a recent magazine, and the matter of punishment without trial put new life into the conversation.

"I should like to see a real lynching," said Gay rather callously.

"Well, I should hardly express it that way," said Fairfax, "but if a real, live lynching were to come my way, I should not avoid it."

"I should," spoke the other from the depths of his chair, where he had been puffing in moody silence. Judged by his hair, which was freely sprinkled with gray, the speaker might have been a man of forty-five or fifty, but his face, though lined and serious, was youthful, the face of a man hardly past thirty.

"What! you, Dr. Melville? Why, I thought that you physicians wouldn't weaken at anything."

"I have seen one such affair," said the doctor gravely; "in fact, I took a prominent part in it."

"Tell us about it," said the reporter, feeling for his pencil and notebook, which he was, nevertheless, careful to hide from the speaker.

The men drew their chairs eagerly up to the doctor's, but for a minute he did not seem to see them, but sat gazing abstractedly into the fire; then he took a long draw upon his cigar and began:

"I can see it all very vividly now. It was in the summertime and about seven years ago. I was practicing at the time down in the little town of Bradford. It was a small and primitive place, just the location for an impecunious medical man, recently out of college.

"In lieu of a regular office, I attended to business in the first of two rooms which I rented from Hiram Daly, one of the more prosperous of the townsmen. Here I boarded and here also came my patients—white and black—whites from every section, and blacks from 'nigger town,' as the west portion of the place was called.

"The people about me were most of them coarse and rough, but they were simple and generous, and as time passed on I had about abandoned my intention of seeking distinction in wider fields and determined to settle into the place of a modest country doctor. This was rather a strange conclusion for a young man to arrive at, and I will not deny that the presence in the house of my host's beautiful young daughter, Annie, had something to do with my decision. She was a girl of seventeen or eighteen, and very far superior to her surroundings. She had a native grace and a pleasing way about her that made everybody that came under her spell her abject slave. White and black who knew her loved her, and none, I thought, more deeply and respectfully than Jube Benson, the black man of all work about the place.

"He was a fellow whom everybody trusted—an apparently steady-going, grinning sort, as we used to call him. Well, he was completely under Miss Annie's thumb, and as soon as he saw that I began to care for Annie, and anybody could see that, he transferred some of his allegiance to me and became my faithful servitor also. Never did a man have a more devoted adherent in his wooing than did I, and many a one of Annie's tasks which he volunteered to do gave her an extra hour with me. You can imagine that I liked the boy, and you need not wonder any more that, as both wooing and my practice waxed apace, I was content to give up my great ambitions and stay just where I was.

"It wasn't a very pleasant thing, then, to have an epidemic of typhoid break out in the town that kept me going so that I hardly had time for the courting that a fellow wants to carry on with his sweetheart while he is still young enough to call her his girl. I fumed, but duty was duty, and I kept to my work night and day. It was now that Jube proved how invaluable he was as coadjutor. He not only took messages to Annie, but brought sometimes little ones from her to me, and he would tell me little secret things that he had overheard her say that made me throb with joy and swear at him for repeating his mistress's conversation. But, best of all, Jube was a perfect Cerberus, and no one on earth could have been more effective in keeping away or deluding the other young fellows who visited the Dalys. He would tell me of it afterwards, chuckling softly to himself, 'An', Doctah, I say to Mistah Hemp Stevens, " 'Scuse us, Mistah Stevens, but Miss Annie, she des gone out," an' den he go outer de gate lookin' moughty lonesome. When Sam Elkins come, I say, "Sh, Mistah Elkins, Miss Annie, she done tuk down," an' he say, "What, Jube, you don' reckon hit de———" Den he stop an' look skeert, an' I say, "I feared hit is, Mistah Elkins," an' sheks my haid ez solemn. He goes outer de gate lookin' lak his bes' frien' done daid, an' all de time Miss Annie behine de cu'tain ovah de po'ch des a-laffin' fit to kill.'

"Jube was a most admirable liar, but what could I do? He knew that I was a young fool of a hypocrite, and when I would rebuke him for these deceptions, he would give way and roll on the floor in an excess of delighted laughter until from very contagion I had to join him—and, well, there was no need of my preaching when there had been no beginning to his repentance and when there must ensue a continuance of his wrong-doing.

"This thing went on for over three months, and then, pouf! I was down like a shot. My patients were nearly all up, but the reaction from overwork made me an easy victim of the lurking germs. Then Jube loomed up as a nurse. He put everyone else aside, and with the doctor, a friend of mine from a neighboring town, took entire charge of me. Even Annie herself was put aside, and I was cared for as tenderly as a baby. Tom, that was my physician and friend, told me all about it afterward with tears in his eyes. Only he was a big, blunt man, and his expressions did not convey all that he meant. He told me how Jube had nursed me as if I were a sick kitten and he my mother. Of how fiercely he guarded his right to be the sole one to 'do' for me, as he called it, and how, when the crisis came, he hovered, weeping but hopeful, at my bedside until it was safely passed, when they drove him, weak and exhausted, from the room. As for me, I knew little about it at the time, and cared less. I was too busy in my fight with death. To my chimerical vision there was only a black but gentle demon that came and went, alternating with a white fairy, who would insist on coming in on her head, growing larger and larger and then dissolving. But the pathos and devotion in the story lost nothing in my blunt friend's telling.

"It was during the period of a long convalescence, however, that I came to know my humble ally as he really was, devoted to the point of abjectness. There were times when, for very shame at his goodness to me, I would beg him to go away, to do something else. He would go, but before I had time to realize that I was not being ministered to, he would be back at my side, grinning and puttering just the same. He manufactured duties for the joy of performing them. He pretended to see desires in me that I never had, because he liked to pander to them, and when I became entirely exasperated and ripped out a good round oath, he chuckled with the remark, 'Dah, now, you sholy is gittin' well. Nevah did hyeah a man anywhaih nigh Jo'dan's sho' cuss lak dat.'

"Why, I grew to love him, love him, oh, yes, I loved him as well—oh, what am I saying? All human love and gratitude are damned poor things; excuse me, gentlemen, this isn't a pleasant story. The truth is usually a nasty thing to stand.

"It was not six months after that that my friendship to Jube, which he had been at such great pains to win, was put to too severe a test.

"It was in the summertime again, and, as business was slack, I had ridden over to see my friend, Dr. Tom. I had spent a good part of the day there, and it was past four o'clock when I rode leisurely into Bradford. I was in a particularly joyous mood and no premonition of the impending catastrophe oppressed me. No sense of sorrow, present or to come, forced itself upon me, even when I saw men hurrying through the almost deserted streets. When I got within sight of my home and saw a crowd surrounding it, I was only interested sufficiently to spur my horse into a jog trot, which brought me up to the throng, when something in the sullen, settled horror in the men's faces gave me a sudden, sick thrill. They whispered a word to me, and without a thought save for Annie, the girl who had been so surely growing into my heart, I leaped from the saddle and tore my way through the people to the house.

"It was Annie, poor girl, bruised and bleeding, her face and dress torn from struggling. They were gathered round her with white faces, and oh! with what terrible patience they were trying to gain from her fluttering lips the name of her murderer. They made way for me and I knelt at her side. She was beyond my skill, and my will merged with theirs. One thought was in our minds.

" 'Who?' I asked.

"Her eyes half opened. 'That black———' She fell back into my arms dead.

"We turned and looked at each other. The mother had broken down and was weeping, but the face of the father was like iron.

" 'It is enough,' he said; 'Jube has disappeared.' He went to the door and said to the expectant crowd, 'She is dead.'

"I heard the angry roar without swelling up like the noise of a flood, and then I heard the sudden movement of many feet as the men separated into searching parties, and laying the dead girl back upon her couch, I took my rifle and went out to join them.

"As if by intuition the knowledge had passed among the men that Jube Benson had disappeared, and he, by common consent, was to be the object of our search. Fully a dozen of the citizens had seen him hastening toward the woods and noted his skulking air, but as he had grinned in his old good-natured way, they had, at the time, thought nothing of it. Now, however, the diabolical reason of his slyness was apparent. He had been shrewd enough to disarm suspicion, and by now was far away. Even Mrs. Daly, who was visiting with a neighbor, had seen him stepping out by a back way, and had said with a laugh, 'I reckon that black rascal's a-running off somewhere.' Oh, if she had only known!

" 'To the woods! To the woods!' that was the cry; and away we went, each with the determination not to shoot, but to bring the culprit alive into town, and then to deal with him as his crime deserved.

"I cannot describe the feelings I experienced as I went out that night to beat the woods for this human tiger. My heart smoldered within me like a coal, and I went forward under the impulse of a will that was half my own, half some more malignant power's. My throat throbbed drily, but water or whisky would not have quenched my thirst. The thought has come to me since, that now I could interpret the panther's desire for blood and sympathize with it, but then I thought nothing. I simply went forward and watched, watched with burning eyes for a familiar form that I had looked for as often before with such different emotions.

"Luck or ill-luck, which you will, was with our party, and just as dawn was graying the sky, we came upon our quarry crouched in the corner of a fence. It was only half light, and we might have passed, but my eyes caught sight of him, and I raised the cry. We leveled our guns and he rose and came toward us.

" 'I t'ought you wa'n't gwine see me,' he said sullenly; 'I didn't mean no harm.'

" 'Harm!'

"Some of the men took the word up with oaths, others were ominously silent.

"We gathered around him like hungry beasts, and I began to see terror dawning in his eyes. He turned to me, 'I's moughty glad you's hyeah, Doc,' he said; 'you ain't gwine let 'em whup me.'

" 'Whip you, you hound,' I said, 'I'm going to see you hanged,' and in the excess of my passion I struck him full on the mouth. He made a motion as if to resent the blow against such great odds, but controlled himself.

" 'W'y, Doctah,' he exclaimed in the saddest voice I have ever heard, 'w'y, Doctah! I ain't stole nuffin' o' yo'n, an' I was comin' back. I only run off to see my gal, Lucy, ovah to de Centah.'

" 'You lie!' I said, and my hands were busy helping others bind him upon a horse. Why did I do it? I don't know. A false education, I reckon, one false from the beginning. I saw his black face glooming there in the half light, and I could only think of him as a monster. It's tradition. At first I was told that the black man would catch me, and when I got over that, they taught me that the devil was black, and when I recovered from the sickness of that belief, here were Jube and his fellows with faces of menacing blackness. There was only one conclusion: This black man stood for all the powers of evil, the result of whose machinations had been gathering in my mind from childhood up. But this has nothing to do with what happened.

"After firing a few shots to announce our capture, we rode back into town with Jube. The ingathering parties from all directions met us as we made our way up to the house. All was very quiet and orderly. There was no doubt that it was, as the papers would have said, a gathering of the best citizens. It was a gathering of stern, determined men, bent on a terrible vengeance.

"We took Jube into the house, into the room where the corpse lay. At the sight of it he gave a scream like an animal's, and his face went the color of storm-blown water. This was enough to condemn him. We divined rather than heard his cry of 'Miss Ann, Miss Ann; oh, my God! Doc, you don't t'ink I done it?'

"Hungry hands were ready. We hurried him out into the yard. A rope was ready. A tree was at hand. Well, that part was the least of it, save that Hiram Daly stepped aside to let me be the first to pull upon the rope. It was lax at first. Then it tightened, and I felt the quivering soft weight resist my muscles. Other hands joined and Jube swung off his feet.

"No one was masked. We knew each other. Not even the culprit's face was covered, and the last I remember of him as he went into the air was a look of sad reproach that will remain with me until I meet him face to face again.

"We were tying the end of the rope to a tree, where the dead man might hang as a warning to his fellows, when a terrible cry chilled us to the marrow.

" 'Cut 'im down, cut 'im down; he ain't guilty. We got de one. Cut him down, fu' Gawd's sake. Here's de man; we foun' him hidin' in de barn!'

"Jube's brother, Ben, and another Negro came rushing toward us, half dragging, half carrying a miserable-looking wretch between them. Someone cut the rope and Jube dropped lifeless to the ground.

" 'Oh, my Gawd, he's daid, he's daid!' wailed the brother, but with blazing eyes he brought his captive into the center of the group, and we saw in the full light the scratched face of Tom Skinner, the worst white ruffian in town; but the face we saw was not as we were accustomed to see it, merely smeared with dirt. It was blackened to imitate a Negro's.

"God forgive me; I could not wait to try to resuscitate Jube. I knew he was already past help; so I rushed into the house and to the dead girl's side. In the excitement they had not yet washed or laid her out. Carefully, carefully, I searched underneath her broken fingernails. There was skin there. I took it out, the little curled pieces, and went with it into my office.

"There, determinedly, I examined it under a powerful glass, and read my own doom. It was the skin of a white man, and in it were embedded strands of short brown hair or beard.

"How I went out to tell the waiting crowd I do not know, for something kept crying in my ears, 'Blood guilty! Blood guilty!'

"The men went away stricken into silence and awe. The new prisoner attempted neither denial nor plea. When they were gone, I would have helped Ben carry his brother in, but he waved me away fiercely. 'You he'ped murder my brothah, you dat was his frien'; go 'way, go 'way! I'll tek him home myse'f.' I could only respect his wish, and he and his comrade took up the dead man and between them bore him up the street on which the sun was now shining full.

"I saw the few men who had not skulked indoors uncover as they passed, and I—I—stood there between the two murdered ones, while all the while something in my ears kept crying, 'Blood guilty! Blood guilty!' "

The doctor's head dropped into his hands and he sat for some time in silence, which was broken by neither of the men; then he rose, saying, "Gentlemen, that was my last lynching."

desire for acceptance
white man can be wrong

On Being Crazy

W. E. B. Du Bois

It was one o'clock and I was hungry. I walked into a restaurant, seated myself, and reached for the bill of fare. My table companion rose.

"Sir," said he, "do you wish to force your company on those who do not want you?"

No, said I, I wish to eat.

"Are you aware, sir, that this is social equality?"

Nothing of the sort, sir, it is hunger—and I ate.

The day's work done, I sought the theatre. As I sank into my seat, the lady shrank and squirmed.

I beg pardon, I said.

"Do you enjoy being where you are not wanted?" she asked coldly.

Oh no, I said.

"Well you are not wanted here."

I was surprised. I fear you are mistaken, I said, I certainly want the music, and I like to think the music wants me to listen to it.

"Usher," said the lady, "this is social equality."

"No, madame," said the usher, "it is the second movement of Beethoven's Fifth Symphony."

After the theatre, I sought the hotel where I had sent my baggage. The clerk scowled.

"What do you want?"

Rest, I said.

"This is a white hotel," he said.

I looked around. Such a color scheme requires a great deal of cleaning, I said, but I don't know that I object.

"We object," said he.

Then why, I began, but he interrupted.

"We don't keep niggers," he said, "we don't want social equality."

Neither do I, I replied gently, I want a bed.

I walked thoughtfully to the train. I'll take a sleeper through Texas. I'm a little bit dissatisfied with this town.

"Can't sell you one."

I only want to hire it, said I, for a couple of nights.

"Can't sell you a sleeper in Texas," he maintained. "They consider that social equality."

I consider it barbarism, I said, and I think I'll walk.

Walking, I met another wayfarer, who immediately walked to the other side of the road, where it was muddy. I asked his reason.

"Niggers is dirty," he said.

So is mud, said I. Moreover, I am not as dirty as you—yet.

"But you're a nigger, ain't you?" he asked.

My grandfather was so called.

"Well then!" he answered triumphantly.

Do you live in the South? I persisted, pleasantly.

"Sure," he growled, "and starve there."

I should think you and the Negroes should get together and vote out starvation.

"We don't let them vote."

We? Why not? I said in surprise.

"Niggers is too ignorant to vote."

But, I said, I am not so ignorant as you.

"But you're a nigger."

Yes, I'm certainly what you mean by that.

"Well then!" he returned, with that curiously inconsequential note of triumph. "Moreover," he said, "I don't want my sister to marry a nigger."

I had not seen his sister, so I merely murmured, let her say no.

"By God, you shan't marry her, even if she said yes."

But—but I don't want to marry her, I answered, a little perturbed at the personal turn.

"Why not!" he yelled, angrier than ever.

Because I'm already married and I rather like my wife.

"Is she a nigger?" he asked suspiciously.

Well, I said again, her grandmother was called that.

"Well then!" he shouted in that oddly illogical way.

I gave up.

Go on, I said, either you are crazy or I am.

"We both are," he said as he trotted along in the mud.

(Lynching of Jube
(desire for acceptance - Jube & white man) 1907

slight protest

The Goophered Grapevine

CHARLES WADDELL CHESNUTT

We alighted from the buggy, walked about the yard for a while, and then wandered off into the adjoining vineyard. Upon Annie's complaining of weariness I led the way back to the yard, where a pine log lying under the spreading elm afforded a shady though somewhat hard seat. One end of the log was already occupied by a venerable-looking colored man. He held on his knees a hat full of grapes, over which he was smacking his lips with great gusto; and a pile of grapeskins near him indicated that the performance was no new thing. We approached him at an angle from the rear, and were close to him before he perceived us. He respectfully rose as we drew near, and was moving away, when I begged him to keep his seat.

"Don't let us disturb you," I said. "There is plenty of room for us all."

He resumed his seat with some embarrassment. While he had been standing, I had observed that he was a tall man, and though slightly bowed by the weight of years, apparently quite vigorous. He was not entirely black, and this fact, together with the quality of his hair, which was about six inches long and very bushy, except on the top of his head, where he was quite bald, suggested a slight strain of other than Negro blood. There was a shrewdness in his eyes, too, which was not altogether African, and which, as we afterwards learned from experience, was indicative of a corresponding shrewdness in his character. He went on eating his grapes, but did not seem to enjoy himself quite so well as he had apparently done before he became aware of our presence.

"Do you live around here?" I asked, anxious to put him at his ease.

"Yas, suh. I lives des ober yander, behine de nex' san'hill, on de Lumberton plank-road."

"Do you know anything about the time when this vineyard was cultivated?"

"Lawd bless you, suh, I knows all about it. Dey ain' na'er a man in dis settlement w'at won' tell you ole Julius McAdoo 'uz bawn en raise' on dis yer same plantation. Is you de Norv'n gemman w'at's gwine ter buy de ole vimya'd?"

"I am looking at it," I replied; "but I don't know that I shall care to buy unless I can be reasonably sure of making something out of it."

"Well, suh, you is a stranger ter me, en I is a stranger to you, en we is bofe strangers ter one anudder, but 'f I 'uz in yo' place, I wouldn't buy dis vimya'd."

"Why not?" I asked.

"Well, I dunno whe'r you b'lieves in conj'in' er not—some er de w'ite folks don't, er says dey don't—but de truf er de matter is dat dis yer ole vimya'd is goophered."

"Is what?" I asked, not grasping the meaning of this unfamiliar word.

"Is goophered—cunju'd, bewitch'."

He imparted this information with such solemn earnestness and with such an air of confidential mystery that I felt somewhat interested, while Annie was evidently much impressed, and drew closer to me.

"How do you know it is bewitched?" I asked.

"I wouldn' spec' fer you ter b'lieve me 'less you know all 'bout de fac's. But ef you en young miss dere doan' min' lis'nin' ter a ole nigger run on a minute er two w'ile you er restin', I kin 'spain to you how it all happen'."

We assured him that we would be glad to hear how it all happened, and he began to tell us. At first the current of his memory—or imagination—seemed somewhat sluggish; but as his embarrassment wore off, his language flowed more freely, and the story acquired perspective and coherence. As he became more and more absorbed in the narrative, his eyes assumed a dreamy expression, and he seemed to lose sight of his auditors, and to be living over again in monologue his life on the old plantation.

"Ole Mars Dugal' McAdoo," he began, "bought dis place long

many years befo' de wah, en I 'member well w'en he sot out all
dis yer part er de plantation in scuppernon's. De vimes growed
monst'us fas', en Mars Dugal' made a thousan' gallon er scuppernon' wine eve'y year.

"Now, ef dey's an'thing a nigger lub, nex' ter 'possum, en
chick'n, en watermillyums, it's scuppernon's. Dey ain' nuffin dat
kin stan' up side'n de scuppernon' fer sweetness; sugar ain't a
suckumstance ter scuppernon'. W'en de season is nigh 'bout
ober, en de grapes begin ter swivel up des a little wid de
wrinkles er ole age—we'n de skin git sof' en brown—den de
scuppernon' make you smack yo' lip en roll yo' eye en wush fer
mo'; so I reckon it ain' very 'stonishin' dat niggers lub scuppernon'.

"Dey wuz a sight er niggers in de naberhood er de vimya'd.
Dere wuz ole Mars Henry Brayboy's niggers, en ole Mars Jeems
McLean's niggers, en Mars Dugal's own niggers; den dey wuz a
settlement er free niggers en po' buckrahs down by de Wim'l'ton
Road, en Mars Dugal' had de only vimya'd in de naberhood. I
reckon it ain' so much so nowadays, but befo' de wah, in slab'ry
times, a nigger didn' mine goin' fi' er ten mile in a night w'en
dey wuz sump'n good ter eat at de yuther een'.

"So atter a w'ile Mars Dugal' begin ter miss his scuppernon's.
Co'se he 'cuse' de niggers er it, but dey all 'nied it ter de las'.
Mars Dugal' sot spring guns en steel traps, en he en de oberseah
sot up nights once't or twice't, tel one night Mars Dugal'—he 'uz
a monst'us keerless man—got his leg shot full er cow-peas. But
somehow er nudder dey couldn' nebber ketch none er de
niggers. I dunner how it happen, but it happen des like I tell
you, en de grapes kep' on a-goin' des de same.

"But bimeby ole Mars Dugal' fix' up a plan ter stop it. Dey wuz
a cunjuh 'oman livin' down 'mongs' de free niggers on de
Wim'l'ton Road, en all de darkies fum Rockfish ter Beaver Crick
wuz feared er her. She could wuk de mos' powerfulles' kin' er
goopher—could make people hab fits, er rheumatiz', er mak 'em
des dwinel away en die; en dey say she went out ridin' de
niggers at night, fer she wuz a witch 'sides bein' a cunjuh
'oman. Mars Dugal' hearn 'bout Aun' Peggy's doin's, en begun ter
'flect whe'r er no he couldn' git her ter he'p him keep de niggers
off'n de grapevimes. One day in de spring er de year, ole miss
pack' up a basket er chick'n en poun'cake, en a bottle er

scuppernon' wine, en Mars Dugal' tuk it in his buggy en driv over ter Aun' Peggy's cabin. He tuk de basket in, en had a long talk wid Aun' Peggy.

"De nex' day Aun' Peggy come up ter de vimya'd. De niggers seed her slippin' 'round, en dey soon foun' out what she 'uz doin' dere. Mars Dugal' had hi'ed her ter goopher de grapevimes. She sa'ntered 'roun' 'mongs' de vimes, en tuk a leaf fum dis one, en a grape-hull fum dat one, en den a little twig fum here, en a little pinch er dirt fum dere—en put it all in a big black bottle, wid a snake's toof en a speckle hen's gall en some ha'rs fum a black cat's tail, en den fill' de bottle wid scuppernon' wine. W'en she got de goopher all ready en fix', she tuk 'n went out in de woods en buried it under de root uv a red oak tree, en den come back en tole one er de niggers she done goopher de grapevimes, en a'er a nigger w'at eat dem grapes 'ud be sho ter die inside'n twel' mont's.

"Atter dat de niggers let de scuppernon's 'lone, en Mars Dugal' didn' hab no 'casion ter fine no mo' fault; en de season wuz mos' gone, w'en a strange gemman stop at de plantation one night ter see Mars Dugal' on some business; en his coachman, seein' de scuppernon's growin' so nice en sweet, slip 'roun' behine de smoke-house en et all de scuppernon's he could hole. Nobody didn' notice it at de time, but dat night, on de way home, de gemman's hoss runned away en kill' de coachman. W'en we hearn de noos, Aun' Lucy, de cook, she up'n say she seed de strange nigger eat'n' er de scuppernon's behine de smoke-house; en den we knowed de goopher had be'en er wukkin'. Den one er de nigger chilluns runned away fum de quarters one day, en got in de scuppernon's, en died de nex' week. White folks say he die' er de fevuh, but de niggers knowed it wuz de goopher. So you k'n be sho de darkies didn' hab much ter do wid dem scuppernon' vimes.

"W'en de scuppernon' season 'uz ober fer dat year, Mars Dugal' foun' he had made fifteen hund'ed gallon er wine; en one er de niggers hearn him laffin' wid de oberseah fit ter kill, en sayin' dem fifteen hund'ed gallon er wine wuz monst'us good intrus' on de ten dollars he laid out on de vimya'd. So I 'low ez he paid Aun' Peggy ten dollars fer to goopher de grapevimes.

"De goopher didn' wuk no mo' tel de nex summer, w'en 'long to'ds de middle er de season one er de fiel' han's died; en ez dat lef' Mars Dugal' sho't er han's, he went off ter town fer ter buy anudder. He fotch de noo nigger home wid 'im. He wuz er ole nigger, er de color er a gingy-cake, en ball ez a hossaple on de top er his head. He wuz a peart ole nigger, do', en could do a big day's wuk.

"Now it happen dat one er de niggers on de nex' plantation, one er ole Mars Henry Brayboy's niggers, had runned away de day befo', en tuk ter de swamp, en ole Mars Dugal' en some er de yuther nabor w'ite folks had gone out wid dere guns en dere dogs fer ter he'p 'em hunt fer de nigger; en de han's on our own plantation wuz all so flusterated dat we fuhgot ter tell de noo han' 'bout de goopher on de scuppernon' vimes. Co'se he smell de grapes en see de vimes, an atter dahk de fus' thing he done wuz ter slip off ter de grapevimes 'dout sayin' nuffin ter nobody. Nex' mawnin' he tole some er de niggers 'bout de fine bait er scuppernon' he et de night befo'.

"W'en dey tole 'im 'bout de goopher on de grapevines, he 'uz dat tarrified dat he turn pale, en look des like he gwine ter die right in his tracks. De oberseah come up en axed w'at 'uz de matter; en w'en dey tole 'im Henry been eatin' er de scuppernon's, en got de goopher on 'im, he gin Henry a big drink er w'iskey, en 'low dat de nex' rainy day he take 'im ober ter Aun' Peggy's, en see ef she wouldn' take de goopher off'n him, seein' ez he didn't know nuffin' erbout it tel he done et de grapes.

"Sho nuff, it rain de nex' day, en de oberseah went ober ter Aun' Peggy's wid Henry. En Aun' Peggy say dat bein' ez Henry didn' know 'bout de goopher, en et de grapes in ign'ance er de conseq'ences, she reckon she mought be able ter take de goopher off'n him. So she fotch out er bottle wid some cunjuh medicine in it, en po'd some out in a go'd fer Henry ter drink. He manage ter git it down; he say it tas'e like w'iskey wid sump'n bitter in it. She 'lowed dat 'ud keep de goopher off'n him tel de spring; but w'en de sap begin ter rise in de grapevimes he ha' ter come en see her ag'in, en she tell him w'at he's ter do.

"Nex' spring, w'en de sap commence' ter rise in de scuppernon' vime, Henry tuk a ham one night. Whar'd he git de ham? *I* doan know; dey wa'n't no hams on de plantation 'cep'n' w'at 'uz in de smokehouse, but *I* never see Henry 'bout de smokehouse. But ez I wuz a-sayin', he tuk de ham ober ter Aun' Peggy's; en Aun' Peggy tole 'im dat w'en Mars Dugal' begin ter prune de grapevimes, he must go en take 'n scrape off de sap what it ooze out'n de cut een's er de vimes, en 'n'int his ball head wid it; en ef he do dat once't a year de goopher wouldn't wuk agin 'im long ez he done it. En bein' ez he fotch her de ham, she fix' it so he kin eat all de scuppernon' he want.

"So Henry 'n'int his head wid de sap out'n de big grapevime des ha'f way 'twix de quarters en de big house, en de goopher nebber wuk agin him dat summer. But the beatenes' thing you eber see happen ter Henry. Up ter dat time he wuz ez ball ez a sweeten' 'tater, but des ez soon ez de young leaves begun ter come out on de grapevimes, de ha'r begun ter grow out on Henry's head, en by de middle er de summer he had de bigges' head er ha'r on de plantation. Befo' dat, Henry had tol'able good ha'r 'roun' de aidges, but soon ez de young grapes begun ter come, Henry's ha'r begun to quirl all up in little balls, des like dis yer reg'lar grapy ha'r, en by de time de grapes got ripe his head look des like a bunch er grapes. Combin' it didn' do no good; he wuk at it ha'f de night wid er Jim Crow, en think he git it straighten' out, but in de mawnin' de grapes 'ud be dere des de same. So he gin it up, en tried ter keep de grapes down by havin' his ha'r cut sho't.

"But dat wa'n't de quares' thing 'bout de goopher. When Henry come ter de plantation, he wuz gittin' a little ole and stiff in de j'ints. But dat summer he got des ez spry en libely ez any young nigger on de plantation; fac', he got so biggity dat Mars Jackson, de oberseah, ha' ter th'eaten ter whip 'im ef he didn' stop cuttin' up his didos en behave hisse'f. But de mos' cur'ouses' thing happen' in de fall, when de sap begin ter go down in de grapevimes. Fus, when de grapes 'uz gethered, de knots begun ter straighten out'n Henry's ha'r; en w'en de leaves begin ter fall, Henry's ha'r commence' ter drap out; en when de vimes 'uz bar', Henry's head wuz baller'n it wuz in de spring, en he begin ter git ole en stiff in de j'ints ag'in, en paid no mo' 'tention ter de gals dyoin' er de whole winter. En nex' spring, w'en he rub de sap on ag'in, he got young ag'in, en so soopl en libely dat none er de young niggers on de plantation couldn' jump, ner dance, ner hoe ez much cotton ez Henry. But in de fall er de year his grapes 'mence' ter straighten out, en his j'ints ter git stiff, en his ha'r drap off, en de rheumatiz begin ter wrastle wid 'im.

"Now, ef you'd 'a' knowed ole Mars Dugal' McAdoo, you'd 'a' knowed dat it ha' ter be a mighty rainy day when he couldn' fine sump'n fer his niggers ter do, en it ha' ter be a mighty little hole he couldn' crawl thoo, en ha'ter be a monst'us cloudy night when a dollar git by him in de dahkness; en w'en he see how Henry git young in de spring en ole in de fall, he 'lowed ter hisse'f ez how he could make mo' money out'n Henry dan by wukkin' him in de cotton-fiel'. 'Long de nex' spring, atter de sap 'mence' ter rise, en Henry 'n'int 'is head en sta'ted fer ter git young en soopl, Mars Dugal' up'n tuk Henry ter down, en sole 'im fer fifteen hunder' dollars. Co'se de man w'at bought Henry didn' know nuffin 'bout de goopher, en Mars Dugal' didn't see no 'casion fer ter tell 'im. Long to'ds de fall, w'en de sap went down, Henry begin ter git ole ag'in same ez yuzhal, en his noo marster begin ter git skeered les'n he gwine ter lose his fifteen-hunder'-dollar nigger. He sent fer a mighty fine doctor, but de med'cine didn' 'pear ter do no good; de goopher had a good holt. Henry tole de doctor 'bout de goopher, but de doctor des laff at 'im.

"One day in de winter Mars Dugal' went ter town, en wuz santerin' 'long de Main Street, w'en who should he meet but Henry's noo master. Dey said 'Hoddy,' en Mars Dugal' ax 'im ter hab a seegyar; en atter dey run on awhile 'bout de craps en de weather, Mars Dugal' ax 'im, sorter keerless, like ez ef he des thought of it—

" 'How you like de nigger I sole you las' spring?'

"Henry's marster shuck his head en knock de ashes off'n his seegyar.

" 'Spec' I made a bad bahgin when I bought dat nigger. Henry done good wuk all de summer, but sence de fall set in he 'pears ter be sorter pinin' away. Dey ain' nuffin pertickler de matter wid 'im—leastways de doctor say so—'cep'n' a tech er de rheumatiz; but his ha'r is all fell out, en ef he don't pick up his strenk mighty soon, I spec' I'm gwine ter lose 'im.'

"Dey smoked on awhile, en bimeby ole mars say, 'Well, a bahgin's a bahgin, but you en me is good fren's, en I doan wan' ter see you lose all de money you paid fer dat nigger; en ef w'at you say is so, en I ain't 'sputin' it, he ain't wuf much now. I spec's you wukked him too ha'd dis summer, er e'se de swamps down here don't agree wid de san'-hill nigger. So you des lemme know, en ef he gits any wusser, I'll be willin' ter gib yer five hund'ed dollars for 'im, en take my chances on his livin'.'

"Sho' nuff, when Henry begun ter draw up wid de rheumatiz en it look like he gwine ter die fer sho, his noo marster sen' fer

Mars Dugal', en Mars Dugal' gin him what he promus, en brung
Henry home ag'in. He tuk good keer uv 'im dyoin' er de
winter—give 'im w'iskey ter rub his rheumatiz, en terbacker ter
smoke, en all he want ter eat—'caze a nigger w'at he could
make a thousan' dollars a year off'n didn' grow on eve'y huckle-
berry bush.

"Nex' spring, w'en de sap rise en Henry's ha'r commence' ter
sprout, Mars Dugal' sole 'im ag'in, down in Robeson County dis
time; en he kep' dat sellin' business up fer five year er mo'.
Henry nebber say nuffin 'bout de goopher ter his noo marsters,
'caze he know he gwine ter be tuk good keer uv de nex' winter,
w'en Mars Dugal' buy him back. En Mars Dugal' made 'nuff
money off'n Henry ter buy anudder plantation ober on Beaver
Crick.

"But 'long 'bout de een 'er dat five year dey come a stranger
ter stop at de plantation. De fus' day he 'uz dere he went out wid
Mars Dugal' en spent all de mawnin' lookin' ober de vimya'd, en
atter dinner dey spent all de evenin' playin' kya'ds. De niggers
soon 'skivver' dat he wuz a Yankee, en dat he come down ter
Norf C'lina fer ter l'arn de w'ite folks how to raise grapes en
make wine. He promus Mars Dugal' he c'd make de grapevimes
b'ar twice't ez many grapes, en dat de noo winepress he wuz a-
sellin' would make mo' d'n twice't ez many gallons er wine. En
ole Mars Dugal' des drunk it all in, des 'peared ter be bewitch'
wid dat Yankee. W'en de darkies see dat Yankee runnin' 'roun'
de vimya'd en diggin' under de grapevimes, dey shuk dere
heads, en 'lowed dat dey feared Mars Dugal' losin' his min'.
Mars Dugal' had all de dirt dug away fum under de roots er all
de scuppernon' vimes, an' let 'em stan' dat away fer a week er
mo'. Den dat Yankee made de niggers fix up a mixtry er lime en
ashes en manyo, en po' it 'roun' de roots er de grapevimes. Den
he 'vise Mars Dugal' fer ter trim de vimes close't, en Mars Dugal'
tuck 'n done eve'ything de Yankee tole him ter do. Dyoin' all er
dis time, mine yer, dis yer Yankee wuz libbin' off'n de fat er de
lan', at de big house, en playin' kya'ds wid Mars Dugal' eve'y
night; en dey say Mars Dugal' los' mo'n a thousan' dollars dyoin'
er de week dat Yankee wuz a-ruinin' de grapevimes.

"W'en de sap ris nex' spring, ole Henry 'n'inted his head ez
yuzhal, en his ha'r 'mence' ter grow des de same ez it done eve'y
year. De scuppernon' vimes growed monst's fas', en de leaves
wuz greener en thicker dan dey eber be'n dyoin' my remem-

b'ance; en Henry's ha'r growed out thicker dan eber, en he 'peared ter git younger 'n younger, en soopler; en seein' ez he wuz sho't er han's dat spring, havin' tuk in consid'able noo groun', Mars Dugal' 'git de crap in en de cotton chop'. So he kep' Henry on de plantation.

"But 'long 'bout time fer de grapes ter come on de scuppernon' vimes, dey 'peared ter come a change ober 'em; de leaves witherd en swivel' up, en de young grapes turn' yaller, en bimeby eve'ybody on de plantation could see dat de whole vimya'd wuz dyin'. Mars Dugal' tuk'n water de vimes en done all he could, but 't wa'n no use; dat Yankee had done bus' de watermillyum. One time de vimes picked up a bit, en Mars Dugal' 'lowed dey wuz gwine ter come out ag'in; but dat Yankee done dug too close under de roots, en prune de branches too close ter de vime, en all dat lime en ashes done burn de life out'm de vimes, en dey des kep' a-with'in' en a-swivelin'.

"All dis time de goopher wuz a-wukkin'. When de vimes sta'ted ter wither, Henry 'mence' ter complain er his rheumatiz; en when de leaves begin ter dry up, his ha'r 'mence' ter drap out. When de vimes fresh' up a bit, Henry'd git peart ag'in, en when de vimes wither' ag'in, Henry'd git ole ag'in, en des kep' gittin' mo' fitten fer nuffin; he des pined away, en pined away, en fin'ly tuk ter his cabin; en when de big vime whar he got de sap ter 'n'int his head withered en turned yaller en died, Henry died too—des went out sorter like a cannel. Dey didn't 'pear ter be nuffin de matter wid 'im, 'cep'n de rheumatiz, but his strenk des dwinel' away 'tel he didn' hab ernuff lef' ter draw his bref. De goopher had got de under holt, en th'owed Henry dat time fer good en all.

"Mars Dugal' tuk on might'ly 'bout losin' his vimes en his nigger in de same year; en he swo' dat ef he could git holt er dat Yankee he'd wear 'im ter a frazzle, en den chaw up de frazzle; en he'd done it, too, for Mars Dugal' 'uz a monst'us brash man w'en he once git started. He sot de vimy'd out ober ag'in, but it wuz th'ee er fo' year befo' de vimes got ter b'arin' any scuppernon's.

"W'en de wah broke out, Mars Dugal' raise' a comp'ny, en went off ter fight de Yankees. He say he wuz mighty glad wah come, en he des want ter kill a Yankee fer eve'y dollar he los' 'long er dat grape-raisin' Yankee. En I 'spec' he would 'a' done it, too, ef de Yankees hadn' s'picioned sump'en en killed him fus'.

Atter de s'render, ole Miss move' ter town, de niggers all scattered 'way fum de plantation, en de vimya'd ain' be'n cultervated sence."

"Is that story true?" asked Annie doubtfully, but seriously, as the old man concluded his narrative.

"It's des ez true ez I'm a-settin' here, miss. Dey's a easy way ter prove it: I kin lead de way right ter Henry's grave ober yonder in de plantation buryin'-groun'. En I tell yer w'at, marster, I wouldn' 'vise you to buy dis yer ole vimya'd, 'caze de goopher's on it yit, en dey ain' no tellin' w'en it's gwine ter crap out."

"But I thought you said all the old vines died."

"Dey did 'pear ter die, but a few un 'em come out ag'in, en is mixed in 'mongs' de yuthers. I ain' skeered ter eat de grapes 'caze I knows de old vimes fum de noo ones, but wid strangers dey ain 'no tellin' w'at mought happen. I wouldn' 'vise yer ter buy dis vimya'd."

I bought the vineyard, nevertheless, and it has been for a long time in a thriving condition, and is often referred to by the local press as a striking illustration of the opportunities open to Northern capital in the development of Southern industries. The luscious scuppernong holds first rank among our grapes, though we cultivate a great many other varieties; and our income from grapes packed and shipped to the Northern markets is quite considerable. I have not noticed any developments of the goopher in the vineyard, although I have a mild suspicion that our colored assistants do not suffer from want of grapes during the season.

I found, when I bought the vineyard, that Uncle Julius had occupied a cabin on the place for many years, and derived a respectable revenue from the product of the neglected grape-vines. This, doubtless, accounted for his advice to me not to buy the vineyard, though whether it inspired the goopher story I am unable to state. I believe, however, that the wages I paid him for his services as coachman, for I gave him employment in that capacity, were more than an equivalent for anything he lost by the sale of the vineyard.

The City of Refuge

RUDOLPH FISHER

I

Confronted suddenly by daylight, King Solomon Gillis stood dazed and blinking. The railroad station, the long, white-walled corridor, the impassable slot-machine, the terrifying subway train—he felt as if he had been caught up in the jaws of a steam-shovel, jammed together with other helpless lumps of dirt, swept blindly along for a time, and at last abruptly dumped.

There had been strange and terrible sounds: "New York! Penn Terminal—all change!" "Pohter, hyer, pohter, suh?" Shuffle of a thousand soles, clatter of a thousand heels, innumerable echoes. Cracking rifle-shots—no, snapping turnstiles. "Put a nickel in!" "Harlem? Sure. This side—next train." Distant thunder, nearing. The screeching onslaught of the fiery hosts of hell, headlong, breathtaking. Car doors rattling, sliding, banging open. "Say, wha' d'ye think this is, a baggage car?" Heat, oppression, suffocation—eternity—"Hundred 'n turdy-fif' next!" More turnstiles. Jonah emerging from the whale.

Clean air, blue sky, bright sunlight.

Gillis set down his tan cardboard extension case and wiped his black, shining brow. Then slowly, spreadingly, he grinned at what he saw: Negroes at every turn; up and down Lenox Avenue, up and down 135th Street; big, lanky Negroes, short, squat Negroes; black ones, brown ones, yellow ones; men standing idle on the curb, women, bundle-laden, trudging reluctantly homeward, children rattle-trapping about the sidewalks; here and there a white face drifting along, but Negroes predominantly, overwhelmingly everywhere. There was assuredly no doubt of his whereabouts. This was Negro Harlem.

Back in North Carolina Gillis had shot a white man and, with the aid of prayer and an automobile, probably escaped a lynching. Carefully avoiding the railroads, he had reached Washington in safety. For his car a Southwest bootlegger had given him a hundred dollars and directions to Harlem; and so he had come to Harlem.

Ever since a traveling preacher had first told him of the place, King Solomon Gillis had longed to come to Harlem. The Uggams were always talking about it; one of their boys had gone to France in the draft and, returning, had never got any nearer home than Harlem. And there were occasional "colored" newspapers from New York: newspapers that mentioned Negroes without comment, but always spoke of a white person as "So-and-so, white." That was the point. In Harlem, black was white. You had rights that could not be denied you; you had privileges, protected by law. And you had money. Everybody in Harlem had money. It was a land of plenty. Why, had not Mouse Uggam sent back as much as fifty dollars at a time to his people in Waxhaw?

The shooting, therefore, simply catalyzed whatever sluggish mental reaction had been already directing King Solomon's fortunes toward Harlem. The land of plenty was more than that now; it was also the city of refuge.

Casting about for direction, the tall newcomer's glance caught inevitably on the most conspicuous thing in sight, a magnificent figure in blue that stood in the middle of the crossing and blew a whistle and waved great white-gloved hands. The Southern Negro's eyes opened wide; his mouth opened wider. If the inside of New York had mystified him, the outside was amazing him. For there stood a handsome brass-buttoned giant directing the heaviest traffic Gillis had ever seen; halting unnumbered tons of automobiles and trucks and wagons and pushcarts and street-cars; holding them at bay with one hand while he swept similar tons peremptorily on with the other; ruling the wide crossing with supreme self-assurance. And he, too, was a Negro!

Yet most of the vehicles that leaped or crouched at his bidding carried white passengers. One of these overdrove bounds a few feet, and Gillis heard the officer's shrill whistle and gruff reproof, saw the driver's face turn red and his car draw back like a threatened pup. It was beyond belief—impossible. Black might be white, but it couldn't be that white!

"Done died an' woke up in Heaven," thought King Solomon, watching, fascinated; and after a while, as if the wonder of it were too great to believe simply by seeing, "Cullud policemans!" he said, half aloud; then repeated over and over, with greater and greater conviction, "Even got cullud policemans—even got cullud—"

"Where y' want to go, big boy?"

Gillis turned. A little, sharp-faced yellow man was addressing him.

"Saw you was a stranger. Thought maybe I could help y' out."

King Solomon located and gratefully extended a slip of paper. "Wha' dis hyeh at, please, suh?"

The other studied it a moment, pushing back his hat and scratching his head. The hat was a tall-crowned, unindented brown felt; the head was brown patent-leather, its glistening brush-back flawless save for a suspicious crimpiness near the clean-grazed edges.

"See that second corner? Turn to the left when you get there. Number forty-five's about halfway down the block."

"Thank y', suh."

"You from—Massachusetts?"

"No, suh, Nawth Ca'lina."

"Is 'at so? You look like a Northerner. Be with us long?"

"Till I die," grinned the flattered King Solomon.

"Stoppin' there?"

"Reckon I is. Man in Washin'ton 'lowed I'd find lodgin' at dis ad-dress."

"Good enough. If y' don't, maybe I can fix y' up. Harlem's pretty crowded. This is me." He proffered a card.

"Thank y', suh," said Gillis, and put the card in his pocket.

The little yellow man watched him plod flat-footedly on down the street, long awkward legs never quite straightened, shouldered extension-case bending him sidewise, wonder upon wonder halting or turning him about. Presently, as he proceeded, a pair of bright green stockings caught and held his attention. Tony, the storekeeper, was crossing the sidewalk with a bushel basket of apples. There was a collision; the apples rolled; Tony exploded; King Solomon apologized. The little yellow man laughed shortly, took out a notebook, and put down the address he had seen on King Solomon's slip of paper.

"Guess you're the shine I been waitin' for," he surmised.

As Gillis, approaching his destination, stopped to rest, a haunting notion grew into an insistent idea. "Dat li'l yaller nigger was a sho' 'nuff gen'man to show me de road. Seem lak I knowed him befo'——" He pondered. That receding brow, that sharp-ridged, spreading nose, that tight upper lip over the two big front teeth, that chinless jaw—— He fumbled hurriedly for the card he had not looked at and eagerly made out the name.

"Mouse Uggam, sho' 'nuff! Well, dog-gone!"

II

Uggam sought out Tom Edwards, once a Pullman porter, now prosperous proprietor of a cabaret, and told him:

"Chief, I got him: a baby jess in from the land o' cotton and so dumb he thinks ante bellum's an old woman."

"Where'd you find him?"

"Where you find all the jaybirds when they first hit Harlem—at the subway entrance. This one come up the stairs, batted his eyes once or twice, an' froze to the spot—with his mouth open. Sure sign he's from 'way down behind the sun and ripe f' the pluckin'."

Edwards grinned a gold-studded, fat-jowled grin. "Gave him the usual line, I suppose?"

"Didn't miss. An' he fell like a ton o' bricks. 'Course I've got him spotted, but damn 'f I know jess how to switch 'em on to him."

"Get him a job around a store somewhere. Make out you're befriendin' him. Get his confidence."

"Sounds good. Ought to be easy. He's from my state. Maybe I know him or some of his people."

"Make out you do, anyhow. Then tell him some fairy tale that'll switch your trade to him. The cops'll follow the trade. We could even let Froggy flop into some dumb white cop's hands and 'confess' where he got it. See?"

"Chief, you got a head, no lie."

"Don't lose no time. And remember, hereafter, it's better to sacrifice a little than to get squealed on. Never refuse a customer. Give him a little credit. Humor him along till you can get rid of him safe. You don't know what that guy that died may have said; you don't know who's on to you now. And if they get you—I don't know you."

"They won't get me," said Uggam.

King Solomon Gillis sat meditating in a room half the size of his hencoop back home, with a single window opening into an airshaft.

An airshaft: cabbage and chitterlings cooking; liver and onions sizzling, sputtering; three player-pianos out-plunking each other; a man and a woman calling each other vile things; a sick, neglected baby wailing; a phonograph broadcasting blues; dishes clacking; a girl crying heartbrokenly; waste noises, waste odors of a score of families, seeking issue through a common channel; pollution from bottom to top—a sewer of sounds and smells.

Contemplating this, King Solomon grinned and breathed, "Dog-gone!" A little later, still gazing into the sewer, he grinned again. "Green stockin's," he said; "loud green!" The sewer gradually grew darker. A window lighted up opposite, revealing a woman in camisole and petticoat, arranging her hair. King Solomon, staring vacantly, shook his head and grinned yet again. "Even got cullud policemans!" he mumbled softly.

III

Uggam leaned out of the room's one window and spat maliciously into the dinginess of the airshaft. "Damn glad you got him," he commented as Gillis finished his story. "They's a thousand shines in Harlem would change places with you in a minute jess f' the honor of killin' a cracker."

"But I didn't go to do it. 'T was a accident."

"That's the only part to keep secret."

"Know whut dey done? Dey killed five o' Mose Joplin's hawses 'fo he lef'. Put groun' glass in de feed-trough. Sam Cheevers come up on three of 'em one night pizenin' his well. Bleesom beat Crinshaw out o' sixty acres o' lan' an' a year's crops. Dass jess how 't is. Soon's a nigger make a li'l sump'n he better git to leavin'. An' fo' long ev'ybody's goin' be lef'!"

"Hope to hell they don't all come here."

The doorbell of the apartment rang. A crescendo of footfalls in the hallway culminated in a sharp rap on Gillis's door. Gillis jumped. Nobody but a policeman would rap like that. Maybe the landlady had been listening and had called in the law. It came again, loud, quick, angry. King Solomon prayed that the policeman would be a Negro.

Uggam stepped over and opened the door. King Solomon's apprehensive eyes saw framed therein, instead of a gigantic officer calling for him, a little blot of a creature, quite black against even the darkness of the hallway, except for a dirty wide-striped silk shirt, collarless, with the sleeves rolled up.

"Ah hahve bill fo' Mr. Gillis." A high, strongly accented Jamaican voice, with its characteristic singsong intonation, interrupted King Solomon's sigh of relief.

"Bill? Bill fo' me? What kin' o' bill?"

"Wan bushel appels. T'ree seventy-fife."

"Apples? I ain' bought no apples." He took the paper and read aloud, laboriously, "Antonio Gabrielli to K. S. Gillis, Doctor——"

"Mr. Gabrielli say, you not pays him, he send policemon."

"What I had to do wid 'is apples?"

"You bumps into him yesterday, no? Scatter appels everywhere—on the sidewalk, in de gutter. Kids pick up an' run away. Others all spoil. So you pays."

Gillis appealed to Uggam. "How 'bout it, Mouse?"

"He's a damn liar. Tony picked up most of 'em; I seen him. Lemme look at that bill—Tony never wrote this thing. This baby's jess playin' you for a sucker."

"Ain' had no apples, ain' payin' fo'none," announced King Solomon, thus prompted. "Didn't have to come to Harlem to git cheated. Plenty o' dat right wha' I come fum."

But the West Indian warmly insisted. "You cahn't do daht, mon. Whaht you t'ink, 'ey? Dis mon loose 'is appels an' 'is money too?"

"What diff'ence it make to you, nigger?"

"Who you call nigger, mon? Ah hahve you understahn'——"

"Oh, well, white folks, den. What all you got t' do wid dis hyeh, anyhow?"

"Mr. Gabrielli send me to collect bill!"

"How I know dat?"

"Do Ah not bring bill? You t'ink Ah steal t'ree dollar, 'ey?"

"Three dollars an' sebenty-fi' cent," corrected Gillis. "Nuther thing: wha' you ever see me befo'? How you know dis is me?"

"Ah see you, sure. Ah help Mr. Gabrielli in de store. When you knocks down de baskette appels, Ah see. Ah follow you. Ah know you comes in dis house."

"Oh, you does? An' how come you know my name an' flat an room so good? How come dat?"

"Ah fin' out. Sometime Ah brings up here vegetables from de store."

"Humph! Mus' be workin' on shares."

"You pays, 'ey? You pays me or de policemon?"

"Wait a minute," broke in Uggam, who had been thoughtfully contemplating the bill. "Now listen, big shorty. You haul hips on back to Tony. We got your menu all right"—he waved the bill—"but we don't eat your kind o' cookin', see?"

The West Indian flared. "Whaht it is to you, 'ey? You can not mind your own business? Ah hahve not spik to you!"

"No, brother. But this is my friend, an' I'll be john-browned if there's a monkey-chaser in Harlem can gyp him if I know it, see? Bes' thing f' you to do is to catch air, toot sweet."

Sensing frustration, the little islander demanded the bill back. Uggam figured he could use the bill himself, maybe. The West Indian hotly persisted; he even menaced. Uggam pocketed the paper and invited him to take it. Wisely enough, the caller preferred to catch air.

When he had gone, King Solomon sought words of thanks.

"Bottle it," said Uggam. "The point is this: I figger you got a job."

"Job? No I ain't! Wha' at?"

"When you show Tony this bill, he'll hit the roof and fire that monk."

"What ef he do?"

"Then you up 'n ask f' the job. He'll be too grateful to refuse. I know Tony some, an' I'll be there to put in a good word. See?"

King Solomon considered this. "Sho' needs a job, but ain' after stealin' none."

"Stealin'? 'T wouldn't be stealin'. Stealin' 's what that damn monkey-chaser tried to do from you. This would be doin' Tony a favor an' gettin' y'self out o' the barrel. What's the holdback?"

"What make you keep callin' him monkey-chaser?"

"West Indian. That's another thing. Any time y' can knife a monk, do it. They's too damn many of 'em here. They're an achin' pain."

"Jess de way white folks feels 'bout niggers."

"Damn that. How 'bout it? Y' want the job?"

"Hm—well—I'd ruther be a policeman."

"Policeman?" Uggam gasped.

"M—hm. Dass all I wants to be, a policeman, so I kin police all the white folks right plumb in jail!"

Uggam said seriously, "Well, y' might work up to that. But it takes time. An' y've got to eat while y're waitin'." He paused to let this penetrate. "Now how 'bout this job at Tony's in the meantime? I should think y'd jump at it."

King Solomon was persuaded.

"Hm—well—reckon I does," he said slowly.

"Now y're tootin'!" Uggam's two big front teeth popped out in a grin of genuine pleasure. "Come on. Let's go."

IV

Spitting blood and crying with rage, the West Indian scrambled to his feet. For a moment he stood in front of the store gesticulating furiously and jabbering shrill threats and unintelligible curses. Then abruptly he stopped and took himself off.

King Solomon Gillis, mildly puzzled, watched him from Tony's doorway. "I jess give him a li'l shove," he said to himself, "an' he roll' clean 'cross de sidewalk." And a little later, disgustedly, "Monkey-chaser!" he grunted, and went back to his sweeping.

"Well, big boy, how y' comin' on?"

Gillis dropped his broom. "Hay-o, Mouse. Wha' you been las' two-three days?"

"Oh, around. Gettin' on all right here? Had any trouble?"

"Deed I ain't—ceptin' jess now I had to throw 'at li'l jigger out."

"Who? The monk?"

"M—hm. He sho' Lawd doan like me in his job. Look like he think I stole it from him, stiddy him tryin' to steal from me. Had to push him down sho' 'nuff 'fo I could get rid of 'im. Den he run off talkin' Wes' Indi'man an' shakin' his fis' at me."

"Ferget it." Uggam glanced about. "Where's Tony?"

"Boss man? He be back direckly."

"Listen—like to make two or three bucks a day extra?"

"Huh?"

"Two or three dollars a day more'n what you're gettin' already?"

"Ain' I near 'nuff in jail now?"

"Listen." King Solomon listened. Uggam hadn't been in France for nothing. Fact was, in France he'd learned about some valuable French medicine. He'd bought some back with him—little white pills—and while in Harlem had found a certain druggist who knew what they were and could supply all he could use. Now there were any number of people who would buy and pay well for as much of this French medicine as Uggam could get. It was good for what ailed them, and they didn't know how to get it except through him. But he had no store in which to set up an agency and hence no single place where his customers could go to get what they wanted. If he had, he could sell three or four times as much as he did.

King Solomon was in a position to help him now, same as he had helped King Solomon. He would leave a dozen packages of the medicine—just small envelopes that could all be carried in a coat pocket—with King Solomon every day. Then he could simply send his customers to King Solomon at Tony's store. They'd make some trifling purchase, slip him a certain coupon which Uggam had given them, and King Solomon would wrap the little envelope of medicine with their purchase. Mustn't let Tony catch on, because he might object, and then the whole scheme would go gaflooey. Of course it wouldn't really be hurting Tony any. Wouldn't it increase the number of his customers?

Finally, at the end of each day, Uggam would meet King Solomon some place and give him a quarter for each coupon he held. There'd be at least ten or twelve a day—two and a half or three dollars plumb extra! Eighteen or twenty dollars a week. "Dog-gone!" breathed Gillis.

"Does Tony ever leave you here alone?"

"M—hm. Jess started dis mawnin'. Doan nobody much come round 'tween ten an' twelve, so he done took to doin' his buyin' right 'long 'bout dat time. Nobody hyeh but me fo' 'n hour or so."

"Good. I'll try to get my folks to come 'round here mostly while Tony's out, see?"

"I doan miss."

"Sure y' get the idea, now?" Uggam carefully explained it all again. By the time he had finished, King Solomon was wallowing in gratitude.

"Mouse, you sho' is been a friend to me. Why, 'f 't hadn't been fo' you——"

"Bottle it," said Uggam. "I'll be round to your room tonight with enough stuff for tomorrer, see? Be sure'n be there."

"Won't be nowha' else."

"An' remember, this is all jess between you 'n me."

"Nobody else but," vowed King Solomon.

Uggam grinned to himself as he went on his way. "Dumb Oscar! Wonder how much can we make before the cops nab him? French medicine—Humph!"

V

Tony Gabrielli, an oblate Neapolitan of enormous equator, wobbled heavily out of his store and settled himself over a soapbox.

Usually Tony enjoyed sitting out front thus in the evening, when his helper had gone home and his trade was slackest. He liked to watch the little Gabriellis playing over the sidewalk with the little Levys and Johnsons; the trios and quartettes of brightly dressed dark-skinned girls merrily out for a stroll; the slovenly gaited darker men, who eyed them up and down and commented to each other with an unsuppressed "Hot damn!" or "Oh no, now!"

But tonight Tony was troubled. Something was wrong in the store; something was different since the arrival of King Solomon Gillis. The new man had seemed to prove himself honest and trustworthy, it was true. Tony had tested him, as he always tested a new man, by apparently leaving him alone in charge for two or three mornings. As a matter of fact, the new man was never under more vigilant observation than during these two or three mornings. Tony's store was a modification of the front rooms of his flat and was in direct communication with it by way of a glass-windowed door in the rear. Tony always managed to get back into his flat via the side-street entrance and watch the new man through this unobtrusive glass-windowed door. If anything excited his suspicion, like unwarranted interest in the cash register, he walked unexpectedly out of this door to sur-

prise the offender in the act. Thereafter he would have no more
such trouble. But he had not succeeded in seeing King Solomon
steal even an apple.

What he had observed, however, was that the number of
customers that came into the store during the morning's slack
hour had pronouncedly increased in the last few days. Before,
there had been three or four. Now there were twelve or fifteen.
The mysterious thing about it was that their purchases totaled
little more than those of the original three or four.

Yesterday and today Tony had elected to be in the store at the
time when, on the other days, he had been out. But Gillis had
not been overcharging or short-changing; for when Tony waited
on the customers himself—strange faces all—he found that
they bought something like a yeast cake or a five-cent loaf of
bread. It was puzzling. Why should strangers leave their own
neighborhoods and repeatedly come to him for a yeast cake or a
loaf of bread? They were not new neighbors. New neighbors
would have bought more variously and extensively and at
different times of day. Living nearby, they would have come in,
the men often in shirtsleeves and slippers, the women in
kimonos, with boudoir caps covering their lumpy heads. They
would have sent in strange children for things like yeast cakes
and loaves of bread. And why did not some of them come in at
night, when the new helper was off duty?

As for accosting Gillis on suspicion, Tony was too wise for
that. Patronage had a queer way of shifting itself in Harlem.
You lost your temper and let slip a single "negre!" A week later
you sold your business.

Spread over his soapbox, with his pudgy hands clasped on his
preposterous paunch, Tony sat and wondered. Two men came
up, conspicuous for no other reason than that they were white.
They displayed extreme nervousness, looking about as if afraid
of being seen; and when one of them spoke to Tony, it was in a
husky, toneless, blowing voice, like the sound of a dirty phonograph record.

"Are you Antonio Gabrielli?"

"Yes, sure." Strange behavior for such lusty-looking fellows.
He who had spoken unsmilingly winked first one eye then the
other, and indicated by a gesture of his head that they should
enter the store. His companion looked cautiously up and down

the avenue, while Tony, wondering what ailed them, rolled to his feet and puffingly led the way.

Inside, the spokesman snuffled, gave his shoulders a queer little hunch, and asked, "Can you fix us up, buddy?" The other glanced restlessly about the place as if he were constantly hearing unaccountable noises.

Tony thought he understood clearly now. "Booze, 'ey?" he smiled. "Sorry—I no got."

"Booze, hell, no!" The voice dwindled to a throaty whisper. "Dope. Coke, milk, dice—anything. Name your price. Got to have it."

"Dope?" Tony was entirely at a loss. "What's a dis, dope?"

"Aw, lay off, brother. We're in on this. Here." He handed Tony a piece of paper. "Froggy gave us a coupon. Come on. You can't go wrong."

"I no got," insisted the perplexed Tony; nor could he be budged on that point.

Quite suddenly the manner of both men changed. "All right," said the first angrily, in a voice as robust as his body. "All right, you're clever. You no got. Well, you will get. You'll get twenty years!"

"Twenty year. Whadda you talk?"

"Wait a minute, Mac," said the second caller. "Maybe the wop's on the level. Look here, Tony, we're officers, see, policemen." He produced a badge. "A couple of weeks ago a guy was brought in dying for the want of a shot, see? Dope—he needed some dope—like this—in his arm. See? Well, we tried to make him tell us where he'd been getting it, but he was too weak. He croaked next day. Evidently he hadn't had money enough to buy any more.

"Well, this morning a little nigger that goes by the name of Froggy was brought into the precinct pretty well doped up. When he finally came to, he swore he got the stuff here at your store. Of course, we've just been trying to trick you into giving yourself away, but you don't bite. Now what's your game? Know anything about this?"

Tony understood. "I dunno," he said slowly; and then his own problem, whose contemplation his callers had interrupted, occurred to him. "Sure!" he exclaimed. "Wait. Maybeso I know somet'ing."

"All right. Spill it."

"I got a new man, work-a for me." And he told them what he had noted since King Solomon Gillis came.

"Sounds interesting. Where is this guy?"

"Here in da store—all day."

"Be here tomorrow?"

"Sure. All day."

"All right. We'll drop in tomorrow and give him the eye. Maybe he's our man."

"Sure. Come ten o'clock. I show you," promised Tony.

VI

Even the oldest and rattiest cabarets in Harlem have sense of shame enough to hide themselves under the ground—for instance, Edwards's. To get into Edwards's you casually enter a dimly lighted corner saloon, apparently—only apparently—a subdued memory of brighter days. What was once the family entrance is now a side entrance for ladies. Supporting yourself against close walls, you crouchingly descend a narrow, twisted staircase until, with a final turn, you find yourself in a glaring, long, low basement. In a moment your eyes become accustomed to the haze of tobacco smoke. You see men and women seated at wire-legged, white-topped tables, which are covered with half-empty bottles and glasses; you trace the slow jazz accompaniment you heard as you came down the stairs to a pianist, a cornetist, and a drummer on a little platform at the far end of the room. There is a cleared space from the foot of the stairs, where you are standing, to the platform where this orchestra is mounted, and in it a tall brown girl is swaying from side to side and rhythmically proclaiming that she has the world in a jug and the stopper in her hand. Behind a counter at your left sits a fat, bald, tea-colored Negro, and you wonder if this is Edwards— Edwards, who stands in with the police, with the political bosses, with the importers of wines and worse. A white-vested waiter hustles you to a seat and takes your order. The song's tempo becomes quicker; the drum and the cornet rip out a fanfare, almost drowning the piano; the girl catches up her dress and begins to dance. . . .

Gillis's wondering eyes had been roaming about. They stopped.

"Look, Mouse!" he whispered. "Look a yonder!"

"Look at what?"

"Dog-gone if it ain' de self-same gal!"

"Wha' d' ye mean, self-same girl?"

"Over yonder, wi' de green stockin's. Dass de gal made me knock over dem apples fust day I come to town. 'Member? Been wishin' I could see her ev'y sence."

"What for?" Uggam wondered.

King Solomon grew confidential. "Ain' but two things in dis world, Mouse, I really wants. One is to be a policeman. Been wantin' dat ev'y sence I seen dat cullud traffic cop dat day. Other is to get myse'f a gal lak dat one over yonder!"

"You'll do it," laughed Uggam, "if you live long enough."

"Who dat wid her?"

"How 'n hell do I know?"

"He cullud?"

"Don't look like it. Why? What of it?"

"Hm—nuthin'——"

"How many coupons y' got tonight?"

"Ten." King Solomon handed them over.

"Y' ought to've slipt 'em to me under the table, but it's all right now, long as we got this table to ourselves. Here's y' medicine for tomorrer."

"Wha'?"

"Reach under the table."

Gillis secured and pocketed the medicine.

"An' here's two-fifty for a good day's work." Uggam passed the money over. Perhaps he grew careless; certainly the passing this time was above the table, in plain sight.

"Thanks, Mouse."

Two white men had been watching Gillis and Uggam from a table nearby. In the tumult of merriment that rewarded the entertainer's most recent and daring effort, one of these men, with a word to the other, came over and took the vacant chair beside Gillis.

"Is your name Gillis?"

" 'Tain' nuthin' else."

Uggam's eyes narrowed.

The white man showed King Solomon a police officer's badge.

"You're wanted for dope-peddling. Will you come along without trouble?"

"Fo' what?"

"Violation of the narcotic law—dope-selling."

"Who—me?"

"Come on, now, lay off that stuff. I saw what happened just now myself." He addressed Uggam. "Do you know this fellow?"

"Nope. Never saw him before tonight."

"Didn't I just see him sell you something?"

"Guess you did. We happened to be sittin' here at the same table and got to talkin'. After a while I says I can't seem to sleep nights, so he offers me sump'n he says'll make me sleep, all right. I don't know what it is, but he says he uses it himself an' I offers to pay him what it cost him. That's how I come to take it. Guess he's got more in his pocket there now."

The detective reached deftly into the coat pocket of the dumfounded King Solomon and withdrew a packet of envelopes. He tore off a corner of one, emptied a half-dozen tiny white tablets into his palm, and sneered triumphantly. "You'll make a good witness," he told Uggam.

The entertainer was issuing an ultimatum to all sweet mammas who dared to monkey around her loving man. Her audience was absorbed and delighted, with the exception of one couple—the girl with the green stockings and her escort. They sat directly in the line of vision of King Solomon's wide eyes, which, in the calamity that had descended upon him, for the moment saw nothing.

"Are you coming without trouble?"

Mouse Uggam, his friend. Harlem. Land of plenty. City of refuge—city of refuge. If you live long enough——

Consciousness of what was happening between the pair across the room suddenly broke through Gillis's daze like flame through smoke. The man was trying to kiss the girl and she was resisting. Gillis jumped up. The detective, taking the act for an attempt at escape, jumped with him and was quick enough to intercept him. The second officer came at once to his partner's aid, blowing his whistle several times as he came.

People overturned chairs getting out of the way, but nobody ran for the door. It was an old crowd. A fight was a treat; and the tall Negro could fight.

"Judas Priest!"

"Did you see that?"

"Damn!"

White—both white. Five of Mose Joplin's horses. Poisoning a

well. A year's crops. Green stockings—white—white——

"That's the time, papa!"

"Do it, big boy!"

"Good night!"

Uggam watched tensely, with one eye on the door. The second cop had blown for help——

Downing one of the detectives a third time and turning to grapple again with the other, Gillis found himself face to face with a uniformed black policeman.

He stopped as if stunned. For a moment he simply stared. Into his mind swept his own words, like a forgotten song suddenly recalled:

"Cullud policemans!"

The officer stood ready, awaiting his rush.

"Even—got—cullud—policemans——"

Very slowly King Solomon's arms relaxed; very slowly he stood erect; and the grin that came over his features had something exultant about it.

The Overcoat

JOHN P. DAVIS

It was late fall. The leaves outside the church lay dead and brown on the frozen earth. There was a smoky greenwood fire in the stove. Somebody, little David didn't know who, was singing *Nearer My God to Thee*. The whole environment was strange to David: Sybil sitting on one side of him and his father on the other, both looking straight ahead. Their mouths were buttoned tight. His was wide open in curiosity. There were so many people there whom he wanted to see. He wished that he dared look around. He just *knew* that old, blind Stephen was back there sitting beside the stove. And the green patches over his eyes looked so funny. Everyone was so quiet. He felt like moving around. He wondered why they had had to take his mother all the way in to town and then bring her back out again in that grey box covered with flowers. She would be ever so much more comfortable at home on the couch. He began to kick his tan boots with brass eyelets against the back of the next pew; but his father looked at him. David had seen that look before. It meant: stop. He stopped. Then he began to think of his mother again. Whenever he did, pictures seemed to flash through his head. He always had a choky feeling in his throat like after eating dry bread from Mother's tin breadbox. He remembered everything.

Now he was thinking of the time when Sybil had sent him for the doctor. There he was now: standing down at the crossroads, kicking his feet into the dusty red clay. He had been angry. He imagined his face had been like Father's when he had hit his thumb with a hammer and said "damn." He had gone for the doctor in a hurry. Gee! but he remembered that well. But why shouldn't he? Hadn't Sybil stopped him from playing "Indian" to say that mother was very, very sick? She had sent him running to get Doctor Parker or if he couldn't be found to get . . . (Sybil had frowned a moment before going on) . . . yes, to get Doctor Benson. How he had scurried off to Doctor Parker's. He hadn't stopped on the way either to see if he could make a stone skip three times over a pool of water. Instead he had run a little bit, and even when all out of breath he had trudged on and on—down through the woods a mile and a half and over a cornfield which had been cut down and ploughed under, reveal- ing only the roots of cornstalks. Finally he had come to the little yellow house of the doctor, sitting back between two rows of tall sycamore trees. His heart had bumped up and down inside of him when he had seen the green shutters on the house closed. He felt a dryness in his throat when nobody answered his knock. But he hadn't given up. No! He had gone on back across the cornfield and then up the hill to Doctor Benson's low rambling white house with a porch all the way round. A dog had barked and a white gardener had yelled to him to go round the back way. Hadn't he resented it though. And he had almost cried when the maid peeking out at him from behind the door of the kitchen had said that Doctor Benson wasn't there and that he would have to go down to Hunt's grocery store to find him. But he had to find a doctor. Sybil said that he must. So he had gone on.

And then standing down there at the crossroads, kicking the
toes off of his tan boots, he had seen thin-lipped Doctor Benson
sitting in Hunt's store, sipping a bottle of pop with his little
yellow-haired boy. He hated the Hunts, who cheated every
Negro who bought things on credit at their store. He hated thin-
lipped, sneering Doctor Benson. Most of all he hated that
Benson boy with his wiry yellow hair. Wasn't he always calling
out after him:

> "Nigger, Nigger never die,
> Snotty nose and shiny eye"?

Hadn't he thrown a stone and hit his spotted white fox terrier?
Could he ever forget that day in early fall when he had been
walking along the road with his grey, fuzzy chincilla overcoat on
his arm—his overcoat that both his mother and father had
picked out for him, with its half-red lining and its pearly grey
buttons? Oh, he remembered well enough. That yellow-haired
Benson brat (that's what he'd heard Father call him) grabbed
his overcoat from his arm and stamped all over it, saying:
"Niggers lak him oughtn't ter have that kind of an overcoat
nohow." And he told him: "Ef he wanted it, to pick it up lak a
common Nigger should."

But he wasn't going to take orders from any poor white trash.
He had thrown his head back, clenched his fists, and walked
away, leaving his overcoat by the side of the road. Hadn't he
been proud at that moment? His mother had sent Sybil to look
for the coat, but it wasn't there. Then she had whipped him and
cried afterwards. She kissed him on his quivering, pouting
mouth. How he remembered that kiss! It made up for the
whipping, it made up for everything except, except that Benson
boy. He didn't care that his mother had had to buy him a drab
second-hand overcoat at a Jew store for a dollar ninety-eight
cents (the other had cost seven dollars). He had been proud. He
had shown that Benson boy that he wouldn't take orders from
poor white trash, even if he were smaller.

And now Sybil had sent him for this "brat's" father. What
good was this poor white doctor, anyway? He didn't know
anything about medicine. Father had said he didn't. All he
would do would be to charge Father a lot of money without
doing Mother any good. He might poison her. He'd be low down
and mean enough to do something like that. What was the use

of getting him anyway? Father had said just that morning that he was going to bring a colored doctor home with him after work. Sybil was just a frightened girl. She was always getting excited about something. What did the father of that little "brat" know about curing people?

He had hesitated and wavered—first deciding to get the doctor and then not to. Even when he was a quarter of a mile up the road he had turned to go back, but again he had visions of his overcoat lying torn and dirty on the ground. And everything went black and then red before him.

He wondered what he would tell Sybil when he got home. He couldn't tell her why he hadn't got Doctor Benson. She wouldn't understand. What could he tell her? Well, he'd better make up his mind soon to a straight tale and stick to it. If Sybil caught him lying, she'd tell Father and he'd get an awful licking. Besides Sybil hadn't really wanted Doctor Benson. Hadn't she said to get Doctor Parker and hadn't she almost *not* said Doctor Benson? Well, he'd better hurry home or she'd be worrying about him.

He remembered just as plainly how Sybil had acted: how she had paled under her cream color as she said, "But, Buddy, couldn't you get any . . . body?" He hated himself a thousand times since for just shaking his head. Sybil had cried and cried until she went in to Mother; then she bit her lips and wiped her eyes on her gingham apron and went in with her face frozen into a smile. How brave Syb had been! He had always thought of her as brave and oldish-like. He felt mean and sorry. He had even tried to make up for not getting the doctor by drawing a bucket of water and filling the woodbox with chips.

Then Sybil came and took him to see Mother. He shuddered. How pale and white she looked as she lay there—whiter than any white woman he had ever seen. Her eyes were dark and filled with tears. The skin on her face seemed tight, like the cream-colored parlor curtains on a stretcher. She looked as if something was hurting inside of her. And then she had told him to kiss her; and when he did, her lips seemed sticky and queer. How mean he felt then. He wanted to run from the room. He wanted to cry and his eyes welled up with tears. He would have cried, too, if Sybil hadn't pinched him and shaken her head. Instead, he smiled a little. Funny, but somehow he always understood Syb.

He could hear his mother just as plainly making Syb promise to take care of "Davy Boy" (that's what she always called him) and to be a good girl for Mother's sake. Then she made him promise to be "good" and mind Sybil and Father, and get in wood and chips whenever Sybil asked him. To him it seemed very much like the times his mother had got ready to go to town and left him in Sybil's care. But he promised. And his mother ran her long, slim fingers through his hair and kissed him again and again.

Then his father had come home from work, bringing with him a tall colored doctor. They had both gone to Mother's room. How well he remembered Sybil and himself huddled together by the kitchen woodbox, listening to the low tones of the doctor and his father. It seemed such a long time. It grew darker and darker. Soon it became all black and Syb lit the coal-oil lamp on the table and came back to sit beside him.

Finally Father, looking tired, with the corners of his mouth twitching and the little wrinkles under his eyes seeming much darker to David than ever before, called them into Mother's room. Mother was there, trying to say something. Tears choked her, and Sybil brushed back a strand of her long, silken hair that was blowing over her eyes. "Mo . . . ther," she said, her whole body quivering, "Mo . . . ther." And then David remembered something like a wind that blew across his face; and when he looked at his mother again, she had closed her eyes.

And he heard the doctor say, shaking his head, "If I'd only been here two hours sooner." David thought of every time his mother had ever kissed him. He thought of himself down at the crossroads watching Doctor Benson sip soda-pop. He fell on the couch and cried and cried and cried, and his father clutched him tightly and tried to soothe him; while Sybil was looking out of the window into the dark night—standing there in her gingham apron, withered like the white flower in the fruit jar on the kitchen table.

David didn't know how much time had passed since he had begun thinking all this, but he had been very quiet. Now he cast sidewide glances about the church. Tall Deacon Gant was praying and Sybil made him bow his head. "We has faith in you, Gawd," droned the old man. The rest was only syllables to David. Old Mother Simms was looking out of dark, heavily lidded eyes into his. She looked so sad as tears rolled down the furrows of her black, wrinkled face. But somehow it seemed funny to see her with fluffy purple feathers on her hat and a black lace collar on her starched white dress. Now David felt that something was going to happen. They were standing up, Sybil, Father, and he. Sybil was guiding him past the grey box. He was looking on his mother's closed eyes. How full her cheeks looked now; not as when she was sick. He could hear voices all around. He thought he heard that Benson boy calling out after him; he almost saw a red tongue poking out of a pale face, topped by yellow hair. He fancied he heard his mother call him "Davy boy." Everything was in a daze. When next he recognized his surroundings, he was in a black coach drawn by two horses. Sybil was crying; Father, stonily silent.

universal theme -death
slight mention of white injustice

Truant

CLAUDE McKAY

The warbling of a mother's melody had just ended, and the audience was in a sentimental state and ready for the scene that the curtain, slowly drawn, disclosed. A mother in calico print jigged on her knee a little baby, crooning the while some Gaelic folk-words. A colleen sat on a red-covered box, mending a chemise; sitting at her feet, a younger sister with a picture book. Three boys in shirt sleeves and patched pantaloons playing with a red-and-green train on a lacquer-black railroad. A happy family. An antique sitting room, torn wallpaper, two comic chairs, and the Holy Virgin on the mantelpiece. A happy family. Father, fat and round like a chianti bottle, skips into the picture and up leaps boys and girls and mother with baby. The Merry Mulligans!

The orchestra starts at the pointing baton. Squeaky-burlesque family singing. Dancing. Stunting. A performing wonder, that little baby. Charming family of seven. American-famous. The Merry Mulligans, beloved of all lovers of clean vaudeville.

With them the show finished. Barclay Oram and his wife
Rhoda descended from Nigger Heaven, walked up to 50th
Street, and caught the local subway train for Harlem. He took
the slower train, hoping there would be seats and the passengers
not jammed together as always.

Perhaps others had hoped for the same thing. The cars were
packed. Rhoda broke up a piece of chewing gum and chewed.
She had a large mouth, and she chewed the gum as if she were
eating food, opening her mouth so wide that people could see
the roof. When they were first married, Barclay had detested her
way of chewing gum and told her so. But she replied that it was
absurd to let a little thing like chewing gum irritate him.

"Oh, you brown baby!" she had cried, taking his face in her
hands and kissing him with the perfumed flavor of her favorite
chewing gum on her breath. . . .

"The show was pretty nice, eh?" said Rhoda.

"I am fed up with them; a cabaret in Harlem is better," replied Barclay.

"I don't think so. Anything downtown for a change is prefer-
able to the cheap old colored shows. I'm dead sick of them."

She chewed the gum vigorously, dropping a few pointless
phrases that were half-swallowed up in the roar of the train
though the enormous gut of the city and the strange staccato
talk of voices half-lifted above and half-caught in the roar.
Barclay gazed moodily at the many straphangers who were
jammed together. None seemed standing on his feet. All seemed
like fat bags and lean boxes piled up indiscriminately in a
warehouse. Penned up like cattle, the standing closely pressing
the seated passengers, kneading them with their knees and
blotting out their sight, so that those who had been fortunate to
find seats were as uncomfortable as those who had not.

"I thought we'd have a little air in this local box," he said.

"It'll be better at 72nd Street," she said. "Some of them will
get out."

"And others will push in. New York City is swarming with
people like a beehive."

"Getting thicker and thicker every day," she agreed.

At 135th Street they left the train. Rhoda, as usual, put her
hand through her husband's arm as they walked home. The
saloons, restaurants, candy stores of the Avenue were crowded.

The Chop Suey Palace was doing a good after-theater business.

"Might have some chop suey," suggested Barclay.

"Not tonight," she said. "Betsy's with the Howlands, and they might want to go to bed."

"Ah yes!" He had forgotten about Betsy, their four-year-old child. Always he forgot about her. Never could he quite realize that he was the father of a family. A railroad waiter, although he was thirty-six, he always felt himself just a boy—a servant boy. His betters whom he served treated him always as a boy—often as a nice dog. And when he grew irritated and snapped, they turned on him as upon a bad dog. It was better for him, then, that, although he was a husband and father, he should feel like an irresponsible boy. Even when sometimes he grew sad, sullen, and disquieted, these were the moods of a boy. Rhoda bossed him a little and never took his moods seriously. . . .

They went straight home. Barclay lighted up the three-room apartment. Rhoda went across the hall to the Howlands' for Betsy. She brought the child in, sleeping on her breast, and bent down that Barclay might kiss her. Then she put her to bed in her little cot beside the dresser.

They had a little supper, cold chicken and beer. . . . They went to bed in the front room that they had made their bedroom. Another room was let to a railroad porter, and the dining room served for eating and sitting room.

Rhoda undressed, rubbed her face and her limbs with cold cream, slipped on a long white gown with pink ribbon around the neck, and lay down against the wall. Barclay laid himself down beside her in his underclothes. During the first six months of their union he had slept regularly in pyjamas. Then he ignored them and began sleeping in his underclothes, returning to the habit of his village boyhood. Rhoda protested at first. Afterwards she accepted it quietly. . . .

Sleep, sweet sleep. . . .

The next morning Rhoda shook Barclay at five o'clock. "O God!" He stretched himself, turned over, and rested his head on her breast.

"Time to get up," she said.

"Yes," he sighed. "God! I feel tired." He stretched his arms, touched, fondled her face, and fell into a slight doze.

Ten minutes more. Rhoda gave him a dig in the back with her knee and cried, "You just must get up, Barclay."

"All right." He turned out of bed. Six o'clock in the Pennsylvania Station for duty, that was life itself. A dutiful black boy among proud and sure white men, so that he could himself be a man in Harlem with purchasing power for wife, child, flat, movie, food, liquor. . . .

He went to the bathroom and washed. Dressed, he entered the dining room, opened a cabinet, and poured out a glass of whisky. That peppered him up and opened his eyes wide. It was not necessary for Rhoda to make coffee. He would breakfast with the other waiters in the dining car. Mechanically he kissed her good-by. She heard him close the door, and she moved over into the middle of the bed, comfortably alone, for an early-morning nap.

It was a disastrous trip for Barclay. On the dining car he was the first waiter and in charge of the pantry. As pantryman he received five dollars a month more than the other waiters. It was his job to get the stores (with the steward and chef) from the commissary. He was responsible for the stuff kept in the pantry. There were some waiters and cooks addicted to petty stealing. Butter, cream, cheese, sugar, fruit. They stole for their women in New York. They stole for their women-on-the-side in the stopover cities. Always Barclay had to mount guard quietly. Between him and the raw-voiced, black-bull chef there was an understanding to watch out for the nimble-fingered among the crew. For if they were short in the checking up of the stores, the steward held them responsible. And the commissary held the steward responsible.

This trip Barclay had one of his moody-boy spells. He would not watch the pantry. Let the boys swipe the stuff. He had no pleasure waiting on the passengers. It was often a pleasure, something of an anticipated adventure, each day to meet new passengers, remark the temperature of their looks, and sometimes make casual conversation with a transient acquaintance. But today it was all wrong from the moment he observed them, impatient, crowding the corridor, and the rushing of the dining room as soon as the doors were opened. They filled him with loathing, made him sick of service. SERVICE. A beautiful word fallen upon bad days. No place for true human service in these automatic-serving days.

Mechanically Barclay picked up the dimes and quarters that were left for service. For Rhoda and Betsy. It pleasured him

when Rhoda wore pretty clothes. And Betsy loved him more
each time he remembered to bring home colored bonbons. What
was he going to do with the child? He wondered if he would be
able to give her a good education like her mother's. And what
would she do? Perhaps marry a railroad waiter like her mother,
and raise up children to carry on the great tradition of black
servitude.

Philadelphia, Harrisburg, Altoona, Pittsburgh. No dice, no
coon-can, this trip. His workmates coaxed. Nothing could lift
him out of himself. He was a moody boy this trip. The afternoon
of the fourth day from New York brought the dining car to
Washington. Washington reminded Barclay of a grave. He had
sharp, hammering memories of his university days there. For
there he had fallen in love. . . .

He went up to 7th Street, loitering through the Negro district,
stopping curiously before a house, leaning against a stoop,
sniffing here and there like a stray hound. He went into a barrel-
house and drank a glass of whisky. The place was sour-smelling,
full of black men, dim and smoky, close, but friendly warm.

The hour of his train's departure, approached. Barclay continued drinking. He felt pleased with himself in doing something irregular. Oh, he had been regular for such a long time! A
good waiter, an honest pantryman. Never once had he sneaked
a packet of sugar nor a pound of butter for his flat. Rhoda would
have flung it in the street. He had never given to the colored
girls who worked in the yards and visited the dining cars with
their teasing smiles. Oh, it was hard to be responsible, hard to
be regular.

What would the steward say about his being left in Washington? Maybe he would be drunk himself, for he was a regular
souser. Barclay recalled the day when he got helplessly stewed
on the Washington run, and the waiters managed the dining
car, handed out checks, made change among themselves, and
gave the best service they ever did as a crew. At Philadelphia an
inspector hopped on the train and took charge of the service.
The dining car was crowded. The steward half-roused himself
out of his stupor and came lurching through the jam of passengers in the corridor into the diner, to dispute the stewardship
with the inspector.

"I'm in charge of this diner," he said in a nerve-biting, imey-
wimey voice. "Give a man a chance; treat me like a gen'leman."

Tears trickled down his cheeks. He staggered and swayed in
the corridor, blocking the entrance and exit of the guests. Like a
challenged mastiff, the inspector eyed him, at the same time
glancing quickly from the waiters to the amazed guests. Then
he gripped the steward by the scruff of the collar and, with the
help of the Pullman conductor, locked him up in a drawing
room until the train reached New York.

The crew did not like the steward and hoped they would be
rid of him at last. But he was back with them the next trip. The
inspector was known as a hard guy, quick to report a waiter if a
flask of gin were discovered in his locker. But it was different
with the steward. Both men were peers, the inspector being a
promoted steward.

"Well, I'm off duty, anyhow," murmured Barclay. He smiled
and ordered another drink. The train must have passed Baltimore by then, on its way to New York. What waiter was waiting
on the first two tables? "I should worry." He had the warm,
luxurious feelings of a truant. He drank himself drunk.

"Something for a change. I've been regular too long. Too
awfully regular," he mused.

He rocked heavily out of the barrel-house to a little fried-
chicken restaurant. He ate. His stomach appeased, his thoughts
turned to a speakeasy. May as well finish the thing in style—be
grandly irregular, he thought. He found a speakeasy. Bold-eyed
chocolate girls, brown girls, yellow girls. Blues. Pianola blues,
gramophone blues. Easy-queasy, daddy-mammy, honey-baby,
brown-gal, black-boy, hot-dog blues. . . .

The next day he reported himself at the restaurant-car department in Washington, and was sent home to New York. There at
the commissary the superintendent looked him over and said:
"Well, you're a case. You wanted a little time off, eh? Well, take
ten days."

That was his punishment—ten idle days. He left the commissary walking on air. For three years he had worked on the
railroad without taking a holiday. Why? He did not himself
know. He had often yearned for a few entirely free days. But he
had never had the courage to take them, not for fear of forfeit-
ing the nominal wages, but the tips—his real wages. Nor had he
wanted to lose his former dining car. He had liked his work-pals
there. A good crew teaming splendidly along together, respectful

to and respected by the steward, who was a decent-minded man. Moreover, there was the flat with Rhoda and Betsy. Every day was precious, every tip necessary. . . . Ten days gratuitously thrust upon him with malicious intent. No wages-and-food, no tips. Let him cool his heels and tighten his belt. Yet he was happy, happy like a truant suspended from school.

Freedom! Ten days. What would he do with them? There would be parties. Rhoda loved parties. She had friends in New York who knew her when she was a schoolteacher. Whist. Dancing. Movies.

He nosed around the tenderloin district. When he first came to New York he had lived in 40th Street.

He met a pal he had once worked with as elevator boy in a department store. They drank two glasses of beer each and walked up to San Juan Hill.

When Barclay got home, Rhoda, in an orange evening dress, was just leaving for a party. They embraced.

"I phoned up the commissary yesterday and they said you were left in Washington. Bad boy!" She laughed. "Guess I'll fix you something to eat."

"Don't bother. I'm not hungry," said Barclay.

"All right. I'm going on to Mame Dixon's for whist and a little dancing afterwards. You might dress up and come on down and have a little fun."

"Not tonight, honey. We'll have plenty of time to go around together. They gave me ten days."

"Ten days!" she cried. "The rent is due on Friday and the insurance on—on—Ten days! But why did you get left, Barclay?"

"I don't know. Felt rotten the whole trip—tired, blue. Been too punctual all along. Just had to break the habit. Feel a little irresponsible."

"But you might get in bad with the company. How could you, when there's Betsy and me to think of and our social position?"

She broke up a stick of chewing gum and vigorously chewed. "Well, anyway, come on along to Mame's if you feel like it." She rolled the gum with her tongue. "But if you don't, you can bring Betsy over from the Howlands'."

Chewing, chewing, she went out.

"Kill-joy," murmured Barclay. Riding on the subway from San Juan Hill to Harlem, he had been guessing chucklingly at what she would say. Perhaps: "All right, honey-stick, why slave every day? Let's play around together for ten days."

Chewing, chewing. Always chewing. Yet that mouth was the enchanting thing about her. . . . Her mouth. It made me marry her. Her skin was brown and beautiful. Like cat's fur, soft to the fingers. But it was not her fruit-ripe skin. It was her mouth that made me.

Ordinary her face would have been, if it were not for the full, large mouth that was mounted on the ample plane of her features like an exquisite piece of bas-relief.

He went across the hall to the Howlands' and brought back Betsy.

"Candy, daddy, candy!" The happy brown thing clapped her hands and pulled at his pantaloons. He set her on his knee and gave her a little paper packet. He danced her up and down: "Betsy, wupsy, mupsy, pretsy, eatsy plentsy candy."

She wriggled off his knee with the packet and dropped the candies one by one into a small glass jar, gurgling over the colors and popping one into her mouth at intervals. . . . She returned again to Barclay's knee, squeezing a brown rubber doll. For a little while she made a rocking horse of him. Then she scratched her head and yawned. Barclay undressed her and put her in the crib.

"Betsy and me and our social position." That social position! Alone he brooded, moody, unreasonable. Resentment gripped his heart. He hated his love of Rhoda's mouth. He hated the flat and his pitiable "social position." He hated fatherhood. He resented the sleeping child.

"Betsy and me and——" Should he go on forever like that? Round the circle of the Eastern field? New York, Boston, Buffalo, Pittsburgh, Harrisburg, Washington, Baltimore, Philadelphia, again New York.

Forever? Getting off nowhere?

Forever fated to the lifelong tasks of the unimaginative? Why was he, a West Indian peasant boy, held prisoner within the huge granite-gray walls of New York? Dreaming of tawny tasseled fields of sugar cane, and silver-gray John-tuhits among clusters of green and glossy-blue berries of pimento. The husbands and fathers of his village were not mechanically driven servant boys. They were hardy, independent tillers of the soil or struggling artisans.

What enchantment had lured him away from the green intimate life that clustered round his village—the simple African-transplanted life of the West Indian hills? Why had he hankered for the hard-slabbed streets, the vertical towers, the gray complex life of this steel-tempered city? Stone and steel! Steel and stone! Mounting in heaven-pursuing magnificence. Feet piled upon feet, miles circling miles, of steel and stone. A tree seemed absurd and a garden queer in this iron-gray majesty of man's imagination. He was a slave to it. A part of him was in love with this piling grandeur. And that was why he was a slave to it.

From the bedroom came a slight stirring and a sleepy murmur of child-language. Barclay was lost in the past. Step by step he retraced his life. . . . His fever-like hunger for book knowledge, for strange lands and great cities. His grand adolescent dream.

The evening of his departure from the village came back star-blue and clear. He had trudged many miles to the railroad with his bright-patterned carpet bag on his shoulder. For three years in the capital of his island he had worked in a rum warehouse. Happy. On the road to his beautiful dream. Later he had crossed over to Santiago in Cuba. And at twenty-five he had reached New York, found his strange land—a great city of great books.

Two years of elevator-running and switchboard-operating had glanced by like a magic arrow against the gaunt gray walls of the city. Time was a radiant servant working for his dream.

His dream, of course, was the Negro university. Now he remembered how he turned green cold like a cucumber when he was told that he could not enter the university course. Two years preparatory work was needed. Undaunted, he had returned to New York and crammed for a year. And the next fall he swept through the entrance examinations.

For Barclay then the highroad to wisdom led necessarily by way of a university. It had never occurred to him that he might have also attained his goal in his own free, informal way.

He had been enchanted by the words: University, Seat of Learning. He had seen young men of the insular island villages returned from the native colleges. They all brought back with them a new style of clothes, a different accent, a new gait, the exciting, intoxicating smell of the city—so much more intriguing than the ever-fresh accustomed smell of the bright-green hill-valley village. Style and accent and exotic smell—all those attractive fruits of college training, fundamental forms of the cultural life. Home study could not give him the stamp. . . . His disillusion had not embittered him. . . .

My college days were happy, he reflected. A symmetrical group of buildings, gray walls supporting in winter stout, dark-brown leafless creepers. An all-Negro body of students—men and women—of many complexions, all intensely active. The booklore was there, housed in a kind of Gothic building with a projecting façade resting on Grecian pillars. The names of Aristotle, Solon, Virgil, Shakespeare, Dante, and Longfellow were cut in the façade. The building was one of the many symbols, scattered over America and the world, summing up the dream of a great romantic king of steel.

Barclay found no romance in textbooks, of course. But he found plenty of it in the company of the jolly girls and chummy chaps of his widened acquaintance. And the barbaric steps of the turkey-trot and the bunny-hug (exciting dances of that period) he had found more enchanting than the library. He was amorously touched by the warm, intimate little dances he attended—the spontaneous outburst of group-singing when the dancers were particularly drunk on a rich, tintinnabulating melody.

Then one day he was abruptly pulled up in his fantastic steps. No more money in the box. He had to wheel round about and begin the heavy steps of working his way through college.

The next fall he met Rhoda. It was at one of those molasses-thick Aframerican affairs that had rendered university life so attractive to him, at the home of a very generous fawn-brown widow who enjoyed giving a few students a nice time at her flat. The widow entertained her guests in a free kind of way. She did not belong to the various divisions that go to the making of nice Negro society, for she was merely the widow of a Pullman porter, who had saved up his tips and paid up on a good insurance policy. She had been too fine for the non-discriminating parlor-social sets, and too secular for the prayer-meeting black ladies. So she had cleverly gone in for the non-snobbish young intellectuals—poor students who could not afford to put on airs.

Barclay recalled the warm roomful of young Negro men and girls. Copper and chocolate and fine anthracite, with here and there a dash of cream, all warmly dancing. One night he was attracted to Rhoda. He danced with her all the time and she was warm to him, loving to him. She was the first American girl with whom he began a steady intimacy. All the ardors of him were stirred to her, and simply, impetuously he had rushed into deep love, like a bee that darts too far into the heart of a flower and, unable to withdraw, dies at the bottom of the juice.

Rhoda, who had been earning her own living as a teacher, helped him, and the problem of money was lifted from his mind. Oh, he was very happy then! Books and parties and Rhoda. . . .

In the middle of his junior year she told him she was with child. They discussed whether she should have the child or operate it away. If she had it without being married, she would lose her job. He remembered a school-teaching girl of his village who had tried to conceal her pregnancy and died under an operation in the city. The other girls, the free peasant girls, always bore their children when they were gotten with child. Perhaps it was better that way.

Rhoda was pleased that Barclay wanted the thing to develop in the natural way. She desired a child. She was at that vague age when some women feel that marriage is more than the grim pursuit of a career. So they went to New York together and got married.

But Barclay did not fully realize the responsibility, perhaps could not, of marriage. Never fully understood its significance.

Barclay remembered now that he was as keen as Rhoda for the marriage. Carried away by the curiosity to take up a new role, there had been something almost of eagerness in his desire to quit the university. And it had seemed a beautiful gesture. Rhoda had helped him when he was in great need, and he felt splendid now to come to her support when she was incapacitated for work. He would have hated to see her drop down to menial tasks. As a Jack-of-all-trades he had met many refined colored girls having a rough time, jammed at the bottom of the common scramble to survive.

He had been happy that Rhoda was not pushed to leave Betsy in one of those dime dumps where poor colored children were guarded while their mothers worked, happy that from his job on the railroad he was earning enough for the family to live simply and comfortably.

About that job he had never taken serious thought. Where was it leading him? What was it making of his character? He had taken it as if he were acting in a play rather than working at a job. It met the necessary bill of being in love. For he was really in love with Rhoda. The autumn-leaf mellowness of her body. Her ripe-ripe accent and richness of laughter. And her mouth: the full form of it, its strength and beauty, its almost unbearable sweetness, magnetic, drawing, sensuous, exquisite, a dark pagan piece of pleasure. . . . How fascinated and enslaved he had been to what was now stale with chewing gum and banal remarks on "social position."

Barclay's attitude to the railroad was about the same toward the modern world in general. He had entered light-heartedly into the whirl and crash and crush, the grand babel of building, the suction and spouting, groaning and whining and breaking of steel—all the riotous, contagious movement around him.

He had entered into the rough camaraderie of the railroad with all the hot energy of youth. It was a rugged, new experience that kindled his vagabonding mind and body. There was rude poetry in the roar and rush and rattle of trains, the sharp whistle of engines and racing landscapes, the charm of a desolate mining town and glimpses of faces lost as soon as seen. He had even tried to capture some of those fleeting piled-up images. Some he had read to his workmates, which they appreciated, but teased him for writing:

> We are out in the field, the vast wide-open field,
> Thundering through from city to city
> Where factories grow like jungle trees
> Yielding new harvests for the world.
> Through Johnstown glowing like a world aflame,
> And Pittsburgh, Negro-black, brooding in iron smoke,
> Philly's Fifteenth street of wenches, speakeasies, and cops.
> Out in the field, new fields of life
> Where machines spin flowers like tropic trees
> And coal and steel are blazing suns—
> And darkly we wonder, night-wrapped in the light.

The steel-framed poetry of cities did not crowd out but rather intensified in him the singing memories of his village life. He loved both, the one complementing the other. Against the intricate stone-and-steel flights of humanity's mass spirit, misty in space and time, hovered the green charm of his village. Yellow-eyed and white-lidded Spanish needles coloring the grassy hillsides, barefooted black girls, straight like young sweet-woods, tramping to market with baskets of mangoes or star-apples poised unsupported on their heads. The native cockish liquor juice of the sugar cane, fermented in bamboo joints for all-night carousal at wakes and tea meetings. Heavy drays loaded with new-made sugar, yams, and plantains, rumbling along the chalky country road away down and over the hills under the starshine and the hot-free love songs of the draymen.

He remembered all, regretting nothing, since his life was a continual fluxion from one state to another. His deepest regret was always momentary, arising from remaining in a rut after he had exhausted the experience.

Rhoda now seemed only another impasse into which he had drifted. Just a hole to pull out of again and away from the road, that arena of steel rushing him round and round in the same familiar circle. He had to evade it and be irresponsible again.

But there was the child and the Moral Law. The cold white law. Rhoda seemed more than he to be subject to it with her constant preoccupation about social position.

Spiritually he was subject to another law. Other gods of strange barbaric glory claimed his allegiance, and not the grim frock-coated gentleman of the Moral Law of the land. The Invisible Law that upheld those magnificent machines and steel-spired temples and new cathedrals erected to the steel-flung traffic plan of man. Oh, he could understand and love the poetry of them, but not their law that held humanity gripped in fear.

His thought fell to a whisper within him. He could never feel himself more than a stranger within these walls. His body went through the mechanical process, but untamed, for his spirit was wandering far. . . .

Rhoda at the party and the child asleep. He could hear her breathing and wondered if it were breath of his breath. For he had often felt to himself a breath of his own related to none. Suppose he should start now on the trail again with that strange burning thought. Related to none.

There were the Liberty Bonds in his trunk. Rhoda would need them. He remembered how he had signed for them. All the waiters herded together in one of the commissary rooms and lectured by one of the special war men.

"Buy a bond, boys. All you boys will buy a bond because you all believe in the Allied cause. We are in the war to make the world safe for Democracy. You boys on the railroad are enjoying the blessings of Democracy like all real Americans. Your service is inestimable. Keep on doing your part and do your best by buying a bond because you believe in the Allied cause and you want America to win the war and the banner of Democracy float over the world. Come on, take your bond."

For the Moral Law. Buy a bond.

Well it was all right; he had subscribed. One way of saving money, although the bonds were worth so much less now. There was the bankbook with a couple hundred dollars. Leave that, too. Insurance policies. Forget them.

He thought he heard the child stir. He dared not look. He clicked the door and stepped out. Where? Destination did not matter. Maybe his true life lay in eternal inquietude.

little concentration on white concern: negro family & employment

A Summer Tragedy

ARNA BONTEMPS

Old Jeff Patton, the black share farmer, fumbled with his bow tie. His fingers trembled and the high, stiff collar pinched his throat. A fellow loses his hand for such vanities after thirty or forty years of simple life. Once a year, or maybe twice if there's a wedding among his kinfolks, he may spruce up; but generally fancy clothes do nothing but adorn the wall of the big room and feed the moths. That had been Jeff Patton's experience. He had not worn his stiff-bosomed shirt more than a dozen times in all his married life. His swallow-tailed coat lay on the bed beside him, freshly brushed and pressed, but it was as full of holes as the overalls in which he worked on weekdays. The moths had used it badly. Jeff twisted his mouth into a hideous toothless grimace as he contended with the obstinate bow. He stamped his good foot and decided to give up the struggle.

"Jennie," he called.

"What's that, Jeff?" His wife's shrunken voice came out of the adjoining room like an echo. It was hardly bigger than a whisper.

"I reckon you'll have to he'p me wid this heah bow tie, baby," he said meekly. "Dog if I can hitch it up."

Her answer was not strong enough to reach him, but presently the old woman came to the door, feeling her way with a stick. She had a wasted, dead-leaf appearance. Her body, as scrawny and gnarled as a string bean, seemed less than nothing in the ocean of frayed and faded petticoats that surrounded her. These hung an inch or two above the tops of her heavy unlaced shoes and showed little grotesque piles where the stockings had fallen down from her negligible legs.

"You oughta could do a heap mo' wid a thing like that'n me—beingst as you got yo' good sight."

"Looks like I oughta could," he admitted. "But my fingers is gone democrat on me. I get all mixed up in the looking glass an' can't tell wicha way to twist the devilish thing."

Jennie sat on the side of the bed, and old Jeff Patton got down on one knee while she tied the bow knot. It was a slow and painful ordeal for each of them in this position. Jeff's bones cracked, his knee ached, and it was only after a half dozen attempts that Jennie worked a semblance of a bow into the tie.

"I got to dress maself now," the old woman whispered. "These is ma old shoes an' stockings, and I ain't so much as unwrapped ma dress."

"Well, don't worry 'bout me no mo', baby," Jeff said. "That 'bout finishes me. All I gotta do now is slip on that old coat 'n ves' an' I'll be fixed to leave."

Jennie disappeared again through the dim passage into the shed room. Being blind was no handicap to her in that black hole. Jeff heard the cane placed against the wall beside the door and knew that his wife was on easy ground. He put on his coat, took a battered top hat from the bed post, and hobbled to the front door. He was ready to travel. As soon as Jennie could get on her Sunday shoes and her old black silk dress, they would start.

Outside the tiny log house, the day was warm and mellow with sunshine. A host of wasps were humming with busy excitement in the trunk of a dead sycamore. Gray squirrels were searching through the grass for hickory nuts, and blue jays were in the trees, hopping from branch to branch. Pine woods stretched away to the left like a black sea. Among them were scattered scores of log houses like Jeff's, houses of black share farmers. Cows and pigs wandered freely among the trees. There was no danger of loss. Each farmer knew his own stock and knew his neighbor's as well as he knew his neighbor's children.

Down the slope to the right were the cultivated acres on which the colored folks worked. They extended to the river, more than two miles away, and they were today green with the unmade cotton crop. A tiny thread of a road, which passed directly in front of Jeff's place, ran through these green fields like a pencil mark.

Jeff, standing outside the door, with his absurd hat in his left hand, surveyed the wide scene tenderly. He had been forty-five years on these acres. He loved them with the unexplained affection that others have for the countries to which they belong.

The sun was hot on his head, his collar still pinched his throat, and the Sunday clothes were intolerably hot. Jeff transferred the hat to his right hand and began fanning with it. Suddenly the whisper that was Jennie's voice came out of the shed room.

"You can bring the car round front whilst you's waitin'," it said feebly. There was a tired pause; then it added, "I'll soon be fixed to go."

"A'right, baby," Jeff answered. "I'll get it in a minute."

But he didn't move. A thought struck him that made his mouth fall open. The mention of the car brought to his mind, with new intensity, the trip he and Jennie were about to take. Fear came into his eyes; excitement took his breath. Lord, Jesus!

"Jeff. . . . O Jeff," the old woman's whisper called.

He awakened with a jolt. "Hunh, baby?"

"What you doin'?"

"Nuthin. Jes studyin'. I jes been turnin' things round 'n round in ma mind."

"You could be gettin' the car," she said.

"Oh yes, right away, baby."

He started round to the shed, limping heavily on his bad leg. There were three frizzly chickens in the yard. All his other chickens had been killed or stolen recently. But the frizzly chickens had been saved somehow. That was fortunate indeed, for these curious creatures had a way of devouring "poison" from the yard and in that way protecting against conjure and black luck and spells. But even the frizzly chickens seemed now to be in a stupor. Jeff thought they had some ailment; he expected all three of them to die shortly.

The shed in which the old T-model Ford stood was only a grass roof held up by four corner poles. It had been built by tremulous hands at a time when the little rattletrap car had been regarded as a peculiar treasure. And, miraculously, despite wind and downpour, it still stood.

Jeff adjusted the crank and put his weight upon it. The engine came to life with a sputter and bang that rattled the old car from radiator to tail light. Jeff hopped into the seat and put his foot on the accelerator. The sputtering and banging increased. The rattling became more violent. That was good. It was good banging, good sputtering and rattling, and it meant that the aged car was still in running condition. She could be depended on for this trip.

Again Jeff's thought halted as if paralyzed. The suggestion of the trip fell into the machinery of his mind like a wrench. He felt dazed and weak. He swung the car out into the yard, made a half turn, and drove around to the front door. When he took his hands off the wheel, he noticed that he was trembling violently. He cut off the motor and climbed to the ground to wait for Jennie.

A few minutes later she was at the window, her voice rattling against the pane like a broken shutter.

"I'm ready, Jeff."

He did not answer, but limped into the house and took her by the arm. He led her slowly through the big room, down the step, and across the yard.

"You reckon I'd oughta lock the do'?" he asked softly.

They stopped and Jennie weighed the question. Finally she shook her head.

"Ne' mind the do'," she said. "I don't see no cause to lock up things."

"You right," Jeff agreed. "No cause to lock up."

Jeff opened the door and helped his wife into the car. A quick shudder passed over him. Jesus! Again he trembled.

"How come you shaking so?" Jennie whispered.

"I don't know," he said.

"You mus' be scairt, Jeff."

"No, baby, I ain't scairt."

He slammed the door after her and went around to crank up again. The motor started easily. Jeff wished that it had not been so responsive. He would have liked a few more minutes in which to turn things around in his head. As it was, with Jennie chiding him about being afraid, he had to keep going. He swung the car into the little pencil-mark road and started off toward the river, driving very slowly, very cautiously.

Chugging across the green countryside, the small battered Ford seemed tiny indeed. Jeff felt a familiar excitement, a thrill, as they came down the first slope to the immense levels on which the cotton was growing. He could not help reflecting that the crops were good. He knew what that meant, too; he had made forty-five of them with his own hands. It was true that he had worn out nearly a dozen mules, but that was the fault of old man Stevenson, the owner of the land. Major Stevenson had the odd notion that one mule was all a share farmer needed to work a thirty-acre plot. It was an expensive notion, the way it killed mules from overwork, but the old man held to it. Jeff thought it killed a good many share farmers as well as mules, but he had no sympathy for them. He had always been strong, and he had been taught to have no patience with weakness in men. Women or children might be tolerated if they were puny, but a weak man was a curse. Of course, his own children——

Jeff's thought halted there. He and Jennie never mentioned their dead children any more. And naturally, he did not wish to dwell upon them in his mind. Before he knew it, some remark would slip out of his mouth and that would make Jennie feel blue. Perhaps she would cry. A woman like Jennie could not easily throw off the grief that comes from losing five grown children within two years. Even Jeff was still staggered by the blow. His memory had not been much good recently. He frequently talked to himself. And, although he had kept it a secret, he knew that his courage had left him. He was terrified by the least unfamiliar sound at night. He was reluctant to venture far from home in the daytime. And that habit of trembling when he felt fearful was now far beyond his control. Sometimes he became afraid and trembled without knowing what had frightened him. The feeling would just come over him like a chill.

The car rattled slowly over the dusty road. Jennie sat erect and silent with a little absurd hat pinned to her hair. Her useless eyes seemed very large, very white in their deep sockets. Suddenly Jeff heard her voice, and he inclined his head to catch the words.

"Is we passed Delia Moore's house yet?" she asked.

"Not yet," he said.

"You must be drivin' mighty slow, Jeff."

"We just as well take our time, baby."

There was a pause. A little puff of steam was coming out of the radiator of the car. Heat wavered above the hood. Delia Moore's house was nearly half a mile away. After a moment Jennie spoke again.

"You ain't really scairt, is you, Jeff?"

"Nah, baby, I ain't scairt."

"You know how we agreed—we gotta keep on goin'."

Jewels of perspiration appeared on Jeff's forehead. His eyes rounded, blinked, became fixed on the road.

"I don't know," he said with a shiver, "I reckon it's the only thing to do."

"Hm."

A flock of guinea fowls, pecking in the road, were scattered by the passing car. Some of them took to their wings; others hid under bushes. A blue jay, swaying on a leafy twig, was annoying a roadside squirrel. Jeff held an even speed till he came near Delia's place. Then he slowed down noticeably.

Delia's house was really no house at all, but an abandoned store building converted into a dwelling. It sat near a crossroads, beneath a single black cedar tree. There Delia, a cattish old creature of Jennie's age, lived alone. She had been there more years than anybody could remember, and long ago had won the disfavor of such women as Jennie. For in her young days Delia had been gayer, yellower, and saucier than seemed proper in those parts. Her ways with menfolks had been dark and suspicious. And the fact that she had had as many husbands as children did not help her reputation.

"Yonder's old Delia," Jeff said as they passed.

"What she doin'?"

"Jes sittin' in the do'," he said.

"She see us?"

"Hm," Jeff said. "Musta did."

That relieved Jennie. It strengthened her to know that her old enemy had seen her pass in her best clothes. That would give the old she-devil something to chew her gums and fret about, Jennie thought. Wouldn't she have a fit if she didn't find out? Old evil Delia! This would be just the thing for her. It would pay her back for being so evil. It would also pay her, Jennie thought, for the way she used to grin at Jeff—long ago, when her teeth were good.

The road became smooth and red, and Jeff could tell by the smell of the air that they were nearing the river. He could see the rise where the road turned and ran along parallel to the stream. The car chugged on monotonously. After a long silent spell, Jennie leaned against Jeff and spoke.

"How many bale o' cotton you think we got standin'?" she said.

Jeff wrinkled his forehead as he calculated.

" 'Bout twenty-five, I reckon."

"How many you make las' year?"

"Twenty-eight," he said. "How come you ask that?"

"I's jes thinkin'," Jennie said quietly.

"It don't make a speck o' difference though," Jeff reflected. "If we get much or if we get little, we still gonna be in debt to old man Stevenson when he gets through counting up agin us. It's took us a long time to learn that."

Jennie was not listening to these words. She had fallen into a trance-like meditation. Her lips twitched. She chewed her gums and rubbed her gnarled hands nervously. Suddenly, she leaned forward, buried her face in the nervous hands, and burst into tears. She cried aloud in a dry, cracked voice that suggested the rattle of fodder on dead stalks. She cried aloud like a child, for she had never learned to suppress a genuine sob. Her slight old frame shook heavily and seemed hardly able to sustain such violent grief.

"What's the matter, baby?" Jeff asked awkwardly. "Why you cryin' like all that?"

"I's jes thinkin'," she said.

"So you the one what's scairt now, hunh?"

"I ain't scairt, Jeff. I's jes thinkin' 'bout leavin' eve'thing like this—eve'thing we been used to. It's right sad-like."

Jeff did not answer, and presently Jennie buried her face again and cried.

The sun was almost overhead. It beat down furiously on the dusty wagon-path road, on the parched roadside grass and the tiny battered car. Jeff's hands, gripping the wheel, became wet with perspiration; his forehead sparkled. Jeff's lips parted. His mouth shaped a hideous grimace. His face suggested the face of a man being burned. But the torture passed and his expression softened again.

"You mustn't cry, baby," he said to his wife. "We gotta be strong. We can't break down."

Jennie waited a few seconds, then said, "You reckon we oughta do it, Jeff? You reckon we oughta go 'head an' do it, really?"

Jeff's voice choked; his eyes blurred. He was terrified to hear Jennie say the thing that had been in his mind all morning. She had egged him on when he had wanted more than anything in the world to wait, to reconsider, to think things over a little longer. Now she was getting cold feet. Actually, there was no need of thinking the question through again. It would only end in making the same painful decision once more. Jeff knew that. There was no need of fooling around longer.

"We jes as well to do like we planned," he said. "They ain't nothin' else for us now—it's the bes' thing."

Jeff thought of the handicaps, the near impossibility, of making another crop with his leg bothering him more and more each week. Then there was always the chance that he would have another stroke, like the one that had made him lame. Another one might kill him. The least it could do would be to leave him helpless. Jeff gasped—Lord, Jesus! He could not bear to think of being helpless, like a baby, on Jennie's hands. Frail, blind Jennie.

The little pounding motor of the car worked harder and harder. The puff of steam from the cracked radiator became larger. Jeff realized that they were climbing a little rise. A moment later the road turned abruptly, and he looked down upon the face of the river.

"Jeff."

"Hunh?"

"Is that the water I hear?"

"Hm. Tha's it."

"Well, which way you goin' now?"

"Down this-a way," he said. "The road runs 'long 'side o' the water a lil piece."

She waited a while calmly. Then she said, "Drive faster."

"A'right, baby," Jeff said.

The water roared in the bed of the river. It was fifty or sixty feet below the level of the road. Between the road and the water there was a long smooth slope, sharply inclined. The slope was dry, the clay hardened by prolonged summer heat. The water below, roaring in a narrow channel, was noisy and wild.

"Jeff."

"Hunh?"

"How far you goin'?"

"Jes a lil piece down the road."

"You ain't scairt, is you, Jeff?"

"Nah, baby," he said trembling. "I ain't scairt."

"Remember how we planned it, Jeff. We gotta do it like we said. Brave-like."

"Hm."

Jeff's brain darkened. Things suddenly seemed unreal, like figures in a dream. Thoughts swam in his mind foolishly, hysterically, like little blind fish in a pool within a dense cave. They rushed again. Jeff soon became dizzy. He shuddered violently and turned to his wife.

"Jennie, I can't do it. I can't." His voice broke pitifully.

She did not appear to be listening. All the grief had gone from her face. She sat erect, her unseeing eyes wide open, strained and frightful. Her glossy black skin had become dull. She seemed as thin, as sharp and bony, as a starved bird. Now, having suffered and endured the sadness of tearing herself away from beloved things, she showed no anguish. She was absorbed with her own thoughts, and she didn't even hear Jeff's voice shouting in her ear.

Jeff said nothing more. For an instant there was light in his cavernous brain. The great chamber was, for less than a second, peopled by characters he knew and loved. They were simple, healthy creatures, and they behaved in a manner that he could understand. They had quality. But since he had already taken leave of them long ago, the remembrance did not break his heart again. Young Jeff Patton was among them, the Jeff Patton of fifty years ago who went down to New Orleans with a crowd of country boys to the Mardi Gras doings. The gay young crowd, boys with candy-striped shirts and rouged brown girls in noisy silks, was like a picture in his head. Yet it did not make him sad. On that very trip Slim Burns had killed Joe Beasley—the crowd had been broken up. Since then Jeff Patton's world had been the Greenbriar Plantation. If there had been other Mardi Gras carnivals, he had not heard of them. Since then there had been no time; the years had fallen on him like waves. Now he was old, worn out. Another paralytic stroke (like the one he had already suffered) would put him on his back for keeps. In that condition, with a frail blind woman to look after him, he would be worse off than if he were dead.

Suddenly Jeff's hands became steady. He actually felt brave. He slowed down the motor of the car and carefully pulled off the road. Below, the water of the stream boomed, a soft thunder in the deep channel. Jeff ran the car onto the clay slope, pointed it directly toward the stream, and put his foot heavily on the accelerator. The little car leaped furiously down the steep incline toward the water. The movement was nearly as swift and direct as a fall. The two old black folks, sitting quietly side by side, showed no excitement. In another instant the car hit the water and dropped immediately out of sight.

A little later it lodged in the mud of a shallow place. One wheel of the crushed and upturned little Ford became visible above the rushing water.

no mention of whites

The Gilded Six-Bits

Zora Neale Hurston

It was a Negro yard around a Negro house in a Negro settlement that looked to the payroll of the G. and G. Fertilizer Works for its support.

But there was something happy about the place. The front yard was parted in the middle by a sidewalk from gate to doorstep, a sidewalk edged on either side by quart bottles driven neck down into the ground on a slant. A mess of homey flowers planted without a plan but blooming cheerily from their helter-skelter places. The fence and house were whitewashed. The porch and steps scrubbed white.

The front door stood open to the sunshine so that the floor of the front room could finish drying after its weekly scouring. It was Saturday. Everything clean from the front gate to the privy house. Yard raked so that the strokes of the rake would make a pattern. Fresh newspaper cut in fancy edge on the kitchen shelves.

Missie May was bathing herself in the galvanized washtub in the bedroom. Her dark-brown skin glistened under the soapsuds that skittered down from her washrag. Her stiff young breasts thrust forward aggressively like broad-based cones with the tips lacquered in black.

She heard men's voices in the distance and glanced at the dollar clock on the dresser.

"Humph! Ah'm way behind time t'day! Joe gointer be heah 'fore Ah git mah clothes on if Ah don't make haste."

She grabbed the clean meal sack at hand and dried herself hurriedly and began to dress. But before she could tie her slippers, there came the ring of singing metal on wood. Nine times.

Missie May grinned with delight. She had not seen the big, tall man come stealing in the gate and creep up the walk, grinning happily at the joyful mischief he was about to commit. But she knew that it was her husband throwing silver dollars in the door for her to pick up and pile beside her plate at dinner. It was this way every Saturday afternoon. The nine dollars hurled into the open door, he scurried to a hiding place behind the cape jasmine bush and waited.

Missie May promptly appeared at the door in mock alarm.

"Who dat chunkin' money in mah do'way?" she demanded. No answer from the yard. She leaped off the porch and began to search the shrubbery. She peeped under the porch and hung over the gate to look up and down the road. While she did this, the man behind the jasmine darted to the chinaberry tree. She spied him and gave chase.

"Nobody ain't gointer be chunkin' money at me and Ah not do 'em nothin'," she shouted in mock anger. He ran around the house with Missie May at his heels. She overtook him at the kitchen door. He ran inside but could not close it after him before she crowded in and locked with him in a rough and tumble. For several minutes the two were a furious mass of male and female energy. Shouting, laughing, twisting, turning, tussling, tickling each other in the ribs; Missie May clutching onto Joe and Joe trying, but not too hard, to get away.

"Missie May, take yo' hand out mah pocket!" Joe shouted out between laughs.

"Ah ain't, Joe, not lessen you gwine gimme whateve' it is good you got in yo' pocket. Turn it go, Joe, do Ah'll tear yo' clothes."

"Go on tear 'em. You de one dat pushes de needles round heah. Move yo' hand, Missie May."

"Lemme git dat paper sack out yo' pocket. Ah bet its candy kisses."

"Tain't. Move yo' hand. Woman ain't got no business in a man's clothes nohow. Go way."

Missie May gouged way down and gave an upward jerk and triumphed.

"Unhhunh! Ah got it. It 'tis so candy kisses. Ah knowed you had somethin' for me in yo' clothes. Now Ah got to see whut's in every pocket you got."

Joe smiled indulgently and let his wife go through all of his pockets and take out the things that he had hidden there for her to find. She bore off the chewing gum, the cake of sweet soap, the pocket handkerchief as if she had wrested them from him, as if they had not been bought for the sake of this friendly battle.

"Whew! dat play-fight done got me all warmed up." Joe exclaimed. "Got me some water in de kittle?"

"Yo' water is on de fire and yo' clean things is cross de bed. Hurry up and wash yo'self and git changed so we kin eat. Ah'm hongry." As Missie said this, she bore the steaming kettle into the bedroom.

"You ain't hongry, sugar," Joe contradicted her. "Youse jes' a little empty. Ah'm de one whut's hongry. Ah could eat up camp meetin', back off 'ssociation, and drink Jurdan dry. Have it on de table when Ah git out de tub."

"Don't you mess wid mah business, man. You git in yo' clothes. Ah'm a real wife, not no dress and breath. Ah might not look lak one, but if you burn me, you won't git a thing but wife ashes."

Joe splashed in the bedroom and Missie May fanned around in the kitchen. A fresh red and white checked cloth on the table. Big pitcher of buttermilk beaded with pale drops of butter from the churn. Hot fried mullet, crackling bread, ham hock atop a mound of string beans and new potatoes, and perched on the window sill, a pone of spicy potato pudding.

Very little talk during the meal, but that little consisted of banter that pretended to deny affection but in reality flaunted it. Like when Missie May reached for a second helping of the tater pone. Joe snatched it out of her reach.

After Missie May had made two or three unsuccessful grabs at the pan, she begged, "Aw, Joe, gimme some mo' dat tater pone."

"Nope, sweetenin' is for us men-folks. Y'all pritty lil frail eels don't need nothin' lak dis. You too sweet already."

"Please, Joe."

"Naw, naw. Ah don't want you to git no sweeter than whut you is already. We goin' down de road a lil piece t'night, so you go put on yo' Sunday-go-to-meetin' things."

Missie May looked at her husband to see if he was playing some prank. "Sho nuff, Joe?"

"Yeah. We goin' to de ice-cream parlor."

"Where de ice-cream parlor at, Joe?"

"A new man done come heah from Chicago and he done got a place and took and opened it up for a ice-cream parlor, and bein' as it's real swell, Ah wants you to be one de first ladies to walk in dere and have some set down."

"Do Jesus. Ah ain't knowed nothin' 'bout it. Who de man done it?"

"Mister Otis D. Slemmons, of spots and places—Memphis, Chicago, Jacksonville, Philadelphia, and so on."

"Dat heavy-set man wid his mouth full of gold teethes?"

"Yeah. Where did you see 'im at?"

"Ah went down to de sto' tuh git a box of lye and Ah seen 'im standin' on de corner talkin' to some of de mens, and Ah come on back and went to scrubbin' de floor, and he passed and tipped his hat whilst Ah was scourin' de steps. Ah thought Ah never seen *him* befo'."

Joe smiled pleasantly. "Yeah, he's up to date. He got de finest clothes Ah ever seen on a colored man's back."

"Aw, he don't look no better in his clothes than you do in

yourn. He got a puzzlegut on 'im and he so chuckle-headed, he got a pone behind his neck."

Joe looked down at his own abdomen and said wistfully: "Wisht Ah had a build on me lak he got. He ain't puzzlegutted, honey. He jes' got a corperation. Dat make 'm look lak a rich white man. All rich mens is got some belly on 'em."

"Ah seen de pitchers of Henry Ford and he's a spare-built man, and Rockefeller look lak he ain't got but one gut. But Ford and Rockefeller and dis Slemmons and all de rest kin be as many-gutted as dey please, Ah's satisfied wid you jes' lak you is, baby. God took pattern after a pine tree and built you noble. Youse a pritty man, and if Ah knowed any way to make you mo' pritty still, Ah'd take and do it."

Joe reached over gently and toyed with Missie May's ear. "You jes' say dat cause you love me, but Ah know Ah can't hold no light to Otis D. Slemmons. Ah ain't never been nowhere and Ah ain't got nothin' but you."

Missie May got on his lap and kissed him and he kissed back in kind. Then he went on. "All de womens is crazy 'bout 'im everywhere he go."

"How you know dat, Joe?"

"He told us so hisself."

"Dat don't make it so. His mouf is cut cross-ways, ain't it? Well, he kin lie jes' lak anybody else."

"Good Lawd, Missie! You womens sho is hard to sense into things. He's got a five-dollar gold piece for a stick-pin and he got a ten-dollar gold piece on his watch chain and his mouf is jes' crammed full of gold teethes. Sho wisht it wuz mine. And whut make it so cool, he got money 'cumulated. And womens give it all to 'im."

"Ah don't see whut de womens see on 'im. Ah wouldn't give 'im a wink if de sheriff wuz after 'im."

"Well, he told us how de white womens in Chicago give 'im all dat gold money. So he don't 'low nobody to touch it at all. Not even put dey finger on it. Dey tole 'im not to. You kin make 'miration at it, but don't tetch it."

"Whyn't he stay up dere where dey so crazy 'bout 'im?"

"Ah reckon dey done made 'im vast-rich and he wants to travel some. He says dey wouldn't leave 'im hit a lick of work. He got mo' lady people crazy 'bout him than he kin shake a stick at."

"Joe, Ah hates to see you so dumb. Dat stray nigger jes' tell y'all anything and y'all b'lieve it."

"Go 'head on now, honey, and put on yo' clothes. He talkin' 'bout his pritty womens—Ah want 'im to see *mine*."

Missie May went off to dress and Joe spent the time trying to make his stomach punch out like Slemmons' middle. He tried the rolling swagger of the stranger, but found that his tall bone-and-muscle stride fitted ill with it. He just had time to drop back into his seat before Missie May came in, dressed to go.

On the way home that night Joe was exultant. "Didn't Ah say ole Otis was swell? Cain't he talk Chicago talk? Wuzn't dat funny whut he said when great big fat ole Ida Armstrong come in? He asted me, 'Who is dat broad wid de forte shake?' Dat's a new word. Us always thought forty was a set of figgers but he showed us where it means a whole heap of things. Sometimes he don't say forty, he jes' say thirty-eight and two, and dat mean de same thing. Know whut he tole me when Ah wuz payin' for our ice cream? He say, 'Ah have to hand it to you, Joe. Dat wife of yours is jes' thirty-eight and two. Yessuh, she's forte!' Ain't he killin'?"

"He'll do in case of a rush. But he sho is got uh heap uh gold on 'im. Dat's de first time Ah ever seed gold money. It lookted good on him sho nuff, but it'd look a whole heap better on you."

"Who, me? Missie May, youse crazy! Where would a po'man lak me git gold money from?"

Missie May was silent for a minute, then she said, "Us might find some goin' long de road some time. Us could."

"Who would be losin' gold money round heah? We ain't even seen none dese white folks wearin' no gold money on dey watch chain. You must be figgerin' Mister Packard or Mister Cadillac goin' pass through heah."

"You don't know whut been lost 'round heah. Maybe somebody way back in memorial times lost they gold money and went on off and it ain't never been found. And then if we wuz to find it, you could wear some 'thout havin' no gang of womens lak dat Slemmons say he got."

Joe laughed and hugged her. "Don't be so wishful 'bout me. Ah'm satisfied de way Ah is. So long as Ah be yo' husband, Ah don't keer 'bout nothin' else. Ah'd ruther all de other womens in de world to be dead than for you to have de toothache. Less we go to bed and git our night rest."

It was Saturday night once more before Joe could parade his wife in Slemmons' ice-cream parlor again. He worked the night shift, and Saturday was his only night off. Every other evening around six o'clock he left home, and dying dawn saw him hustling home around the lake, where the challenging sun flung a flaming sword from east to west across the trembling water.

That was the best part of life—going home to Missie May. Their whitewashed house, the mock battle on Saturday, the dinner and ice-cream parlor afterwards, church on Sunday nights, when Missie out-dressed any woman in town—all, everything, was right.

One night around eleven the acid ran out at the G. and G. The foreman knocked off the crew and let the steam die down. As Joe rounded the lake on his way home, a lean moon rode the lake in a silver boat. If anybody had asked Joe about the moon on the lake, he would have said he hadn't paid it any attention. But he saw it with his feelings. It made him yearn painfully for Missie. Creation obsessed him. He thought about children. They had been married more than a year now. They had money put away. They ought to be making little feet for shoes. A little boy-child would be about right.

He saw a dim light in the bedroom and decided to come in through the kitchen door. He could wash the fertilizer dust off himself before presenting himself to Missie May. It would be nice for her not to know that he was there until he slipped into his place in bed and hugged her back. She always liked that.

He eased the kitchen door open slowly and silently, but when he went to set his dinner bucket on the table he bumped into a pile of dishes, and something crashed to the floor. He heard his wife gasp in fright and hurried to reassure her.

"Iss me, honey. Don't git skeered."

There was a quick, large movement in the bedroom. A rustle, a thud, and a stealthy silence. The light went out.

What? Robbers? Murderers? Some varmint attacking his helpless wife, perhaps. He struck a match, threw himself on guard, and stepped over the door-sill into the bedroom.

The great belt on the wheel of Time slipped and eternity stood still. By the match light he could see the man's legs fighting with his breeches in his frantic desire to get them on. He had both chance and time to kill the intruder in his helpless condition—half in and half out of his pants—but he was too weak to take action. The shapeless enemies of humanity that live in the hours of Time had waylaid Joe. He was assaulted in his weakness. Like Samson awakening after his haircut. So he just opened his mouth and laughed.

The match went out, and he struck another and lit the lamp. A howling wind raced across his heart, but underneath its fury he heard his wife sobbing and Slemmons pleading for his life. Offering to buy it with all that he had. "Please, suh, don't kill me. Sixty-two dollars at de sto'. Gold money."

Joe just stood. Slemmons looked at the window, but it was screened. Joe stood out like a rough-backed mountain between him and the door. Barring him from escape, from sunrise, from life.

He considered a surprise attack upon the big clown that stood there, laughing like a chessy cat. But before his fist could travel an inch, Joe's own rushed out to crush him like a battering ram. Then Joe stood over him.

"Git into yo' damn rags, Slemmons, and dat quick."

Slemmons scrambled to his feet and into his vest and coat. As he grabbed his hat, Joe's fury overrode his intentions and he grabbed at Slemmons with his left hand and struck at him with his right. The right landed. The left grazed the front of his vest. Slemmons was knocked a somersault into the kitchen and fled through the open door. Joe found himself alone with Missie May, with the golden watch charm clutched in his left fist. A short bit of broken chain dangled between his fingers.

Missie May was sobbing. Wails of weeping without words. Joe stood, and after awhile he found out that he had something in his hand. And then he stood and felt without thinking and without seeing with his natural eyes. Missie May kept on crying and Joe kept on feeling so much; and not knowing what to do with all his feelings, he put Slemmons' watch charm in his pants pocket and took a good laugh and went to bed.

"Missie May, whut you cryin' for?"

"Cause Ah love you so hard and Ah know you don't love *me* no mo'."

Joe sank his face into the pillow for a spell, then he said huskily, "You don't know de feelings of dat yet, Missie May."

"Oh Joe, honey, he said he wuz gointer give me dat gold money and he jes' kept on after me——"

Joe was very still and silent for a long time. Then he said, "Well, don't cry no mo', Missie May. Ah got yo' gold piece for you."

The hours went past on their rusty ankles. Joe still and quiet on one bed-rail and Missie May wrung dry of sobs on the other. Finally the sun's tide crept upon the shore of night and drowned all its hours. Missie May with her face, stiff and streaked, towards the window saw the dawn come into her yard. It was day. Nothing more. Joe wouldn't be coming home as usual. No need to fling open the front door and sweep off the porch, making it nice for Joe. Never no more breakfasts to cook; no more washing and starching of Joe's jumper-jackets and pants. No more nothing. So why get up?

With this strange man in her bed, she felt embarrassed to get up and dress. She decided to wait till he had dressed and gone. Then she would get up, dress quickly, and be gone forever beyond reach of Joe's looks and laughs. But he never moved. Red light turned to yellow, then white.

From beyond the no-man's land between them came a voice. A strange voice that yesterday had been Joe's.

"Missie May, ain't you gonna fix me no breakfus'?"

She sprang out of bed. "Yeah, Joe. Ah didn't reckon you wuz hongry."

No need to die today. Joe needed her for a few more minutes anyhow.

Soon there was a roaring fire in the cook stove. Water bucket full and two chickens killed. Joe loved fried chicken and rice. She didn't deserve a thing and good Joe was letting her cook him some breakfast. She rushed hot biscuits to the table as Joe took his seat.

He ate with his eyes in his plate. No laughter, no banter.

"Missie May, you ain't eatin' yo breakfus'."

"Ah don't choose none. Ah thank yuh."

His coffee cup was empty. She sprang to refill it. When she turned from the stove and bent to set the cup beside Joe's plate, she saw the yellow coin on the table between them.

She slumped into her seat and wept into her arms.

Presently Joe said calmly, "Missie May, you cry too much. Don't look back lak Lot's wife and turn to salt."

The sun, the hero of every day, the impersonal old man that beams as brightly on death as on birth, came up every morning and raced across the blue dome and dipped into the sea of fire every evening. Water ran down hill and birds nested.

Missie knew why she didn't leave Joe. She couldn't. She loved him too much, but she could not understand why Joe didn't leave her. He was polite, even kind at times, but aloof.

There were no more Saturday romps. No ringing silver dollars to stack beside her plate. No pockets to rifle. In fact the yellow coin in his trousers was like a monster hiding in the cave of his pockets to destroy her.

She often wondered if he still had it, but nothing could have induced her to ask nor yet to explore his pockets to see for herself. Its shadow was in the house whether or no.

One night Joe came home around midnight and complained of pains in the back. He asked Missie to rub him down with liniment. It had been three months since Missie had touched his body and it all seemed strange. But she rubbed him. Grateful for the chance. Before morning, youth triumphed and Missie exulted. But the next day, as she joyfully made up their bed, beneath her pillow she found the piece of money with the bit of chain attached.

Alone to herself, she looked at the thing with loathing, but look she must. She took it into her hands with trembling and saw first thing that it was no gold piece. It was a gilded half dollar. Then she knew why Slemmons had forbidden anyone to touch his gold. He trusted village eyes at a distance not to recognize his stick-pin as a gilded quarter and his watch charm as a four-bit piece.

She was glad at first that Joe had left it there. Perhaps he was through with her punishment. They were man and wife again. Then another thought came clawing at her. He had come home to buy from her as if she were any woman in the long house. Fifty cents for her love. As if to say that he could pay as well as Slemmons. She slid the coin into his Sunday pants pocket and dressed herself and left his house.

Halfway between her house and the quarters she met her husband's mother, and after a short talk she turned and went back home. Never would she admit defeat to that woman, who prayed for it nightly. If she had not the substance of marriage she had the outside show. Joe must leave *her*. She let him see she didn't want his old gold four-bits too.

She saw no more of the coin for some time, though she knew that Joe could not help finding it in his pocket. But his health kept poor, and he came home at least every ten days to be rubbed.

The sun swept around the horizon, trailing its robes of weeks and days. One morning as Joe came in from work, he found Missie May chopping wood. Without a word he took the ax and chopped a huge pile before he stopped.

"You ain't got no business choppin' wood, and you know it."

"How come? Ah been choppin' it for de last longest."

"Ah ain't blind. You makin' feet for shoes."

"Won't you be glad to have a li'l baby chile, Joe?"

"You know dat 'thout astin' me."

"Iss gointer be a boy chile and de very spit of you."

"You reckon, Missie May?"

"Who else could it look lak?"

Joe said nothing, but he thrust his hand deep into his pocket and fingered something there.

It was almost six months later Missie May took to bed, and Joe went and got his mother to come wait on the house.

Missie May was delivered of a fine boy. Her travail was over when Joe came in from work one morning. His mother and the old women were drinking great bowls of coffee around the fire in the kitchen.

The minute Joe came into the room his mother called him aside.

"How did Missie May make out?" he asked quickly.

"Who, dat gal? She strong as a ox. She gointer have plenty mo'. We done fixed her wid de sugar and lard to sweeten her for de nex' one."

Joe stood silent awhile.

"You ain't ast 'bout de baby, Joe. You oughter be mighty proud cause he sho is de spittin' image of yuh, son. Dat's yourn all right, if you never git another one, dat un is yourn. And you know Ah'm mighty proud too, son, cause Ah never thought well of you marryin' Missie May cause her ma used tuh fan her foot round right smart and Ah been mighty skeered dat Missie May wuz gointer git misput on her road."

Joe said nothing. He fooled around the house till late in the day, then, just before he went to work, he went and stood at the foot of the bed and asked his wife how she felt. He did this every day during the week.

On Saturday he went to Orlando to make his market. It had been a long time since he had done that.

Meat and lard, meal and flour, soap and starch. Cans of corn and tomatoes. All the staples. He fooled around town for awhile and bought bananas and apples. Way after while he went around to the candy store.

"Hello, Joe," the clerk greeted him. "Ain't seen you in a long time."

"Nope, Ah ain't been heah. Been round in spots and places."

"Want some of them molasses kisses you always buy?"

"Yessuh." He threw the gilded half dollar on the counter. "Will dat spend?"

"Whut is it, Joe? Well, I'll be doggone! A gold-plated four-bit piece. Where'd you git it, Joe?"

"Offen a stray nigger dat come through Eatonville. He had it on his watch chain for a charm—goin' round making out iss gold money. Ha ha! He had a quarter on his tie pin and it wuz all golded up too. Tryin' to fool people. Makin' out he so rich and everything. Ha! Ha! Tryin' to tole off folkses wives from home."

"How did you git it, Joe? Did he fool you, too?"

"Who, me? Naw suh! He ain't fooled me none. Know whut Ah done? He come round me wid his smart talk. Ah hauled off and knocked 'im down and took his old four-bits way from 'im. Gointer buy my wife some good ole lasses kisses wid it. Gimme fifty cents worth of dem candy kisses."

"Fifty cents buys a mighty lot of candy kisses, Joe. Why don't you split it up and take some chocolate bars, too. They eat good, too."

"Yessuh, dey do, but Ah wants all dat in kisses. Ah got a li'l boy chile home now. Tain't a week old yet, but he kin suck a sugar tit and maybe eat one them kisses hisself."

Joe got his candy and left the store. The clerk turned to the next customer. "Wisht I could be like these darkies. Laughin' all the time. Nothin' worries 'em.'

Back in Eatonville, Joe reached his own front door. There was the ring of singing metal on wood. Fifteen times. Missie May couldn't run to the door, but she crept there as quickly as she could.

"Joe Banks, Ah hear you chunkin' money in mah do'way. You wait till Ah got mah strength back and Ah'm gointer fix you for dat."

Bright and Morning Star

RICHARD WRIGHT

I

She stood with her black face some six inches from the moist windowpane and wondered when on earth would it ever stop raining. It might keep up like this all week, she thought. She heard rain droning upon the roof, and high up in the wet sky her eyes followed the silent rush of a bright shaft of yellow that swung from the airplane beacon in far-off Memphis. Momently she could see it cutting through the rainy dark; it would hover a second like a gleaming sword above her head, then vanish. She sighed, troubling, *Johnny-Boys been trampin in this slop all day wid no decent shoes on his feet.* . . . Through the window she could see the rich black earth sprawling outside in the night. There was more rain than the clay could soak up; pools stood everywhere. She yawned and mumbled: "Rains good n bad. It kin make seeds bus up thu the groun, er it kin bog things down lika watah-soaked coffin." Her hands were folded loosely over her stomach and the hot air of the kitchen traced a filmy veil of sweat on her forehead. From the cook stove came the soft singing of burning wood, and now and then a throaty bubble rose from a pot of simmering greens.

"Shucks, Johnny-Boy coulda let somebody else do all tha runnin in the rain. Theres others bettah fixed fer it than he is. But, naw! Johnny-Boy ain the one t trust nobody t do nothin. Hes gotta do it *all* hissef. . . ."

She glanced at a pile of damp clothes in a zinc tub. *Waal, Ah bettah git t work.* She turned, lifted a smoothing iron with a thick pad of cloth, touched a spit-wet finger to it with a quick, jerking motion: *smiiitz!* *Yeah; its hot!* Stooping, she took a blue work-shirt from the tub and shook it out. With a deft twist of her shoulder she caught the iron in her right hand; the fingers of her left hand took a piece of wax from a tin box and a frying sizzle came as she smeared the bottom. She was thinking of nothing now; her hands followed a life-long ritual of toil. Spreading a sleeve, she ran the hot iron to and fro until the wet cloth became stiff. She was deep in the midst of her work when a song rose up out of the far-off days of her childhood and broke through half-parted lips:

> *Hes the Lily of the Valley, the Bright n Mawnin Star*
> *Hes the Fariest of Ten Thousan t mah soul . . .*

A gust of wind dashed rain against the window. Johnny-Boy oughta c mon home n eat his suppah. Aw, Lawd! Itd be fine ef Sug could eat wid us tonight! Itd be like ol times! Mabbe aftah all it won't be long fo he comes back. Tha lettah Ah got from im las week said *Don give up hope*. . . . Yeah; we gotta live in hope. Then both of her sons, Sug and Johnny-Boy, would be back with her.

With an involuntary nervous gesture, she stopped and stood still, listening. But the only sound was the lulling fall of rain. Shucks, ain no usa me ackin this way, she thought. Ever time they gits ready to hol them meetings Ah gits jumpity. Ah been a lil scared ever since Sug went t jail. She heard the clock ticking and looked. Johnny-Boys a *hour* late! He sho mus be havin a time doin all tha trampin, trampin thu the mud. . . . But her fear was a quiet one; it was more like an intense brooding than a fear; it was a sort of hugging of hated facts so closely that she could feel their grain, like letting cold water run over her hand from a faucet on a winter morning.

She ironed again, faster now, as if she felt the more she engaged her body in work the less she would think. But how could she forget Johnny-Boy out there on those wet fields rounding up white and black Communists for a meeting tomorrow? And that was just what Sug had been doing when the sheriff had caught him, beat him, and tried to make him tell who and where his comrades were. Po Sug! They sho musta beat the boy somethin awful! But, thank Gawd, he didnt talk! He ain no weaklin, Sug ain! Hes been lion-hearted all his life long.

That had happened a year ago. And now each time those meetings came around, the old terror surged back. While shoving the iron, a cluster of toiling days returned; days of washing

and ironing to feed Johnny-Boy and Sug so they could do party
work; days of carrying a hundred pounds of white folks' clothes
upon her head across fields sometimes wet and sometimes dry.
But in those days a hundred pounds was nothing to carry carefully balanced upon her head while stepping by instinct over the
corn and cotton rows. The only time it had seemed heavy was
when she had heard of Sug's arrest. She had been coming home
one morning with a bundle upon her head, her hands swinging
idly by her sides, walking slowly with her eyes in front of her,
when Bob, Johnny-Boy's pal, had called from across the fields
and had come and told her that the sheriff had got Sug. That
morning the bundle had become heavier than she could ever
remember.

And with each passing week now, though she spoke of it to no
one, things were becoming heavier. The tubs of water and the
smoothing iron and the bundle of clothes were becoming harder
to lift, with her back aching so; and her work was taking longer,
all because Sug was gone and she didn't know just when Johnny-
Boy would be taken too. To ease the ache of anxiety that was
swelling her heart, she hummed, then sang softly:

> *He walks wid me, He talks wid me*
> *He tells me Ahm His own. . . .*

Guiltily, she stopped and smiled. Looks like Ah jus cant seem
t fergit them ol songs, no mattah how hard Ah tries. . . . She
had learned them when she was a little girl living and working
on a farm. Every Monday morning from the corn- and cotton-
fields the slow strains had floated from her mother's lips, lonely
and haunting; and later, as the years had filled with gall, she
had learned their deep meaning. Long hours of scrubbing floors
for a few cents a day had taught her who Jesus was, what a
great boon it was to cling to Him, to be like Him and suffer
without a mumbling word. She had poured the yearning of her
life into the songs, feeling buoyed with a faith beyond this
world. The figure of the Man nailed in agony to the Cross, His
burial in a cold grave, His transfigured Resurrection, His being
breath and clay, God and Man—all had focused her feelings
upon an imagery which had swept her life into a wondrous
vision.

But as she had grown older, a cold white mountain, the white
folks and their laws, had swum into her vision and shattered her

songs and their spell of peace. To her that white mountain was temptation, something to lure her from her Lord, a part of the world God had made in order that she might endure it and come through all the stronger, just as Christ had risen with greater glory from the tomb. The days crowded with trouble had enhanced her faith and she had grown to love hardship with a bitter pride; she had obeyed the laws of the white folks with a soft smile of secret knowing.

After her mother had been snatched up to heaven in a chariot of fire, the years had brought her a rough workingman and two black babies, Sug and Johnny-Boy, all three of whom she had wrapped in the charm and magic of her vision. Then she was tested by no less than God; her man died, a trial which she bore with the strength shed by the grace of her vision; finally even the memory of her man faded into the vision itself, leaving her with two black boys growing tall, slowly into manhood.

Then one day grief had come to her heart when Johnny-Boy and Sug had walked forth, demanding their lives. She had sought to fill their eyes with her vision, but they would have none of it. And she had wept when they began to boast of the strength shed by a new and terrible vision.

But she had loved them, even as she loved them now; bleeding, her heart had followed them. She could have done no less, being an old woman in a strange world. And day by day her sons had ripped from her startled eyes her old vision, and image by image had given her a new one, different, but great and strong enough to fling her into the light of another grace. The wrongs and sufferings of black men had taken the place of Him nailed to the Cross; the meager beginnings of the party had become another Resurrection; and the hate of those who would destroy her new faith had quickened in her a hunger to feel how deeply her new strength went.

"Lawd, Johnny-Boy," she would sometimes say, "Ah jus wan them white folks t try t make me tell *who* is *in* the party n who *ain!* Ah jus wan em t try, n Ahll show em somethin they never thought a black woman could have!"

But sometimes, like tonight, while lost in the forgetfulness of work, the past and the present would become mixed in her; while toiling under a strange star for a new freedom, the old songs would slip from her lips with their beguiling sweetness.

The iron was getting cold. She put more wood into the fire,

stood again at the window, and watched the yellow blade of light cut through the wet darkness. Johnny-Boy ain here yit. . . . Then, before she was aware of it, she was still, listening for sounds. Under the drone of rain she heard the slosh of feet in mud. Tha ain Johnny-Boy. She knew his long, heavy footsteps in a million. She heard feet come on the porch. Some woman. . . . She heard bare knuckles knock three times, then once. Thas some of them comrades! She unbarred the door, cracked it a few inches, and flinched from the cold rush of damp wind.

"Whos tha?"

"Its me!"

"Who?"

"Me, Reva!"

She flung the door open.

"Lawd, chile c mon in!"

She stepped to one side and a thin, blond-haired white girl ran through the door; as she slid the bolt she heard the girl gasping and shaking her wet clothes. Somethings wrong! Reva wouldna walked a mile t mah house in all this slop fer nothin! Tha gals stuck onto Johnny-Boy. Ah wondah ef anythin happened t im?

"Git on inter the kitchen, Reva, where its warm."

"Lawd, Ah sho is wet!"

"How yuh reckon yuhd be, in all tha rain?"

"Johnny-Boy ain here *yit*?" asked Reva.

"Naw! N ain no usa yuh worryin bout im. Jus yuh git them shoes off! Yuh wanna ketch yo deatha col?" She stood looking absently. Yeah; its somethin about the party er Johnny-Boy thas gone wrong. Lawd, Ah wondah ef her pa knows how she feels bout Johnny-Boy? "Honey, yuh hadnt oughta come out in sloppy weather like this."

"Ah had t come, An Sue."

She led Reva to the kitchen.

"Git them shoes off n git close t the stove so yuhll git dry!"

"An Sue, Ah got somethin t tell yuh . . ."

The words made her hold her breath. Ah bet its somethin bout Johnny-Boy!

"Whut, honey?"

"The sheriff wuz by our house tonight. He come t see pa."

"Yeah?"

"He done got word from somewheres bout tha meetin tomorrow."

"Is it Johnny-Boy, Reva?"

"Aw, naw, An Sue! Ah ain hearda word bout im. Ain yuh seen im tonight?"

"He ain come home t eat yit."

"Where kin he be?"

"Lawd knows, chile."

"Somebodys gotta tell them comrades tha meetings off," said Reva. "The sheriffs got men watchin our house. Ah had t slip out t git here widout em followin me."

"Reva?"

"Hunh?"

"Ahma ol woman n Ah wans yuh t tell me the truth."

"Whut, An Sue?"

"Yuh ain tryin t fool me, is yuh?"

"*Fool* yuh?"

"Bout Johnny-Boy?"

"Lawd, naw, An Sue!"

"Ef theres anythin wrong jus tell me, chile. Ah kin stan it."

She stood by the ironing board, her hands as usual folded loosely over her stomach, watching Reva pull off her water-clogged shoes. She was feeling that Johnny-Boy was already lost to her; she was feeling the pain that would come when she knew it for certain; and she was feeling that she would have to be brave and bear it. She was like a person caught in a swift current of water and knew where the water was sweeping her and did not want to go on but had to go on to the end.

"It ain nothin bout Johnny-Boy, An Sue," said Reva. "But we gotta do somethin er we'll all git inter trouble."

"How the sheriff know about tha meetin?"

"Thas whut pa wans t know."

"Somebody done turned Judas."

"Sho looks like it."

"Ah bet it wuz some of them new ones," she said.

"Its hard t tell," said Reva.

"Lissen, Reva, yuh oughta stay here n git dry, but yuh bettah git back n tell yo pa Johnny-Boy ain here n Ah don know when hes gonna show up. *Some*bodys gotta tell them comrades t stay erway from yo pas house."

She stood with her back to the window, looking at Reva's wide blue eyes. Po critter! Gotta go back thu all tha slop! Though she felt sorry for Reva, not once did she think that it would not have to be done. Being a woman, Reva was not suspect; she would *have* to go. It was just as natural for Reva to go back through the cold rain as it was for her to iron night and day, or for Sug to be in jail. Right now, Johnny-Boy was out there on those dark fields trying to get home. Lawd, don let em git im tonight! In spite of herself her feelings became torn. She loved her son, and loving him, she loved what he was trying to do. Johnny-Boy was happiest when he was working for the party, and her love for him was for his happiness. She frowned, trying hard to fit something together in her feelings: for her to try to stop Johnny-Boy was to admit that all the toil of years meant nothing; and to let him go meant that sometime or other he would be caught, like Sug. In facing it this way she felt a little stunned, as though she had come suddenly upon a blank wall in the dark. But outside in the rain were people, white and black, whom she had known all her life. Those people depended upon Johnny-Boy, loved him, and looked to him as a man and leader. Yeah; hes gotta keep on; he cant stop now. . . . She looked at Reva; she was crying and pulling her shoes back on with reluctant fingers.

"Whut yuh carryin on tha way fer, chile?"

"Yuh done los Sug, now yuh sending Johnny-Boy . . ."

"Ah got t, honey."

She was glad she could say that. Reva believed in black folks and not for anything in the world would she falter before her. In Reva's trust and acceptance of her she had found her first feelings of humanity; Reva's love was her refuge from shame and degradation. If in the early days of her life the white mountain had driven her back from the earth, then in her last days Reva's love was drawing her toward it, like the beacon that swung through the night outside. She heard Reva sobbing.

"Hush, honey!"

"Mah brothers in jail too! Ma cries ever day . . ."

"Ah know, honey."

She helped Reva with her coat; her fingers felt the scant flesh of the girl's shoulders. She don git ernuff t eat, she thought. She slipped her arms around Reva's waist and held her close for a moment.

"Now, yuh stop that cryin."

"A-a-ah c-c-cant hep it. . . ."

"Everythingll be awright; Johnny-Boyll be back."

"Yuh think so?"

"Sho, chile. Cos he will."

Neither of them spoke again until they stood in the doorway. Outside they could hear water washing through the ruts of the street.

"Be sho n send Johnny-Boy t tell the folks t stay erway from pas house," said Reva.

"Ahll tell im. Don yuh worry."

"Good-by!"

"Good-by!"

Leaning against the door jamb, she shook her head slowly and watched Reva vanish through the falling rain.

II

She was back at her board, ironing, when she heard feet sucking in the mud of the back yard; feet she knew from long years of listening were Johnny-Boy's. But tonight, with all the rain and fear, his coming was like a leaving, was almost more than she could bear. Tears welled to her eyes and she blinked them away. She felt that he was coming so that she could give him up; to see him now was to say good-by. But it was a good-by she knew she could never say; they were not that way toward each other. All day long they could sit in the same room and not speak; she was his mother and he was her son. Most of the time a nod or a grunt would carry all the meaning that she wanted to convey to him, or he to her. She did not even turn her head when she heard him come stomping into the kitchen. She heard him pull up a chair, sit, sigh, and draw off his muddy shoes; they fell to the floor with heavy thuds. Soon the kitchen was full of the scent of his drying socks and his burning pipe. Tha boys hongry! She paused and looked at him over her shoulder; he was puffing at his pipe with his head tilted back and his feet propped up on the edge of the stove; his eyelids drooped and his wet clothes steamed from the heat of the fire. Lawd, tha boy gits mo like his pa ever day he lives, she mused, her lips breaking in a slow faint smile. Hols tha pipe in his mouth just like his pa usta hol his. Wondah how they woulda got erlong ef his pa hada lived? They oughta liked each other, they so mucha like. She wished there could have been other children besides Sug, so

Johnny-Boy would not have to be so much alone. A man needs a woman by his side. . . . She thought of Reva; she liked Reva; the brightest glow her heart had ever known was when she had learned that Reva loved Johnny-Boy. But beyond Reva were cold white faces. Ef theys caught it means *death*. . . . She jerked around when she heard Johnny-Boy's pipe clatter to the floor. She saw him pick it up, smile sheepishly at her, and wag his head.

"Gawd, Ahm sleepy," he mumbled.

She got a pillow from her room and gave it to him.

"Here," she said.

"Hunh," he said, putting the pillow between his head and the back of the chair.

They were silent again. Yes, she would have to tell him to go back out into the cold rain and slop; maybe to get caught; maybe for the last time; she didn't know. But she would let him eat and get dry before telling him that the sheriff knew of the meeting to be held at Lem's tomorrow. And she would make him take a big dose of soda before he went out; soda always helped to stave off a cold. She looked at the clock. It was eleven. Theres time yit. Spreading a newspaper on the apron of the stove, she placed a heaping plate of greens upon it, a knife, a fork, a cup of coffee, a slab of cornbread, and a dish of peach cobbler.

"Yo suppahs ready," she said.

"Yeah," he said.

He did not move. She ironed again. Presently, she heard him eating. When she could no longer hear his knife tinkling against the edge of the plate, she knew he was through. It was almost twelve now. She would let him rest a little while longer before she told him. Till one er'clock, mabbe. Hes so tired. . . . She finished her ironing, put away the board, and stacked the clothes in her dresser drawer. She poured herself a cup of black coffee, drew up a chair, sat down, and drank.

"Yuh almos dry," she said, not looking around.

"Yeah," he said, turning sharply to her.

The tone of voice in which she had spoken had let him know that more was coming. She drained her cup and waited a moment longer.

"Reva wuz here."

"Yeah?"

"She lef bout a hour ergo."

"Whut she say?"

"She said ol man Lem hada visit from the sheriff today."

"Bout the meetin?"

"Yeah."

She saw him stare at the coals glowing red through the crevices of the stove and run his fingers nervously through his hair. She knew he was wondering how the sheriff had found out. In the silence he would ask a wordless question and in the silence she would answer wordlessly. Johnny-Boys too trustin, she thought. Hes trying t make the party big n hes takin in folks fastern he kin git t know em. You cant trust ever white man yuh meet. . . .

"Yuh know, Johnny-Boy, yuh been takin in a lotta them white folks lately . . ."

"Aw, ma!"

"But, Johnny-Boy . . ."

"Please, don talk t me bout tha now, ma."

"Yuh ain t ol t lissen n learn, son," she said.

"Ah know whut yuh gonna say, ma. N yuh wrong. Yuh cant judge folks jus by how yuh feel bout em n by how long yuh done knowed em. Ef we start tha we wouldn't have *no*body in the party. When folks pledge they word t be with us, then we gotta take em in. Wes too weak t be choosy."

He rose abruptly, rammed his hands into his pockets, and stood facing the window; she looked at his back in a long silence. She knew his faith; it was deep. He had always said that black men could not fight the rich bosses alone; a man could not fight with every hand against him. But he believes so hard hes blind, she thought. At odd times they had had these arguments before; always she would be pitting her feelings against the hard necessity of his thinking, and always she would lose. She shook her head. Po Johnny-Boy; he don know . . .

"But ain nona our folks tol, Johnny-Boy," she said.

"How yuh know?" he asked. His voice came low and with a tinge of anger. He still faced the window, and now and then the yellow blade of light flicked across the sharp outline of his black face.

"Cause Ah know em," she said.

"*Any*body mighta tol," he said.

"It wuznt nona *our* folks," she said again.

She saw his hand sweep in a swift arc of disgust.

"*Our* folks! Ma, who in Gawds name is *our* folks?"

"The folks we wuz born n raised wid, son. The folks we *know!*"

"We cant make the party grow tha way, ma."

"It mighta been Booker," she said.

"Yuh don know."

". . . er Blattberg . . ."

"Fer Chrissakes!"

". . . er any of the fo-five others whut joined las week."

"Ma, yuh jus don wan me t go out tonight," he said.

"Yo ol ma wans yuh t be careful, son."

"Ma, when yuh start doubtin folks in the party, then there ain no end."

"Son, Ah knows ever black man n woman in this parta the county," she said, standing too. "Ah watched em grow up; Ah even heped birth n nurse some of em; Ah knows em *all* from way back. There ain none of em that *coulda* tol! The folks Ah know jus don open they dos n ast death t walk in! Son, it wuz some of them *white* folks! Yuh jus mark mah word n wait n see!"

"Why is it gotta be *white* folks?" he asked. "Ef they tol, then theys jus Judases, thas all."

"Son, look at whuts befo yuh."

He shook his head and sighed.

"Ma, Ah done tol yuh a hundred times. Ah cant see white n Ah cant see black," he said. "Ah sees rich men n Ah sees po men."

She picked up his dirty dishes and piled them in a pan. Out of the corners of her eyes she saw him sit and pull on his wet shoes. Hes goin! When she put the last dish away he was standing, fully dressed, warming his hands over the stove. Jus a few mo minutes now n he'll be gone, like Sug, mabbe. Her throat tightened. This black mans fight takes *everthin!* Looks like Gawd put us in this world jus t beat us down!

"Keep this, ma," he said.

She saw a crumpled wad of money in his outstretched fingers.

"Naw; yuh keep it. Yuh might need it."

"It ain mine, ma. It berlongs t the party."

"But, Johnny-Boy, yuh might hafta go erway!"

"Ah kin make out."

"Don fergit yosef too much, son."

"Ef Ah don come back theyll need it."

He was looking at her face and she was looking at the money.

"Yuh keep tha," she said slowly. "Ahll give em the money."

"From where?"

"Ah got some."

"Where yuh git it from?"

She sighed.

"Ah been savin a dollah a week fer Sug ever since hes been in jail."

"Lawd, ma!"

She saw the look of puzzled love and wonder in his eyes. Clumsily, he put the money back into his pocket.

"Ahm gone," he said.

"Here; drink this glass of soda watah."

She watched him drink, then put the glass away.

"Waal," he said.

"Take the stuff outta yo pockets!"

She lifted the lid of the stove and he dumped all the papers from his pocket into the fire. She followed him to the door and made him turn round.

"Lawd, yuh tryin to maka revolution n yuh cant even keep yo coat buttoned." Her nimble fingers fastened his collar high around his throat. "There!"

He pulled the brim of his hat low over his eyes. She opened the door, and with the suddenness of the cold gust of wind that struck her face, he was gone. She watched the black fields and the rain take him, her eyes burning. When the last faint footstep could no longer be heard, she closed the door, went to her bed, lay down, and pulled the cover over her while fully dressed. Her feelings coursed with the rhythm of the rain: Hes gone! Lawd, Ah *know* hes gone! Her blood felt cold.

III

She was floating in a grey void somewhere between sleeping and dreaming and then suddenly she was wide awake, hearing and feeling in the same instant the thunder of the door crashing in and a cold wind filling the room. It was pitch black and she stared, resting on her elbows, her mouth open, not breathing, her ears full of the sound of tramping feet and booming voices. She knew at once: They lookin fer im! Then, filled with her will, she was on her feet, rigid, waiting, listening.

"The lamps burnin!"
"Yuh see her?"
"Naw!"
"Look in the kitchen!"
"Gee, this place smells like niggers!"
"Say, somebodys here er been here!"
"Yeah; theres fire in the stove!"
"Mabbe hes been here n gone?"
"Boy, look at these jars of jam!"
"Niggers make good jam!"
"Git some bread!"
"Heres some cornbread!"
"Say, lemme git some!"
"Take it easy! Theres plenty here!"
"Ahma take some of this stuff home!"
"Look, heres a pota greens!"
"N some hot cawffee!"

"Say, yuh guys! C mon! Cut it out! We didnt come here fer a feas!"

She walked slowly down the hall. They lookin fer im, but they ain got im yit! She stopped in the doorway, her gnarled black hands as always, folded over her stomach, but tight now, so tightly the veins bulged. The kitchen was crowded with white men in glistening raincoats. Though the lamp burned, their flashlights still glowed in red fists. Across her floor she saw the muddy tracks of their boots.

"Yuh white folks git outta mah house!"

There was quick silence; every face turned toward her. She saw a sudden movement, but did not know what it meant until something hot and wet slammed her squarely in the face. She gasped, but did not move. Calmly, she wiped the warm, greasy liquor of greens from her eyes with her left hand. One of the white men had thrown a handful of greens out of the pot at her.

"How they taste, ol bitch?"
"Ah ast yuh t git outta mah house!"

She saw the sheriff detach himself from the crowd and walk toward her.

"Now, Anty . . ."
"White man, don yuh *Anty* me!"
"Yuh ain got the right sperit!"
"Sperit hell! Yuh git these men outta mah house!"

"Yuh ack like yuh don like it!"

"Naw, Ah don like it, n yuh knows dam waal Ah don!"

"Whut yuh gonna do bout it?"

"Ahm tellin yuh t git outta mah house!"

"Gittin sassy?"

"Ef telling yuh t git outta mah house is sass, then Ahm sassy!"

Her words came in a tense whisper; but beyond, back of them, she was watching, thinking, judging the men.

"Listen, Anty," the sheriff's voice came soft and low. "Ahm here t hep yuh. How come yah wanna ack this way?"

"Yuh ain never heped yo *own* sef since yuh been born," she flared. "How kin the likes of yuh hep me?"

One of the white men came forward and stood directly in front of her.

"Lissen, nigger woman, yuh talkin t *white* men!"

"Ah don care who Ahm talkin t!"

"Yuhll wish some day yuh did!"

"Not t the likes of yuh!"

"Yuh need somebody t teach yuh how t be a good nigger!"

"*Yuh* cant teach it t me!"

"Yuh gonna change yo tune."

"Not longs mah bloods warm!"

"Don git smart now!"

"Yuh git outta mah house!"

"Spose we don go?" the sheriff asked.

They were crowded around her. She had not moved since she had taken her place in the doorway. She was thinking only of Johnny-Boy as she stood there, giving and taking words; and she knew that they, too, were thinking of Johnny-Boy. She knew they wanted him, and her heart was daring them to take him from her.

"Spose we don go?" the sheriff asked again.

"Twenty of yuh runnin over one ol woman! Now, ain yuh white men glad yuh so brave?"

The sheriff grabbed her arm.

"C mon, now! Yuh done did ernuff sass fer one night. Wheres tha nigger son of yos?"

"Don yuh wished yuh knowed?"

"Yuh wanna git slapped?"

"Ah ain never seen one of yo kind tha wuznt too low fer . . ."

The sheriff slapped her straight across her face with his open palm. She fell back against a wall and sank to her knees.

"Is tha whut white men do t nigger women?"

She rose slowly and stood again, not even touching the place that ached from his blow, her hands folded over her stomach.

"Ah ain never seen one of yo kind tha wuznt too low fer . . ."

He slapped her again; she reeled backward several feet and fell on her side.

"Is tha whut we too low t do?"

She stood before him again, dry-eyed, as though she had not been struck. Her lips were numb and her chin was wet with blood.

"Aw, let her go! Its the nigger we wan!" said one.

"Wheres that nigger son of yos?" the sheriff asked.

"Find im," she said.

"By Gawd, ef we hafta find im we'll kill im!"

"He wont be the only nigger yuh ever killed," she said.

She was consumed with a bitter pride. There was nothing on this earth, she felt then, that they could not do to her but that she could take. She stood on a narrow plot of ground from which she would die before she was pushed. And then it was, while standing there, feeling warm blood seeping down her throat, that she gave up Johnny-Boy, gave him up to the white folks. She gave him up because they had come tramping into her heart, demanding him, thinking they could get him by beating her, thinking they could scare her into making her tell where he was. She gave him up because she wanted them to know that they could not get what they wanted by bluffing and killing.

"Wheres this meetin gonna be?" the sheriff asked.

"Don yuh wish yuh knowed?"

"Ain there gonna be a meetin?"

"How come yuh astin me?"

"There *is* gonna be a meetin," said the sheriff.

"Is it?"

"Ah gotta great mind t choke it outta yuh!"

"Yuh so smart," she said.

"We ain playin wid yuh!"

"Did Ah say yuh wuz?"

"Tha nigger son of yos is erroun here somewheres n we aim t find im," said the sheriff. "Ef yuh tell us where he is n ef he

talks, mabbe he'll git off easy. But ef we hafta find im, we'll kill
im! Ef we hafta find im, then yuh git a sheet t put over im in the
mawnin, see? Gut yuh a sheet, cause hes gonna be dead!"

"He wont be the only nigger yuh ever killed," she said again.

The sheriff walked past her. The others followed. Yuh didnt
git whut yuh wanted! she thought exultingly. N yuh ain gonna
never git it! Hotly, something ached in her to make them feel
the intensity of her pride and freedom; her heart groped to turn
the bitter hours of her life into words of a kind that would make
them feel that she had taken all they had done to her in her
stride and could still take more. Her faith surged so strongly in
her she was all but blinded. She walked behind them to the
door, knotting and twisting her fingers. She saw them step to the
muddy ground. Each whirl of the yellow beacon revealed
glimpses of slanting rain. Her lips moved, then she shouted:

"Yuh didnt git whut yuh wanted! N yuh ain gonna nevah
git it!"

The sheriff stopped and turned; his voice came low and hard.

"Now, by Gawd, thas ernuff outta yuh!"

"Ah know when Ah done said ernuff!"

"Aw, naw, yuh don!" he said. "Yuh don know when yuh done
said ernuff, but Ahma teach yuh ternight!"

He was up the steps and across the porch with one bound.
She backed into the hall, her eyes full on his face.

"Tell me when yuh gonna stop talkin!" he said, swinging his
fist.

The blow caught her high on the cheek; her eyes went blank;
she fell flat on her face. She felt the hard heel of his wet shoes
coming into her temple and stomach.

"Lemme hear yuh talk some mo!"

She wanted to, but could not; pain numbed and choked her.
She lay still, and somewhere out of the grey void of uncon-
sciousness she heard someone say: *aw fer chrissakes leave her
erlone its the nigger we wan. . . .*

IV

She never knew how long she had lain huddled in the dark
hallway. Her first returning feeling was of a nameless fear
crowding the inside of her, then a deep pain spreading from her
temple downward over her body. Her ears were filled with the

drone of rain and she shuddered from the cold wind blowing through the door. She opened her eyes and at first saw nothing. As if she were imagining it, she knew she was half-lying and half-sitting in a corner against a wall. With difficulty she twisted her neck, and what she saw made her hold her breath—a vast white blur was suspended directly above her. For a moment she could not tell if her fear was from the blur or if the blur was from her fear. Gradually the blur resolved itself into a huge white face that slowly filled her vision. She was stone still, conscious really of the effort to breathe, feeling somehow that she existed only by the mercy of that white face. She had seen it before; its fear had gripped her many times; it had for her the fear of all the white faces she had ever seen in her life. *Sue* . . . As from a great distance, she heard her name being called. She was regaining consciousness now, but the fear was coming with her. She looked into the face of a white man, wanting to scream out for him to go, yet accepting his presence because she felt she had to. Though some remote part of her mind was active, her limbs were powerless. It was as if an invisible knife had split her in two, leaving one half of her lying there helpless, while the other half shrank in dread from a forgotten but familiar enemy. *Sue its me Sue its me* . . . Then all at once the voice came clearly.

"Sue, its me! Its Booker!"

And she heard an answering voice speaking inside of her, Yeah, its Booker . . . The one whut jus joined . . . She roused herself, struggling for full consciousness; and as she did so she transferred to the person of Booker the nameless fear she felt. It seemed that Booker towered above her as a challenge to her right to exist upon the earth.

"Yuh awright?"

She did not answer; she started violently to her feet and fell.

"Sue, yuh hurt!"

"Yeah," she breathed.

"Where they hit yuh?"

"Its mah head," she whispered.

She was speaking even though she did not want to; the fear that had hold of her compelled her.

"They beat yuh?"

"Yeah."

"Them bastards! Them Gawddam bastards!"

She heard him saying it over and over; then she felt herself being lifted.

"Naw!" she gasped.

"Ahma take yuh t the kitchen!"

"Put me down!"

"But yuh cant stay here like this!"

She shrank in his arms and pushed her hands against his body; when she was in the kitchen she freed herself, sank into a chair, and held tightly to its back. She looked wonderingly at Booker. There was nothing about him that should frighten her so, but even that did not ease her tension. She saw him go to the water bucket, wet his handkerchief, wring it, and offer it to her. Distrustfully, she stared at the damp cloth.

"Here; put this on yo fohead . . ."

"Naw!"

"C mon; itll make yuh feel bettah!"

She hesitated in confusion. What right had she to be afraid when someone was acting as kindly as this toward her? Reluctantly, she leaned forward and pressed the damp cloth to her head. It helped. With each passing minute she was catching hold of herself, yet wondering why she felt as she did.

"Whut happened?"

"Ah don know."

"Yuh feel bettah?"

"Yeah."

"Who all wuz here?"

"Ah don know," she said again.

"Yo head still hurt?"

"Yeah."

"Gee, Ahm sorry."

"Ahm awright," she sighed and buried her face in her hands. She felt him touch her shoulder.

"Sue, Ah got some bad news fer yuh . . ."

She knew; she stiffened and grew cold. It had happened; she stared dry-eyed, with compressed lips.

"Its mah Johnny-Boy," she said.

"Yeah; Ahm awful sorry t hafta tell yuh this way. But Ah thought yuh oughta know . . ."

Her tension eased and a vacant place opened up inside of her. A voice whispered, Jesus, hep me!

"W-w-where is he?"

"They got im out t Foleys Woods tryin t make im tell who the others is."

"He ain gonna tell," she said. "They just as waal kill im, cause he ain gonna nevah tell."

"Ah hope he don," said Booker. "But he didnt hava chance t tell the others. They grabbed im jus as he got t the woods."

Then all the horror of it flashed upon her; she saw flung out over the rainy countryside an array of shacks where white and black comrades were sleeping; in the morning they would be rising and going to Lem's; then they would be caught. And that meant terror, prison, and death. The comrades would have to be told; she would have to tell them; she could not entrust Johnny-Boy's work to another, and especially not to Booker as long as she felt toward him as she did. Gripping the bottom of the chair with both hands, she tried to rise; the room blurred and she swayed. She found herself resting in Booker's arms.

"Lemme go!"

"Sue, yuh too weak t walk!"

"Ah gotta tell em!" she said.

"Set down, Sue! Yuh hurt! Yuh sick!"

When seated, she looked at him helplessly.

"Sue, lissen! Johnny-Boys caught. Ahm here. Yuh tell me who they is n Ahll tell em."

She stared at the floor and did not answer. Yes; she was too weak to go. There was no way for her to tramp all those miles through the rain tonight. But should she tell Booker? If only she had somebody like Reva to talk to! She did not want to decide alone; she must make no mistake about this. She felt Booker's fingers pressing on her arm and it was as though the white mountain was pushing her to the edge of a sheer height; she again exclaimed inwardly, Jesus, hep me! Booker's white face was at her side, waiting. Would she be doing right to tell him? Suppose she did not tell and then the comrades were caught? She could not ever forgive herself for doing a thing like that. But maybe she was wrong; maybe her fear was what Johnny-Boy had always called "jus foolishness." She remembered his saying, Ma we cant make the party grow ef we start doubtin everybody . . .

"Tell me who they is, Sue, n Ahll tell em. Ah jus joined n Ah don know who they is."

"Ah don know who they is," she said.

"Yuh *gotta* tell me who they is, Sue!"

"Ah tol yuh Ah don know!"

"Yuh *do* know! C mon! Set up n talk!"

"Naw!"

"Yuh wan em all t git *killed?*"

She shook her head and swallowed. Lawd, Ah don blieve in this man!

"Lissen, Ahll call the names n yuh tell me which ones is in the party n which ones ain, see?"

"Naw!"

"Please, Sue!"

"Ah don know," she said.

"Sue, yuh ain doin right by em. Johnny-Boy wouldnt wan yuh t be this way. Hes out there holdin up his end. Les hol up ours . . ."

"Lawd, Ah don know . . ."

"Is yuh scareda me cause Ahm *white?* Johnny-Boy ain like tha. Don let all the work we done go fer nothin."

She gave up and bowed her head in her hands.

"Is it Johnson? Tell me, Sue?"

"Yeah," she whispered in horror; a mounting horror of feeling herself being undone.

"Is it Green?"

"Yeah."

"Murphy?"

"Lawd, Ah don know!"

"Yuh gotta tell me, Sue!"

"Mistah Booker, please leave me erlone . . ."

"Is it Murphy?"

She answered yes to the names of Johnny-Boy's comrades; she answered until he asked her no more. Then she thought, How he know the sheriffs men is watchin Lems house? She stood up and held onto her chair, feeling something sure and firm within her.

"How yuh know bout Lem?"

"Why . . . How Ah know?"

"Whut yuh doin here this tima night? How yuh know the sheriff got Johnny-Boy?"

"Sue, don yuh blieve in me?"

She did not, but she could not answer. She stared at him until her lips hung open; she was searching deep within herself for certainty.

"You meet Reva?" she asked.

"Reva?"

"Yeah; Lems gal?"

"Oh, yeah. Sho, Ah met Reva."

"She tell yuh?"

She asked the question more of herself than of him; she longed to believe.

"Yeah," he said softly. "Ah reckon Ah oughta be goin t tell em now."

"Who?" she asked. "Tell *who*?"

The muscles of her body were stiff as she waited for his answer; she felt as though life depended upon it.

"The comrades," he said.

"Yeah," she sighed.

She did not know when he left; she was not looking or listening. She just suddenly saw the room empty and from her the thing that had made her fearful was gone.

V

For a space of time that seemed to her as long as she had been upon the earth, she sat huddled over the cold stove. One minute she would say to herself, They both gone now; Johnny-Boy n Sug . . . Mabbe Ahll never see em ergin. Then a surge of guilt would blot out her longing. "Lawd, Ah shouldna tol!" she mumbled. "But no man kin be so lowdown as t do a think like tha . . ." Several times she had an impulse to try to tell the comrades herself; she was feeling a little better now. But what good would that do? She had told Booker the names. He jus couldnt be a Judas t po folks like us . . . He *couldnt!*

"An Sue!"

Thas Reva! Her heart leaped with an anxious gladness. She rose without answering and limped down the dark hallway. Through the open door, against the background of rain, she saw Reva's face, lit now and then to whiteness by the whirling beams of the beacon. She was about to call, but a thought checked her. Jesus, hep me! Ah gotta tell her bout Johnny-Boy . . . Lawd, Ah cant!

"An Sue, yuh there?"

"C mon in, chile!"

She caught Reva and held her close for a moment without speaking.

"Lawd, Ahm sho glad yuh here," she said at last.

"Ah thought somethin had happened t yuh," said Reva, pulling away. "Ah saw the do open . . . Pa tol me to come back n stay wid yuh tonight . . ." Reva paused and started, "W-w-whuts the mattah?"

She was so full of having Reva with her that she did not understand what the question meant.

"Hunh?"

"Yo neck . . ."

"Aw, it ain nothin, chile. C mon in the kitchen."

"But theres blood on yo neck!"

"The sheriff wuz here . . ."

"Them fools! Whut they wanna bother yuh fer? Ah could kill em! So hep me Gawd, Ah could!"

"It ain nothin," she said.

She was wondering how to tell Reva about Johnny-Boy and Booker. Ahll wait a lil while longer, she thought. Now that Reva was here, her fear did not seem as awful as before.

"C mon, lemme fix yo head, An Sue. Yuh hurt."

They went to the kitchen. She sat silent while Reva dressed her scalp. She was feeling better now; in just a little while she would tell Reva. She felt the girl's finger pressing gently upon her head.

"Tha hurt?"

"A lil, chile."

"Yuh po thing."

"It ain nothin."

"Did Johnny-Boy come?"

She hesitated.

"Yeah."

"He done gone t tell the others?"

Reva's voice sounded so clear and confident that it mocked her. Lawd, Ah cant tell this chile . . .

"Yuh tol im, didn't yuh, An Sue?"

"Y-y-yeah . . ."

"Gee! Thas good! Ah tol pa he didnt hafta worry ef Johnny-Boy got the news. Mabbe thingsll come out awright."

"Ah hope . . ."

She could not go on; she had gone as far as she could. For the first time that night she began to cry.

"Hush, An Sue! Yuh awways been brave. Itll be awright!"

"Ain nothin awright, chile. The worls jus too much fer us, Ah reckon."

"Ef yuh cry that way itll make me cry."

She forced herself to stop. Naw; Ah cant carry on way in fronta Reva . . . Right now she had a deep need for Reva to believe in her. She watched the girl get pine-knots from behind the stove, rekindle the fire, and put on the coffee pot.

"Yuh wan some cawffee?" Reva asked.

"Naw, honey."

"Aw, c mon, An Sue."

"Jusa lil, honey."

"Thas the way to be. Oh, say, Ah fergot," said Reva, measuring out spoonsful of coffee. "Pa tol me t tell yuh t watch out fer tha Booker man. Hes a stool."

She showed not one sign of outward movement or expression, but as the words fell from Reva's lips she went limp inside.

"Pa tol me soon as Ah got back home. He got word from town . . ."

She stopped listening. She felt as though she had been slapped to the extreme outer edge of life, into a cold darkness. She knew now what she had felt when she had looked up out of her fog of pain and had seen Booker. It was the image of all the white folks, and the fear that went with them, that she had seen and felt during her lifetime. And again, for the second time that night, something she had felt had come true. All she could say to herself was, Ah didnt like im! Gawd knows, Ah didnt! Ah tol Johnny-Boy it wuz some of them white folks . . .

"Here; drink yo cawffee . . ."

She took the cup; her fingers trembled, and the steaming liquid spilt onto her dress and leg.

"Ahm sorry, An Sue!"

Her leg was scalded, but the pain did not bother her.

"Its awright," she said.

"Wait; lemme put some lard on tha burn!"

"It don hurt."

"Yuh worried bout somethin."

"Naw, honey."

"Lemme fix yuh so mo cawffee."

"Ah don wan nothin now, Reva."

"Waal, buck up. Don be tha way . . ."

They were silent. She heard Reva drinking. No; she would not
tell Reva; Reva was all she had left. But she had to do something, some way, somehow. She was undone too much as it was;
and to tell Reva about Booker or Johnny-Boy was more than she
was equal to; it would be too coldly shameful. She wanted to be
alone and fight this thing out with herself.

"Go t bed, honey. Yuh tired."

"Naw; Ahm awright, An Sue."

She heard the bottom of Reva's empty cup clank against the
top of the stove. Ah *got* t make her go t bed! Yes; Booker would
tell the names of the comrades to the sheriff. If she could only
stop him some way! That was the answer, the point, the star
that grew bright in the morning of new hope. Soon, maybe half
an hour from now, Booker would reach Foley's Woods. Hes boun
t go the long way, cause he don know no short cut, she thought.
Ah could wade the creek n beat im there. . . . But what would
she do after that?

"Reva, honey, go t bed. Ahm awright. Yuh need res."

"Ah ain sleepy, An Sue."

"Ah knows whuts bes fer yuh, chile. Yuh tired n wet."

"Ah wanna stay up wid yuh."

She forced a smile and said:

"Ah don think they gonna hurt Johnny-Boy . . ."

"Fer *real*, An Sue?"

"Sho, honey."

"But Ah wanna wait up wid yuh."

"Thas mah job, honey. Thas whut a mas fer, t wait up fer her
chullun."

"Good night, An Sue."

"Good night, honey."

She watched Reva pull up and leave the kitchen; presently
she heard the shucks in the mattress whispering, and she knew
that Reva had gone to bed. She was alone. Through the cracks of
the stove she saw the fire dying to grey ashes; the room was
growing cold again. The yellow beacon continued to flit past the
window and the rain still drummed. Yes; she was alone; she had
done this awful thing alone; she must find some way out, alone.
Like touching a festering sore, she put her finger upon that
moment when she had shouted her defiance to the sheriff, when

she had shouted to feel her strength. She had lost Sug to save others; she had let Johnny-Boy go to save others; and then in a moment of weakness that came from too much strength she had lost all. If she had not shouted to the sheriff, she would have been strong enough to have resisted Booker; she would have been able to tell the comrades herself. Something tightened in her as she rememberd and understood the fit of fear she had felt on coming to herself in the dark hallway. A part of her life she thought she had done away with forever had had hold of her then. She had thought the soft, warm past was over; she had thought that it did not mean much when now she sang: *"Hes the Lily of the Valley, the Bright n Mawnin Star"* . . . The days when she had sung that song were the days when she had not hoped for anything on this earth, the days when the cold mountain had driven her into the arms of Jesus. She had thought that Sug and Johnny-Boy had taught her to forget Him, to fix her hope upon the fight of black men for freedom. Through the gradual years she had believed and worked with them, had felt strength shed from the grace of their terrible vision. That grace had been upon her when she had let the sheriff slap her down; it had been upon her when she had risen time and again from the floor and faced him. But she had trapped herself with her own hunger; to water the long, dry thirst of her faith her pride had made a bargain which her flesh could not keep. Her having told the names of Johnny-Boy's comrades was but an incident in a deeper horror. She stood up and looked at the floor while call and counter-call, loyalty and counter-loyalty struggled in her soul. Mired she was between two abandoned worlds, living, but dying without the strength of the grace that either gave. The clearer she felt it the fuller did something well up from the depths of her for release; the more urgent did she feel the need to fling into her black sky another star, another hope, one more terrible vision to give her the strength to live and act. Softly and restlessly she walked about the kitchen, feeling herself naked against the night, the rain, the world; and shamed whenever the thought of Reva's love crossed her mind. She lifted her empty hands and looked at her writhing fingers. Lawd, whut kin Ah do now? She could still wade the creek and get to Foley's Woods before Booker. And then what? How could she manage to see Johnny-Boy or Booker? Again she heard the sheriff's threatening voice: Git yuh

a sheet, cause hes gonna be dead! The sheet! Thas it, the *sheet!*
Her whole being leaped with will; the long years of her life bent
toward a moment of focus, a point. Ah kin go wid mah sheet!
Ahll be doin whut he said! Lawd Gawd in Heaven, Ahma go lika
nigger woman wid mah windin sheet t git mah dead son! But
then what? She stood straight and smiled grimly; she had in her
heart the whole meaning of her life; her entire personality was
poised on the brink of a total act. Ah know! Ah *know!* She
thought of Johnny-Boy's gun in the dresser drawer. Ahll hide the
gun in the sheet n go aftah Johnny-Boys body. . . . She tiptoed
to her room, eased out the dresser drawer, and got a sheet. Reva
was sleeping; the darkness was filled with her quiet breathing.
She groped in the drawer and found the gun. She wound the
gun in the sheet and held them both under her apron. Then she
stole to the bedside and watched Reva. Lawd, hep her! But
mabbe shes bettah off. This had t happen sometimes . . . She
n Johnny-Boy couldna been together in this here South . . . N
Ah couldnt tell her bout Booker. Itll come out awright n she
wont nevah know. Reva's trust would never be shaken. She
caught her breath as the shucks in the mattress rustled dryly;
then all was quiet and she breathed easily again. She tiptoed to
the door, down the hall, and stood on the porch. Above her the
yellow beacon whirled through the rain. She went over muddy
ground, mounted a slope, stopped, and looked back at her house.
The lamp glowed in her window, and the yellow beacon that
swung every few seconds seemed to feed it with light. She
turned and started across the fields, holding the gun and sheet
tightly, thinking, Po Reva . . . Po critter . . . Shes fas
ersleep . . .

VI

For the most part she walked with her eyes half shut, her lips
tightly compressed, leaning her body against the wind and the
driving rain, feeling the pistol in the sheet sagging cold and
heavy in her fingers. Already she was getting wet; it seemed that
her feet found every puddle of water that stood between the
corn rows.

She came to the edge of the creek and paused, wondering at
what point was it low. Taking the sheet from under her apron,
she wrapped the gun in it so that her finger could be upon the

trigger. Ahll cross here, she thought. At first she did not feel the
water; her feet were already wet. But the water grew cold as it
came up to her knees; she gasped when it reached her waist.
Lawd, this creeks high! When she had passed the middle, she
knew that she was out of danger. She came out of the water,
climbed a grassy hill, walked on, turned a bend, and saw the
lights of autos gleaming ahead. Yeah; theys still there! She
hurried with her head down. Wondah did Ah beat im here?
Lawd, Ah *hope* so! A vivid image of Booker's white face hovered
a moment before her eyes, and a surging will rose up in her so
hard and strong that it vanished. She was among the autos now.
From nearby came the hoarse voices of the men.

"Hey, yuh!"

She stopped, nervously clutching the sheet. Two white men
with shotguns came toward her.

"Whut in hell yuh doin out here?"

She did not answer.

"Didnt yuh hear somebody speak t yuh?"

"Ahm comin aftah mah son," she said humbly.

"Yo *son*?"

"Yessuh."

"Whut yo son doin out here?"

"The sheriffs got im."

"Holy Scott! Jim, its the niggers ma!"

"Whut yuh got there?" asked one.

"A sheet."

"A *sheet*?"

"Yessuh."

"Fer whut?"

"The sheriff tol me t bring a sheet t git his body."

"Waal, waal . . ."

"Now, ain tha somethin?"

The white men looked at each other.

"These niggers sho love one ernother," said one.

"N tha ain no lie," said the other.

"Take me t the sheriff," she begged.

"Yuh ain givin us *orders*, is yuh?"

"Nawsuh."

"We'll take yuh when wes good n ready."

"Yessuh."

"So yuh wan his body?"

"Yessuh."

"Waal, he ain dead yit."

"They gonna kill im," she said.

"Ef he talks they wont."

"He ain gonna talk," she said.

"How yuh know?"

"Cause he ain."

"We got ways of makin niggers talk."

"Yuh ain got no way fer im."

"Yuh thinka lot of that black Red, don yuh?"

"Hes mah son."

"Why don yuh teach im some sense?"

"Hes mah son," she said again.

"Lissen, ol nigger woman, yuh stand there wid yo hair white. Yuh got bettah sense than t blieve tha niggers kin make a revolution . . ."

"A black republic," said the other one, laughing.

"Take me t the sheriff," she begged.

"Yuh his ma," said one. "Yuh kin make im talk n tell whos in this thing wid im."

"He ain gonna talk," she said.

"Don yuh wan im t live?"

She did not answer.

"C mon, les take her t Bradley."

They grabbed her arms, and she clutched hard at the sheet and gun; they led her toward the crowd in the woods. Her feelings were simple; Booker would not tell; she was there with the gun to see to that. The louder became the voices of the men the deeper became her feeling of wanting to right the mistake she had made; of wanting to fight her way back to solid ground. She would stall for time until Booker showed up. Oh, ef theyll only lemme git close t Johnny-Boy! As they led her near the crowd she saw white faces turning and looking at her and heard a rising clamor of voices.

"Whos tha?"

"A nigger woman!"

"Whut she doin out here?"

"This is his ma!" called one of the men.

"Whut she wans?"

"She brought a sheet t cover his body!"

"He ain dead yit!"

"They tryin t make im talk!"

"But he will be dead soon ef he don open up!"

"Say, look! The niggers ma brought a sheet t cover up his body!"

"Now, ain that sweet?"

"Mabbe she wans t hol a prayer meetin!"

"Did she git a preacher?"

"Say, go git Bradley!"

"O.K.!"

The crowd grew quiet. They looked at her curiously; she felt their cold eyes trying to detect some weakness in her. Humbly, she stood with the sheet covering the gun. She had already accepted all that they could do to her.

The sheriff came.

"So yuh brought yo sheet, hunh?"

"Yessuh," she whispered.

"Looks like them slaps we gave yuh learned yuh some sense, didnt they?"

She did not answer.

"Yuh don need tha sheet. Yo son ain dead yit," he said, reaching toward her.

She backed away, her eyes wide.

"Naw!"

"Now, lissen, Anty!" he said. "There ain no use in yuh ackin a fool! Go in there n tell tha nigger son of yos t tell us whos in this wid im, see? Ah promise we won't kill im ef he talks. We'll let im git outta town."

"There ain nothin Ah kin tell im," she said.

"Yuh wan us t kill im?"

She did not answer. She saw someone lean toward the sheriff and whisper.

"Bring her erlong," the sheriff said.

They led her to a muddy clearing. The rain streamed down through the ghostly glare of the flashlights. As the men formed a semi-circle she saw Johnny-Boy lying in a trough of mud. He was tied with rope; he lay hunched, and one side of his face rested in a pool of black water. His eyes were staring questioningly at her.

"Speak t im," said the sheriff.

If she could only tell him why she was here! But that was impossible; she was close to what she wanted and she stared straight before her with compressed lips.

"Say, nigger!" called the sheriff, kicking Johnny-Boy. "Heres yo ma!"

Johnny-Boy did not move or speak. The sheriff faced her again.

"Lissen, Anty," he said. "Yuh got mo say wid im than anybody. Tell im t talk n hava chance. Whut he wanna pertect the other niggers n white folks fer?"

She slid her finger about the trigger of the gun and looked stonily at the mud.

"Go t him," said the sheriff.

She did not move. Her heart was crying out to answer the amazed question in Johnny-Boy's eyes. But there was no way now.

"Waal, yuhre astin fer it. By Gawd, we gotta way to *make* yuh talk t im," he said, turning away. "Say, Tim, git one of them logs n turn that nigger upside-down n put his legs on it!"

A murmur of assent ran through the crowd. She bit her lips; she knew what that meant.

"Yuh wan yo nigger son crippled?" she heard the sheriff ask.

She did not answer. She saw them roll the log up; they lifted Johnny-Boy and laid him on his face and stomach, then they pulled his legs over the log. His kneecaps rested on the sheer top of the log's back and the toes of his shoes pointed groundward. So absorbed was she is watching that she felt that it was she who was being lifted and made ready for torture.

"Git a crowbar!" said the sheriff.

A tall, lank man got a crowbar from a nearby auto and stood over the log. His jaws worked slowly on a wad of tabacco.

"Now, its up t yuh, Anty," the sheriff said. "Tell the man wuht t do!"

She looked into the rain. The sheriff turned.

"Mabbe she think wes playin. Ef she don say nothin, then break em at the kneecaps!"

"O.K., Sheriff!"

She stood waiting for Booker. Her legs felt weak; she wondered if she would be able to wait much longer. Over and over she said to herself, Ef he came now Ahd kill em both!

"She ain sayin nothin, Sheriff!"

"Waal, Gawddammit, let im have it!"

The crowbar came down and Johnny-Boy's body lunged in the mud and water. There was a scream. She swayed, holding tight to the gun and sheet.

"Hol im! Git the other leg!"

The crowbar fell again. There was another scream.

"Yuh break em?" asked the sheriff.

The tall man lifted Johnny-Boy's legs and let them drop limply again, dropping rearward from the kneecaps. Johnny-Boy's body lay still. His head had rolled to one side and she could not see his face.

"Jus lika broke sparrow wing," said the man, laughing softly.

Then Johnny-Boy's face turned to her; he screamed.

"Go way, ma! Go way!"

It was the first time she had heard his voice since she had come out to the woods; she all but lost control of herself. She started violently forward, but the sheriff's arm checked her.

"Aw, naw! Yuh had yo chance!" He turned to Johnny-Boy. "She kin go ef yuh talk."

"Mistah, he ain gonna talk," she said.

"Go way, ma!" said Johnny-Boy.

"Shoot im! Don make im suffah so," she begged.

"He'll either talk or he'll never hear yuh ergin," the sheriff said. "Theres other things we kin do t im."

She said nothing.

"What yuh come here fer, ma?" Johnny-Boy sobbed.

"Ahm gonna split his eardrums," the sheriff said. "Ef yuh got anythin t say t im yuh bettah say it *now!*"

She closed her eyes. She heard the sheriff's feet sucking in mud. Ah could save im! She opened her eyes; there were shouts of eagerness from the crowd as it pushed in closer.

"Bus em, Sheriff!"

"Fix im so he cant hear!"

"He knows how t do it, too!"

"He busted a Jew boy tha way once!"

She saw the sheriff stoop over Johnny-Boy, place his flat palm over one ear, and strike his fist against it with all his might. He placed his palm over the other ear and struck again. Johnny-Boy moaned, his head rolling from side to side, his eyes showing white amazement in a world without sound.

"Yuh wouldnt talk t im when yuh had the chance," said the sheriff. "Try n talk now."

She felt warm tears on her cheeks. She longed to shoot Johnny-Boy and let him go. But if she did that they would take the gun from her, and Booker would tell who the others were. Lawd, hep me! The men were talking loudly now, as though the main business was over. It seemed ages that she stood there watching Johnny-Boy roll and whimper in his world of silence.

"Say, Sheriff, heres somebody lookin fer yuh!"

"Who is it?"

"Ah don know!"

"Bring em in!"

She stiffened and looked around wildly, holding the gun tight. Is tha Booker? Then she held still, feeling that her excitement might betray her. Mabbe Ah kin shoot em both! Mabbe Ah kin shoot *twice!* The sheriff stood in front of her, waiting. The crowd parted and she saw Booker hurrying forward.

"Ah know em all, Sheriff!" he called.

He came full into the muddy clearing where Johnny-Boy lay.

"Yuh mean yuh got the names?"

"Sho! The ol nigger . . ."

She saw his lips hang open and silent when he saw her. She stepped forward and raised the sheet.

"Whut . . ."

She fired, once; then, without pausing, she turned, hearing them yell. She aimed at Johnny-Boy, but they had their arms around her, bearing her to the ground, clawing at the sheet in her hand. She glimpsed Booker lying sprawled in the mud, on his face, his hands stretched out before him; then a cluster of yelling men blotted him out. She lay without struggling, looking upward through the rain at the white faces above her. And she was suddenly at peace; they were not a white mountain now; they were not pushing her any longer to the edge of life. Its awright . . .

"She shot Booker!"

"She hada gun in the sheet!"

"She shot im right thu the head!"

"Whut she shoot im fer?"

"Kill the bitch!"

"Ah *thought* somethin wuz wrong bout her!"

"Ah wuz fer givin it t her from the firs!"

"Thas whut yuh git for treatin a nigger nice!"

"Say, Bookers dead!"

She stopped looking into the white faces, stopped listening. She waited, giving up her life before they took it from her; she had done what she wanted. Ef only Johnny-Boy . . . She looked at him; he lay looking at her with tired eyes. Ef she could only tell im! But he lay already buried in a grave of silence.

"Whut yuh kill im fer, hunh?"

It was the sheriff's voice; she did not answer.

"Mabbe she wuz shootin at yuh, Sheriff?"

"Whut yuh kill im fer?"

She felt the sheriff's foot come into her side; she closed her eyes.

"Yuh black bitch!"

"Let her have it!"

"Yuh reckon she foun out bout Booker?"

"She mighta."

"Jesus Chris, whut yuh dummies *waitin* on!"

"Yeah; kill her!"

"Kill em *both!*"

"Let her know her nigger sons dead firs!"

She turned her head toward Johnny-Boy; he lay looking puzzled in a world beyond the reach of voices. At leas he cant hear, she thought.

"C mon, let im have it!"

She listened to hear what Johnny-Boy could not. They came, two of them, one right behind the other, so close together that they sounded like one shot. She did not look at Johnny-Boy now; she looked at the white faces of the men, hard and wet in the glare of the flashlights.

"Yuh hear tha, nigger woman?"

"Did tha surprise im? Hes in hell now, wonderin whut hit im!"

"C mon! Give it t her, Sheriff!"

"Lemme shoot her, Sheriff! It wuz mah pal she shot!"

"Awright, Pete! Thas fair ernuff!"

She gave up as much of her life as she could before they took it from her. But the sound of the shot and the streak of fire that tore its way through her chest forced her to live again, intensely. She had not moved, save for the slight jarring impact of the bullet. She felt the heat of her own blood warming her cold, wet back. She yearned suddenly to talk. "Yuh didnt git whut yuh wanted! N yuh ain gonna nevah git it! Yuh didnt kill me; Ah come here by mahsef . . ." She felt rain falling into her wide-open, dimming eyes and heard faint voices. Her lips moved soundlessly. *Yuh didnt git yuh didnt yuh didnt . . .* Focused and pointed she was, buried in the depths of her star, swallowed in its peace and strength, and not feeling her flesh growing cold, cold as the rain that fell from the invisible sky upon the doomed living and the dead that never dies.

See p. 85 - dream

unjust treatment by white pride

The Boy Who Painted Christ Black

JOHN HENRIK CLARKE

He was the smartest boy in the Muskogee County School—for colored children. Everybody even remotely connected with the school knew this. The teacher always pronounced his name with profound gusto as she pointed him out as the ideal student. Once I heard her say: "If he were white he might, some day, become President." Only Aaron Crawford wasn't white; quite the contrary. His skin was so solid black that it glowed, reflecting an inner virtue that was strange, and beyond my comprehension.

In many ways he looked like something that was awkwardly put together. Both his nose and his lips seemed a trifle too large for his face. To say he was ugly would be unjust and to say he was handsome would be gross exaggeration. Truthfully, I could never make up my mind about him. Sometimes he looked like something out of a book of ancient history . . . looked as if he was left over from that magnificent era before the machine age came and marred the earth's natural beauty.

His great variety of talent often startled the teachers. This caused his classmates to look upon him with a mixed feeling of awe and envy.

Before Thanksgiving, he always drew turkeys and pumpkins on the blackboard. On George Washington's birthday, he drew large American flags surrounded by little hatchets. It was these small masterpieces that made him the most talked-about colored boy in Columbus, Georgia. The Negro principal of the Muskogee County School said he would some day be a great painter, like Henry O. Tanner.

For the teacher's birthday, which fell on a day about a week before commencement, Aaron Crawford painted the picture that caused an uproar, and a turning point, at the Muskogee County School. The moment he entered the room that morning, all eyes fell on him. Besides his torn book holder, he was carrying a large-framed concern wrapped in old newspapers. As he went to his seat, the teacher's eyes followed his every motion, a curious wonderment mirrored in them conflicting with the half-smile that wreathed her face.

Aaron put his books down, then smiling broadly, advanced toward the teacher's desk. His alert eyes were so bright with joy that they were almost frightening. The children were leaning forward in their seats, staring greedily at him; a restless anticipation was rampant within every breast.

Already the teacher sensed that Aaron had a present for her. Still smiling, he placed it on her desk and began to help her unwrap it. As the last piece of paper fell from the large frame, the teacher jerked her hand away from it suddenly, her eyes flickering unbelievingly. Amidst the rigid tension, her heavy breathing was distinct and frightening. Temporarily, there was no other sound in the room.

Aaron stared questioningly at her and she moved her hand back to the present cautiously, as if it were a living thing with vicious characteristics. I am sure it was the one thing she least expected.

With a quick, involuntary movement I rose up from my desk. A series of submerged murmurs spread through the room, rising to a distinct monotone. The teacher turned toward the children, staring reproachfully. They did not move their eyes from the present that Aaron had brought her. . . . It was a large picture of Christ—painted black!

Aaron Crawford went back to his seat, a feeling of triumph reflecting in his every movement.

The teacher faced us. Her curious half-smile had blurred into a mild bewilderment. She searched the bright faces before her and started to smile again, occasionally stealing quick glances at the large picture propped on her desk, as though doing so were forbidden amusement.

"Aaron," she spoke at last, a slight tinge of uncertainty in her tone, "this is a most welcome present. Thanks. I will treasure it." She paused, then went on speaking, a trifle more coherent than before. "Looks like you are going to be quite an artist. . . . Suppose you come forward and tell the class how you came to paint this remarkable picture."

When he rose to speak, to explain about the picture, a hush fell tightly over the room, and the children gave him all of their attention . . . something they rarely did for the teacher. He did not speak at first; he just stood there in front of the room, toying absently with his hands, observing his audience carefully, like a great concert artist.

"It was like this," he said, placing full emphasis on every word. "You see, my uncle who lives in New York teaches classes in Negro History at the Y.M.C.A. When he visited us last year he was telling me about the many great black folks who have made history. He said black folks were once the most powerful people on earth. When I asked him about Christ, he said no one ever proved whether he was black or white. Somehow a feeling came over me that he was a black man, 'cause he was so kind and forgiving, kinder than I have ever seen white people be. So, when I painted his picture I couldn't help but paint it as I thought it was."

After this, the little artist sat down, smiling broadly, as if he had gained entrance to a great storehouse of knowledge that ordinary people could neither acquire nor comprehend.

The teacher, knowing nothing else to do under prevailing circumstances, invited the children to rise from their seats and come forward so they could get a complete view of Aaron's unique piece of art.

When I came close to the picture, I noticed it was painted with the kind of paint you get in the five and ten cent stores. Its shape was blurred slightly, as if someone had jarred the frame before the paint had time to dry. The eyes of Christ were deepset and sad, very much like those of Aaron's father, who was a deacon in the local Baptist Church. This picture of Christ looked much different from the one I saw hanging on the wall when I was in Sunday School. It looked more like a helpless Negro, pleading silently for mercy.

For the next few days, there was much talk about Aaron's picture.

The school term ended the following week and Aaron's picture, along with the best handwork done by the students that year, was on display in the assembly room. Naturally, Aaron's picture graced the place of honor.

There was no book work to be done on commencement day and joy was rampant among the children. The girls in their brightly colored dresses gave the school the delightful air of Spring awakening.

In the middle of the day all the children were gathered in the small assembly. On this day we were always favored with a visit from a man whom all the teachers spoke of with mixed esteem and fear. Professor Danual, they called him, and they always pronounced his name with reverence. He was supervisor of all the city schools, including those small and poorly equipped ones set aside for colored children.

The great man arrived almost at the end of our commencement exercises. On seeing him enter the hall, the children rose, bowed courteously, and sat down again, their eyes examining him as if he were a circus freak.

He was a tall white man with solid gray hair that made his lean face seem paler than it actually was. His eyes were the clearest blue I have ever seen. They were the only life-like things about him.

As he made his way to the front of the room the Negro principal, George Du Vaul, was walking ahead of him, cautiously preventing anything from getting in his way. As he passed me, I heard the teachers, frightened, sucking in their breath, felt the tension tightening.

A large chair was in the center of the rostrum. It had been daintily polished and the janitor had laboriously recushioned its bottom. The supervisor went straight to it without being guided, knowing that this pretty splendor was reserved for him.

Presently the Negro principal introduced the distinguished guest and he favored us with a short speech. It wasn't a very important speech. Almost at the end of it, I remember him saying something about he wouldn't be surprised if one of us boys grew up to be a great colored man, like Booker T. Washington.

After he sat down, the school chorus sang two spirituals and the girls in the fourth grade did an Indian folk dance. This brought the commencement program to an end.

After this the supervisor came down from the rostrum, his

eyes tinged with curiosity, and began to view the array of handwork on display in front of the chapel.

Suddenly his face underwent a strange rejuvenation. His clear blue eyes flickered in astonishment. He was looking at Aaron Crawford's picture of Christ. Mechanically he moved his stooped form closer to the picture and stood gazing fixedly at it, curious and undecided, as though it were a dangerous animal that would rise any moment and spread destruction.

We waited tensely for his next movement. The silence was almost suffocating. At last he twisted himself around and began to search the grim faces before him. The fiery glitter of his eyes abated slightly as they rested on the Negro principal, protestingly.

"Who painted this sacrilegious nonsense?" he demanded sharply.

"I painted it, sir." These were Aaron's words, spoken hesitantly. He wetted his lips timidly and looked up at the supervisor, his eyes voicing a sad plea for understanding.

He spoke again, this time more coherently. "Th' principal said a colored person have jes as much right paintin' Jesus black as a white person have paintin' him white. And he says. . . ." At this point he halted abruptly, as if to search for his next words. A strong tinge of bewilderment dimmed the glow of his solid black face. He stammered out a few more words, then stopped again.

The supervisor strode a few steps toward him. At last color had swelled some of the lifelessness out of his lean face.

"Well, go on!" he said, enragedly, ". . . I'm still listening."

Aaron moved his lips pathetically but no words passed them. His eyes wandered around the room, resting finally, with an air of hope, on the face of the Negro principal. After a moment, he jerked his face in another direction, regretfully, as if something he had said had betrayed an understanding between him and the principal.

Presently the principal stepped forward to defend the school's prize student.

"I encouraged the boy in painting that picture," he said firmly. "And it was with my permission that he brought the picture into this school. I don't think the boy is so far wrong in painting Christ black. The artists of all other races have painted whatsoever God they worship to resemble themselves. I see no reason why we should be immune from that privilege. After all, Christ was born in that part of the world that had always been predominantly populated by colored people. There is a strong possibility that he could have been a Negro."

But for the monotonous lull of heavy breathing, I would have sworn that his words had frozen everyone in the hall. I had never heard the little principal speak so boldly to anyone, black or white.

The supervisor swallowed dumfoundedly. His face was aglow in silent rage.

"Have you been teaching these children things like that?" he asked the Negro principal, sternly.

"I have been teaching them that their race has produced great kings and queens as well as slaves and serfs," the principal said. "The time is long overdue when we should let the world know that we erected and enjoyed the benefits of a splendid civilization long before the people of Europe had a written language."

The supervisor coughed. His eyes bulged menacingly as he spoke. "You are not being paid to teach such things in this school, and I am demanding your resignation for overstepping your limit as principal."

George Du Vaul did not speak. A strong quiver swept over his sullen face. He revolved himself slowly and walked out of the room towards his office.

The supervisor's eyes followed him until he was out of focus. Then he murmured under his breath: "There'll be a lot of fuss in this world if you start people thinking that Christ was a nigger."

Some of the teachers followed the principal out of the chapel, leaving the crestfallen children restless and in a quandary about what to do next. Finally we started back to our rooms. The supervisor was behind me. I heard him murmur to himself: "Damn, if niggers ain't getting smarter."

A few days later I heard that the principal had accepted a summer job as art instructor of a small high school somewhere in south Georgia and had gotten permission from Aaron's parents to take him along so he could continue to encourage him in his painting.

I was on my way home when I saw him leaving his office. He was carrying a large briefcase and some books tucked under his arm. He had already said good-by to all the teachers. And strangely, he did not look brokenhearted. As he headed for the large front door, he readjusted his horn-rimmed glasses, but did not look back. An air of triumph gave more dignity to his soldierly stride. He had the appearance of a man who had done a great thing, something greater than any ordinary man would do.

Aaron Crawford was waiting outside for him. They walked down the street together. He put his arms around Aaron's shoulder affectionately. He was talking sincerely to Aaron about something, and Aaron was listening, deeply earnest.

I watched them until they were so far down the street that their forms had begun to blur. Even from this distance I could see they were still walking in brisk, dignified strides, like two people who had won some sort of victory.

Black in religion
v. white
pride

One Friday Morning

LANGSTON HUGHES

The thrilling news did not come directly to Nancy Lee, but it came in little indirections that finally added themselves up to one tremendous fact: she had won the prize! But being a calm and quiet young lady, she did not say anything, although the whole high school buzzed with rumors, guesses, reportedly authentic announcements on the part of students who had no right to be making announcements at all—since no student really knew yet who had won this year's art scholarship.

But Nancy Lee's drawing was so good, her lines so sure, her colors so bright and harmonious, that certainly no other student in the senior art class at George Washington High was thought to have very much of a chance. Yet you never could tell. Last year nobody had expected Joe Williams to win the Artist Club scholarship with that funny modernistic water color he had done of the high-level bridge. In fact, it was hard to make out there was a bridge until you had looked at the picture a long time. Still, Joe Williams got the prize, was feted by the community's leading painters, club women, and society folks at a big banquet at the Park-Rose Hotel, and was now an award student at the Art School—the city's only art school.

Nancy Lee Johnson was a colored girl, a few years out of the South. But seldom did her high-school classmates think of her as colored. She was smart, pretty, and brown, and fitted in well with the life of the school. She stood high in scholarship, played a swell game of basketball, had taken part in the senior musical in a soft, velvety voice, and had never seemed to intrude or stand out, except in pleasant ways, so it was seldom even mentioned—her color.

Nancy Lee sometimes forgot she was colored herself. She liked her classmates and her school. Particularly she liked her art teacher, Miss Dietrich, the tall red-haired woman who taught her law and order in doing things; and the beauty of working step by step until a job is done; a picture finished; a design created; or a block print carved out of nothing but an idea and a smooth square of linoleum, inked, proofs made, and finally put down on paper—clean, sharp, beautiful, individual, unlike any other in the world, thus making the paper have a meaning nobody else could give it except Nancy Lee. That was the wonderful thing about true creation. You made something nobody else on earth could make—but you.

Miss Dietrich was the kind of teacher who brought out the best in her students—but their own best, not anybody else's copied best. For anybody else's best, great though it might be, even Michelangelo's, wasn't enough to please Miss Dietrich, dealing with the creative impulses of young men and women living in an American city in the Middle West, and being American.

Nancy Lee was proud of being American, a Negro American with blood out of Africa a long time ago, too many generations back to count. But her parents had taught her the beauties of Africa, its strength, its song, its mighty rivers, its early smelting of iron, its building of the pyramids, and its ancient and important civilizations. And Miss Dietrich had discovered for her the sharp and humorous lines of African sculpture, Benin, Congo, Makonde. Nancy Lee's father was a mail carrier, her mother a social worker in a city settlement house. Both parents had been to Negro colleges in the South. And her mother had gotten a further degree in social work from a Northern university. Her parents were, like most Americans, simple, ordinary people who had worked hard and steadily for their education. Now they were trying to make it easier for Nancy Lee to achieve learning than it had been for them. They would be very happy when they heard of the award to their daughter—yet Nancy did not tell them. To surprise them would be better. Besides, there had been a promise.

Casually, one day, Miss Dietrich asked Nancy Lee what color frame she thought would be best on her picture. That had been the first inkling.

"Blue," Nancy Lee said. Although the picture had been entered in the Artist Club contest a month ago, Nancy Lee did not hesitate in her choice of a color for the possible frame, since she could still see her picture clearly in her mind's eye—for that picture waiting for the blue frame had come out of her soul, her own life, and had bloomed into miraculous being with Miss Dietrich's help. It was, she knew, the best water color she had painted in her four years as a high-school art student, and she was glad she had made something Miss Dietrich liked well enough to permit her to enter in the contest before she graduated.

It was not a modernistic picture in the sense that you had to look at it a long time to understand what it meant. It was just a simple scene in the city park on a spring day, with the trees still leaflessly lacy against the sky, the new grass fresh and green, a flag on a tall pole in the center, children playing, and an old Negro woman sitting on a bench with her head turned. A lot for one picture, to be sure, but it was not there in heavy and final detail like a calendar. Its charm was that everything was light and airy, happy like spring, with a lot of blue sky, paper-white clouds, and air showing through. You could tell that the old Negro woman was looking at the flag, and that the flag was proud in the spring breeze, and that the breeze helped to make the children's dresses billow as they played.

Miss Dietrich had taught Nancy Lee how to paint spring, people, and a breeze on what was only a plain white piece of paper from the supply closet. But Miss Dietrich had not said make it like any other spring-people-breeze ever seen before. She let it remain Nancy Lee's own. That is how the old Negro woman happened to be there looking at the flag—for in her mind the flag, the spring, and the woman formed a kind of triangle holding a dream Nancy Lee wanted to express. White stars on a blue field, spring, children, ever-growing life, and an old woman. Would the judges at the Artist Club like it?

One wet, rainy April afternoon Miss O'Shay, the girls' vice-principal, sent for Nancy Lee to stop by her office as school closed. Pupils without umbrellas or raincoats were clustered in doorways, hoping to make it home between showers. Outside the skies were gray. Nancy Lee's thoughts were suddenly gray, too.

She did not think she had done anything wrong, yet that tight little knot came in her throat just the same as she approached Miss O'Shay's door. Perhaps she had banged her locker too often and too hard. Perhaps the note in French she had written to Sallie halfway across the study hall just for fun had never gotten to Sallie but into Miss O'Shay's hands instead. Or maybe she was failing in some subject and wouldn't be allowed to graduate. Chemistry! A pang went through the pit of her stomach.

She knocked on Miss O'Shay's door. That familiarly solid and competent voice said, "Come in."

Miss O'Shay had a way of making you feel welcome, even if you came to be expelled.

"Sit down, Nancy Lee Johnson," said Miss O'Shay. "I have something to tell you." Nancy Lee sat down. "But I must ask you to promise not to tell anyone yet."

"I won't, Miss O'Shay," Nancy Lee said, wondering what on earth the principal had to say to her.

"You are about to graduate," Miss O'Shay said. "And we shall miss you. You have been an excellent student, Nancy, and you will not be without honors on the senior list, as I am sure you know."

At that point there was a light knock on the door. Miss O'Shay called out, "Come in," and Miss Dietrich entered. "May I be a part of this, too?" she asked, tall and smiling.

"Of course," Miss O'Shay said. "I was just telling Nancy Lee what we thought of her. But I hadn't gotten around to giving her the news. Perhaps, Miss Dietrich, you'd like to tell her yourself."

Miss Dietrich was always direct. "Nancy Lee," she said, "your picture has won the Artist Club scholarship."

The slender brown girl's eyes widened, her heart jumped,

then her throat tightened again. She tried to smile, but instead tears came to her eyes.

"Dear Nancy Lee," Miss O'Shay said, "we are so happy for you." The elderly white woman took her hand and shook it warmly while Miss Dietrich beamed with pride.

Nancy Lee must have danced all the way home. She never remembered quite how she got there through the rain. She hoped she had been dignified. But certainly she hadn't stopped to tell anybody her secret on the way. Raindrops, smiles, and tears mingled on her brown cheeks. She hoped her mother hadn't yet gotten home and that the house was empty. She wanted to have time to calm down and look natural before she had to see anyone. She didn't want to be bursting with excitement—having a secret to contain.

Miss O'Shay's calling her to the office had been in the nature of a preparation and a warning. The kind, elderly vice-principal said she did not believe in catching young ladies unawares, even with honors, so she wished her to know about the coming award. In making acceptance speeches she wanted her to be calm, prepared, not nervous, overcome, and frightened. So Nancy Lee was asked to think what she would say when the scholarship was conferred upon her a few days hence, both at the Friday morning high-school assembly hour, when the announcement would be made, and at the evening banquet of the Artist Club. Nancy Lee promised the vice-principal to think calmly about what she would say.

Miss Dietrich had then asked for some facts about her parents, her background, and her life, since such material would probably be desired for the papers. Nancy Lee had told her how, six years before, they had come up from the Deep South, her father having been successful in achieving a transfer from the one post office to another, a thing he had long sought in order to give Nancy Lee a chance to go to school in the North. Now they lived in a modest Negro neighborhood, went to see the best plays when they came to town, and had been saving to send Nancy Lee to art school, in case she were permitted to enter. But the scholarship would help a great deal, for they were not rich people.

"Now Mother can have a new coat next winter," Nancy Lee thought, "because my tuition will all be covered for the first year. And once in art school, there are other scholarships I can win."

Dreams began to dance through her head, plans and ambitions, beauties she would create for herself, her parents, and the Negro people—for Nancy Lee possessed a deep and reverent race pride. She could see the old woman in her picture (really her grandmother in the South) lifting her head to the bright stars on the flag in the distance. A Negro in America! Often hurt, discriminated against, sometimes lynched—but always there were the stars on the blue body of the flag. Was there any other flag in the world that had so many stars? Nancy Lee thought deeply, but she could remember none in all the encyclopedias or geographies she had ever looked into.

"Hitch your wagon to a star," Nancy Lee thought, dancing home in the rain. "Who were our flag-makers?"

Friday morning came, the morning when the world would know—her high-school world, the newspaper world, her mother and dad. Dad could not be there at the assembly to hear the announcement, nor see her prize picture displayed on the stage, nor listen to Nancy Lee's little speech of acceptance, but Mother would be able to come, although Mother was much puzzled as to why Nancy Lee was so insistent she be at school on that particular Friday morning.

When something is happening, something new and fine, something that will change your very life, it is hard to go to sleep at night for thinking about it, and hard to keep your heart from pounding, or a strange little knot of joy from gathering in your throat. Nancy Lee had taken her bath, brushed her hair until it glowed, and had gone to bed thinking about the next day, the big day, when before three thousand students, she would be the one student honored, her painting the one painting to be acclaimed as the best of the year from all the art classes of the city. Her short speech of gratitude was ready. She went over it in her mind, not word for word (because she didn't want it to sound as if she had learned it by heart), but she let the thoughts flow simply and sincerely through her consciousness many times.

When the president of the Artist Club presented her with the medal and scroll of the scholarship award, she would say:

"Judges and members of the Artist Club. I want to thank you

for this award that means so much to me personally and through me to my people, the colored people of this city, who, sometimes, are discouraged and bewildered, thinking that color and poverty are against them. I accept this award with gratitude and pride, not for myself alone, but for my race that believes in American opportunity and American fairness—and the bright stars in our flag. I thank Miss Dietrich and the teachers who made it possible for me to have the knowledge and training that lie behind this honor you have conferred upon my painting. When I came here from the South a few years ago, I was not sure how you would receive me. You received me well. You have given me a chance and helped me along the road I wanted to follow. I suppose the judges know that every week here at assembly the students of this school pledge allegiance to the flag. I shall try to be worthy of that pledge, and of the help and friendship and understanding of my fellow citizens of whatever race or creed, and of our American dream of 'Liberty and justice for all!' "

That would be her response before the students in the morning. How proud and happy the Negro pupils would be, perhaps almost as proud as they were of the one colored star on the football team. Her mother would probably cry with happiness. Thus Nancy Lee went to sleep dreaming of a wonderful to-morrow.

The bright sunlight of an April morning woke her. There was breakfast with her parents—their half-amused and puzzled faces across the table, wondering what could be this secret that made her eyes so bright. The swift walk to school; the clock in the tower almost nine; hundreds of pupils streaming into the long, rambling old building that was the city's largest high school; the sudden quiet of the homeroom after the bell rang; then the teacher opening her record book to call the roll. But just before she began, she looked across the room until her eyes located Nancy Lee.

"Nancy," she said, "Miss O'Shay would like to see you in her office, please."

Nancy Lee rose and went out while the names were being called and the word *present* added its period to each name. Perhaps, Nancy Lee thought, the reporters from the papers had already come. Maybe they wanted to take her picture before assembly, which wasn't until ten o'clock. (Last year they had

had the photograph of the winner of the award in the morning papers as soon as the announcement had been made.)

Nancy Lee knocked at Miss O'Shay's door.

"Come in."

The vice-principal stood at her desk. There was no one else in the room. It was very quiet.

"Sit down, Nancy Lee," she said. Miss O'Shay did not smile. There was a long pause. The seconds went by slowly. "I do not know how to tell you what I have to say," the elderly woman began, her eyes on the papers on her desk. "I am indignant and ashamed for myself and for this city." Then she lifted her eyes and looked at Nancy Lee in the neat blue dress, sitting there before her. "You are not to receive the scholarship this morning."

Outside in the hall the electric bells announcing the first period rang, loud and interminably long. Miss O'Shay remained silent. To the brown girl there in the chair, the room grew suddenly smaller, smaller, smaller, and there was no air. She could not speak.

Miss O'Shay said, "When the committee learned that you were colored, they changed their plans."

Still Nancy Lee said nothing, for there was no air to give breath to her lungs.

"Here is the letter from the committee, Nancy Lee." Miss O'Shay picked it up and read the final paragraph to her.

" 'It seems to us wiser to arbitrarily rotate the award among the various high schools of the city from now on. And especially in this case since the student chosen happens to be colored, a circumstance which unfortunately, had we known, might have prevented this embarrassment. But there have never been any Negro students in the local art school, and the presence of one there might create difficulties for all concerned. We have high regard for the quality of Nancy Lee Johnson's talent, but we do not feel it would be fair to honor it with the Artist Club award.' " Miss O'Shay paused. She put the letter down.

"Nancy Lee, I am very sorry to have to give you this message."

"But my speech," Nancy Lee said, "was about. . . ." The words stuck in her throat. ". . . about America. . . ."

Miss O'Shay had risen; she turned her back and stood looking out the window at the spring tulips in the school yard.

"I thought, since the award would be made at assembly right after our oath of allegiance," the words tumbled almost hysterically from Nancy Lee's throat now, "I would put part of the flag salute in my speech. You know, Miss O'Shay, that part about 'liberty and justice for all.' "

"I know," said Miss O'Shay, slowly facing the room again. "But America is only what we who believe in it make it. I am Irish. You may not know, Nancy Lee, but years ago we were called the dirty Irish, and mobs rioted against us in the big cities, and we were invited to go back where we came from. But we didn't go. And we didn't give up, because we believed in the American dream, and in our power to make that dream come true. Difficulties, yes. Mountains to climb, yes. Discouragements to face, yes. Democracy to make, yes. That is it, Nancy Lee! We still have in this world of ours democracy to *make*. You and I, Nancy Lee. But the premise and the base are here, the lines of the Declaration of Independence and the words of Lincoln are here, and the stars in our flag. Those who deny you this scholarship do not know the meaning of those stars, but it's up to us to make them know. As a teacher in the public schools of this city, I myself will go before the school board and ask them to remove from our system the offer of any prizes or awards denied to any student because of race or color."

Suddenly Miss O'Shay stopped speaking. Her clear, clear blue eyes looked into those of the girl before her. The woman's eyes were full of strength and courage. "Lift up your head, Nancy Lee, and smile at me."

Miss O'Shay stood against the open window with the green lawn and the tulips beyond, the sunlight tangled in her gray hair, her voice an electric flow of strength to the hurt spirit of Nancy Lee. The Abolitionists who believed in freedom when there was slavery must have been like that. The first white teachers who went into the Deep South to teach the freed slaves must have been like that. All those who stand against ignorance, narrowness, hate, and mud on stars must be like that.

Nancy Lee lifted her head and smiled. The bell for assembly rang. She went through the long hall filled with students, toward the auditorium.

"There will be other awards," Nancy Lee thought. "There're schools in other cities. This won't keep me down. But when I'm a woman, I'll fight to see that these things don't happen to other girls as this has happened to me. And men and women like Miss O'Shay will help me."

She took her seat among the seniors. The doors of the auditorium closed. As the principal came onto the platform, the students rose and turned their eyes to the flag on the stage.

One hand went to the heart, the other outstretched toward the flag. Three thousand voices spoke. Among them was the voice of a dark girl whose cheeks were suddenly wet with tears, ". . . one nation indivisible, with liberty and justice for all."

"That is the land we must make," she thought.

pride

So Peaceful in the Country

CARL RUTHVEN OFFORD

Viola got up before the sun, and through the kitchen window she watched the slow rolling away of mountain mist. She felt a lot better. She still thought of Jim, but the thinking now wasn't as sharp as last night.

Last night was awful. Last night was the first night in two years that she'd slept without him. After they'd agreed on her taking a country job it seemed that they'd slept even tighter. Something about their having to part for the summer drew them even more tightly together. So it had seemed. Then last night . . . almost a hundred miles from Jim.

Sleeping alone was terrible. Mr. and Mrs. Christian had gone to the village, and the strange place had seemed too still, the room too large, the bed too different. It wasn't like Harlem. The bed hadn't seemed like a bed at all after the light was turned off. She woke up when it was still too dark and turned on the light and wrote to Jim. It was a long, long letter, very tender, about herself and him. And now the day was coming on fast and the place was beginning to feel a lot better.

In the grayish distance of early morning the rolling mist peeled off the high mountains like pillars of steam. Viola stared out in a deep quiet of feeling, her mind stretching back to Jim. He probably wasn't awake yet, she thought. Perhaps he would oversleep, she thought. That would be bad. She suddenly smiled. If Jim got up late for his class, he'd be tearing around the room like a crazy fool. The smile stayed in wrinkles around her full mouth as she pictured Jim getting up late and finding himself all alone and tearing around the room like mad.

From the dining room came the sound of padded footsteps and she turned in surprise. Did they get up this early? The electric clock on the kitchen wall said ten minutes to seven. She left the window and started to prepare coffee, then she heard the padded steps coming toward the kitchen. Without looking up she saw the bottom of his pyjama pants and his bare white feet on the floor.

Mr. George Christian, Jr., stood at the kitchen door and stretched and yawned and grumbled.

"Good morning, suh," she replied. She didn't look up. Her eyes went back to his naked feet and she thought they were awfully white. She noticed the long white toes and decided to herself that black toes were much better than white ones. That was one thing nobody could argue about, she thought.

Mr. Christian ambled into the kitchen and over to the window. The sun was just breaking over the mountains. Waves of glorious orange splashed like a fan across the sky. Stretching and yawning at the window, he said, "That coffee smells good." He turned and sniffed, his hands comically holding his head. "Certainly smells good."

"It'll be ready in a minute, suh."

"That's fine," he mumbled. "That's fine."

Viola thought she smelled liquor on his breath. She was almost sure of it.

Mr. Christian stuck his head out the window again, then he withdrew and ambled out of the kitchen, and as he went he began to warble, "She'll be coming round the mountain when she comes. Oh, she'll be coming round the mountain when she comes."

He was tight, Viola thought. Yes. He had a hangover from last night in the village. She wondered how people could get themselves plastered smack in the middle of the week.

When she served the coffee in the dining room she noticed that there were swollen puffs under his eyes.

"Should I fix some toast, suh?'

"No, thank you. Nothing more."

She returned to the kitchen, guessing and wondering about them. How many times a week did they get themselves plastered? Yesterday they had seemed so upright and orderly. His little freckle-faced wife had struck her as being gayish, but she hadn't thought . . .

"Viola!"

She put down her coffee cup and hurried in.

"Yes, suh."

He glanced at her and sighed. He didn't look so well, she thought.

"Well," he said. He spread an arm with what appeared to be a great effort. "How do you like it out here?"

"Seems very nice," she answered softly.

He pressed his face in his hands, sighed, then he took a sip of the hot coffee. Viola waited, standing awkwardly to one side.

"I've got an awful head," he said. "I guess I tried to drink the village dry. Did you ever get drunk?"

"No," she answered shortly.

"Not even once in your life?"

"No, suh."

"That's fine. That's fine. I don't as a rule, but last night was the exception."

"Drink the coffee while it's hot," she advised. "It'll make you feel better." She remembered that Jim had had a hangover once, and strong coffee had helped to straighten him out.

Mr. Christian took a couple of sips, closing his eyes with each sip as if he were taking a bitter medicine.

"What did you do in the city?"

"Work," she answered.

"At what?"

"Anything. Housework, factory work. Anything."

"Your husband's unemployed?"

"He's studying."

"Studying?"

"He's studying engineering. Electrical engineering." She emphasized the words with pride.

"That's interesting." He stared at the cup and saucer, then he suddenly burped. "I'm sorry."

Viola shifted awkwardly from one foot to the other. She looked impatiently toward the kitchen.

"You'll have it pretty easy today," he said. "So don't worry about anything. It's only me now and I'm no bother."

"Just you?" She was startled.

"My wife will be back in a couple of days. Maybe tomorrow. It's nothing too serious. Nothing at all, as a matter of fact." It appeared that he was about to burp again but he didn't. His eyes stared wide and he seemed to bite his pale lips. Abruptly he got up from the table and made for the bathroom.

Viola went to the kitchen, her eyes misty with thought. This thing of his wife's absence wasn't so good. She didn't like it at all. Evidently he and his wife had quarreled in the village. She heard Mr. Christian come out from the bathroom, then he called to her in a broken, throaty voice. "I'm going back to bed! I'll be all right later!"

Good Lord, she thought. What was this she was getting into? Could she stay in this country house with him alone? She hadn't counted on anything like that. What would Jim say? What would he think? She stood at the window, looking out upon the range of mountains, now bright green in the sunlight, and for a long time she pondered just what she should do.

It was after twelve when Mr. Christian got up, and he was totally sober. He came out, a blue beach robe tied loosely around his waist, and he looked a lot different. The puffs under his eyes had melted down and his face was no longer stark white. He ate hungrily, in sober silence. A sad silence, Viola thought, and she actually felt sorry for him. Love was an awful mess of a thing, she thought. In few cases did it stand up as wonderfully as with Jim and herself.

After he'd finished eating he sat there smoking a cigarette in silence. Viola gathered the dishes quietly, not looking at him directly, but watching him from the corner of her eyes. The blue beach robe was opened from the neck in a long V that stopped at the waist, and she couldn't help noticing the little ringlets of sandy hair on his bare chest. Jim didn't have hair on his chest. Jim's chest was broad and clean and copper-colored. Jim was so different. Except for worries over money Jim was never sad and long-faced.

She went back to the kitchen, feeling sorry for Mr. Christian and feeling angry at herself for caring at all. She had made up her mind to tell him she was quitting, but she had gone back and forth without saying a word. Sorry for him or not, she couldn't stay. She had coached herself as to just the exact way she would put it to him—but she hadn't. She stood over the dishes in the sink, fighting with herself, condemning herself, then she heard him coming to the kitchen.

"Viola," he said, and now she stared at his calling her name. "There's no need to stick to the kitchen. Take the afternoon off." His face was calm and very serious as he stood in the doorway. Watching him, she began to frame the words in her mouth. She must tell him now. And yet, she felt very foolish about it. He turned, the beach robe swishing as he went to the door.

"Skip, jump, or swim!" he called back. "Do whatever you like!"

After a second she went to the window and looked after him. He took the winding grass-beaten trail that led to the boathouse, and she kept her eyes on the back of his head and parts of his broad shoulders that showed through the high foliage until she couldn't see him any more.

Staring out on the expanse of green mountains, she thought of Jim. If Jim were here they could do things, she thought. Down below, the lake shimmered in the bright sunlight. If only Jim were here, she thought. They could hike up the hills and just fool around, picking flowers and just fooling. Or they could go down to the lake. Or just sit under a big tree somewhere. The place was so beautiful and so peaceful. She sighed and turned from the window. Afternoon off or not, there were the dishes.

She washed the dishes leisurely, idly soaping them over as she thought. Then there were no more dishes and only the sink. She earnestly tackled the stains on the enamel, and when they were all off, the white sink made her think of Mr. Christian's feet.

Some afternoon off, she thought, going back to the window. Where could she go, what could she do? The village was miles away. And what could she do in the village? She might go down to the lake, she thought. The water down below glistened warmly in the sun. Even better, she might put on her bathing suit and go in. Why not?

She changed into her one-piece bathing suit and went to the full-length mirror in Mrs. Christian's room. She thought she looked all right. The past winter hadn't altered her waistline any, and her breasts were holding up fine. Approvingly she eyed her long, graceful legs. Only in a bathing suit did they get a decent break, she thought.

She stepped lightly through the big empty house and out through the door, towel and bathing cap swinging in one hand. The grass crunched softly under her feet, and the taller blades nicked at her brown legs as she followed the winding downhill path to the lake.

Before she quite reached the lake she saw Mr. Christian in a rowboat. She couldn't see much of him at first. He was stretched out in the boat, and she was thinking he might be asleep when he raised himself and shouted, "Ahoy, there!"

She didn't think she could shout back that far. She didn't think she could shout back at all. She lifted a hand in a quick, timid way and didn't look at him again. She sat down by the lake for a minute, speculating on the coldness of the water; then she kicked off her slippers and waded in.

She walked out gradually, tentatively feeling the muddy bottom of the lake with every step. The water rose like a cold band around her legs, then her thighs. When it rose to her chest she stopped. This was far enough. After all, she couldn't swim. She made sure that the bathing cap was securely adjusted, then she threw herself forward. She splashed and paddled about, feeling the water shockingly cold at first, then feeling as though the water itself grew pleasantly warmer. She didn't notice Mr. Christian paddle over in the small rowboat, and when he spoke, his voice startled her. "You're swimming in mud. Why don't you swim out?"

She stopped splashing and looked at him. He was laughing. "Don't let me stop you. You're doing very well."

Self-conscious, she stood still in the water up to her waist.

"I think your stroke is really good," he said. "But your legs sink."

She liked what he said about her stroke. Jim had been working on her stroke for two summers in the public swimming pool. Suddenly Mr. Christian dived from the rowboat and swam over to her.

"This is how you should kick." He swam for her to see, his strong legs working up, down, up, down, like a pair of scissors. "Now try it."

She stood still.

"Come on, I'll help you." He lifted her easily by the waist. "Now stretch out. Not rigidly. Relax. The water here's too shallow anyway." She felt him carrying her out with giant strides.

"Please," she said. "I can't swim."

"It's all right. I'm here. I'm holding you." He laughed as he talked, and she felt his warm breath on her face. "Now, do as I said. Relax."

"Not here," she pleaded. "It's too deep here."

"Don't be afraid. I'm with you."

"No," she pleaded, but just then he released her. She felt herself sink into a heavy, watery world and she tried to scream. She came up clutching frantically to his neck and spouting water.

"You didn't even try," he said. "Now just be calm."

"No," she begged, shaking her head, her eyes blinking wet. Her face brushed against his and it was like receiving a sudden shock. "Take me back," she pleaded. "Please."

He shook her gently. "You'll never learn by being afraid. Now, listen to me. Look at me."

She brought her face around fearfully and looked at him. He didn't speak. Not speaking, his deep eyes suddenly held a burning that frightened her. Suddenly she thought of Jim in a way that brought his dark face right up to the watery surface of the lake.

"Please," she begged, looking away from his eyes. "Take me back now." For a long moment he neither spoke nor moved, and she waited fearfully, her gaze turned away, but still feeling his eyes, feeling his warm arms, his warm body. Tears suddenly filled her eyes and her body trembled.

"Are you crying?" he said hoarsely. Then he abruptly moved and she knew he was taking her out. He set her down in shallow water, and as soon as her feet touched the wet earth she began to run.

She didn't look back and she didn't stop running. Up the winding path she went and into her room, the tears streaming down her face. Hastily she dressed and packed her work things in the small suitcase. Jim, she thought. Jim. Jim. Jim. She thought of nothing in connection with Jim more than seeing him. She saw him in the room and in the suitcase and in everything she did, and she wanted only to get to him.

As she started out from the house, along the driveway, she saw Mr. Christian coming up from the lake.

"Viola!" he called. "Say—what are you doing?"

She hurried on without answering. She couldn't stay another minute.

He came up the pathway to the house on the run. "Wait!" he called. "Wait a minute!"

She kept on, a fresh flow of tears coming to her eyes. The dirt road felt hard under her thin high-heeled shoes, and as she hurried, a small cloud of dust trailed behind. Mr. Christian called to her once more, then she rounded a bend in the dirt road and was out of sight.

Her blurry eyes focused on the brown dirt road, she kept going, the suitcase swinging to her stride. Then she heard his automobile coming behind.

"Come on," he said, stopping the car just ahead of her. "I'll take you to the station."

Standing in the grass beside the road, she eyed him indirectly. He was wearing his beach robe, and his face was set in that serious look he had had in the kitchen.

"Don't be impractical," he urged. "The station's five miles away. Get in." He flung the rear door open.

Avoiding his eyes, she got in and sat huddled in the corner of the rear seat. The car shot along on the small dirt road and neither of them spoke. Once she looked into the mirror above the steering wheel and thought she caught him looking at her. After that she avoided the mirror. In a silence that was taut he drove her to the station, but as she was getting out he pressed an envelope in her hand.

"It shouldn't be said that you worked for nothing." He tried to smile, but it was a strained, awkward thing on his face as he drove away.

She opened the envelope and saw two ten-dollar bills. She stared at the money with a dazed expression. It was too much for one day's work. It was ridiculously too much.

white man as a good

And / Or

STERLING BROWN

For safety's sake, though he is a lieutenant in the army now and may never come back to the South, let us call him Houston. He was short and frail, with a dark brown sensitive face. I first met him at the FEPC hearings in Birmingham when, on short acquaintance, he revealed to me how he was burned up by conditions in Dixie. To judge from his twang, he was southern-born, and he was Tuskegee trained, but he had the rather dicty restaurant on edge when he went into his tirades. The brown burghers, some of them a bit jittery anyway at FEPC and especially at the influx of a bunch of young "foreign" and radical Negroes into dynamite-loaded Birmingham, eyed him carefully over their glasses of iced tea.

I ran into him again in the small Alabama town where he was teaching. He was still quite a talker, in his high-pitched voice with a quaver in it—though he didn't quaver in other respects. He was brimming over with facts and consequent bitterness, deeper than I expected in a graduate of Tuskegee. To him, as to so many college men, the Negro's great need was the ballot. He had made a thoughtful study of the disenfranchising techniques and political shenanigans of Alabama in general. He laughed sardonically at the Negro's being asked to interpret such "constitutional" questions as "What is *non compos mentis* when it is applied to a citizen in legal jeopardy?" But he knew also how deeply engraved was the symbol at the head of the Democratic column on the official ballot used in all elections in Alabama: a rooster with the words "White Supremacy" arched over its head, and the words under it: "For the Right." White supremacy was well symbolized by the rooster, he thought; and he was afraid that Negro purposefulness was too well symbolized by a chicken. And a chicken with pip, lethargic, gaping, and trembling. He was determined to vote himself, and he told me with gusto the tragicomedy, at times the farce, of his experiences with the county board of registrars.

Knowing the ropes, Houston's first strategic step to get the vote was to buy a radio at a white store and charge it. This was his first charge account in the town, but it meant a possible white sponsor to vouch for him when the polls opened. Two weeks later he applied to the Board of Registrars. He was asked, "Do you have three hundred dollars worth of taxable property?"

Houston said no, but added that he understood that the property qualification was alternative to the literacy qualification. He was told that he was wrong: he had to have three hundred dollars worth of property or forty acres of land. That seemed to end the matter as far as the Board was concerned. Houston waited a few minutes and then asked if he would be permitted to make out an application. He was granted permission with the warning that the Board would have to pass on his case, and that as he did not have the property qualification, the chances were against him. He was also told that he needed two residents of the town to vouch for his character. He named the merchant from whom he had bought the radio and a clothing merchant.

When approached, the first merchant said that he would be glad to go over and sign, but that he couldn't leave his store just then. He would go over late that afternoon. Houston thanked him. The next day he telephoned the merchant, who hadn't quite managed it the day before but would try to get over some time that day. Houston thanked him again. The next day the merchant hadn't seen his way clear, either, things being so busy, but he gave his word that he wouldn't let the polls close on Houston. Three days later, the merchant told Houston that he had just got tied up and the polls had closed. A week later, Houston went to the store and paid the balance on the radio. The merchant said that he was sorry; he just hadn't been able to get around to doing that little favor, but he gave his word again that he would be glad indeed to go over when the polls opened again. Yessir, glad. That would be just the next month, Houston told him.

When the polls opened the next month, Houston called the merchant, who made an appointment with him for "about 2 P.M." At the store on the dot, Houston was told that the merchant was out of town. Yessir, a quick trip.

Houston then applied to the second merchant, with whom he

had had even more dealings, but on a cash basis. The run-around here was also efficient. He didn't know Houston well enough "to take an oath about his character," but he promised that if men at the Post Office and Bank said O.K., he would vouch for him. Every time the Post Office superintendent called, the merchant was out. Finally, the banker caught him, and the appointment was made.

"I understand you have an application for R. T. Houston, who has been working out at the school for the last three years or so." The board informed the merchant that investigation showed that Houston did not have either three hundred dollars worth of property or forty acres of land. The merchant said, "Oh, I don't know anything about that." He wanted to get out of there quick. Houston stated again his understanding about the alternative literacy qualification.

"It doesn't make any difference whether you graduated from Harvard. If you don't have the property, you can't register," the merchant offered. Houston remembered that he seemed to cheer up, saying it.

The merchant and Houston left the office, Houston thanking him for his time, and the merchant saying jocularly, "Well, you got to get your three hundred dollars worth of property or forty acres of land somewhere. What are you going to do?"

"I'm going to register," said Houston. "There is a provision in the Constitution for having your qualifications determined." Houston was partly compensated for the long runaround by the look of amazement on the merchant's face.

With two other colleagues, both acquainted with the law, Houston approached the Board again to thresh out the matter of qualifications. The registrar, a woman, stated that somebody else had asked the same question and that she had "marked it in the book." She was told that the property qualification was an alternative.

"No," she said, "you must have the property."

"When was the amendment passed making both qualifications necessary?"

This question was ignored. In triumph, the registrar read the second qualification. ". . . owner or husband of woman who is owner . . . of forty acres of land, or personal property or real estate assessed . . . at value of three hundred dollars or more," etc.

She was then asked to read the first qualification. She complied, hesitantly. Another registrar horned in: "This board will have to pass on you, and we register who we want to register."

The first qualification set up the requirement of "reading and writing any article of the Constitution of the United States in the English language . . ." and of being "regularly engaged in some lawful employment the twelve months next preceding the time they offer to register . . . etc." The word linking this to the second qualification is *or*.

On being asked what the word *or* meant, the registrar said that it meant *in addition to,* based on an interpretation from the Attorney General. Houston and his colleagues asked for this ruling, but it was not produced. Instead the three trouble-makers were shunted across the hall to the Probate Judge's office. The Judge was asked point blank if "or" in the state constitution meant "and." The Judge replied point-blank that it did. "You must have both the property as well as the literacy qualification," he said. The registrars got their ruling from the Attorney General; the Judge knew nothing of any law that had been made. Questioned closely on whether all the list of voters owned three hundred dollars worth of property, the Judge hedged. He complained that his questioners were only trying to get him into an argument with the Board of Registrars.

"What steps should we take to get an interpretation of the disputed passage?" was the straw breaking the camel's back.

"Find out for yourself," the Judge yelled, and stormed out of his office.

A few hours later, while preparing papers for an appeal to the Circuit Court to clarify the problem of qualification, Houston learned that the Board of Registrars had been busy telephoning him. Another call, unidentified but "from someone in touch with the Judge," informed Houston that he would get his registration papers.

When he walked into the office, there was a decided stir. One of the women on the Board said, "Here he is now." The spokes-man of the Board was polite. "We decided to let you register," he said.

"Thank you very much," said Houston. The certificate was signed and dated as of the preceding day, when the Judge had ruled on "And / Or."

Houston was told that it would be wise to get two good people of the town to vouch for him.

He named colleagues of his at the school.

"We mean white people," said the registrar. "Don't you know two good white people?"

"Nossir," said Houston politely. "I don't know two good white people . . . to vouch for me."

peaceful resistance

Fighter

JOHN CASWELL SMITH

Poke's bed groaned and squeaked as he twisted spasmodically to avoid the big, faceless man in his dream who leveled a pistol at him. He shrank back, frightened and defenseless. But when the bullet hit him, he laughed to himself with the realization that it does not hurt to get shot. Just a heavy thud like a fist hitting you. Poke felt a detachment from the fight that had started it all. The whole thing seemed ended and far away, now that the great noise of the gun had ended all the lesser noises. He could feel that his right leg was soaking wet, and that the sticky, warm blood was filling his shoe.

As he began to sag and drop weakly where he stood, there came the banging at the door, and the noise of feet stamping about in the hallway. A muffle of voices was trying to penetrate down through his sleep to his tired mind, calling his name; and as he heard the back window raised, he heard frightened voices saying, "They're breaking that door in! Hurry up and jump! Never mind the dog. He's tied up."

The hammering at the door kept on, and it seemed to Poke that it was an especial torment designed only for him, to keep him from dozing off into a peaceful sleep. It grew louder and more insistent until at last, in revengeful anger, he gave one final surge and raised his head to shout. It was only then that he heard his name called, clearly this time, and he sat up straight, gasping for breath and clutching through the bedcovers at his leg. He looked around the room and saw that it was daytime, when again there came that heavy thumping of a fist against the door.

"Poke!" The voice called him. "Poke! Wake up, man!"

Poke grinned to himself. "Wait a minute," he called, and drew his big frame out of bed. He stopped cautiously before putting his hand on the latch. "That you, Country Boy?" he asked.

"Yeah, man. Open up. Damn!"

As Country strode into the room, Poke was already back in bed, as though trying to recover some of the heat his body had lost during the moment he had been standing at the door in his underwear. Country was a rustic-looking, flabby youth whose clothes hung loosely on his body. "You jus' a sleepin' po' boy, ain't yuh," he said to the hunched-up shape in the bed. Poke grunted and drew the covers tighter.

Country walked over to the window and raised the shade. The afternoon sun streamed through the window. He tapped lightly on the pane at a shapely brown girl who was passing at the moment.

She turned. "Hello, Country!" she yelled. He raised his hat in mock grandeur and bowed. The girl hurried on with a gesture of feigned impatience. He returned his hat to his head and reached into both pockets of his long, shapeless overcoat. From one pocket he drew out several partially smoked cigarettes, from the other a match. Without turning from the window, he lighted a cigarette and returned the others to his pocket. "That Hattie sho' kin truck, you know that, Poke?" he said.

Poke turned over to squint at the figure standing by the window. "Hunh?" he groaned, still half asleep. He shaded his eyes from the winter sunlight that found its way past the window.

"I say that Hattie sho' kin walk fine."

"Yeah." He saw the blue clouds of smoke floating in the sunshine. "Gimme a smoke."

"Ain't got nothin' but stumps."

"Well, gimme a stump, then! Damn, I wanna smoke. Not a lotta yo' mouth."

Country turned and sauntered over to the bed, groping in his pockets. He lighted the cigarette butt he placed between Poke's lips, blew out the match, and seated himself on a chair nearby. Poke reached from the bed and flicked the first ash of his cigarette into an ash tray on a small table beside him.

"I ain't never noticed that table before." Country sat forward to place his hand appraisingly on the shining top of the table.

"Jessie bought that. She tryin' to fix this place up a little."

Country pushed his hat back on his head and looked around the small room. "Sho' looks nice," he said quietly. "Jessie comin' in tonight?" He leaned forward to crush out the half inch of cigarette.

"Yeah. S'posed to, anyhow."

"You'n her goin' tuh th' dance?"

"What dance?"

"What dance! You mean you ain't heard about th' stomp's gonna be at the Blue Moon t'night?" Country's face was a study in disbelief.

"Aw, *that* ole dance. Yeah, I 'most fuhgot about it." Poke looked gravely at his own cigarette stub before mashing it out on the ash tray. "Naw, man. I ain't goin' to no dance tonight."

"How come yuh ain't goin'? You broke?"

"Naw, I ain't broke. I jus' ain' goin', thass all." Poke was becoming belligerent. Country stood up slowly and stretched himself without feeling any real need for it. "Le's get outta here," he said softly, and walked back over to the window to look aimlessly at the people walking by. He felt not a little satisfaction with himself, for now he knew at least that he didn't have to worry about Poke going to that dance. It wouldn't help Poke's parole record any if he should tie up with any of those tough hombres from across town. House parties, where you knew everybody, were easier; but public dances were something else again, because nobody was in his own neighborhood, and there were always cops at public dances.

All Poke had to do was just be *seen* where there was a fight and back he'd go to the reformatory to do some more time. Well, he wasn't going to the dance, and that was one worry off Country's mind. He could tell that to Jessie when she came in off her job tonight, and she could take over from there. He often wondered to himself why he bothered about Poke, but he always told himself he just liked the guy.

Besides that, Jessie was his cousin and if he could look out for Poke during the week, it sort of helped; gave him a tie to somebody. When she put her hand on his arm each week and said, "Country, look out fo' Poke and see he don't get in no more trouble," he always laughed softly at her, but he knew he was going to keep on helping. Standing at the window, he smiled again to himself and turned around to look at his responsibility.

Poke was nearly dressed and had removed from his head the section of stocking, knotted at one end, that kept his hair from getting mussed while he slept. He walked to the foot of the bed and slid a necktie from the white iron rail of the bed and began knotting it around his neck. The two were silent, both thinking of the fact that it would not be very long now before they would meet Jessie at the subway station. It had become a sort of ritual on Thursdays, and from this point on there was not much need of conversation. Some lunch and a game of "61" at the poolroom would take care of their thoughts until late afternoon.

II

Jessie pushed through the crowd that surged through the turnstiles and hurried up the stairs. She did hope Poke hadn't got himself in any trouble; but of course he hadn't—otherwise Country would have called her. Yet she couldn't keep the nagging little worry out of her mind.

Poke wasn't really bad. He didn't even carry a knife; hadn't ever carried one. If he could only get a good job. But he always had such bad luck, and besides, nobody wanted to hire a fellow with a prison record. Trouble always seemed to follow him around so. The cops kept such a close watch on him. He couldn't even take a quick ride over to Jersey without asking permission to leave the state. If only she didn't have to be away from him so much.

She reached the top of the stairs and looked anxiously at the crowd of people standing in front of the cigar store. There they were: faithful, slow-talking Country and her tall, broad-shouldered Poke. Poke saw her and walked over to meet her in the middle of the sidewalk, while Country lagged behind with a show of indifference. Poke kissed her roughly and took the small handbag she was carrying. "Hello, Baby," he said, and made a soft, punching motion at her with his free hand.

"How're you, Poke? Hello, Country—whatcha know good?" Relief and positive happiness flowed into her voice.

"Ev'ything's good. 'At's why I knock awn wood." Country snapped his fingers and pushed his hat forward over his eyes. Jessie laughed and took him by the arm as she walked between the two men.

Music blared at them from radio shops as they walked leisurely along, and there was loud, friendly talk all about them. Jessie liked it. Country's easy-going languidness reassured her, too, and she could know that Poke had not been in any fights.

For his part, Poke seemed unaware of everything around him. He was frequently like this, wordless and presenting a stolid, enigmatic exterior. He never talked much under any circumstances. Silence and muscular expression were his way of life. It seemed useless to him to try to explain about the things that went on inside his head. He knew people would laugh, so he laughed it away himself and put a hard-boiled front in its place.

Sometimes, all the things he felt inside would well up into his arms and hands and they would grow taut, feeling the need to strike out at something visible—something that could be solved or conquered in terms of his limited powers. Tangible energy was what he understood; and whenever he had hit a man and felt him deaden and drop, it gave him a strange sense of triumph and release. Violence offered a crazy kind of peace because he was familiar with it without understanding it.

As they approached a tenement entrance, the door suddenly flew open, and a short, heavy man hurtled through it, leaning dangerously forward. He lost his balance and fell face downward on the sidewalk, but scrambled to his feet cursing and started back furiously toward the building. He was met at the door by a slender, wiry black man who lifted a knee to his stomach and ripped an uppercut into his face. The stout man fell backward with a groan and rolled over into a pile of dirty paper.

Jessie screamed involuntarily and held tighter to Poke's arm, which she felt stiffening like a steel coil. Country looked quickly up and down the street and stepped over to take hold of Poke's other arm. "Shut up, Jessie," he said, and pulled persistently on Poke's arm. "Just keep awn walkin'. Goddammit, Poke, keep walkin', willya! 'F a cop shows up now, he'll swear t' Christ *you* hit 'im." Poke felt as though they were holding open the jaws of a trap, permitting him to escape. Jessie was clinging to his arm, her eyes wide and frightened. Halfway down the block they looked back. A crowd had gathered, and they couldn't see what was going on.

At the corner, the trio turned into a side street, and halfway down the block they entered a place called "Pearly's Bar-B-Que." There was a bar along one side, and a long row of booths on the other. A music box near the door was sending out blues from a deep-throated contralto voice. There was a low hum of voices coming from the booths, occasionally broken into by high-pitched laughter. Somewhere, in the back of the room, a young girl was singing with the music, and at the far end of the bar a small knot of men stood talking in desultory tones.

Up near the door, the bartender brightened as the three people entered. He was a slender, yellow-skinned man with sandy-colored, woolly hair. "Whatcha know, Country?" he said. "Are you in the groove, Smooth?"

Country grinned. "Yeah, man. Groovie as a ten-cent movie." He walked over and leaned on the bar. Poke and Jessie kept on into the room and slid into one of the booths at the end.

The bartender's face sobered for a moment and he leaned forward. "Ain't that Poke Benson?" he whispered.

"Yeah—why?" Country kept his voice down and glanced at the booth where his two friends were seated. Jessie was facing him and talking earnestly to Poke, who sat across from her.

"Nothin', oney I don' want no trouble in here. The pay-off's tough enough as it is." The bartender looked anxiously at Country.

"You ain' goin' tuh have no trouble. 'At boy's awright."

The bartender wiped a section of the bar with a damp cloth. "He may be awright to you, but I heard about that ghee—plenty. You git 'im the hell outta here. I'm doin' awright wit this little hustle I got, and don' wanna git it all broke up."

"Aw man, fuhgit it. 'At boy ain' go' hurt nobody. I bin knowin' Poke fuh long time. You jus' g'wan an' sell yo' li'l bit a whiskey, an' ev'vything's gonna be groovy." Country began a rhythmic jerk of his shoulders from side to side to keep time with the music. He waved at Jessie, who had looked up at him when he had begun swaying his shoulders and snapping his fingers. She smiled and waved back at him. Country stepped closer to the bar. "Trouble is," he said, "all you cats go bristlin' up when Poke comes round. He ain' go' start nothin' lessen somebody else starts gittin' bad. 'At boy ain' never bin in no trouble he made hisself."

A fat waitress in a maroon-colored uniform stepped up to the bar, near the small group of men. "Draw two!" she shouted. The bartender turned half toward her but lingered a moment where he stood.

"Well, you jus' stick aroun' an' keep your boy straight. I do' wanna take no chances. 'At baby's poison." He turned away then, and sauntered over to the beer taps. Country walked slowly to the booth where Jessie and Poke were sitting. The fat waitress stepped across in front of him, placed two glasses of beer on the table, and looked expectantly up at Country. Ignoring her, he slid into the seat beside Poke.

"Whatchawl gonna do?" he asked, and drummed lightly on the table with his fingers. The waitress walked away and resumed her seat at the end of the room.

Jessie looked nervously at Country and tried to smile. "I dunno, Country," she said. "Me an' Poke ain't decided yet." Country looked at Poke and decided not to say anything. He went on drumming on the table and whistling a tune that he made up as he went along.

"Well, I guess I'll mosey along," he said presently, and stood up. "I got me a little run tuh make, an' I'll pick y'awl up later awn." He nudged Poke gently. "Take it easy, Greasy," he said, and started toward the door. He could tell that Poke needed woman's talk now. There wasn't any place in particular for him to go, but he knew he could find them later on if he wanted to. He waved at the bartender on the way out, and winked reassuringly at him.

III

Jessie sipped at her beer and looked at Poke, who kept looking at a spot on the table. "Then what did the man say, Honey?" she asked.

"Said he didn' need no help."

"Did he say why?"

"Nope. Jus' said he didn' need no help."

"Did yuh show 'im that card the man gave yuh?"

"Yeah, but he didn' even read it." Poke made a helpless motion with his big right hand, coiled it into a fist, and brought it softly down on the table.

Jessie was trying to be cheerful, but her voice was tight and tense. "Well, maybe you c'n get somethin' nex' week, huh?"

Poke didn't answer. It was always like this whenever he tried to talk. There was too much to talk about and there were no words for some of the things he felt. Besides, there was the dull pounding in him that never seemed to stop. He knew, in some vague, intuitive way, that it was all made from old childhood hurts; from the times when he first felt like crying whenever anyone spoke harshly to him. He knew it was made from the beatings his father gave him that made him run away from home, and from being chased and beaten in white boys' neighborhoods the times he had crossed the ghetto boundaries.

Mixed with the bitter memories were all his futile yearnings; it was all stirred up in him now, each part indistinguishable, flavored with shame and fear and anger and the crushing endlessness of walking up and down in a prison cell. The power and the impotence were a distorting combination, resolving themselves into an uncertain and aimless strength.

"Poke. Ain't you goin' t' speak tuh me?" She could feel his distance, and touched his hand as though to bring him back to consciousness. "Poke," she said again, "did I say somethin' yuh didn' like?" He looked up at her and smiled.

"Pay it no mind, Baby," he said, "I jus' don' feel like talkin' now, thass all. Le's go do somethin'."

"I gotta go get muh hair done, Poke." It relieved her some to see him smile. This was more like him, and she wanted to hurry to the hairdresser's so that they could go to supper. She reached into her pocketbook and took out a couple of one-dollar bills. "Pay for the beer and le's go. Miss Sally's gonna be lookin' fuh me at six o'clock, an' it'll *be* six in a little bit."

Poke picked up the money carelessly. "You g'wan over there, an' I'll drop by that way in about a hour," he said.

Jessie looked uncertainly at him for an instant. "O.K.," she said, and hurried out.

Poke took a cigarette from the package that lay in front of him. As he lighted it, the waitress came to his table to remove the two empty glasses. "Gimme another one," Poke said. She walked away without saying anything. As she strode over to the bar, the front door opened and three men walked in.

They were all dressed alike, and were of about equal stature. Each wore an almost white, wide-brimmed hat, a long, double-breasted dark-blue overcoat, and in each outside breast pocket there gleamed the carefully folded points of a white silk handkerchief. All three wore bright-yellow kid gloves and all had whites scarves neatly folded around their necks. They stepped up to the bar and pretended to be oblivious to the stir their entrance caused in the room. The bartender looked uneasily out of the window, and with a half smile walked to a spot directly opposite them.

"Whatchawl gonna have?" he asked quietly.

The waitress arrived at the bar and drawled, "Draw one." The white hat in the middle, at the sound of her voice, looked around. "Hello, Jelly-Belly," he said. White Hat Number One, on his left, looked at the woman and smirked. The waitress ignored them. White Hat Number Three kept looking straight at the bartender, who dropped his glance and drew a glass of beer from the tap in front of him. The other two snickered and broke finally into a guffaw as the woman walked away from them toward Poke's table.

"Y'ole lady ain' payin' you no min' t'night," said Number One. Number Three kept looking steadily at the bartender.

Several people got up to put their wraps on in preparation for leaving. The knot of men at the bar had become tense and silent. The bartender spoke politely again to the three. "Y'awl gonna have something?" he asked. Number Two looked astonished and turned to Number Three.

"Yalla Boy wants tuh know do we wants somethin'," he said. "Whyn't yuh tell the man we don' drinks nothin'?" Number One snickered, but Number Three continued to hold the bartender with his impudent stare.

The bartender shifted his feet and prepared to walk away from the position he had taken in front of the three. "Gimme a glassa whisky," said Number One suddenly, and leaned farther forward.

The harassed man selected a bottle and poured a drink from it into a small glass. He poured some ginger ale into a larger glass and placed it alongside the whisky. Number One picked up the small glass and was about to drink when Number Two reached over and knocked the glass out of his hand. It went clattering over the bar with a loud noise, breaking other glasses in the process.

Everyone in the room came to a sudden and watchful silence. Poke turned carelessly to follow the anxious glances he saw on every face around him. The white hats were all laughing and taking in the attention of the rapt audience they had created, noting that everyone seemed not a little uneasy. Poke turned back to his glass of beer.

The middle white hat began apologizing; with feigned seriousness, to his companion. The bartender was wiping up the
moisture and tossing pieces of broken glass into a trash can at
his feet. Someone had started the music box going again, and
the shrill, high sound of a clarinet screeched into the smoky air
of the room.

"Give muh frien' another glassa whisky, Yalla Boy," said the
offending white hat.

The bartender turned an injured look upon him. "Who's goin'
tuh pay for th' first drink?" he asked.

Number Two, a malicious grin on his face, said, "Yalla Boy,
you git him another drink, an' don' be so busy with yo' mouth."
He flashed his right hand toward the white handkerchief in his
breast pocket, and there suddenly appeared in his gloved hand a
long, slender knife, with an open gleaming blade. He kept grinning and looking at the bartender while he fondled the weapon,
as though it had nothing to do with his conversation.

"Now listen, fellas, you-all treat me right, an' ev'vything's
gonna be awright," said the bartender in a placating tone.

"Ev'vything's gonna be awright anyhow, Yalla Boy," said
Number Two. "Git muh buddy anothuh drink." He closed the
knife and slipped it back into his pocket as the bartender turned
and reached for the bottle again. At that moment, Country
appeared at the doorway. He peered in, opened the door, and
started for the booth where he had left Poke and Jessie. Just at
that moment, the nearest white hat stepped backward to brush
off his coat, and the two collided gently.

" 'Scuse me, pal," said Country, and started forward again, but
found himself facing the other two, who had stepped over to
block his path. Country was surprised for a moment, and
somewhat bewildered as he found himself surrounded by the
three men. He smiled and tried to walk past the two in front of
him, but one of them pushed him back.

IV

Country was trying to think of an easier way of dealing with this
situation when suddenly he saw the big form of Poke walking
purposefully toward him. The bartender, stung to action, was
moving swiftly around the bar in an attempt to intercept Poke.
One of the two men facing Country wheeled to follow this

movement and found himself face to face with Poke, who stopped just short of the group.

"Now where in hell you think you're goin'!" the white hat facing Poke challenged. Poke paid no attention to him. Instead, he looked over his head and said easily, "Whatsa matter, Country?" The bartender had reached a spot just behind Poke and was attempting to keep peace.

"Take it easy, Poke. Ev'vything's gonna be awright," he said and tried to take Poke by the arm. But he was a minor character in the play by now, and Poke flung him off. Country was terrified as he saw the situation gaining more and more momentum.

"You betta keep the hell outta this, Big Boy," said the white hat, but Poke kept his attention on Country. The devils in him were turning the screws now, tightening the drumhead, and slowly they began to beat out an impelling cadence. He swept the three with a disdainful glance.

"You goddamn punks betta let 'at boy alone," he said, and looked back at his friend. "C'mere, Country. Walk awn over heah."

"Aw, Poke, these ole boys ain' go' hurt nobody. Dey jus' playin' aroun', man." There was no conviction in Country's voice. The bartender was still trying weakly to avoid trouble.

"C'mon, you guys," he said anxiously, "lay offa this stuff. You-all gonna git me in trouble. Look—whyn't you-all take a drink awn th' house, an' fuhgit this mess."

Nobody even looked at him. Poke was standing silently, watching the whole array in front of him; and as the pounding inside him reached a crashing crescendo, the taut spring in him snapped, and he sent his hard, angry fist smashing into the leering, confident face in front of him. The man's eyes went back, showing only whites, and as his body sped backward it crashed into the bar, upsetting glasses and a cardboard cigarette advertisement. Country turned to attack the man behind him, but was met by a vicious kick in the groin that doubled him over in excruciating pain.

The man who now faced Poke reached toward his white handkerchief, but Poke grabbed the hand, and as he twisted the fist in his vise-like grip, the unopened knife it held rattled to the floor. Having lost his weapon, the white hat lifted his knee to kick at this devil of a man, but as he did so, Poke sidestepped adroitly, grasped the uplifted leg, and lifted the cursing man off the floor to send him crashing down beside his unconscious companion.

He had only time to throw up his hand to ward off the blow he saw coming at him, out of the corner of his eye, as he turned toward the man who had kicked Country. The bottle glanced off his upthrown elbow and crashed to the floor as he lunged forward and grasped the man by the collar of his coat with one hand. With his free hand he drove a hammer-like blow into the terrified face, and as he reversed the direction of his fist he crooked his arm and hit the bloody mouth a hard blow with his elbow and again with his fist as it followed the elbow outward and down in a piston action that rained blows all over the broken face he held before him.

And as he pounded, the release came suddenly in him and he felt free and satisfied. He let the man fall from his grip and for the first time became aware that Country and the bartender were pulling at his arms, attempting to stop him.

By this time the room was full of excited people, and fear came suddenly on the heels of the great peace he had begun to feel. Country was pleading with him, almost crying. "Poke," he was saying, "Poke, c'mon an' le's git outta here. Damn, man, the law gonna be all ovuh this place." He turned dazedly to look at Country, whose face had been kicked in the fracas. Blood was streaking the corner of his mouth, and there were deep lines of pain around his eyes.

The bartender was cursing and groaning over the damage. Outside, a police whistle sounded, and as though it were a special signal, the crowd ran out into the street to disperse. Instantly, Poke too was alert and ready for flight, and at last gave himself over to Country's urging.

They were running toward the back of the room even as the police car's siren lowered to a growl at the front door. They heard the hammering on the locked door of the lavatory as they slid over the window sill and dropped to the ground. Somewhere a dog was barking, and as Poke ran through the alley he had a vague feeling that he had done all this before, in precisely the same way. A pistol shot should come next, he thought, and as he and Country separated at the end of the alley he heard a shot, and the bullet pinged off the bricks overhead. He reached down to his thigh and was surprised to find he had not been hit. In daylight the police might not have missed.

When he reached the avenue, Poke slowed to a steady,

panther-like gait. He crossed the street against the lights and carefully moved toward the next avenue. He tried to formulate a plan as he walked along, but flight was too strong in him still for his imagination to call up anything but the most familiar of faces and feelings.

He reached up to pull his hat further down. Something in the gesture made him halt, burning him with the impossibility and futility of hiding. He turned and looked up and down the dark street and then moved again, aimlessly now and with less purposefulness in his stride, certain that the police would be alert and hunting for him everywhere. The heat and drive of the fight had dwindled now and gone out of him; and the old fears and confusions were flooding back into his consciousness, taking the place that the opiates of anger had so briefly filled.

He began to hear the arrogant voice of the judge droning blamefully through the courtroom, Jessie's repressed weeping, and the clumsy, mumbled words of Country's indignation and sympathy. Already he could feel the terrifying loneliness of the womanless prison cell. He kept walking, and the dead click of his heels was accompaniment to his old, cruel sorrow; and as he huddled away from the chilly night air, he shrank deeply into himself, feeling small like a child, and hurt, and wanting somehow to find a way to let himself cry.

The Homecoming

Frank Yerby

The train stretched itself out long and low against the tracks and ran very fast and smooth. The drive rods flashed out of the big pistons like blades of light, and the huge counter-weighted wheels were blurred solid with the speed. Out of the throat of the stack, the white smoke blasted up in stiff, hard pants, straight up for a yard; then the backward rushing mass of air caught it, trailing it out over the cars like a veil.

In the Jim Crow coach, just back of the mail car, Sergeant

Willie Jackson pushed the window up a notch higher. The heat came blasting in the window in solid waves, bringing the dust with it, and the cinders. Willie mopped his face with his handkerchief. It came away stained with the dust and sweat.

"Damn," he said without heat, and looked out at the parched fields that were spinning backward past his window. Up on the edge of the skyline, a man stopped his plowing to wave at the passing train.

"How come we always do that?" Willie speculated idly. "Don't know a soul on this train—not a soul—but he got to wave. Oh, well . . ."

The train was bending itself around a curve, and the soft, long, lost, lonesome wail of the whistle cried out twice. Willie stirred in his seat, watching the cabins with the whitewash peeling off spinning backward past the train, lost in the immensity of sun-blasted fields under a pale, yellowish white sky, the blue washed out by the sun swath, and no cloud showing.

Up ahead, the water tower was rushing toward the train. Willie grinned. He had played under that tower as a boy. Water was always leaking out of it, enough water to cool a hard, skinny, little black body even in the heat of summer. The creek was off somewhere to the south, green and clear under the willows, making a little laughing sound over the rocks. He could see the trees that hid it now, the lone clump standing up abruptly in the brown and naked expanse of the fields.

Now the houses began to thicken, separated by only a few hundred yards instead of by miles. The train slowed, snorting tiredly into another curve. Across the diagonal of the bend, Willie could see the town, all of it—a few dozen buildings clustered around the Confederate Monument, bisected by a single paved street. The heat was pushing down on it like a gigantic hand, flattening it against the rust-brown earth.

Now the train was grinding to a stop. Willie swung down from the car, carefully keeping his left leg off the ground, taking the weight on his right. Nobody else got off the train.

The heat struck him in the face like a physical blow. The sunlight brought great drops of sweat out on his forehead, making his black face glisten. He stood there in the full glare, the light pointing up the little strips of colored ribbon on his tunic. One of them was purple, with two white ends. Then there was a yellow one with thin red, white, and blue stripes in the middle and red and white stripes near the two ends. Another was red with three white stripes near the ends. Willie wore his collar loose, and his uniform was faded, but he still stood erect, with his chest out and his belly sucked in.

He started across the street toward the Monument, throwing one leg a little stiffly. The white men who always sat around it on the little iron benches looked at him curiously. He came on until he stood in the shadow of the shaft. He looked up at the statue of the Confederate soldier, complete with knapsack and holding the musket with the little needle-type bayonet ready for the charge. At the foot of the shaft there was an inscription carved in stone. Willie spelled out the words:

"No nation rose so white and pure; none fell so free of stain."

He stood there, letting the words sink into his brain.

One of the tall loungers took a sliver of wood out of his mouth and grinned. He nudged his companion.

"What do it say, boy?" he asked.

Willie looked past him at the dusty, unpaved streets straggling out from the Monument.

"I ask you a question, boy." The white man's voice was very quiet.

"You talking to me?" Willie said softly.

"You know Goddamn well I'm talking to you. You got ears, ain't you?"

"You said boy," Willie said. "I didn't know you was talking to me."

"Who the hell else could I been talking to, nigger?" the white man demanded.

"I don't know," Willie said. "I didn't see no boys around."

The two white men got up.

"Ain't you forgetting something, nigger?" one of them asked, walking toward Willie.

"Not that I knows of," Willie declared.

"Ain't nobody ever told you to say sir to a white man?"

"Yes," Willie said. "They told me that."

"Yes what?" the white man prompted.

"Yes nothing." Willie said quietly. "Jus plain yes. And I don't think you better come any closer, white man."

"Nigger, do you know where you're at?"

"Yes," Willie said. "Yes, I knows. And I knows you can have

me killed. But I don't care about that. Long time now I don't care. So please don't come no closer, white man. I'm asking you kindly."

The two men hesitated. Willie started toward them, walking very slowly. They stood very still, watching him come. Then at the last moment, they stood aside and let him pass. He limped across the street and went into the town's lone Five and Ten Cent Store.

"How come I come in here?" he muttered. "Ain't got nobody to buy nothing for." He stood still a moment, frowning. "Reckon I'll get some post cards to send the boys," he decided. He walked over to the rack and made his selections carefully: the new Post Office Building, the Memorial Bridge, the Confederate Monument. "Make this look like a real town," he said. "Keep that one hoss outa sight." Then he was limping over to the counter, the cards and the quarter in his hand. The salesgirl started toward him, her hand outstretched to take the money. But just before she reached him, a white woman came toward the counter, so the girl went on past Willie, smiling sweetly, saying, "Can I help you?"

"Look a here, girl," Willie said sharply. "I was here first."

The salesgirl and the woman both turned toward him, their mouths dropping open.

"My money the same color as hers," Willie said. He stuffed the cards in his pocket. Then deliberately he tossed the quarter on the counter and walked out the door.

"Well, I never!" the white woman gasped.

When Willie came out on the sidewalk, a little knot of men had gathered around the Monument. Willie could see the two men in the center talking to the others. Then they all stopped talking at once and looked at him. He limped on down the block and turned the corner.

At the next corner he turned again, and again at the next. Then he slowed. Nobody was following him.

The houses thinned out again. There were no trees shading the dirt road, powder-dry under the hammer blows of the sun. Willie limped on, the sweat pouring down his black face, soaking his collar. Then at last he was turning into a flagstone driveway curving toward a large, very old house, set well back from the road in a clump of pine trees. He went up on the broad, sweeping veranda, and rang the bell.

A very old black man opened the door. He looked at Willie with a puzzled expression, squinting his red, mottled old eyes against the light.

"Don't you remember me, Uncle Ben?" Willie said.

"Willie!" the old man said. "The Colonel sure be glad to see you! I go call him—right now!" Then he was off, trotting down the hall. Willie stood still, waiting.

The Colonel came out of the study, his hand outstretched.

"Willie," he said. "You little black scoundrel! Damn! You aren't little any more, are you?"

"No," Willie said. "I done growed."

"So I see! So I see! Come on back in the kitchen, boy. I want to talk to you."

Willie followed the lean, bent figure of the old white man through the house. In the kitchen Martha, the cook, gave a squeal of pleasure.

"Willie! My, my, how fine you's looking! Sit down! Where you find him, Colonel Bob?"

"I just dropped by," Willie said.

"Fix him something to eat, Martha," the Colonel said, "while I pry some military information out of him."

Martha scurried off, her white teeth gleaming in a pleased smile.

"You've got a mighty heap of ribbons, Willie," the Colonel said. "What are they for?"

"This here purple one is the Purple Heart," Willie explained. "That was for my leg."

"Bad?" the Colonel demanded.

"Hand grenade. They had to take it off. This here leg's a fake."

"Well, I'll be damned! I never would have known it."

"They make them good now. And they teaches you before you leaves the hospital."

"What are the others for?"

"The yellow one means Pacific Theater of War," Willie said. "And the red one is the Good Conduct Medal."

"I knew you'd get that one," the Colonel declared. "You always were a good boy, Willie."

"Thank you," Willie said.

Martha was back now with coffee and cake. "Dinner be ready in a little," she said.

"You're out for good, aren't you, Willie?"

"Yes."

"Good. I'll give you your old job back. I need an extra man on the place."

"Begging your pardon, Colonel Bob," Willie said, "I ain't staying here. I'm going North."

"What! What the clinking ding dang ever gave you such an idea?"

"I can't stay here, Colonel Bob. I ain't suited for here no more."

"The North is no place for niggers, Willie. Why, those dang-blasted Yankees would let you starve to death. Down here a good boy like you always got a white man to look after him. Any time you get hungry you can always come up to most anybody's back door and they'll feed you."

"Yes," Willie said. "They feed me all right. They say that's Colonel Bob's boy, Willie, and they give me a swell meal. That's how come I got to go."

"Now you're talking riddles, Willie."

"No, Colonel Bob, I ain't talking riddles. I seen men killed. My friends. I done growed inside, too, Colonel Bob."

"What's that got to do with your staying here?"

Martha came over to the table, bearing the steaming food on the tray. She stood there holding the tray, looking at Willie. He looked past her out the doorway where the big pines were shredding the sunlight.

"I done forgot too many things," he said slowly. "I done forgot how to scratch my head and shuffle my feet and grin when I don't feel like grinning."

"Willie!" Martha said. "Don't talk like that! Don't you know you can't talk like that?"

Colonel Bob silenced her with a lifted hand.

"Somebody's been talking to you," he declared, "teaching you the wrong things."

"No. Just had a lot of time for thinking. Thought it up all by myself. I done fought and been most killed and now I'm a man. Can't be a boy no more. Nobody's boy. Not even yours, Colonel Bob."

"Willie!" Martha moaned.

"Got to be a man. My own man. Can't let my kids cut a buck and wing on the sidewalk for pennies. Can't ask for handouts round the back door. Got to come in the front door. Got to git it myself. Can't git it, then I starves proud, Colonel Bob."

Martha's mouth was working, forming the words, but no sound came out of it, no sound at all.

"Do you think it's right," Colonel Bob asked evenly, "for you to talk to a white man like this—any white man—even me?"

"I don't know. All I know is I got to go. I can't even say yessir no more. Ever time I do, it choke up in my throat like black vomit. Ain't coming to no more back doors. And when I gits old, folks going to say Mister Jackson—not no Uncle Willie."

"You're right, Willie," Colonel Bob said. "You better go. In fact, you'd better go right now."

Willie stood up and adjusted his overseas cap.

"Thank you, Colonel Bob," he said. "You been awful good to me. Now I reckon I be going."

Colonel Bob did not answer. Instead he got up and held the screen door open. Willie went past him out the door. On the steps he stopped.

"Good-by, Colonel Bob," he said softly.

The old white man looked at Willie as though he were going to say something, but then he thought better of it and closed his jaw down tight.

Willie turned away to go, but Uncle Ben was scurrying through the kitchen like an ancient rabbit.

"Colonel Bob!" he croaked. "There's trouble up in town. Man want you on the phone right now! Say they's after some colored soldier. Lawdy!"

"Yes," Willie said. "Maybe they after me."

"You stay right there," Colonel Bob growled, "and don't move a muscle! I'll be back in a minute." He turned and walked rapidly toward the front of the house.

Willie stood very still, looking up through a break in the trees at the pale, whitish blue sky. It was very high and empty. And in the trees, no bird sang. But Colonel Bob was coming back now, his face very red, and knotted into hard lines.

"Willie," he said, "did you tell two white men you'd kill them if they came nigh you?"

"Yes. I didn't say that, but that's what I meant."

"And did you have some kind of an argument with a white *woman*?"

"Yes, Colonel Bob."

"My God!"

"He crazy, Colonel Bob," Martha wailed. "He done gone plum outa his mind!"

"You better not go back to town," the Colonel said. "You better stay here until I can get you out after dark."

Willie smiled a little.

"I'm gonna ketch me a train," he said. "Two o'clock today, I'm gonna ketch it."

"You be kilt!" Martha declared. "They kill you sure!"

"We done run too much, Martha," Willie said slowly. "We done run and hid and anyhow we done got caught. And then we goes down on our knees and begs. I ain't running. Done forgot how. Don't know how to run. Don't know how to beg. Just knows how to fight, that's all, Martha."

"Oh, Jesus, he crazy! Told you he crazy, Colonel Bob!"

Colonel Bob was looking at Willie, a slow, thoughtful look.

"Can't sneak off in the dark, Colonel Bob. Can't steal away to Jesus. Got to go marching. And don't a man better touch me." He turned and went down the steps. "Good-by Colonel Bob," he called.

"Crazy," Martha wept. "Out of his mind!"

"Stop your blubbering!" Colonel Bob snapped. "Willie's no more crazy than I am. Maybe it's the world that's crazy. I don't know. I thought I did, but I don't." His blue eyes looked after the retreating figure. "Three hundred years of wounded pride," he mused. "Three centuries of hurt dignity. Going down the road marching. What would happen if we let them—no, it's God-damned impossible. . . ."

"Looney!" Martha sobbed. "Plum tetched!"

"They'll kill him," Colonel Bob said. "And they'll do it in the meanest damned way they can think of. His leg won't make any difference. Not all the dang blasted ribbons in the world. Crazy thing. Willie, a soldier of the republic—wounded, and this thing to happen. Crazy." He stopped suddenly, his blue eyes widening in his pale, old face. "Crazy!" he roared. "That's it! If I can make them think—That's it, that's it, by God!"

Then he was racing through the house toward the telephone.

Willie had gone on around the house toward the dirt road, where the heat was a visible thing, and turned his face in the direction of town.

When he neared the one paved street, the heat was lessening. He walked very slowly, turning off the old country road into Lee Avenue, the main street of the town. Then he was moving toward the station. There were many people in the street, he noticed, far more than usual. The sidewalk was almost blocked with men with eyes of blue ice, and a long, slow slouch to their walk. He went on quietly, paying no attention to them. He walked in an absolutely straight line, turning neither to the right nor the left, and each time they opened up their ranks to let him pass through. But afterwards came the sound of their footsteps falling in behind him, each man that he passed swelling the number until the sound of them walking was loud in the silent street.

He did not look back. He limped on his artificial leg making a scraping rustle on the sidewalk, and behind him, steadily, beat upon beat, not in perfect time, a little ragged, moving slowly, steadily, no faster nor slower than he was going, the white men came. They went down the street until they had almost reached the station. Then, moving his lips in prayer that had no words, Willie turned and faced them. They swung out into a broad semicircle, without hastening their steps, moving in toward him in the thick hot silence.

Willie opened his mouth to shriek at them, curse them, goad them into haste, but before his voice could rush past his dried and thickened tongue, the stillness was split from top to bottom by the wail of a siren. They all turned then, looking down the road, to where the khaki-colored truck was pounding up a billowing wall of dust, hurling straight toward them.

Then it was upon them, screeching to a stop, the great red crosses gleaming on its sides. The two soldiers were out of it almost before it was still, grabbing Willie by the arms, dragging him toward the ambulance. Then the young officer with the single silver bar on his cap was climbing down, and with him an old man with white hair.

"This the man, Colonel?" the young officer demanded.

Colonel Bob nodded.

"All right," the officer said. "We'll take over now. This man is a combat fatigue case—not responsible for his actions."

"But I got to go!" Willie said. "Got to ketch that train. Got to go North where I can be free, where I can be a man. You hear me, lieutenant, I got to go!"

The young officer jerked his head in the direction of the ambulance.

"Let me go!" Willie wept. "Let me go!"

But the soldiers were moving forward now, dragging the slim form with them, with one leg sticking out very stiffly, the heavy heel drawing a line through the heat-softened asphalt as they went.

How John Boscoe Outsung the Devil

ARTHUR P. DAVIS

Well, suh, speaking about singing, the folks down in my section of Virginny still talk about Ol' John Boscoe and how he outsung the Devil hisself.

Now this John Boscoe, no doubt about it, was a singing fool. John was a bass singer, and he had the sweetest and the deepest bass anybody had ever listened to on this earth. There ain't never been no voice like it before nor since.

A tall black fellow—John wasn't no great big man—he was just tall and lank and sort of rangy-like. And he didn't have no great bellows of a chest like some singers; he was just tall and hollow-looking, like one of them big pipes on a pipe organ. There was nothing particular-looking about him 'cept his eyes. He had deep-sunken eyes—the eyes of a fanatic; and John was a fanatic on this bass singing business.

But as I said—no doubt about it—John was a songster from his heart; he could really sing. When he hit them high notes— and he could make 'em just as good as a tenor—his voice was as sweet and as silver-toned as a sleigh bell. Some folks say that even the birds used to shut up when John sung them sweet high notes—used to shut up and just listen, with their heads cocked on the side like they was trying to learn how to sing from Ol' John.

And when he went down the scale to them low notes, there

was something in his singing just tore at your innards. John
wasn't one of these basses that twisted his mouth and rolled his
eyes when he made the low ones. He just opened his mouth and
the music came rolling out just as natural as water over a dam;
and he went down the scale so far you could feel yourself just a-
throbbing and everything around you a-shaking. Even the
church used to tremble and quiver when John hit them *real* low
ones.

But the preacher had to caution John about that—careful-
like, of course, without offending, because John Boscoe was a
sensitive one and didn't take no foolishness. Besides, the
preacher knew John brought more folks to church by his singing
than *he* did by his preaching. The whole county, white and
black alike, used to come out to hear John sing. And them as
couldn't get in the church could hear just as well outside or at
home for that matter, but they all come to hear him, and he
never sung enough for 'em. So the preacher cautioned John
kinda quiet-like; he wasn't taking no chance on riling him up
and running him out of the choir.

Of course, the other choir members didn't like John, because
everything they sung ended in a solo for John Boscoe. He just
drowned the rest of them out. Besides, John knew he was good
and he made no bones about it. You could see how little he
thought of the other voices by the way he looked and snorted
when somebody else wanted to sing a solo. And when some of
the boys asked John to sing in a quartette with them, he just
looked at 'em and laughed. Yessuh, John knew how good he was
and every day he showed it more and more.

In fact, Ol' John got vainer and vainer, and prouder and
prouder, and harder than ever to get along with. And he began
to lose friends because his pride was taking possession of him
and making him into a changed man. He had always been a
friendly, Christian sort of a man. Now he was becoming hard
and bitter, with a fanatic look in his deep-set eyes. People began
to avoid them eyes. John's own wife and children begun to fear
him and hate to see him come in the house.

Well, the Pastor saw John changing too, so one Sunday he
preached a red-hot sermon on pride. He told how the Devil got
kicked out of heaven because of pride. He mentioned how Ol'
Satan had tried to tempt Jesus through pride up there on that
mountain—offering to make Him ruler of the world.

And then the Pastor brought that sermon right home to John Boscoe. He told how a man could let a voice—a voice that God had given him to do good—go to his head and turn him against his friends. And when he got to this point, he turned around and looked right at John Boscoe up there in the choir while everybody else in the church held their breath.

But it didn't register none with John. He didn't even hear what the Pastor was saying. He was just waiting for the sermon to be over so he could pump bass on the next hymn.

But John's wife didn't miss a word. Deep down she was praying it would have some effect on John. But she knew that John was so wrapped up in hisself, he hadn't heard a word. She could tell by his eyes. So, when they got home, she told John what the minister had said, starting off with a few womanish tears, about how humiliated she had been, having the Pastor preach right at her husband up there in public.

John hit the ceiling. He raved and he ranted. He damned the church and the preacher and everybody in it. He swore a great oath that he would never set foot in the church again. Who'd the preacher think he was, criticizing him? What did he care about the preacher and all the rest of them little jealous folks? He didn't need 'em, he didn't need nobody! To hell with 'em! God damn 'em! Well, suh, Ol' John carried on so, his wife thought he was losing his mind, and in one way he was.

After that, John's pride just took complete possession of him. He wasn't hisself no more. He'd always been a hard-working man and a good provider for his family, but he got so he didn't care whether he worked or not. He didn't care whether his family had food or not, and John's wife for the first time in her life had to take in washing to make both ends meet. John had such a terrible look in his eye she was just plain scairt to tell him how bad off they really was.

All John thought about was his singing, how good he was, and what a pity he didn't have the kind of people in the county that could appreciate him. What did these country folks know about singing? He spent days dreaming about getting away to the city, where he could give a concert to all the best singers and listeners in the world; and in his dream, he could see them all coming down the aisles of some fine hall to congratulate *him,* John Boscoe, the bass singer.

When John went to the field to plow—which he seldom did

now—he spent most of his time daydreaming like that. He would stand up on a hill, and as his eyes swept over the cornfields, he would imagine all the stalks was grand folks in a fine, big city hall. He would sing to them by the hour, and you could hear him all over the county. Sometimes, when he made them low notes, the folks even over in the next county heard him and thought it was the rumble of thunder.

John's pride as he daydreamed grew so fast it became a great big bitterness inside him. "I am the best bass singer in the county," he used to boast even before he left the church. But that was plain to everybody; no one bothered to argue about what he was saying. No one even disputed him when he began bragging, "I'm the best bass singer in the state," because deep down all the folks felt that too. But when John got to boasting, with that fanatic look in his eye, "I'm the best bass singer in the United States," folks began to look at each other and get oneasy. Some of them believed that too, but they didn't like to hear a man get so braggadocious.

But John's pride, now a raging fire inside him, made him bolder and bolder. One Saturday, he walked into the store and announced, out of the clear blue sky, to all the folks there, "I'm the best bass singer in the whole world, and I know it."

Well, that was just too much for the folks to swallow. So one of the men who had known John all his life spoke up sorta quiet-like. "That's a mighty lot of territory you're covering, John," he said. Well, suh, this remark was like a red rag to a bull. John turned on the doubter and fixed his deep-sunk eyes on him. "In fact, I'm the best damn bass singer in the universe—including the stars above and the regions below," John said.

That was going too far. The folks in the store that Saturday run from John Boscoe and his blasphemous talk like he was the plague. They was scairt God was a-going to cut him down, and they felt God shoulda cut him down, but they didn't want to be around when He did. They got as far away from John Boscoe as they could get, and they stayed away.

But even though God didn't take no notice right then of Ol' John's wild talk, there was somebody else who did. Ol' Satan had had his eye on John for quite a spell. And when Ol' John bust out with this blasphemous talk about the "stars above and the regions below," he took it as a direct insult. It riled him.

"You hear that fool?" he said to the closest imp. "He getting 'side hisself. I'm gonna step up there and teach him a thing or two. He worsen I was when I was up in heaven."

Then the Devil, thinking about the good old days when he was in glory, sorta sighed and said, "Pride sho is a terrible thing. Get you down quickern anything *I* know."

So, pretty soon, as John Boscoe walked out in the fields by hisself, as he always was by now, he met Ol' Satan. Even though he looked like any other dirt farmer, John knew right away it was the Devil. He felt it in his bones, and he was scairt.

But scairt or not, John Boscoe was a stiff-necked one. He wasn't going to run, even from the Devil. At the same time, though, he decided to be mighty polite to Ol' Satan; he wasn't going to take no chances on riling him if he could help it.

"How de do, suh," said John pleasantly to Satan.

The Devil didn't bother to be polite, as he is most of the time. "I hear you *think* you can sing bass," he said to John, sneerified-like.

Devil or no Devil John didn't like that crack. "I don't *think* I can sing bass," John flashed right back. "I *know* I can sing bass—more bass than anybody—" and here he hesitated; he wasn't going to pull that universe business on the Devil, so he ended with—"anybody in the world."

"How about the universe, including the stars above and the regions below?" sneered the Devil.

Ol' John was stung right down to the quick, and forgetting everything but the great ball of pride all knotted inside him, he blurted right out, "Yessuh, I mean just that—no less!"

The Devil smiled a nasty kind of smile, and said sorta quiet and soft-like, "Then you think you can beat *me* singing bass?"

"That I do," answered John, drawing hisself up to his fullest height, filled with all the fanaticism of his great pride. And as he fixed the Devil with his eye, it was hard to say which had the fieriest look. The Devil didn't flinch and John didn't flinch as they stood there eyeing each other.

"You willing to put your money where your mouth is," finally asked the Devil, "or you just a *talking* and not a *betting* man?"

"I'll bet you till I can't see you," said John Boscoe angrily. "Put *your* money where your mouth is."

"Well, let's make it something interesting." The Devil was talking as polite as you please now, because he had John where he wanted him. "If you sing a deeper bass than I do, I'll give you anything you name. And if I beat you, I take your soul right now." Then he laughed. "Of course, I gon' get it anyhow pretty soon, but thisaway I can put a stop right now to all this big talk I been hearing. You ain't gonna feel like singing down in my place, I can tell you in front."

Ol' John Boscoe swelled up like a bullfrog, and glaring at Ol' Satan, he said, "I ain't the talking kind; I'm the *doing* kind. Let's get down to business."

"Jest a minute," the Devil said. "You ain't told me what you want in case you win. Of course, I know you ain't goin' win, but I want to keep the record straight. Will it be money or pretty women or power or all three?"

"I don't want none of them things," answered John. "I ain't never had no money, and I been gettin' 'long all right. I got a good wife, and I got all the power I want—the power to sing more bass than anybody in the universe."

"Well, what *do* you want?" asked the Devil.

"If I beat you," John said, and he had that faraway look in his eye, "if I beat you—and I gon' beat you just as sure as I'm standing here—I just want you to give me one chance to sing under my conditions—to sing the way I been dreaming about."

"How is that?"

"I want a hall," said John, now on fire with the dream in him. "I want a hall that will hold a million people. I want an orchestray of one thousand pieces, with one thousand of the finest players to 'company me. And then I want a chorus of one thousand of the best singers in the world behind me to be a kinda background for me, and then I'm gonna give a concert that all the history books will write about, and all the generations that ain't yet born will talk about—the concert of John Boscoe, the greatest bass singer in the universe."

John's face was all lit up with the splendor of his dream. The Devil just said, "It's a deal; let's bind it," and with that he took out his penknife and scratched John Boscoe's arm. In his left hand suddenly appeared a contract and a pen. John signed.

"Now, that's over," said the Devil, all business. "What'll we sing?"

Quick as a flash, John answered, *"Asleep in the Deep."*

"Agreed," said the Devil. "I like that song myself. You sing first, and beingst you ain't got a chance nohow, I'll give you three tries at it."

John began, and he sung that first pretty part—"loudly the bell in the old tower rings"—he sung it so sweet that all the angels must have been listening and envious. Then he started down the scale on the chorus where it goes "Sailor, beware; sailor, take care"—well, suh, when Ol' John hit them "bewares," you could hear him clean over in the next state, and he was down so low the rumbling shook every house for miles around. The church steeple was shaking so hard the bell was ringing like a fire alarm. Folks knew it was John Boscoe a-singing, and though they worried about their houses falling down, they was enjoying it too much to be scairt.

But then they heard another voice when John finished, and when that second voice sung that pretty first part of the song, folks got an oneasy look in their eyes. The voice was sweet, they had to admit, sweeter even than John's, but there was something too sweet about it, kinda sinfully sweet, like tasting forbidden fruit, and it disturbed them.

Then when this second singer hit them low "bewares," all hell seemed to break loose. The earth started to quiver and shake and heave and toss like a woman in labor. The trees in the woods and the houses and churches seemed to be skipping about like young lambs. The rumble was so low and so great, it was like ninety-nine earthquakes rolled into one. Some folks swear that the very ground itself opened up and you could see smack down into the fires of hell—see all the imps dancing around and clapping their hands and carrying on, 'cause they knew their Master had beaten Ol' John Boscoe.

When John Boscoe heard that last "beware" of the Devil, he knew he was whipped; he knew he was a goner unless he could get some help. There was only one place now where he could get help, and that was from on high. John was plenty scairt. He saw hell staring him in the face; he thought of all them eternal fires and the imps jabbing him with red-hot pitchforks, and he thought most how he couldn't do no singing in hell. Yessuh, John was plumb scairt and getting scairter by the minute.

Falling on his knees, he raised his eyes to God and tried to pray, but he couldn't say a word. His tongue and throat had turned to ashes, and his heart was beating like a hammer. John was so full of misery he felt he was going to bust open, but he couldn't unburden hisself; he couldn't say nary a word.

John was still thinking about John Boscoe, and the Lord— who had watched all these goings-on, as He always does—the Lord didn't want to hear no more selfish prayers. He was tired of them kind, so he just threw a handful of ashes in Ol' John's mouth. The Devil understood what had happened. He just stood there, grinning at John and gloating—and waiting.

Then John started to think about his pride and how it had brought him down to this fix he was in. For the first time in many a day, he remembered his wife and his children and what trouble he had caused them. He saw like a drowning man all they had suffered because of his pride and selfishness. Now he was going to leave them unprovided for—all because he had been a stiff-necked fool. He began to cry—not because of his fear of hell, but because he was thinking of his wife and children. His heart was moved for them, and the tears came flowing down. All of a sudden, his mouth was no longer ashes and dirt, and he could pray.

Lifting his hands and his eyes to heaven, he cried, "O Lord, I know I been a sinful and a prideful man! I know I been bragga-docious and 'side myself with my own biggityness! I been mean and ornery and selfish. I done run my friends from me, I done left and damned the church, and I done deserted my own wife and children.

"And, Lord, that voice you gave me to bring souls to you, I done used to feed my own vanity and pride; I done bragged about how much I could sing and never give You no credit for it—You the one that gave me the power to sing.

"O Lord, I been wrong—I been mighty wrong. I been a fool, Lord, and I deserve all I gon' get. Save me, Lord, if that ain't asking too much, but if You don't save me, look out for my wife and poor fatherless children. That's all I ask, Lord."

The Lord answered John—not by so many words or signs, but John knew the Lord had answered. He felt a new power within him that started at his fingertips and went singing through every vein in his body right down to his toes. His body shook and tingled like he had electricity in him, and the goodness of the Lord made him feel like he had just been shouting in church. The Lord was with him, and he knew it, and as he rose from his knees, he fixed his eye on Ol' Satan and said kinda polite-like, "I believe I got a second chance coming to me. In fact, two more, but I don't need the third."

And then John Boscoe sung again. His voice at first was so natural-born sweet that folks just naturally fell on their knees and started to pray. It sounded like all the harps of heaven was playing while the morning stars was singing together. Then John took it down the scale, and when he hit that last "beware"—well, some folks say it was the deepest roll of thunder that the ear of mortal man had heard. But John—and he ought to know—said twarn't no thunder; 'twas God's voice all mixed up with his own voice, and the power of God was so strong within him, John said he couldn't rightly tell whether he was singing hisself or whether God was singing *through* him. And he said when he made that last real low note, he felt happy all over; he felt so good, so much at peace with the world, so free and so glorious, that he had love in his heart even for Ol' Satan.

But Satan had gone. When he heard John's last note, he knew what had happened, and Satan ain't one to be around when God is speaking. All John saw when he turned to look for the Devil was a cloud of smoke.

John Boscoe came home a humbled and a changed man that afternoon. There was no more bragging about how much he could sing. He became a model husband and the same good provider he had once been. He went back to church and to the choir, and he sung more folks to God than any fifty preachers could have brought. And he became a friend and a Christian helpmate to his brothers in the county. He was a good steward in the vineyard of the Lord until he was gathered to the bosom of his Father.

But even now down in my section of Virginny, on quiet afternoons, when the air is hushed and still, and there ain't no sign of a cloud in the sky, you can hear what sounds like the deep rumble of distant thunder. Folks down there know it ain't no thunder. It's the voice of Ol' John Boscoe singing up in heaven, where he is the bass soloist in the senior choir—a choir of a thousand angel voices with an orchestray of a thousand harps— the choir that sings around the throne of the Almighty.

no mention of white or black problems

Solo on the Drums

ANN PETRY

The orchestra had a week's engagement at the Randlert Theater
at Broadway and Forty-second Street. His name was picked out
in lights on the marquee. The name of the orchestra and then
his name underneath by itself.

There had been a time when he would have been excited by
it. And stopped to let his mind and his eyes linger over it lov-
ingly. Kid Jones. The name—his name—up there in lights that
danced and winked in the brassy sunlight. And at night his
name glittered up there on the marquee as though it had been
sprinkled with diamonds. The people who pushed their way
through the crowded street looked up at it and recognized it and
smiled.

He used to eat it up. But not today. Not after what happened
this morning. He just looked at the sign with his name on it.
There it was. Then he noticed that the sun had come out, and he
shrugged, and went on inside the theater to put on one of the
cream-colored suits and get his music together.

After he finished changing his clothes, he glanced in the long
mirror in his dressing room. He hadn't changed any. Same face.
No fatter and no thinner. No gray hair. Nothing. He frowned.
Because he felt that the things that were eating him up inside
ought to show. But they didn't.

When it was time to go out on the stage, he took his place
behind the drums, not talking, just sitting there. The orchestra
started playing softly. He made a mental note of the fact that
the boys were working together as smoothly as though each one
had been oiled.

The long gray curtains parted. One moment they were closed.
And then they were open. Silently. Almost like magic. The high-
powered spots flooded the stage with light. He could see specks

of dust gliding down the wide beams of light. Under the bands of light the great space out front was all shadow. Faces slowly emerged out of it—disembodied heads and shoulders that slanted up and back, almost to the roof.

He hit the drums lightly. Regularly. A soft, barely discernible rhythm. A background. A repeated emphasis for the horns and the piano and the violin. The man with the trumpet stood up, and the first notes came out sweet and clear and high.

Kid Jones kept up the drum accompaniment. Slow. Careful. Soft. And he felt his left eyebrow lift itself and start to twitch as the man played the trumpet. It happened whenever he heard the trumpet. The notes crept up, higher, higher, higher. So high that his stomach sucked in against itself. Then a little lower and stronger. A sound sustained. The rhythm of it beating against his ears until he was filled with it and sighing with it.

He wanted to cover his ears with his hands because he kept hearing a voice that whispered the same thing over and over again. The voice was trapped somewhere under the roof— caught and held there by the trumpet. "I'm leaving I'm leaving I'm leaving."

The sound took him straight back to the rain, the rain that had come with the morning. He could see the beginning of the day—raw and cold. He was at home. But he was warm because he was close to her, holding her in his arms. The rain and the wind cried softly outside the window.

And now—well, he felt as though he were floating up and up and up on that long blue note of the trumpet. He half closed his eyes and rode up on it. It had stopped being music. It was that whispering voice, making him shiver. Hating it and not being able to do anything about it. "I'm leaving it's the guy who plays the piano I'm in love with him and I'm leaving now today." Rain in the streets. Heat gone. Food gone. Everything gone because a woman's gone. It's everything you ever wanted, he thought. It's everything you never got. Everything you ever had, everything you ever lost. It's all there in the trumpet—pain and hate and trouble and peace and quiet and love.

The last note stayed up in the ceiling. Hanging on and on. The man with the trumpet had stopped playing but Kid Jones could still hear that last note. In his ears. In his mind.

The spotlight shifted and landed on Kid Jones—the man

behind the drums. The long beam of white light struck the top of his head and turned him into a pattern of light and shadow. Because of the cream-colored suit and shirt, his body seemed to be encased in light. But there was a shadow over his face, so that his features blended and disappeared. His hairline receding so far back that he looked like a man with a face that never ended. A man with a high, long face and dark, dark skin.

He caressed the drums with the brushes in his hands. They responded with a whisper of sound. The rhythm came over but it had to be listened for. It stayed that way for a long time. Low, insidious, repeated. Then he made the big bass drum growl and pick up the same rhythm.

The Marquis of Brund, pianist with the band, turned to the piano. The drums and the piano talked the same rhythm. The piano high. A little more insistent than the drums. The Marquis was turned sideway on the piano bench. His left foot tapped out the rhythm. His cream-colored suit sharply outlined the bulkiness of his body against the dark gleam of the piano. The drummer and the pianist were silhouetted in two separate brilliant shafts of light. The drums slowly dominated the piano.

The rhythm changed. It was faster. Kid Jones looked out over the crowded theater as he hit the drums. He began to feel as though he were the drums and the drums were he.

The theater throbbed with the excitement of the drums. A man sitting near the front shivered, and his head jerked to the rhythm. A sailor put his arm around the girl sitting beside him, took his hand and held her face still and pressed his mouth close over hers. Close. Close. Close. Until their faces seemed to melt together. Her hat fell off and neither of them moved. His hand dug deep into her shoulder and still they didn't move.

A kid sneaked in through a side door and slid into an aisle seat. His mouth was wide open, and he clutched his cap with both hands, tight and hard against his chest as he listened.

The drummer forgot he was in the theater. There was only he and the drums and they were far away. Long gone. He was holding Lulu, Helen, Susie, Mamie close in his arms. And all of them—all those girls blended into that one girl who was his wife. The one who said, "I'm leaving." She had said it over and over again, this morning, while rain dripped down the window panes.

no mention whites injustices

When he hit the drums again it was with the thought that he was fighting with the piano player. He was choking the Marquis of Brund. He was putting a knife in clean between his ribs. He was slitting his throat with a long straight blade. Take my woman. Take your life.

The drums leaped with the fury that was in him. The men in the band turned their heads toward him—a faint astonishment showed in their faces.

He ignored them. The drums took him away from them, took him back, and back, and back, in time and space. He built up an illusion. He was sending out the news. Grandma died. The foreigner in the litter has an old disease and will not recover. The man from across the big water is sleeping with the chief's daughter. Kill. Kill. Kill. The war goes well with the men with the bad smell and the loud laugh. It goes badly with the chiefs with the round heads and the peacock's walk.

It is cool in the deep track in the forest. Cool and quiet. The trees talk softly. They speak of the dance tonight. The young girl from across the lake will be there. Her waist is slender and her thighs are rounded. Then the words he wanted to forget were all around Kid Jones again. "I'm leaving I'm leaving I'm leaving."

He couldn't help himself. He stopped hitting the drums and stared at the Marquis of Brund—a long, malevolent look, filled with hate.

There was a restless, uneasy movement in the theater. He remembered where he was. He started playing again. The horn played a phrase. Soft and short. The drums answered. The horn said the same thing all over again. The drums repeated it. The next time it was more intricate. The phrase was turned around, it went back and forth and up and down. And the drums said it over, exactly the same.

He knew a moment of panic. This was where he had to solo again and he wasn't sure he could do it. He touched the drums lightly. They quivered and answered him.

And then it was almost as though the drums were talking about his own life. The woman in Chicago who hated him. The girl with the round, soft body who had been his wife and who had walked out on him, this morning, in the rain. The old woman who was his mother, the same woman who lived in Chicago, and who hated him because he looked like his father, his father who had seduced her and left her, years ago.

He forgot the theater, forgot everything but the drums. He

was welded to the drums, sucked inside them. All of him. His pulse beat. His heart beat. He had become part of the drums. They had become part of him.

He made the big bass rumble and reverberate. He went a little mad on the big bass. Again and again he filled the theater with a sound like thunder. The sound seemed to come not from the drums but from deep inside himself; it was a sound that was being wrenched out of him—a violent, raging, roaring sound. As it issued from him he thought, this is the story of my love, this is the story of my hate, this is all there is left of me. And the sound echoed and re-echoed far up under the roof of the theater.

When he finally stopped playing, he was trembling; his body was wet with sweat. He was surprised to see that the drums were sitting there in front of him. He hadn't become part of them. He was still himself. Kid Jones. Master of the drums. Greatest drummer in the world. Selling himself a little piece at a time. Every afternoon. Twice every evening. Only this time he had topped all his other performances. This time, playing like this after what had happened in the morning, he had sold all of himself—not just a little piece.

Someone kicked his foot. "Bow, you ape. Whassamatter with you?"

He bowed from the waist, and the spotlight slid away from him, down his pants legs. The light landed on the Marquis of Brund, the piano player. The Marquis' skin glistened like a piece of black seaweed. Then the light was back on Kid Jones.

He felt hot and he thought, I stink of sweat. The talcum he had dabbed on his face after he shaved felt like a constricting layer of cement. A thin layer but definitely cement. No air could get through to his skin. He reached for his handkerchief and felt the powder and the sweat mix as he mopped his face.

Then he bowed again. And again. Like a—like one of those things you pull the string and it jerks, goes through the motion of dancing. Pull it again and it kicks. Yeah, he thought, you were hot all right. The jitterbugs ate you up and you haven't any place to go. Since this morning you haven't had any place to go. "I'm leaving it's the guy who plays the piano I'm in love with the Marquis of Brund he plays such sweet piano I'm leaving leaving leaving—"

He stared at the Marquis of Brund for a long moment.

Then he stood up and bowed again. And again.

Mama's Missionary Money

CHESTER HIMES

"You Lem-u-welllllll! You-u-uuuu Lem-u-wellllllLLLLLLLLL!"

Lemuel heard his ma call him. Always wanting him to go to the store. He squirmed back into the corner of the chicken house, out of sight of the yard. He felt damp where he had sat in some fresh chicken manure, and he cursed.

Through a chink in the wall he saw his ma come out of the house, shading the sun from her eyes with her hand, looking for him. Let her find Ella, his little sister, or get somebody else. Tired of going to the store all the time. If it wasn't for his ma it was for Miss Mittybelle next door. Most every morning soon's he started out the house here she come to her door. "Lem-u-well, would you lak t' go to t' the sto' for me lak a darlin' li'l boy?" Just as soon's he got his glove and started out to play. Why din she just say, "Here, go to the sto'." Why'd she have to come on with that old "would you lak t' go" stuff? She knew his ma 'ud beat the stuffin's outen him if he refused.

He watched his ma looking around for him. She didn't call anymore, trying to slip up on him. Old chicken came in the door and looked at him. "Goway, you old tattle tale," he thought, but he was scared to move, scared to breathe. His ma went on off, 'round the house; he saw her going down the picket fence by Miss Mittybelle's sun flowers, going on to the store herself.

He got up and peeped out the door, looked around. He felt like old Daniel Boone. Wasn't nobody in sight. He went out in the yard. The dust was deep where the hens had burrowed hollows. It oozed up twixt the toes of his bare feet and felt hot and soft as flour. His long dark feet were dust-powdered to a tan color. The dust was thick on his ankles, thinning up his legs. There were numerous small scars on the black skin. He was always getting bruised or scratched or cut. There were scars on his hands too and on his long black arms.

He wondered where everybody was. Sonny done gone fishing with his pa. More like Bubber's ma kept him in 'cause he was feeling a little sick. From over toward Mulberry Street came sounds of yelling and screaming. He cocked his long egg-shaped head to listen; his narrow black face was stolid, black skin dusty dry in the noonday sun. Burrhead was getting a licking. Everybody knew everybody's else's cry. He was trying to tell whether it was Burrhead's ma or pa beating him.

Old rooster walked by and looked at him. "Goan, old buzzard!" he whispered, kicking dust at it. The rooster scrambled back, ruffling up, ready to fight.

Lemuel went on to the house, opened and shut the screen door softly, and stood for a moment in the kitchen. His ma'd be gone about fifteen minutes. He wiped the dust off his feet with his hands and started going through the house, searching each room systematically, just looking to see what he could find. He went upstairs to his ma's and pa's room, sniffed around in the closet, feeling in the pockets of his pa's Sunday suit, then knelt down and looked underneath the bed. He stopped and peeped out the front window, cautiously pulling back the curtains. Old Mr. Diggers was out in his yard 'cross the street, fooling 'round his fence. His ma wasn't nowhere in sight.

He turned back into the room and pulled open the top dresser drawer. There was a big rusty black pocketbook with a snap fastener back in the corner. He poked it with a finger. It felt hard. He lifted it up. It was heavy. He opened it. There was money inside, all kinds of money, nickels and dimes and quarters and paper dollars and even ten dollar bills. He closed it up, shoved it back into the corner, slammed shut the drawer, and ran and looked out the front window. Then he ran and looked out the back window. He ran downstairs and went from room to room, looking out all the windows in the house. No one was in sight. Everybody stayed inside during the hot part of the day.

He ran back upstairs, opened the drawer, and got to the pocketbook. He opened it, took out a quarter, closed it, put it away, closed the drawer, ran downstairs and out the back door and across the vacant lot to Mulberry Street. He started downtown, walking fast as he could without running. When he came to the paved sidewalks, they were hot on his feet and he walked half dancing, lifting his feet quickly from the pavement. At the

Bijou he handed up his quarter, got a dime in change, and went into the small, hot theatre to watch a gangster film. Pow! Pow! Pow! That was him shooting down the cops. Pow! Pow! Pow!

"Where you been all day, Lem-u-well?" his ma asked as she bustled 'round the kitchen fixing supper.

"Over tuh the bayou. Fishin'. Me 'n Bluebelly went."

His ma backhanded at him but he ducked out of range. "Told you t' call Francis by his name."

"Yas'm. Francis, Me 'n Francis."

His pa looked up from the hydrant, where he was washing his hands and face. "Ummmmp?" he said. His pa seldom said more than "Ummmmp." It meant most everything. Now it meant did he catch any fish. "Nawsuh," Lemuel said.

His little sister, Ella, was setting the table. Lemuel washed his hands and sat down and his pa sat down and said the blessing while his ma stood bowed at the stove. It was very hot in the kitchen and the sun hadn't set. The reddish glow of the late sun came in through the windows, and they sat in the hot kitchen and ate greens and side meat and rice and baked sweet potatoes and drank the potliquor with the corn bread and had molasses and corn bread for dessert. Afterwards Lemuel helped with the dishes, and they went and sat on the porch in the late evening while the people passed and said hello.

Nothing was said about the quarter. Next day Lemuel took four dimes, three nickels, and two half dollars. He went and found Burrhead. "What you got beat 'bout yesdiddy?"

"Nutton. Ma said I sassed her."

"I got some money." Lemuel took the coins from his pocket and showed them.

"Where you git it?" Burrhead's eyes were big as saucers.

"Ne you mind. I got it. Les go tuh the show."

" 'Gangster Guns' at the Bijou."

"I been there. Les go downtown tuh the Grand."

On the way they stopped in front of Zeke's Grill. It was too early for the show. Zeke was in his window turning flapjacks on the grill. They were big, round flapjacks, golden brown on both sides, and he'd serve 'em up with butter gobbed between. Lemuel never had no flapjacks like that at home. Burrhead neither. They looked like the best tasting flapjacks in the world.

They went inside and had an order, then they stopped at Missus Harris's and each got double ice-cream cones and a bag

of peanut brittle. Now they were ready for the show. It was
boiling hot way up in the balcony next to the projection room,
but what'd they care. They crunched happily away at their
brittle and laughed and carried on. . . . "Watch out, man, he
slippin' up 'hind yuh."

Time to go home Lemuel had a quarter, two nickels, and a
dime left. He gave Burrhead the nickels and dime and kept the
quarter. That night after supper his ma let him go over to the lot
and play catch with Sonny, Bluebelly, and Burrhead. They kept
on playing until it was so dark they couldn't see and they lost
the ball over in the weeds by the bayou.

Next day Lemuel slipped up to his ma's dresser and went into
the magic black pocketbook again. He took enough to buy a real
big-league ball and enough for him and Burrhead to get some
more flapjacks and ice cream too. His ma hadn't said nothing
yet.

As the hot summer days went by and didn't nobody say
nothing at all, he kept taking a little more each day. He and
Burrhead ate flapjacks every day. He set up all the boys in the
neighborhood to peanut brittle and ice cream and rock candy
and took them to the show. Sundays, after he'd put his nickel in
the pan, he had coins left to jingle in his pocket, although he
didn't let his ma or pa hear him jingling them. All his gang
knew he was stealing the money from somewhere. But nobody
tattled on him and they made up lies at home so their parents
wouldn't get suspicious. Lemuel bought gloves and balls and
bats for the team and now they could play regular ball out on
the lot all day.

His ma noticed the new mitt he brought home and asked him
where he got it. He said they'd all been saving their money all
summer and had bought the mitt and some balls. She looked at
him suspiciously. "Doan you dast let me catch you stealin'
nothin', boy."

About this time he noticed the magic black bag was getting
flat and empty. The money was going. He began getting scared.
He wondered how long it was going to be before his ma found
out. But he had gone this far, so he wouldn't stop. He wouldn't
think about what was going to happen when it was all gone. He
was the king of the neighborhood. He had to keep on being
king.

One night after supper he and his pa were sitting on the

porch. Ella was playing with the cat 'round the side. He was sitting on the bottom step, wiggling his toes in the dust. He heard his ma come downstairs. He could tell something was wrong by the way she walked. She came out on the porch.

"Isaiah, somebody's tuk all my missionary money," she said. "Who you reckin it was?"

Lemuel held his breath. "Ummmmp!" his pa said.

"You reckin it were James?" He was her younger brother who came around sometimes.

"Ummmmp! Now doan you worry, Lu'belle. We find it."

Lemuel was too scared to look around. His pa didn't move. Nobody didn't say anything to him. After a while he got up. "I'm goin' tuh bed, ma," he said.

"Ummmmp!" his pa noticed.

Lemuel crawled into bed in the little room he had off the kitchen downstairs. But he couldn't sleep. Later he heard Doris Mae crying from way down the street. He just could barely hear her but he knew it was Doris Mae. Her ma was beating her. He thought Doris Mae's ma was always beating her. Later on he heard his ma and pa go up to bed. All that night he lay half awake, waiting for his pa to come down. He was so scared he just lay there and trembled.

Old rooster crowed. The sun was just rising. Clump-clump-clump. He heard his pa's footsteps on the stairs. Clump-clump-clump. It was like the sound of doom. He wriggled down in the bed and pulled the sheet up over his head. He made like he was sleeping. Clump-clump-clump. He heard his pa come into the room. He held his breath. He felt his pa reach down and pull the sheet off him. He didn't wear no bottoms in the summer. His rear was like a bare tight knot. He screwed his eyes 'round and saw his pa standing tall in mudstained overalls beside the bed, with the cord to his razor strop doubled over his wrist and the strop hanging poised at his side. His pa had on his reformer's look, like he got on when he passed the dance hall over on Elm Street.

"Lem-u-well, I give you uh chance tuh tell the truth. What you do with yo' ma's missionary money?"

"I didn't take it, pa. I swear I didn', pa."

"Ummmmp!" his pa said.

Whack! The strap came down. Lemuel jumped off the bed and tried to crawl underneath it. His pa caught him by the arm.

Whack! Whack! Whack! went the strap. The sound hurt Lemuel
as much as the licks. "Owwwwwwww-owwwwwwwWWWW!" he
began to bawl. All over the neighborhood folks knew that
Lemuel was getting a beating. His buddies knew what for. The
old folks didn't know yet but they'd know before the day was
over.

"God doan lak thieves," his pa said, beating him across the
back and legs.

Lemuel darted toward the door. His pa headed him off. He
crawled between his pa's legs, getting whacked as he went
through. He ran out into the kitchen. His ma was waiting for
him with a switch. He tried to crawl underneath the table. His
head got caught in the legs of a chair. His ma started working
on his rear with the switch.

"MURDER!" he yelled at the top of his voice. "HELP!
POLICE! Please, ma, I ain't never gonna steal nothin' else, ma.
If you jes let me off this time, ma. I swear, ma."

"I'm gonna beat the truth into you," his ma said. "Gonna beat
out the devil."

He pulled out from underneath the table and danced up and
down on the floor, trying to dodge the licks aimed at his leg.

"He gone, ma! Oh, he gone!" he yelled, dancing up and down.
"Dat ol' devil gone, ma! I done tuk Christ Jesus to my heart!"

Well, being as he done seen the light, she sighed and let him
off. Her missionary money wasn't gone clean to waste nohow if
it'd make him mend his stealin' ways. She guessed them
heathens would just have to wait another year; as Isaiah always
say, they done wanted this long 'n it ain't kilt 'em.

The way Lemuel's backsides stung and burned he figured
them ol' heathens was better off than they knew 'bout.

A beautiful story

See How They Run

MARY ELIZABETH VROMAN

A bell rang. Jane Richards squared the sheaf of records decisively in the large Manila folder, placed it in the right-hand corner of her desk, and stood up. The chatter of young voices subsided, and forty-three small faces looked solemnly and curiously at the slight young figure before them. The bell stopped ringing.

I wonder if they're as scared of me as I am of them. She smiled brightly.

"Good morning, children, I am Miss Richards." As if they don't know—the door of the third-grade room had a neat new sign pasted above it with her name in bold black capitals; and anyway, a new teacher's name is the first thing that children find out about on the first day of school. Nevertheless, she wrote it for their benefit in large white letters on the blackboard.

"I hope we will all be happy working and playing together this year." *Now why does that sound so trite?* "As I call the roll will you please stand, so that I may get to know you as soon as possible, and if you like you may tell me something about yourselves, how old you are, where you live, what your parents do, and perhaps something about what you did during the summer."

Seated, she checked the names carefully. "Booker T. Adams."

Booker stood, gangling and stoop-shouldered; he began to recite tiredly, "My name is Booker T. Adams, I'se ten years old." *Shades of Uncle Tom!* "I live on Painter's Path." He paused, the look he gave her was tinged with something very akin to contempt. "I didn't do nothing in the summer," he said deliberately.

"Thank you, Booker." Her voice was even. "George Allen." *Must remember to correct that stoop.* . . . *Where is Painter's Path?* . . . *How to go about correcting those speech defects?*

. . . Go easy, Jane, don't antagonize them. . . . They're clean enough, but this is the first day. . . . How can one teacher do any kind of job with a load of forty-three? . . . Thank heaven the building is modern and well built even though it is overcrowded, not like some I've seen—no potbellied stove.

"Sarahlene Clover Babcock." *Where do these names come from? . . . Up from slavery. . . . How high is up?* Jane smothered a sudden desire to giggle. Outside she was calm and poised and smiling. Clearly she called the names, listening with interest, making a note here and there, making no corrections—not yet.

She experienced a moment of brief inward satisfaction: *I'm doing very well, this is what is expected of me . . .* Orientation to Teaching . . . Miss Murray's voice beat a distant tattoo in her memory. Miss Murray with the Junoesque figure and the moon face. . . . "The ideal teacher personality is one which, combining in itself all the most desirable qualities, expresses itself with quiet assurance in its endeavor to mold the personalities of the students in the most desirable patterns." . . . Dear dull Miss Murray.

She made mental estimates of the class. *What a cross section of my people they represent,* she thought. *Here and there signs of evident poverty, here and there children of obviously well-to-do parents.*

"My name is Rachel Veronica Smith. I am nine years old. I live at Six-oh-seven Fairview Avenue. My father is a Methodist minister. My mother is a housewife. I have two sisters and one brother. Last summer mother and daddy took us all to New York to visit my Aunt Jen. We saw lots of wonderful things. There are millions and millions of people in New York. One day we went on a ferryboat all the way up the Hudson River—that's a great big river as wide as this town, and——"

The children listened wide-eyed. Jane listened carefully. *She speaks good English. Healthy, erect, and even perhaps a little smug. Immaculately well dressed from the smoothly braided hair, with two perky bows, to the shiny brown oxford. . . . Bless you, Rachel, I'm so glad to have you.*

"—— and the buildings are all very tall, some of them nearly reach the sky."

"Haw-haw"—this from Booker, cynically.

"Well, they are too." Rachel swung around, fire in her eyes and insistence in every line of her round, compact body.

"Ain't no buildings as tall as the sky, is dere, Miz Richards?"

Crisis No. 1. Jane chose her answer carefully. *As high as the sky . . . mustn't turn this into a lesson in science . . . all in due time.* "The sky is a long way out, Booker, but the buildings in New York are very tall indeed. Rachel was only trying to show you how very tall they are. In fact, the tallest building in the whole world is in New York City."

"They call it the Empire State Building," interrupted Rachel, heady with her new knowledge and Jane's corroboration.

Booker wasn't through. "You been dere, Miz Richards?"

"Yes, Booker, many times. Someday I shall tell you more about it. Maybe Rachel will help me. Is there anything you'd like to add, Rachel?"

"I would like to say that we are glad you are our new teacher, Miss Richards." Carefully she sat down, spreading her skirt with her plump hands, her smile angelic.

Now I'll bet me a quarter her reverend father told her to say that. "Thank you, Rachel."

The roll call continued. . . . Tanya, slight and pinched, with the toes showing through the very white sneakers, the darned and faded but clean blue dress, the gentle voice like a tinkling bell, and the beautiful sensitive face. . . . Boyd and Lloyd, identical in their starched overalls, and the slightly vacant look. . . . Marjorie Lee, all of twelve years old, the well-developed body moving restlessly in the childish dress, the eyes too wise, the voice too high. . . . Joe Louis, the intelligence in the brilliant black eyes gleaming above the threadbare clothes. *Lives of great men all remind us——— Well, I have them all . . . Frederick Douglass, Franklin Delano, Abraham Lincoln, Booker T., Joe Louis, George Washington. . . . What a great burden you bear, little people, heirs to all your parents' stillborn dreams of greatness. I must not fail you.* The last name on the list . . . C. T. Young. Jane paused, small lines creasing her forehead. She checked the list again.

"C. T., what is your name? I only have your initials on my list."

"Dat's all my name, C. T. Young."

"No, dear, I mean what does C. T. stand for? Is it Charles or Clarence?"

"No'm, jest C. T."

"But I can't put that in my register, dear."

Abruptly Jane rose and went to the next room. Rather timidly she waited to speak to Miss Nelson, the second-grade teacher, who had the formidable record of having taught all of sixteen years. Miss Nelson was large and smiling.

"May I help you, dear?"

"Yes, please. It's about C. T. Young. I believe you had him last year."

"Yes, and the year before that. You'll have him two years too."

"Oh? Well, I was wondering what name you registered him under. All the information I have is C. T. Young."

"That's all there is, honey. Lots of these children only have initials."

"You mean . . . can't something be done about it?"

"What?" Miss Nelson was still smiling, but clearly impatient.

"I . . . well . . . thank you." Jane left quickly.

Back in Room 3 the children were growing restless. Deftly Jane passed out the rating tests and gave instructions. Then she called C. T. to her. He was as small as an eight-year-old, and hungry-looking, with enormous guileless eyes and a beautifully shaped head.

"How many years did you stay in the second grade, C. T.?"

"Two."

"And in the first?"

"Two."

"How old are you?"

" 'Leven."

"When will you be twelve?"

"Nex' month."

And they didn't care . . . nobody ever cared enough about one small boy to give him a name.

"You are a very lucky little boy, C. T. Most people have to take the name somebody gave them whether they like it or not, but you can choose your very own."

"Yeah?" The dark eyes were belligerent. "My father named me C. T. after hisself, Miz Richards, an dat's my name."

Jane felt unreasonably irritated. "How many children are there in your family, C. T.?"

" 'Leven."

"How many are there younger than you?" she asked.

"Seven."

Very gently, "Did you have your breakfast this morning, dear?"

The small figure in the too-large trousers and the too-small shirt drew itself up to full height. "Yes'm, I had fried chicken, and rice, and coffee, and rolls, and oranges too."

Oh, you poor darling. You poor proud lying darling. Is that what you'd like for breakfast?

She asked, "Do you like school, C. T.?"

"Yes'm," he told her suspiciously.

She leafed through the pile of records. "Your record says you haven't been coming to school very regularly. Why?"

"I dunno."

"Did you eat last year in the lunchroom?"

"No'm."

"Did you ever bring a lunch?"

"No'm, I eats such a big breakfast, I doan git hungry at lunchtime."

"Children need to eat lunch to help them grow tall and strong, C. T. So from now on you'll eat lunch in the lunchroom"—an afterthought: *Perhaps it's important to make him think I believe him*—"and from now on maybe you'd better not eat such a big breakfast."

Decisively she wrote his name at the top of what she knew to be an already too-large list. "Only those in absolute necessity," she had been told by Mr. Johnson, the kindly, harassed principal. "We'd like to feed them all, so many are underfed, but we just don't have the money." Well, this was absolute necessity if she ever saw it.

"What does your father do, C. T.?"

"He work at dat big factory cross-town, he make plenty money, Miz Richards." The record said "unemployed."

"Would you like to be named Charles Thomas?"

The expressive eyes darkened, but the voice was quiet. "No'm."

"Very well." Thoughtfully Jane opened the register; she wrote firmly: *C. T. Young.*

October is a witching month in the Southern United States. The richness of the golds and reds and browns of the trees forms an enchanted filigree through which the lilting voices of children at play seem to float, embodied like so many nymphs of Pan.

Jane had played a fast-and-furious game of tag with her class and now she sat quietly under the gnarled old oak, watching the tireless play, feeling the magic of the sun through the leaves warmly dappling her skin, the soft breeze on the nape of her neck like a lover's hands, and her own drowsy lethargy. *Paul, Paul my darling . . . how long for us now?* She had worshiped Paul Carlyle since they were freshmen together. On graduation day he had slipped the small circlet of diamonds on her finger. . . . "A teacher's salary is small, Jane. Maybe we'll be lucky enough to get work together, then in a year or so we can be married. Wait for me, darling, wait for me!"

But in a year or so Paul had gone to war, and Jane went out alone to teach. . . . Lansing Creek—one year . . . the leaky roof, the potbellied stove, the water from the well. . . . Mary-weather Point—two years . . . the tight-lipped spinster principal with the small, vicious face and the small, vicious soul. . . . Three hard, lonely years and then she had been lucky.

The superintendent had praised her. "You have done good work, Miss—ah—Jane. This year you are to be placed at Center-town High—that is, of course, if you care to accept the position."

Jane had caught her breath. Centertown was the largest and best equipped of all the schools in the county, only ten miles from home and Paul—for Paul had come home, older, quieter, but still Paul. He was teaching now more than a hundred miles away, but they went home every other week end to their families and each other. . . . "Next summer you'll be Mrs. Paul Carlyle, darling. It's hard for us to be apart so much. I guess we'll have to be for a long time till I can afford to support you. But, sweet, these little tykes need us so badly." He had held her close, rubbing the nape of the neck under the soft curls. "We have a big job, those of us who teach," he had told her, "a never-ending and often thankless job, Jane, to supply the needs of these kids who lack so much."

They wrote each other long letters, sharing plans and problems. She wrote him about C. T. "I've adopted him, darling. He's so pathetic and so determined to prove that he's not. He learns nothing at all, but I can't let myself believe that he's stupid, so I keep trying."

"Miz Richards, please, ma'am." Tanya's beautiful amber eyes

sought hers timidly. Her brown curls were tangled from playing, her cheeks a bright red under the tightly-stretched olive skin. The elbows jutted awkwardly out of the sleeves of the limp cotton dress, which could not conceal the finely chiseled bones in their pitiable fleshlessness. As always when she looked at her, Jane thought, *What a beautiful child!* So unlike the dark, gaunt, morose mother, and the dumpy, pasty-faced father who had visited her that first week. A fairy's changeling. *You'll make a lovely angel to grace the throne of God, Tanya! Now what made me think of that?*

"Please, ma'am, I'se sick."

Gently Jane drew her down beside her. She felt the parchment skin, noted the unnaturally bright eyes. *Oh, dear God, she's burning up!* "Do you hurt anywhere, Tanya?"

"My head, ma'am, and I'se so tired." Without warning she began to cry.

"How far do you live, Tanya?"

"Two miles."

"You walk to school?"

"Yes'm."

"Do any of your brothers have a bicycle?"

"No'm."

"Rachel!" *Bless you for always being there when I need you.* "Hurry, dear, to the office and ask Mr. Johnson please to send a big boy with a bicycle to take Tanya home. She's sick."

Rachel ran.

"Hush now, dear, we'll get some cool water, and then you'll be home in a little while. Did you feel sick this morning?"

"Yes'm, but Mot Dear sent me to school anyway. She said I just wanted to play hooky." *Keep smiling, Jane. Poor, ambitious, well-meaning parents, made bitter at the seeming futility of dreaming dreams for this lovely child . . . willing her to rise above the drabness of your own meager existence . . . too angry with life to see that what she needs most is your love and care and right now medical attention.*

Jane bathed the child's forehead with cool water at the fountain. *Do the white schools have a clinic? I must ask Paul. Do they have a lounge or a couch where they can lay one wee sick head? Is there anywhere in this town free medical service for one small child . . . born black?*

The boy with the bicycle came. "Take care of her now, ride

slowly and carefully, and take her straight home. . . . Keep the newspaper over your head, Tanya, to keep out the sun, and tell your parents to call the doctor." But she knew they wouldn't—because they couldn't!

The next day Jane went to see Tanya.

"She's sho' nuff sick, Miz Richards," the mother said. "She's always been a puny child, but this time she's took real bad, throat's all raw, talk all out of her haid las' night. I been using a poultice and some herb brew but she ain't got no better."

"Have you called a doctor, Mrs. Fulton?"

"No'm, we cain't afford it, an' Jake, he doan believe in doctors nohow."

Jane waited till the tide of high bright anger welling in her heart and beating in her brain had subsided. When she spoke, her voice was deceptively gentle. "Mrs. Fulton, Tanya is a very sick little girl. She is your only little girl. If you love her, I advise you to have a doctor to her, for if you don't . . . Tanya may die."

The wail that issued from the thin figure seemed to have no part in reality.

Jane spoke hurriedly. "Look, I'm going into town, I'll send a doctor out. Don't worry about paying him. We can see about that later." Impulsively she put her arms around the taut, motionless shoulders. "Don't you worry, honey, it's going to be all right."

There was a kindliness in the doctor's weatherbeaten face that warmed Jane's heart, but his voice was brusque. "You sick, girl? Well?"

"No, sir. I'm not sick." *What long sequence of events has caused even the best of you to look on even the best of us as menials?* "I'm a teacher at Centertown High. There's a little girl in my class who is very ill. Her parents are very poor. I came to see if you would please go to see her."

He looked at her, amused.

"Of course I'll pay the bill, doctor," she added hastily.

"In that case . . . well . . . where does she live?"

Jane told him. "I think it's diphtheria, doctor."

He raised his eyebrows. "Why?"

Jane sat erect. *Don't be afraid, Jane! You're as good a teacher as he is a doctor, and you made an* A *in that course in childhood diseases.* "High fever, restlessness, sore throat, headache, croupy cough, delirium. It could, of course, be tonsillitis or scarlet fever, but that cough—well, I'm only guessing, of course," she finished lamely.

"Hmph." The doctor's face was expressionless. "Well, we'll see. Have your other children been inoculated?"

"Yes, sir. Doctor, if the parents ask, please tell them that the school is paying for your services."

This time he was wide-eyed.

The lie haunted her. She spoke to the other teachers about it the next day at recess. "She's really very sick, maybe you'd like to help?"

Mary Winters, the sixth-grade teacher, was the first to speak. "Richards, I'd like to help, but I've got three kids of my own, and so you see how it is?"

Jane saw.

"Trouble with you, Richards, is you're too emotional." This from Nelson. "When you've taught as many years as I have, my dear, you'll learn not to bang your head against a stone wall. It may sound hardhearted to you, but one just can't worry about one child more or less when one has nearly fifty."

The pain in the back of her eyes grew more insistent. "I can," she said.

"I'll help, Jane," said Marilyn Andrews, breathless, bouncy newlywed Marilyn. "Here's two bucks. It's all I've got, but nothing's plenty for me." Her laughter pealed echoing down the hall.

"I've got a dollar, Richards"—this from mousy, severe little Miss Mitchell—"though I'm not sure I agree with you."

"Why don't you ask the high-school faculty?" said Marilyn. "Better still, take it up in teachers' meeting."

"Mr. Johnson has enough to worry about now," snapped Nelson. *Why, she's mad*, thought Jane, *mad because I'm trying to give a helpless little tyke a chance to live, and because Marilyn and Mitchell helped.*

The bell rang. Wordlessly Jane turned away. She watched the children troop in noisily, an ancient nursery rhyme running through her head:

> *Three blind mice, three blind mice,*
> *See how they run, see how they run,*
> *They all ran after the farmer's wife,*

> *She cut off their tails with a carving knife.*
> *Did you ever see such a sight in your life*
> *As three blind mice?*

Only this time, it was forty-three mice. Jane giggled. *Why, I'm hysterical,* she thought in surprise. *The mice thought the sweet-smelling farmer's wife might have bread and a wee bit of cheese to offer poor blind mice, but the farmer's wife didn't like poor, hungry, dirty blind mice. So she cut off their tails. Then they couldn't run anymore, only wobble. What happened then? Maybe they starved, those that didn't bleed to death. Running round in circles. Running where, little mice?*

She talked to the high-school faculty, and Mr. Johnson. Altogether she got eight dollars.

The following week she received a letter from the doctor:

Dear Miss Richards:

> I am happy to inform you that Tanya is greatly improved, and with careful nursing will be well enough in about eight weeks to return to school. She is very frail, however, and will require special care. I have made three visits to her home. In view of the peculiar circumstances, I am donating my services. The cost of the medicines, however, amounts to the sum of $15. I am referring this to you as you requested. What a beautiful child!

> Yours sincerely,
> JONATHAN H. SINCLAIR, M.D.

P.S. *She had diphtheria.*

Bless you forever and ever, Jonathan H. Sinclair, M.D. For all your long Southern heritage, "a man's a man for a' that . . . and a' that!"

Her heart was light that night when she wrote to Paul. Later she made plans in the darkness. *You'll be well and fat by Christmas, Tanya, and you'll be a lovely angel in my pageant. . . . I must get the children to save pennies. . . . We'll send you milk and oranges and eggs, and we'll make funny little get-well cards to keep you happy.*

But by Christmas Tanya was dead!

The voice from the dark figure was quiet, even monotonous. "Jake an' me, we always work so hard, Miz Richards. We didn't

neither one have no schooling much when we was married—
folks never had much money, but we was happy. Jake, he tenant
farm. I tuk in washing—we plan to save and buy a little house
and farm of our own someday. Den the children come. Six boys,
Miz Richards—all in a hurry. We both want the boys to finish
school, mebbe go to college. We try not to keep them out to work
the farm, but sometimes we have to. Then come Tanya. Just like
a little yellow rose she was, Miz Richards, all pink and gold
. . . and her voice like a silver bell. We think when she grow
up an' finish school she take voice lessons—be like Marian
Anderson. We think mebbe by then the boys would be old
enough to help. I was kinda feared for her when she get sick,
but then she start to get better. She was doing so well, Miz
Richards. Den it get cold, an' the fire so hard to keep all night
long, an' eben the newspapers in the cracks doan keep the win'
out, an' I give her all my kivver; but one night she jest tuk to
shivering an' talking all out her haid—sat right up in bed, she
did. She call your name onc't or twice, Miz Richards, then she
say, 'Mot Dear, does Jesus love me like Miz Richards say in
Sunday school?' I say, 'Yes, honey.' She say, 'Effen I die will I
see Jesus?' I say, 'Yes, honey, but you ain't gwine die.' But she
did, Miz Richards . . . jest smiled an' laid down—jest smiled
an' laid down."

It is terrible to see such hopeless resignation in such tearless
eyes. . . . One little mouse stopped running. . . . *You'll make
a lovely angel to grace the throne of God, Tanya!*

Jane did not go to the funeral. Nelson and Rogers sat in the
first pew. Everyone on the faculty contributed to a beautiful
wreath. Jane preferred not to think about that.

C. T. brought a lovely potted rose to her the next day. "Miz
Richards, ma'am, do you think this is pretty enough to go on
Tanya's grave?"

"Where did you get it, C. T.?"

"I stole it out Miz Adams' front yard, right out of that li'l'
glass house she got there. The door was open, Miz Richards, she
got plenty, she won't miss this li'l' one."

You queer little bundle of truth and lies. What do I do now?
Seeing the tears blinking back in the anxious eyes, she said
gently, "Yes, C. T., the rose is nearly as beautiful as Tanya is
now. She will like it."

"You mean she will know I put it there, Miz Richards? She ain't daid at all?"

"Maybe she'll know, C. T. You see, nothing that is beautiful ever dies as long as we remember it."

So you loved Tanya, little mouse? The memory of her beauty is yours to keep now forever and always, my darling. Those things money can't buy. They've all been trying, but your tail isn't off yet, is it, brat? Not by a long shot. Suddenly she laughed aloud.

He looked at her wonderingly. "What you laughing at, Miz Richards?"

"I'm laughing because I'm happy, C. T.," and she hugged him.

Christmas with its pageantry and splendor came and went. Back from the holidays, Jane had an oral English lesson.

"We'll take this period to let you tell about your holidays, children."

On the weekends that Jane stayed in Centertown she visited different churches, and taught in the Sunday schools when she was asked. She had tried to impress on the children the reasons for giving at Christmastime. In class they had talked about things they could make for gifts, and ways they could save money to buy them. Now she stood by the window, listening attentively, reaping the fruits of her labors.

"I got a doll and a doll carriage for Christmas. Her name is Gladys, and the carriage has red wheels, and I got a tea set and——"

"I got a bicycle and a catcher's mitt."

"We all went to a party and had ice cream and cake."

"I got——"

"I got——"

"I got——"

Score one goose egg for Jane. She was suddenly very tired. "It's your turn, C. T." *Dear God, please don't let him lie too much. He tears my heart. The children never laugh. It's funny how polite they are to C. T. even when they know he's lying. Even that day when Boyd and Lloyd told how they had seen him take food out of the garbage cans in front of the restaurant, and he said he was taking it to some poor hungry children, they didn't laugh. Sometimes children have a great deal more insight than grownups.*

C. T. was talking. "I didn't get nothin' for Christmas, because mamma was sick, but I worked all that week before for Mr. Bondel what owns the store on Main Street. I ran errands an' swep' up an' he give me three dollars, and so I bought mamma a real pretty handkerchief an' a comb, an' I bought my father a tie pin, paid a big ole fifty cents for it too . . . an' I bought my sisters an' brothers some candy an' gum an' I bought me this whistle. Course I got what you give us, Miz Richards" (she had given each a small gift) "an' mamma's white lady give us a whole crate of oranges, an' Miz Smith what live nex' door give me a pair of socks. Mamma she was so happy she made a cake with eggs an' butter an' everything; an' then we ate it an' had a good time."

Rachel spoke wonderingly. "Didn't Santa Claus bring you anything at all?"

C. T. was the epitome of scorn. "Ain't no Santa Claus," he said and sat down.

Jane quelled the age-old third-grade controversy absently, for her heart was singing. *C. T. . . . C. T., son of my own heart, you are the bright new hope of a doubtful world, and the gay new song of a race unconquered. Of them all—Sarahlene, sole heir to the charming stucco home on the hill, all fitted for gracious living; George, whose father is a contractor; Rachel, the minister's daughter; Angela, who has just inherited ten thousand dollars—of all of them who got, you, my dirty little vagabond, who have never owned a coat in your life, because you say you don't get cold; you, out of your nothing, found something to give, and in the dignity of giving found that it was not so important to receive. . . . Christ Child, look down in blessing on one small child made in Your image and born black!*

Jane had problems. Sometimes it was difficult to maintain discipline with forty-two children. Busy as she kept them, there were always some not busy enough. There was the conference with Mr. Johnson.

"Miss Richards, you are doing fine work here, but sometimes your room is a little . . . well—ah—well, to say the least, noisy. You are new here, but we have always maintained a record of having fine discipline here at this school. People have said that it used to be hard to tell whether or not there were children in the building. We have always been proud of that. Now take Miss Nelson. She is an excellent disciplinarian." He smiled. "Maybe if you ask her she will give you her secret. Do not be too proud to accept help from anyone who can give it, Miss Richards."

"No, sir, thank you, sir, I'll do my best to improve, sir." *Ah, you dear, well-meaning, shortsighted, round, busy little man. Why are you not more concerned about how much the children have grown and learned in these past four months than you are about how much noise they make? I know Miss Nelson's secret. Spare not the rod and spoil not the child. Is that what you want me to do? Paralyze these kids with fear so that they will be afraid to move? afraid to question? afraid to grow? Why is it so fine for people not to know there are children in the building? Wasn't the building built for children?* In her room Jane locked the door against the sound of the playing children, put her head on the desk, and cried.

Jane acceded to tradition and administered one whipping. Booker had slapped Sarahlene's face because she had refused to give up a shiny little music box that played a gay little tune. He had taken the whipping docilely enough, as though used to it; but the sneer in his eyes that had almost gone returned to haunt them. Jane's heart misgave her. *From now on I positively refuse to impose my will on any of these poor children by reason of my greater strength.* So she had abandoned the rod in favor of any other means she could find. They did not always work.

There was a never-ending drive for funds. Jane had a passion for perfection. Plays, dances, concerts, bazaars, suppers, parties followed one on another in staggering succession.

"Look here, Richards," Nelson told her one day, "it's true that we need a new piano, and that science equipment, but, honey, these drives in a colored school are like the poor: with us always. It doesn't make too much difference if Suzy forgets her lines, or if the ice cream is a little lumpy. Cooperation is fine, but the way you tear into things you won't last long."

"For once in her life Nelson's right, Jane," Elise told her later. "I can understand how intense you are because I used to be like that; but, pet, Negro teachers have always had to work harder than any others and till recently have always got paid less, so for our own health's sake we have to let up wherever possible. Believe me, honey, if you don't learn to take it easy, you're going to get sick."

Jane did. Measles!

"Oh, no," she wailed, "not in my old age!" But she was glad of the rest. Lying in her own bed at home, she realized how very tired she was.

Paul came to see her that weekend, and sat by her bed and read aloud to her the old classic poems they both loved so well. They listened to their favorite radio programs. Paul's presence was warm and comforting. Jane was reluctant to go back to work.

What to do about C. T. was a question that daily loomed larger in Jane's consciousness. Watching Joe Louis' brilliant development was a thing of joy, and Jane was hard pressed to find enough outlets for his amazing abilities. Jeanette Allen was running a close second, and even Booker, so long a problem, was beginning to grasp fundamentals, but C. T. remained static.

"I always stays two years in a grade, Miz Richards," he told her blandly. "I does better the second year."

"Do you *want* to stay in the third grade two years, C. T.?"

"I don't keer." His voice had been cheerful.

Maybe he really is slow, Jane thought. But one day something happened to make her change her mind.

C. T. was possessed of an unusually strong tendency to protect those he considered to be poor or weak. He took little Johnny Armstrong, who sat beside him in class, under his wing. Johnny was nearsighted and nondescript, his one outstanding feature being his hero-worship of C. T. Johnny was a plodder. Hard as he tried, he made slow progress at best.

The struggle with multiplication tables was a difficult one, in spite of all the little games Jane devised to make them easier for the children. On this particular day there was the uneven hum of little voices trying to memorize. Johnny and C. T. were having a whispered conversation about snakes.

Clearly Jane heard C. T.'s elaboration. "Man, my father caught a moccasin long as that blackboard, I guess, an' I held him while he was live right back of his ugly head—so."

Swiftly Jane crossed the room. "C. T. and Johnny, you are supposed to be learning your tables. The period is nearly up and you haven't even begun to study. Furthermore, in more than five months you haven't even learned the two-times table. Now you will both stay in at the first recess to learn it, and every day after this until you do."

Maybe I should make up some problems about snakes, Jane mused, *but they'd be too ridiculous. . . . Two nests of four snakes—Oh, well, I'll see how they do at recess.* Her heart smote her at the sight of the two little figures at their desks, listening wistfully to the sound of the children at play, but she busied herself and pretended not to notice them. Then she heard C. T.'s voice:

"Lissen, man, these tables is easy if you really want to learn them. Now see here. Two times one is two. Two times two is four. Two times three is six. If you forgit, all you got to do is add two like she said."

"Sho' nuff, man?"

"Sho'. Say them with me . . . two times one——" Obediently Johnny began to recite. Five minutes later they came to her. "We's ready, Miz Richards."

"Very well. Johnny, you may begin."

"Two times one is two. Two times two is four. Two times three is. . . . Two times three is——"

"Six," prompted C. T.

In sweat and pain, Johnny managed to stumble through the two-times table with C. T.'s help.

"That's very poor, Johnny, but you may go for today. Tomorrow I shall expect you to have it letter perfect. Now it's your turn, C. T."

C. T.'s performance was a fair rival to Joe Louis's. Suspiciously she took him through in random order.

"Two times nine?"

"Eighteen."

"Two times four?"

"Eight."

"Two times seven?"

"Fourteen."

"C. T., you could have done this long ago. Why didn't you?"

"I dunno. . . . May I go to play now, Miz Richards?"

"Yes, C. T. Now learn your three-times table for me tomorrow."

But he didn't, not that day, or the day after that, or the day after that. . . . *Why doesn't he? Is it that he doesn't want to? Maybe if I were as ragged and deprived as he I wouldn't want to learn either.*

Jane took C. T. to town and bought him a shirt, a sweater, a pair of dungarees, some underwear, a pair of shoes, and a pair of socks. Then she sent him to the barber to get his hair cut. She gave him the money so he could pay for the articles himself and figure up the change. She instructed him to take a bath before putting on his new clothes, and told him not to tell anyone but his parents that she had bought them.

The next morning the class was in a dither.

"You seen C. T.?"

"Oh, boy, ain't he sharp!"

"C. T., where'd you get them new clothes?"

"Oh, man, I can wear new clothes any time I feel like it, but I can't be bothered with being a fancypants all the time like you guys."

C. T. strutted in new confidence, but his work didn't improve.

Spring came in its virginal green gladness and the children chafed for the out-of-doors. Jane took them out as much as possible on nature studies and excursions.

C. T. was growing more and more mischievous, and his influence began to spread throughout the class. Daily his droll wit became more and more edged with impudence. Jane was at her wit's end.

"You let that child get away with too much, Richards," Nelson told her. "What he needs is a good hiding."

One day Jane kept certain of the class in at the first recess to do neglected homework, C. T. among them. She left the room briefly. When she returned C. T. was gone.

"Where is C. T.?" she asked.

"He went out to play, Miz Richards. He said couldn't no ole teacher keep him in when he didn't want to stay."

Out on the playground C. T. was standing in a swing, gently swaying to and fro, surrounded by a group of admiring youngsters. He was holding forth.

"I gets tired of stayin' in all the time. She doan pick on nobody but me, an' today I put my foot down. 'From now on,' I say, 'I ain't never goin' to stay in, Miz Richards.' Then I walks out." He was enjoying himself immensely. Then he saw her.

"You will come with me, C. T." She was quite calm except for the telltale veins throbbing in her forehead.

"I ain't comin'." The sudden fright in his eyes was veiled quickly by a nonchalant belligerence. He rocked the swing gently.

She repeated, "Come with me, C. T."

The children watched breathlessly.

"I done told you I ain't comin', Miz Richards." His voice was patient, as though explaining to a child. "I ain't . . . comin' . . . a . . . damn . . . tall!"

Jane moved quickly, wrenching the small but surprisingly strong figure from the swing. Then she bore him bodily, kicking and screaming, to the building.

The children relaxed and began to giggle. "Oh, boy! Is he goin' to catch it!" they told one another.

Panting, she held him, still struggling, by the scruff of his collar before the group of teachers gathered in Marilyn's room. "All right, now *you* tell me what to do with him!" she demanded. "I've tried everything." The tears were close behind her eyes.

"What'd he do?" Nelson asked.

Briefly she told them.

"Have you talked to his parents?"

"Three times I've had conferences with them. They say to beat him."

"That, my friend, is what you ought to do. Now he never acted like that with me. If you'll let me handle him, I'll show you how to put a brat like that in his place."

"Go ahead," Jane said wearily.

Nelson left the room, and returned with a narrow but sturdy leather thong. "Now, C. T."—she was smiling, tapping the strap in her open left palm—"go to your room and do what Miss Richards told you to."

"I ain't gonna, an' you can't make me." He sat down with absurd dignity at a desk.

Still smiling, Miss Nelson stood over him. The strap descended without warning across the bony shoulders in the thin shirt. The whip became a dancing demon, a thing possessed, bearing no relation to the hand that held it. The shrieks grew louder. Jane closed her eyes against the blurred fury of a singing lash, a small boy's terror, and a smiling face.

Miss Nelson was not tired. "Well, C. T.?"

"I won't. Yer can kill me but I *won't!*"

The sounds began again. Red welts began to show across the small arms and through the clinging sweat-drenched shirt.

"Now will you go to your room?"

Sobbing and conquered, C. T. went. The seated children stared curiously at the little procession. Jane dismissed them.

In his seat C. T. found pencil and paper.

"What's he supposed to do, Richards?"

Jane told her.

"All right, now write!"

C. T. stared at Nelson through swollen lids, a curious smile curving his lips. Jane knew suddenly that come hell or high water, C. T. would not write. *I mustn't interfere. Please, God, don't let her hurt him too badly. Where have I failed so miserably? . . . Forgive us our trespasses.* The singing whip and the shrieks became a symphony from hell. Suddenly Jane hated the smiling face with an almost unbearable hatred. She spoke, her voice like cold steel.

"That's enough, Nelson."

The noise stopped.

"He's in no condition to write now anyway."

C. T. stood up. "I hate you. I hate you all. You're mean and I hate you." Then he ran. No one followed him. *Run, little mouse!* They avoided each other's eyes.

"Well, there you are," Nelson said as she walked away. Jane never found out what she meant by that.

The next day C. T. did not come to school. The day after that he brought Jane the fatal homework, neatly and painstakingly done, and a bunch of wild flowers. Before the bell rang, the children surrounded him. He was beaming.

"Did you tell yer folks you got a whipping, C. T.?"

"Naw! I'd 'a' only got another."

"Where were you yesterday?"

"Went fishin'. Caught me six cats long as your haid, Sambo."

Jane buried her face in the sweet-smelling flowers. *Oh, my brat, my wonderful resilient brat. They'll never get your tail, will they?*

It was seven weeks till the end of term when C. T. brought Jane a model wooden boat.

Jane stared at it. "Did you make this? It's beautiful, C. T."

"Oh, I make them all the time . . . an' airplanes an' houses too. I do 'em in my spare time," he finished airily.

"Where do you get the models, C. T.?" she asked.

"I copies them from pictures in the magazines."

Right under my nose . . . right there all the time, she thought wonderingly. "C. T., would you like to build things when you grow up? Real houses and ships and planes?"

"Reckon I could, Miz Richards," he said confidently.

The excitement was growing in her. "Look, C. T. You aren't going to do any lessons at all for the rest of the year. You're going to build ships and houses and airplanes and anything else you want to."

"I am, huh?" He grinned. "Well, I guess I wasn't goin' to get promoted nohow."

"Of course, if you want to build them the way they really are, you might have to do a little measuring, and maybe learn to spell the names of the parts you want to order. All the best contractors have to know things like that, you know."

"Say, I'm gonna have real fun, huh? I always said lessons wussent no good nohow. Pop say too much study eats out yer brains anyway."

The days went by. Jane ran a race with time. The instructions from the model companies arrived. Jane burned the midnight oil planning each day's work:

Learn to spell the following words: ship, sail, steamer—boat, anchor, airplane wing, fly.

Write a letter to the lumber company, ordering some lumber.

The floor of our model house is ten inches wide and fourteen inches long. Multiply the length by the width and you'll find the area of the floor in square inches.

Read the story of Columbus and his voyages.

Our plane arrives in Paris in twenty-eight hours. Paris is the capital city of a country named France across the Atlantic Ocean.

Long ago sailors told time by the sun and the stars. Now, the earth goes around the sun——

Work and pray, work and pray!

C. T. learned. Some things vicariously, some things directly. When he found that he needed multiplication to plan his models to scale, he learned to multiply. In three weeks he had mastered simple division.

Jane bought beautifully illustrated stories about ships and planes. He learned to read.

He wrote for and received his own materials.

Jane exulted.

The last day! Forty-two faces waiting anxiously for report cards. Jane spoke to them briefly, praising them collectively, and admonishing them to obey the safety rules during the holidays. Then she passed out the report cards.

As she smiled at each childish face, she thought, *I've been wrong. The long arm of circumstance, environment, and heredity is the farmer's wife that seeks to mow you down, and all of us who touch your lives are in some way responsible for how successful she is. But you aren't mice, my darlings. Mice are hated, hunted pests. You are normal, lovable children. The knife of the farmer's wife is double-edged for you because you are Negro children, born mostly in poverty. But you are wonderful children, nevertheless, for you wear the bright protective cloak of laughter, the strong shield of courage, and the intelligence of children everywhere. Some few of you may indeed become as the mice—but most of you shall find your way to stand fine and tall in the annals of men. There's a bright new tomorrow ahead. For every one of us whose job it is to help you grow that is insensitive and unworthy there are hundreds who daily work that you may grow straight and whole. If it were not so, our world could not long endure.*

She handed C. T. his card.

"Thank you, ma'am."

"Aren't you going to open it?"

He opened it dutifully. When he looked up, his eyes were wide with disbelief. "You didn't make no mistake?"

"No mistake, C. T. You're promoted. You've caught up enough to go to the fourth grade next year."

She dismissed the children. They were a swarm of bees released from a hive. " 'By, Miss Richards." . . . "Happy holidays, Miss Richards."

C. T. was the last to go.

"Well, C. T.?"

"Miz Richards, you remember what you said about a name being important?"

"Yes, C. T."

"Well, I talked to mamma, and she said if I wanted a name it would be all right, and she'd go to the courthouse about it."

"What name have you chosen, C. T.?" she asked.

"Christopher Turner Young."

"That's a nice name, Christopher," she said gravely.

"Sho' nuff, Miz Richards?"

"Sure enough, C. T."

"Miz Richards, you know what?"

"What, dear?"

"I love you."

She kissed him swiftly before he ran to catch his classmates

She stood at the window and watched the running, skipping figures, followed by the bold mimic shadows. *I'm coming home, Paul. I'm leaving my forty-two children, and Tanya there on the hill. My work with them is finished now.* The laughter bubbled up in her throat. *But Paul, oh Paul. See how straight they run!*

Exodus

JAMES BALDWIN

She had always seemed to Florence the oldest woman in the world—for she often spoke of Florence and Gabriel as the children of her old age; and she had been born, innumerable years ago, during slavery, on a plantation in another state. On this plantation she had grown up, one of the field workers, for she was very tall and strong; and by-and-by she had married, and raised children, all of whom had been taken from her, one by sickness, and two by auction, and one whom she had not been allowed to call her own, who had been raised in the master's house. When she was a woman grown, well past thirty as she reckoned it, with one husband buried—but the master had given her another—armies, plundering and burning, had come from the North to set them free. This was in answer to the prayers of the faithful, who had never ceased, both day and night, to cry out for deliverance.

For it had been the will of God that they should hear, and pass it, thereafter, one to another, the story of the Hebrew children, who had been held in bondage in the land of Egypt;

and how the Lord had heard their groaning, and how His heart
was moved; and how He bid them wait but a little season till He
should send deliverance. She had known this story, so it
seemed, from the day that she was born. And while life ran,
rising in the morning before the sun came up, standing and
bending in the fields when the sun was high, crossing the fields
homeward while the sun went down at the gates of heaven far
away—hearing the whistle of the foreman, and his eerie cry
across the fields; in the whiteness of winter when hogs and
turkeys and geese were slaughtered, and lights burned bright in
the big house, and Bathsheba, the cook, sent over in a napkin
bits of ham and chicken and cakes left over by the white folks;
in all that befell, in her joys—her pipe in the evening, her man
at night, the children she suckled, and guided on their first short
steps—and in her tribulations, death, and parting, and the lash;
she did not forget that deliverance was promised, and would
surely come. She had only to endure and trust in God. She knew
that the big house, the house of pride where the white folks
lived, would come down: it was written in the Word of God.
And they, who walked so proudly now, yet had not fashioned,
for themselves, or their children, so sure a foundation as was
hers. They walked on the edge of a steep place and their eyes
were sightless—God would cause them to rush down, as the
herd of swine had once rushed down, into the sea. For all that
they were so beautiful, and took their ease, she knew them, and
she pitied them, who would have no covering in the great day of
His wrath.

Yet, she told her children, God was just, and He struck no
people without first giving many warnings. God gave men time,
but all the times were in His hand, and, one day, the time to
forsake evil and do good would all be finished: then only the
whirlwind, death riding on the whirlwind, awaited those people
who had forgotten God. In all the days that she was growing up,
signs failed not, but none heeded. *Slaves done riz,* was whispered in the cabin, and at the master's gate: slaves in another
county had fired the master's house and fields, and dashed their
children to death against the stones. *Another slave in hell,*
Bathsheba might say one morning, shooing the pickaninnies
away from the great porch: a slave had killed his master, or his
overseer, and had gone down to hell to pay for it. *I ain't got long*

to stay here, someone crooned beside her in the fields: who would be gone by morning on his journey North. All these signs, like the plagues with which the Lord had afflicted Egypt, only hardened the hearts of these people against the Lord. They thought the lash would save them, and they used the lash; or the knife, or the gallows, or the auction block; they thought that kindness would save them, and the master and mistress came down, smiling, to the cabins, making much of the pickaninnies, and bearing gifts. These were great days, and they all, black and white, seemed happy together. But when the Word has gone forth from the mouth of God nothing can turn it back.

The word was fulfilled one morning before she was awake. Many of the stories her mother told meant nothing to Florence, she knew them for what they were, tales told by an old black woman in a cabin in the evening to distract her children from their cold and hunger. But the story of this day she was never to forget, it was a day like the day for which she lived. There was a great running and shouting, said her mother, everywhere outside, and, as she opened her eyes to the light of that day, so bright, she said, and cold, she was certain that the judgment trump had sounded. While she still sat, amazed, and wondering what, on the judgment day, would be the best behavior, in rushed Bathsheba, and behind her many tumbling children, and field hands, and house niggers, all together, and Bathsheba shouted, "Rise up, rise up, Sister Rachel, and see the Lord's deliverance! He done brought us out of Egypt, just like He promised, and we's free at last!"

Bathsheba grabbed her, tears running down her face; she, dressed in the clothes in which she had slept, walked to the door to look out on the new day God had given them.

On that day she saw the proud house humbled, green silk and velvet blowing out of windows, and the garden trampled by many horsemen, and the big gates open. The master and mistress, and their kin, and one child she had borne were in that house—which she did not enter. Soon it occurred to her that there was no reason any more to tarry here. She tied her things in a cloth, which she put on her head, and walked out through the big gate, never to see that country any more.

And this, as Florence grew, became her deep ambition: to

walk out one morning through the cabin door, never to return. . . .

II

In 1900, when she was twenty-six, Florence walked out through the cabin door. she had thought to wait until her mother, who was so ill now that she no longer stirred out of bed, should be buried—but suddenly she knew that she would wait no longer, the time had come. She had been working as cook and serving girl for a large white family in town, and it was on the day that her master proposed that she become his concubine that she knew that her life among these wretched had come to its destined end. She left her employment that same day (leaving behind her a most vehement conjugal bitterness) and with part of the money which, with cunning, cruelty, and sacrifice, she had saved over a period of years, bought a railroad ticket to New York. When she bought it, in a kind of scarlet rage, she held, like a talisman at the back of her mind, the thought: "I can give it back, I can sell it. This don't mean I got to go." But she knew that nothing could stop her.

And it was this leave-taking which came to stand, in Florence's latter days, and with many another witness, at her bedside. Gray clouds obscured the sun that day, and outside the cabin window she saw that mist still covered the ground. Her mother lay in bed, awake; she was pleading with Gabriel, who had been out drinking the night before, and who was not really sober now, to mend his ways and come to the Lord. And Gabriel, full of the confusion, and pain, and guilt which were his whenever he thought of how he made his mother suffer, but which became nearly insupportable when she taxed him with it, stood before the mirror, head bowed, buttoning his shirt. Florence knew that he could not unlock his lips to speak; he could not say Yes to his mother, and to the Lord; and he could not say No.

"Honey," their mother was saying, "don't you *let* your old mother die without you look her in the eye and tell her she going to see you in glory. You hear me, boy?"

In a moment, Florence thought with scorn, tears would fill his eyes, and he would promise to "do better." He had been promising to "do better" since the day he had been baptized.

She put down her bag in the center of the hateful room.

"Ma," she said, "I'm going. I'm a-going this morning."

Now that she had said it, she was angry with herself for not having said it the night before, so that they would have had time to be finished with their weeping and their arguments. She had not trusted herself to withstand, the night before; but now there was almost no time left. The center of her mind was filled with the image of the great, white clock at the railway station, on which the hands did not cease to move.

"You going where?" her mother asked, sharply. But she knew that her mother had understood, had, indeed, long before this moment, known that this moment would come. The astonishment with which she stared at Florence's bag was not altogether astonishment, but a startled, wary attention. A danger imagined had become present and real, and her mother was already searching for a way to break Florence's will. All this Florence, in a moment, knew, and it made her stronger. She watched her mother, waiting.

But at the tone of his mother's voice, Gabriel, who had scarcely heard Florence's announcement, so grateful had he been that something had occurred to distract from him his mother's attention, dropped his eyes, and saw Florence's traveling bag. And he repeated his mother's question in a stunned, angry voice, understanding it only as the words hit the air:

"Yes, girl. Where you think you going?"

"I'm going," she said, "to New York. I got my ticket."

And her mother watched her. For a moment no one said a word. Then, Gabriel, in a changed and frightened voice, asked:

"And when you done decide that?"

She did not look at him, nor answer his question. She continued to watch her mother. "I got my ticket," she repeated. "I'm going on the morning train."

"Girl," asked her mother, quietly, "is you sure you know what you's doing?"

She stiffened, seeing in her mother's eyes a mocking pity. "I'm a woman grown," she said. "I know what I'm doing."

"And you going," cried Gabriel, "this morning—just like that? And you going to walk off and leave your mother—just like that?"

"You hush," she said, turning to him for the first time; "she got you, ain't she?"

This was indeed, she realized, as he dropped his eyes, the bitter, troubling point. He could not endure the thought of being left alone with his mother, with nothing whatever to put between himself and his guilty love. With Florence gone, time would have swallowed up all his mother's children, except himself; and *he*, then, must make amends for all the pain that she had borne, and sweeten her last moments with all his proofs of love. And his mother required of him one proof only, that he tarry no longer in sin. With Florence gone, his stammering time, his playing time, contracted with a bound to the sparest interrogative second; when he must stiffen himself, and answer to his mother, and all the host of heaven, Yes, or No.

Florence smiled inwardly a small, malicious smile, watching his slow bafflement, and panic, and rage; and she looked at her mother again. "She got you," she repeated. "She don't need me."

"You going North," her mother said, then. "And when you reckon on coming back?"

"I don't reckon on coming back," she said.

"You come crying back soon enough," said Gabriel, with malevolence, "soon as they whip your butt up there four or five times."

She looked at him again. "Just don't you try to hold your breath till then, you hear?"

"Girl," said her mother, "you mean to tell me the devil's done made your heart so hard you can just leave your mother on her dying bed, and you don't care if you don't never see her in this world no more? Honey, you can't tell me you done got so evil as all that?"

She felt Gabriel watching her to see how she would take this question—the question, which, for all her determination, she had dreaded most to hear. She looked away from her mother, and straightened, catching her breath, looking outward through the small, cracked window. There, outside, beyond the slowly rising mist, and farther off than her eyes could see, her life awaited her. The woman on the bed was old, her life was fading as the mist rose. She thought of her mother as already in the grave; and she would not let herself be strangled by the hands of the dead.

"I'm going, Ma," she said. "I got to go."

Her mother leaned back, face upward to the light, and began to cry. Gabriel moved to Florence's side and grabbed her arm.

She looked up into his face and saw that his eyes were full of tears.

"You can't go," he said. "You can't go. You can't go and leave your mother thisaway. She need a woman, Florence, to help look after her. What she going to do here, all alone with me?"

She pushed him from her and moved to stand over her mother's bed.

"Ma," she said, "don't be like that. Ain't a blessed thing for you to cry about so. Ain't a thing can happen to me up North can't happen to me here. God's everywhere, Ma. Ain't no need to worry."

She knew that she was mouthing words; and she realized suddenly that her mother scorned to dignify these words with her attention. She had granted Florence the victory—with a promptness which had the effect of making Florence, however dimly and unwillingly, wonder if her victory was real; and she was not weeping for her daughter's future; she was weeping for the past, and weeping in an anguish in which Florence had no part. And all of this filled Florence with a terrible fear, which was immediately transformed into anger.

"Gabriel can take care of you," she said, her voice shaking with malice; "Gabriel ain't never going to leave you. Is you, boy?" and she looked at him. He stood, stupid with bewilderment and grief, a few inches from the bed. "But me," she said, "I got to go." She walked to the center of the room again, and picked up her bag.

"Girl," Gabriel whispered, "ain't you got no feelings at *all?*"

"*Lord!*" her mother cried; and at the sound her heart turned over; she and Gabriel, arrested, stared at the bed. "Lord, Lord, Lord! Lord, have mercy on my sinful daughter! Stretch out your hand and hold her back from the lake that burns forever! Oh, my Lord, my Lord!" and her voice dropped, and broke, and tears ran down her face. "Lord, I done my best with all the children what you give me. Lord, have mercy on my children, and my children's children."

"Florence," said Gabriel, "please don't go. Please don't go. You ain't really fixing to go and leave her like this?"

Tears stood suddenly in her own eyes, though she could not have said what she was crying for. "Leave me be," she said to Gabriel, and picked up her bag again. She opened the door; the

cold morning air came in. "Good-by," she said. And then to
Gabriel: "Tell her I said good-by." She walked through the cabin
door and down the short steps into the frosty yard. Gabriel
watched her, standing magnetized between the door and the
weeping bed. Then, as her hand was on the gate, he ran before
her, and slammed the gate shut.

"Girl, where you going? What you doing? You reckon on
finding some men up North to dress you in pearls and diamonds?"

Violently, she opened the gate and moved out into the road.
He watched her with his jaw hanging, until the dust and the
distance swallowed her up.

God Bless America

JOHN O. KILLENS

Joe's dark eyes searched frantically for Cleo as he marched with
the other Negro soldiers up the long thoroughfare towards the
boat. Women were running out to the line of march, crying and
laughing and kissing the men good-by. But where the hell was
Cleo?

Beside him Luke Robinson, big and fat, nibbled from a carton
of Baby Ruth candy as he walked. But Joe's eyes kept traveling
up and down the line of civilians on either side of the street. She
would be along here somewhere; any second now she would
come calmly out of the throng and walk alongside him till they
reached the boat. Joe's mind made a picture of her, and she
looked the same as last night when he left her. As he had
walked away, with the brisk California night air biting into his
warm body, he had turned for one last glimpse of her in the
doorway, tiny and smiling and waving good-by.

They had spent last night sitting in the little two-by-four room
where they had lived for three months with hardly enough space
to move around. He had rented it and sent for her when he

came to California and learned that his outfit was training for immediate shipment to Korea, and they had lived there fiercely and desperately, like they were trying to live a whole lifetime. But last night they had sat on the side of the big iron bed, making conversation, half-listening to a portable radio, acting like it was just any night. Play-acting like in the movies.

It was late in the evening when he asked her, "How's little Joey acting lately?"

She looked down at herself. "Oh, pal Joey is having himself a ball." She smiled, took Joe's hand, and placed it on her belly; and he felt movement and life. His and her life, and he was going away from it and from her, maybe forever.

Cleo said, "He's trying to tell you good-by, darling." And she sat very still and seemed to ponder over her own words. And then all of a sudden she burst into tears.

She was in his arms and her shoulders shook. "It isn't fair! Why can't they take the ones that aren't married?"

He hugged her tight, feeling a great fullness in his throat. "Come on now, stop crying, hon. Cut it out, will you? I'll be back home before little Joey sees daylight."

"You may never come back. They're killing a lot of our boys over there. Oh, Joe, Joe, why did they have to go and start another war?"

In a gruff voice he said, "Don't you go worrying about Big Joey. He'll take care of himself. You just take care of little Joey and Cleo. That's what you do."

"Don't take any chances, Joe. Don't be a hero!"

He forced himself to laugh, and hugged her tighter. "Don't you worry about the mule going blind."

She made herself stop crying and wiped her face. "But I don't understand, Joe. I don't understand what colored soldiers have to fight for—especially against other colored people."

"Honey," said Joe gently, "we got to fight like anybody else. We can't just sit on the sidelines."

But she just looked at him and shook her head.

"Look," he said, "when I get back I'm going to finish college. I'm going to be a lawyer. That's what I'm fighting for."

She kept shaking her head as if she didn't hear him. "I don't know, Joe. Maybe it's because we were brought up kind of different, you and I. My father died when I was four. My mother worked all her life in white folks' kitchens. I just did make it through high school. You had it a whole lot better than most

Negro boys." She went over to the box of Kleenex and blew her nose.

"I don't see where that has a thing to do with it."

He stared at her, angry with her for being so obstinate. Couldn't she see any progress at all? Look at Jackie Robinson. Look at Ralph Bunche. Goddamn it! they'd been over it all before. What did she want him to do about it anyway? Become a deserter?

She stood up over him. "Can't see it, Joe—just can't see it! I want you here, Joe. Here with me where you belong. Don't leave me, Joe! Please——" She was crying now. "Joe, Joe, what're we going to do? Maybe it would be better to get rid of little Joey——" Her brown eyes were wide with terror. "No, Joe, No! I didn't mean that! I didn't mean it, darling! Don't know what I'm saying . . ."

She sat down beside him, bent over, her face in her hands. It was terrible for him, seeing her this way. He got up and walked from one side of the little room to the other. He thought about what the white captain from Hattiesburg, Mississippi, had said. "Men, we have a job to do. Our outfit is just as damn important as any outfit in the United States Army, white or colored. And we're working towards complete integration. It's a long, hard pull, but I guarantee you every soldier will be treated equally and without discrimination. Remember, we're fighting for the dignity of the individual." Luke Robinson had looked at the tall, lanky captain with an arrogant smile.

Joe stopped in front of Cleo and made himself speak calmly. "Look, hon, it isn't like it used to be at all. Why can't you take my word for it? They're integrating colored soldiers now. And anyhow, what the hell's the use of getting all heated up about it? I *got* to go. That's all there is to it."

He sat down beside her again. He wanted fiercely to believe that things were really changing for his kind of people. Make it easier for him—make it much easier for him and Cleo, if they both believed that colored soldiers had a stake in fighting the war in Korea. Cleo wiped her eyes and blew her nose, and they changed the subject, talked about the baby, suppose it turned out to be a girl, what would her name be? A little after midnight he kissed her good-night and walked back to the barracks.

The soldiers were marching in full field dress, with packs on their backs, duffle-bags on their shoulders, and carbines and rifles. As they approached the big white ship, there was talking and joke-cracking and nervous laughter. They were the leading Negro outfit, immediately following the last of the white troops. Even at route step there was a certain uniform cadence in the sound of their feet striking the asphalt road as they moved forward under the midday sun, through a long funnel of people and palm trees and shrubbery. But Joe hadn't spotted Cleo yet, and he was getting sick from worry. Had anything happened?

Luke Robinson, beside him, was talking and laughing and grumbling. "Boy, I'm telling you, these peoples is a bitch on wheels. Say, Office Willie, what you reckon I read in your Harlem paper last night?" Office Willie was his nickname for Joe because Joe was the company clerk—a high-school gradu- ate, two years in college, something special. "I read where some of your folks' leaders called on the President and demanded that colored soldiers be allowed to fight at the front instead of in quartermaster. Ain't that a damn shame?"

Joe's eyes shifted distractedly from the line of people to Luke, and back to the people again.

"Percy Johnson can have my uniform any day in the week," said Luke. "He want to fight so bad. Them goddamn Koreans ain't done me nothing. I ain't mad with a living ass."

Joe liked Luke Robinson, only he was so damn sensitive on the color question. Many times Joe had told him to take the chip off his shoulder and be somebody. But he had no time for Luke now. Seeing the ship plainly, and the white troops getting aboard, he felt a growing fear. Fear that maybe he had passed Cleo and they hadn't seen each other for looking so damn hard. Fear that he wouldn't get to see her at all—never-ever again. Maybe she was ill, with no way to let him know, too sick to move. He thought of what she had said last night, about little Joey. Maybe . . .

And then he saw her, up ahead, waving at him, with the widest and prettiest and most confident smile anybody ever smiled. He was so goddamn glad he could hardly move his lips to smile or laugh or anything else.

She ran right up to him. "Hello, soldier boy, where you think you're going?"

"Damn," he said finally in as calm a voice as he could manage. "I thought for a while you had forgotten what day it was. Thought you had forgotten to come to my going-away party."

"Now, how do you sound?" She laughed at the funny look on his face, and told him he looked cute with dark glasses on, needing a shave and with the pack on his back. She seemed so cheerful, he couldn't believe she was the same person who had completely broken down last night. He felt the tears rush out of his eyes and spill down his face.

She pretended not to notice, and walked with him till they reached the last block. The women were not allowed to go any further. Looking at her, he wished somehow that she would cry, just a little bit anyhow. But she didn't cry at all. She reached up and kissed him quickly. "Good-by, darling, take care of yourself. Little Joey and I will write every day, beginning this afternoon." And then she was gone.

The last of the white soldiers were boarding the beautiful white ship, and a band on board was playing *God Bless America*. He felt a chill, like an electric current, pass across his slight shoulders, and he wasn't sure whether it was from *God Bless America* or from leaving Cleo behind. He hoped she could hear the music; maybe it would make her understand why Americans, no matter what their color, had to go and fight so many thousands of miles away from home.

They stopped in the middle of the block and stood waiting till the white regiment was all aboard. He wanted to look back for one last glimpse of Cleo, but he wouldn't let himself. Then they started again, marching toward the ship. And suddenly the band stopped playing *God Bless America* and jumped into another tune—*The Darktown Strutters' Ball* . . .

He didn't want to believe his ears. He looked up at the ship and saw some of the white soldiers on deck waving and smiling at the Negro soldiers, yelling "Yeah, Man!" and popping their fingers. A taste of gall crept up from his stomach into his mouth.

"Goddamn," he heard Luke say, "that's the kind of music I like." The husky soldier cut a little step. "I guess Mr. Charlie want us to jitterbug onto his pretty white boat. Equal treatment. . . . We ain't no soldiers, we're a bunch of goddamn clowns."

Joe felt an awful heat growing inside his collar. He hoped fiercely that Cleo was too far away to hear.

Luke grinned at him. "What's the matter, good kid? Mad about something? Damn—that's what I hate about you colored folks. Take that goddamn chip off your shoulder. They just trying to make you people feel at home. Don't you recognize the Negro national anthem when you hear it?"

Joe didn't answer. He just felt his anger mounting and he wished he could walk right out of the line and to hell with everything. But with *The Darktown Strutters' Ball* ringing in his ears, he put his head up, threw his shoulders back, and kept on marching towards the big white boat.

hope - crushed

*Train Whistle Guitar**

ALBERT MURRAY

Lil' Buddy's color was that sky blue in which hens cackled; it was that smoke blue in which dogs barked and mosquito hawks lit on barbed-wire fences. It was the color above meadows. It was my color too because it was a boy's color. It was whistling blue and hunting blue, and it went with baseball, and that was old Lil' Buddy again, and that blue beyond outfields was exactly what we were singing about when we used to sing that old one about it ain't gonna rain no more no more.

Steel blue was a man's color. That was the clean, oil-smelling color of rifle barrels and railroad iron. That was the color that went with Luzana Cholly, and he had a steel-blue 32-20 on a 44 frame. His complexion was not steel blue but leather brown like dark rawhide, but steel blue was the color that went with what he was. His hands were just like rawhide, and when he was not dressed up he smelled like green oak steam. He had on slick starched blue denim overalls then, and when he was dressed up he wore a black broadcloth box-back coat with hickory-striped peg-top pants, and he smelled like the barber shop and new money.

Luzana Cholly was there in that time and place as far back as

* Originally published in *New World Writing IV* as "The Luzana Cholly Kick."

I can remember, even before Lil' Buddy was. Because I can remember when I didn't know Lil' Buddy at all. I can remember when that house they moved to was built (Lil' Buddy's papa and mama were still living together when they came to Gasoline Point from Choctaw County, which was near the Mississippi line), and I can also remember when that street (which was called Chattanooga Lookout Street) was pushed all the way through to the AT&N cut. That was before I had ever even heard of Lil' Buddy, and my buddy then was old Willie Marlowe. Lil' Buddy didn't come until after Willie Marlowe had gone to Detroit, Michigan, and that was not until after Mister One-Arm Will had been dead and buried for about nine months.

I can remember him there in that wee time when I couldn't even follow the stories I knew later they were telling about him, when it was only just grown folks talking, and all I could make of it was *Luzana, they are talking something about old Luzana again, and I didn't know what, to say nothing of where Louisiana was.* But old Luze was there even then and I could see him very clearly when they said his name because I had already seen him coming up that road that came by that house with the chinaberry yard, coming from around the bend and down in the railroad bottom; and I had already heard whatever that was he was picking on his guitar and heard that holler too. That was always far away and long coming. It started low like it was going to be a song, and then it jumped all the way to the very top of his voice and broke off, and then it started again, and this time was already at the top, and then it gave some quick jerking squalls and died away in the woods, the water, and the darkness (you always heard it at night), and Mama always said he was whooping and hollering like somebody back in the rosin-woods country, and Papa said it was one of them old Luzana swamp hollers. I myself always thought it was like a train, like a bad train saying look out this is me, and here I come, and I'm coming through.

That was even before I was big enough to climb the chinaberry tree. That was when they used to talk about the war and the Kaiser, and I can remember that there was a war book with Germans in it, and I used to see sure-enough soldiers marching in the Mardi Gras parades. Soldier Boy Crawford was still wearing his Army coat then, and he was the one who used to tell about how Luze used to play his guitar in France, telling about

how they would be going through some French town like the
ones called Nancy and Saint Die and old Luze would drop out of
the company and go and play around in the underground wine
shops until he got as much cognac and as many French Frogs as
he wanted and then he would turn up in the company again and
Capt'n would put him out by himself on the worst outpost he
could find in No Man's Land and old Luze would stay out there
sometimes for three or four days and nights knocking off patrol
after patrol, and one time in another place, which was the
Hindenburg Line, old Luze was out there again and there were a
few shots late in the afternoon and then it was quiet until about
three o'clock the next morning and then all hell broke loose, and
the Capt'n thought that a whole German battalion was about to
move in, and he sent five patrols out to find out what was
happening, but when they got there all they found was old Luze
all dug in and bristling with enough ammunition to blow up
kingdom come; he had crawled around all during the afternoon
collecting hand grenades and a mortar and two machine guns
and even a light two-wheel cannon, and when they asked him
what was going on he told them that he had fallen off to sleep
and when he woke up he didn't know whether or not any
Germans had snuck up so he thought he'd better lay himself
down a little light barrage. The next morning they found out
that old Luze had wiped out a whole German platoon but when
the Capt'n sent for him to tell him he was going to give him a
medal, old Luze had cut out and was off somewhere picking the
guitar and drinking cognac and chasing the mademoiselles
again. He went through the whole war like that and he came out
of the Army without a single scratch, didn't even get flat feet.

I heard a lot of stories about the war and I used to draw
pictures of them fighting with bayonets in the Argonne Forest,
and Soldier Boy Crawford used to look at them and shake his
head and give me a nickel and say that some day I was going to
be a soldier too.

I used to draw automobiles too, especially the Hudson Super-
Six, like old Long George Nisby had; he said it would do sixty on
a straightaway, and he had a heavy blasting cut-out on it that
jarred the ground. Old Man Perc Stranahan had a Studebaker
but he was a white man and he didn't have a cut-out, and he
drove as slow as a hearse. Old Gander said Old Man Perc always
drove like he was trying to sneak up on something but he never

was going to catch it like that. The cars I didn't like then were the flat-engine Buick and the old humpbacked Hupmobile. I liked the Maxwell and the Willys Knight and the Pierce Arrow.

I was playing train then too, and the trains were there before the automobiles were (there were many more horses and buggies in that part of town than there were automobiles then). I couldn't sit up in my nest in the chinaberry tree and see the trains yet, because I could not climb it yet, but I saw them when Papa used to take me to the L&N bottom to see them come by and I knew them all, and the Pan American was the fastest and Number Four was the fastest that ran in the daytime. Old Luzana could tell you all about the Southern Pacific and the Santa Fe, but that was later. But I already knew something about the Southern Pacific because Cousin Roberta had already gone all the way to Los Angeles, California, on the Sunset Limited.

I used to be in bed and hear the night trains coming by. The Crescent came by at nine-thirty and if you woke up way in the middle of the night you could hear Number Two. I was in my warm bed in that house, and I could hear the whistle coming even before it got to Chickasabogue Bridge and it had a bayou sound then, and then I could hear the engine batting it hell-for-leather on down the line bound for Mobile and New Orleans, and the next time the whistle came it was for Three Mile Creek. It was getting on into the beel then. I played train by myself in the daytime then, looking out the window along the side of the house like an engineer looking down along the drivers.

I used to hear old Stagolee playing the piano over in Hot Water Shorty's jook at night too, even then, especially on Saturday night. They rocked all night long, and I was lying in my warm quilted bed by the window. Uncle Jimmy's bed was by the window on the other side of the fireplace. When it was cold, you could wake up way in the night and still see the red embers in the ashes, and hear the wind whining outside, and sometimes you could hear the boat whistles too, and I could lie listening from where I was and tell you when it was a launch pulling a log raft or a tugboat pulling a barge or a riverboat like the *Nettie Queen*, and sometimes it was a big ship like the *Luchenback* called the Looking Back, which was all the way down at the city wharf at the foot of Government Street.

I knew a lot about the big ships because Uncle Jimmy worked

on the wharf. That was before the state docks were built and the big Gulf-going and ocean-going ships didn't come on past Mobile then unless they were going up to Chickasaw to be overhauled, but I had already seen them and had been on ships from England and France and Holland and naturally there were always ships from the Caribbean and South America because that was where the fruit boats came from.

All I could do was see old Luzana Cholly and hear him coming. I didn't really know him then, but I knew that he was blue steel and that he was always going and coming and that he had the best walk in the world, because I had learned how to do that walk and was already doing the stew out of it long before Lil' Buddy ever saw it. They were calling me Mister Man, and that was when somebody started calling me The Little Blister, because they said I was calling myself blister trying to say Mister. Aun Tee called me My Mister and Mama called me My Little Man, but she had to drop the little part off when Lil' Buddy came, and that was how everybody started calling me The Man, although I was still nothing but a boy, and I said to myself old Luzana is the man, old Luzana is the one I want to be like.

Then I was getting to be big enough to go everywhere by myself and I was going to school. That was when I knew about Dunkin's Hill and going up through Egerton Lane. That was the short way to school, because that was the way the bell sound came. Buddy Babe and Sister Babe and old double-jointed, ox-jawed Jack Johnson all went that way too, but when it rained you couldn't get across the bottom, and that was when everybody went the Shelton way, going through behind Stranahan's store and Good Hope Baptist to the old car line and then along that red clay road by the Hillside store.

Then Lil' Buddy was there and it was sky blue and we were blue hunters and every day was for whistling and going somewhere to do something you had to be rawhide to do, and some day we were going to live in times and places that were blue steel too. We found out a lot about old Luzana then, and then we not only knew him we knew how to talk to him.

The best time (except when he was just sitting somewhere strumming on his guitar) was when he was on his way to the Gambling Woods. (So far as anybody knew, gambling and guitar picking and grabbing freight trains were the only steady jobs he ever had or ever would have, except during the time he was in the Army and the times he was in jail—and he not only had been in jail, he had been in the penitentiary!) We were his good luck when he was headed for a skin game, and we always used to catch him late Saturday afternoon right out there where Gins Alley came into the oil-tank road, because he would be coming from Miss Pauline's cookshop then. The Gambling Woods trail started right out across from Sargin' Jeff's. Sometimes old Luze would have the guitar slung across his back even then, and naturally he had his famous 32-20 in the holster under his right arm.

"Say now hey Mister Luzana," I would holler at him.

"Mister Luzana Cholly one-time," Lil' Buddy always said, and he said that was what old Luze's swamp holler said too.

"Mister Luzana Cholly all night long," I would say then.

"Nobody else!" he would holler back at us then, "nobody else but."

"The one and only Mister Luzana Cholly from Booze Ana Bolly come Solly go Molly hit 'em with the fun folly."

"Talk to me, little ziggy, talk to me."

"Got the world in a jug," I might say then.

"And the stopper in your hand," old Lil' Buddy would say.

"You tell 'em, little crust busters, 'cause I ain't got the heart."

"He's a man among men."

"And Lord God among women!"

"Well tell the dy ya," old Luze would say then, standing wide-legged, laughing, holding a wad of Brown's Mule chewing tobacco in with his tongue at the same time. Then he would skeet a stream of amber juice to one side like a batter does when he steps up to the plate and then he would wipe the back of his leathery hand across his mouth and squint his eyes.

"Tell the dy-damn-ya!"

"Cain't tell no more," Lil' Buddy would say then, and old Luze would frown and wink at me.

"How come, little sooner, how goddam come?"

"Cause money talks."

"Well shut my mouth and call me suitcase."

"Ain't nobody can do that."

"I knowed you could tell 'em little ziggabo, I knowed good and damn well you could tell 'em."

"But we ain't gonna tell 'em no more."

"We sure ain't."

"Talk ain't no good if you ain't got nothing to back it up with."

Old Luze would laugh again and we would stand waiting and then he would run his hands deep down into his pockets and come out with two quarters between his fingers. He would throw them into the air and catch them again, one in each hand, and then he would cross his hands and flip one to me and one to Lil' Buddy.

"Now talk," he would say then. "Now talk, but don't say too much and don't talk too loud, and handle your money like the white folks does."

We were going to be like him even before we were going to be like cowboys. And we knew that blue steel was also root hog or die poor, which was what we were going to have to do whether we liked it or not. Lil' Buddy said it was not just how rough-and-ready old hard-cutting Luze was and how nobody, black or white, was going to do him any dirt and get away with it, and all that. It was that too, but it was also something else. It was also the way he could do whatever he was doing and make it look so easy that he didn't even seem to have to think about it, and once he did it, that seemed to be just about the only real way to do it.

Old Luze did everything his own way just like old Satch played baseball his way. But we knew that we wanted to be like him for more reasons than that too. Somehow or other just as he always seemed to be thirty-five years old and blue steel because he had already been so many places and done so many things you'd never heard of before, he also always seemed to be absolutely alone and not needing anybody else, self-sufficient, independent, dead sure, and at the same time so unconcerned.

Mama said he was don't-carified, and that was it too (if you know the full meaning of the Negro meaning of that expression). He was living in blue steel and his way was don't-carified, because he was blue steel too. Lil' Buddy said hellfied, and he didn't mean hell-defying either, you couldn't say he was hell-defying all the time, and you couldn't say he went for bad either, not even when he was doing that holler he was so notorious for. That *was* hell-defying in a way, but it was

really I don't give a damn if I *am* hell-defying, and he was not
going for bad because he didn't need to, since everybody,
black and white, who knew anything about him at all already
knew that when he made a promise it meant if it's the last
thing I do, if it's the last thing I do on this earth—and they
knew that could mean I'll kill you and pay for you as much
as it meant anything else. Because the idea of going to jail
didn't scare him at all, and the idea of getting shot at didn't
seem to scare him either. *Because all he ever said about that
was if they shoot at me they sure better not miss me, they sure
better get me the first time.*

He was a Negro who was an out and out Nigger in the very
best meaning of the word as Negroes use it among themselves
(who are the only ones who can), and nobody in that time and
that place seemed to know what to make of him. White folks
said he was crazy, but what they really meant or should have
meant was that he was confusing to them, because if they knew
him well enough to say he was crazy they also had to know
enough about him to know that he wasn't even foolhardy, not
even careless, not even what they wanted to mean by biggity.
The funny thing, as I remember it now, was how their confusion made them respect him in spite of themselves. Somehow or
other it was as if they respected him precisely because he didn't
care anything about them one way or the other. They certainly
respected the fact that he wasn't going to take any foolishness
off of them.

Negroes said he was crazy too, but they meant their own
meaning. They did not know what to make of him, but when
they said he was crazy they almost did, because when they said
it they really meant something else. They were not talking so
much about what he did, but how he was doing it. They were
talking about something like poetic madness, and that was the
way they had of saying that he was doing something unheard of,
doing the hell out of it, and getting away with whatever it was.
You could tell that was what they meant by the very way they
said it, by the sound of it, and by the way they were shaking
their heads and laughing when they said it.

The way he always operated as a lone wolf and the uncon-
cerned-, not the Negro-ness as such, were the main things then.
(Naturally Lil' Buddy and I knew about Negroes and white
folks, and we knew that there was something generally wrong

with white folks, but it didn't seem so very important then. We knew that if you hit a white boy he would turn red and call you nigger that did not sound like the Nigger the Negroes said and he would run and get as many other white boys as he could and come back at you, and we knew that a full-grown white had to get somebody to back him up too, but we didn't really think about it much, because there were so many other things we were doing then.)

Nobody ever said anything about old Luzana's papa and mama, and when you suddenly wondered about them you realized that he didn't seem to have or need any family at all, it really was as if he had come full-grown out of the swamp somewhere. And he didn't seem to need a wife either. But that was because he was not going to settle down yet. Because he had lived with more women from time to time and place to place than the average man could even shake a stick at.

We knew somehow or other that the Negro-ness had something to do with the way we felt about him too, but except for cowboys and the New York Yankees and one or two other things, almost everything was Negro then; that is, everything that mattered was. So the Negro part was only natural, although I can see something special about it too now.

When you boil it all down, I guess the main thing was how when you no more than just said his name, *Louisiana Charlie, old Luzana Cholly, old Luze,* that was enough to make you know not only him and how he looked and talked and walked that sporty limp walk, but his whole way of being, and how you knew right off the bat that he all alone and unconcerned in his sharp-edged and rough-backed steel had made it what it was himself.

That was what old Lil' Buddy and I were going to do too, make a name for ourselves. Because we knew even then (and I already knew it before he came) that doing that was exactly what made you the kind of man we wanted to be. Mama said I was her little man, and Aun Tee always called me her little mister, but I wasn't anybody's man and mister yet and I knew it, and when I heard the sound of the name that Mama taught me how to write I always felt funny, and I always jumped even when I didn't move. That was in school, and I wanted to hide, and I always said *they are looking for me, they are trying to see who I am,* and I had to answer because it would be the teacher calling the roll, and I said Present, and it sounded like somebody else.

And when I found out what I found out about me and Aun Tee and knew that she was my flesh and blood mama, I also found out that I didn't know my real name at all, because I didn't know who my true father was. So I said *My name is Reynard the Fox,* and Lil' Buddy said *My name is Jack the Rabbit and my home is in the briar patch.* That was old Luzana too, and when you heard that holler coming suddenly out of nowhere just as old Luze himself always seemed to come, it was just like it was coming from the briar patch.

So when Mama said what she said about me and Aun Tee at that wake that time and I heard it and had to believe it, I wished that old Luzana had been my real papa, but I didn't tell anybody that, not even Lil' Buddy although Lil' Buddy was almost in the same fix because he didn't have a mama any more and he didn't really love his papa because it was his papa that ran his mama away.

But we were buddies and we both did old Luzana's famous walk and we were going to be like him, and the big thing that you had to do to really get like him was to grab yourself a fast armful of fast freight train and get long gone from here. That was the real way to learn about the world, and we wanted to learn everything about it that we could. That was when we started practicing on the switch engine. That was down in the oilyards. You had to be slick to do even that because naturally your folks didn't want you doing stuff like that, because there was old Peg Leg Nat. Old Peg Leg butt-headed Nat could hop a freight almost as good as old Luzana could. He called himself mister-some-big-shit-on-a-stick. He spent most of his time fishing and sometimes he would come around pushing a wheelbarrow selling fresh fish, shrimps, and crabs, but every now and then he would strike out for somewhere on a freight just like old Luze did. Mama used to try to scare us with old Nat, telling us that a peg leg was just what messing around with freight trains would get you, and for a while she did scare us, but not for long, because then we found out that it never would have happened to old Nat if he hadn't been drunk and showing off. And anybody could see that getting his leg cut off hadn't stopped old Nat himself anyway since he could still beat any two-legged man we knew doing it except old Luze himself. Naturally we had to think about it, and naturally it did slow us up for a while, but it didn't really stop us. Because there was still old Luze, and that was who we were anyway, not old Peg Leg Nat.

Then that time when I found out all about me and Aun Tee, I was going to run away, and Lil' Buddy was ready too. Then old Lil' Buddy found out that old Luze was getting ready to get moving again and we were all set and just waiting and then it was the day itself.

I will always remember that one.

I had on my brogan shoes and I had on my corduroy pants under my overalls with my jumper tucked in. I had on my blue baseball cap too and my rawhide wristband and I had my pitching glove folded in my hip pocket. Lil' Buddy had on just about the same thing except that he was carrying his first-base pad instead of his catcher's mitt. We had our other things and something to eat rolled up in our blanket rolls so that we could sling them over our shoulders and have our arms free.

Lil' Buddy had gotten his papa's pearl-handled .38 Smith & Wesson, and we both had good jackknives. We had some hooks and twine to fish with too, just in case, and of course we had our trusty old slingshots for birds.

It was May and school was not out yet, and so not only were we running away, we were playing hooky too. It was hot, and with that many clothes on we were sweating, but you had to have them, and that was the best way to carry them.

There was a thin breeze that came across the railroad from the river, the marsh, and Pole Cat Bay, but the sun was hot and bright, and you could see the rails downright shimmering under the high and wide open sky. We had always said that we were going to wait until school was out, but this was our chance now, and we didn't care about school much any more anyhow. This was going to be school now anyway, except it was going to be much better.

We were waiting in the thicket under the hill. That was between where the Dodge mill road came down and where the oil spur started, and from where we were, we could see up and down the clearing as far as we needed to, to the south all the way across Three Mile Creek bridge to the roundhouse, and where Mobile was, and to the north all the way up past that mill to the Chickasabogue bridge. We knew just about from where old Luzana was going to come running, because we had been watching him do it for a long time now. We had that part down pat.

I don't know how long we had been waiting because we didn't have a watch but it had been a long time, and there was nothing to do but wait then.

"I wish it would hurry up and come on," Lil' Buddy said.

"Me too," I said.

"Got to get to splitting."

We were squatting on the blanket rolls, and Lil' Buddy was smoking another Lucky Strike, smoking the way we both used to smoke them in those old days, letting it hang dangling in the corner of your mouth, and tilting your head to one side with one eye squinted up like a gambler.

"Goddam it, watch me nail that sapsucker," he said.

"Man, you watch me."

You could smell the May woods there then, the dogwood, the honeysuckle, and the warm smell of the undergrowth; and you could hear the birds too, the jays, the thrushes, and even a woodpecker somewhere on a dead tree. I felt how moist and cool the soft dark ground was there in the shade, and you could smell that smell too, and smell the river and the marsh too.

Lil' Buddy finished the cigarette and flipped it out into the sunshine, and then sat with his back against a sapling and sucked his teeth. I looked out across the railroad to where the gulls were circling over the marsh and the river.

"Goddam it, when I come back here to this burg, I'm goddam man and a half," Lil' Buddy said all of a sudden.

"And don't care who knows it," I said.

"Boy, Chicago."

"Man, Detroit."

"Man, Philadelphia."

"Man, New York."

"Boy, I kinda wish old Gander was going too."

"I kinda wish so too."

"Old cat-eyed Gander."

"Old big-toed Gander."

"Old Gander is all right."

"Man, who you telling."

"That son of a bitch know his natural stuff."

"That bastard can steal lightning if he have to."

"Boy, how about that time."

"Man, hell yeah."

"Boy, but old Luze though."

"That Luze takes the cake for everything."

"Hot damn, boy we going!"

"It won't be long now."

"Boy, Los Angeles."

"Boy, St. Louis."

"Man, you know we going."

"Boy, you just watch me swing the sapsucker."

"Boy, snag it."

"Goddam."

"I'm going to natural-born kick that son of a bitch."

"Kick the living guts out of it."

"Boy and when we get back!" I said that and I could see it, coming back on the Pan American I would be carrying two suitcases and have a money belt and an underarm holster, and I would be dressed fit to kill.

"How long you think it will take us to get fixed to come back?" I said.

"Man, I don't know and don't care."

"You coming back when old Luze come back?"

"I don't know."

I didn't say anything else then. Because I was trying to think about how it was really going to be then. Because what I had been thinking about before was how I wanted it to be. I didn't say anything because I was thinking about myself then, think-ing: *I always said I was going but I don't really know whether I want to go or not now. I want to go and I don't want to go.* I tried to see what was really going to happen and I couldn't, and I tried to forget it and think about something else, but I couldn't do that either.

I looked over at Lil' Buddy again. Who was lying back against the tree with his hands behind his head and his eyes closed. Whose legs were crossed, and who was resting easy like a ball-player rests before time for the game to start. I wondered what he was really thinking. Did he really mean it when he said he did not know and didn't care? You couldn't tell what he was thinking, but you could tell that he wasn't going to back out now, no matter how he was feeling about it.

So I said to myself goddam it if Lil' Buddy can make it I can too, and I had more reason to be going away than he did anyway. *I had forgotten about that. I had forgotten all about it. And then I knew that I still loved Papa and they had always loved me and they had always known about me and Aun Tee.*

But I couldn't back out then, because what I had found out wasn't the real reason for going anyway. Old Luze was really the reason, old Luze and blue steel, old Luze and rawhide, old Luze and ever-stretching India Rubber.

"Hey Lebud."

"Hey."

"Going to the big league."

"You said it."

"Skipping city."

"You tell 'em."

"Getting further."

"Ain't no lie."

"Long gone."

"No crap."

That was when Lil' Buddy said my home is in the briar patch. My name is Jack the Rabbit and my natural home is in the briar patch. And I said it too, and I said that was where I was bred and born.

"Goddam it to hell," Lil' Buddy said then, "why don't it come on?"

"Son of a bitch," I said.

Then I was leaning back against my tree looking out across the sandy clearing at the sky and there were clean white pieces of clouds that looked like balled-up sheets in a washtub, and the sky was blue like rinse water with bluing in it, and I was thinking about Mama again, and hoping that it was all a dream.

But then the train was really coming and it wasn't a dream at all, and Lil' Buddy jumped up.

"Come on."

"I'm here."

The engine went by, and we were running across the clearing. My ears were ringing and I was sweating, and my collar was hot and my pants felt as if the seat had been ripped away. There was nothing but the noise and we were running into it, and then we were climbing up the hill and running along the slag and cinders. We were trotting along in reach of it then. We remembered to let an empty boxcar go by, and when the next gondola came, Lil' Buddy grabbed the front end and I got the back. I hit the hotbox with my right foot and stepped onto the step and pulled up. The wind was in my ears then, but I knew about that from practicing. I climbed on up the ladder and got down on the inside, and there was Lil' Buddy coming back toward me.

"Man, what did I tell you!"

"Did you see me lam into that sucker?"

"Boy, we low more nailed it."

"I bet old Luze will be kicking it any minute now."

"Cool hanging it."

"Boy, yair," I said, but I was thinking I hope old Luze didn't change his mind. I hope we don't miss him. I hope we don't have to start out all by ourselves.

"Going boy."

"Yeah."

"*Going,*
don't know where I'm going
but I'm going
Say now I'm going
don't know when I'm going
but I'm going."

We crawled up into the left front corner out of the wind, and there was nothing to do but wait then. We knew that she was going to have to pull into the hole for Number Four when she got twelve miles out, and that was when we were going to get to the open boxcar.

We got the cigarettes out and lit up, and there was nothing but the rumbling noise that the wide-open car made then, and the faraway sound of the engine and the low-rolling smoke coming back. That was just sitting there, and after we got a little more used to the vibration, nothing at all was happening except being there. You couldn't even see the scenery going by.

It was just being there and being in that time, and you never really remember anything about things like that except the sameness and the way you felt, and all I can remember now about that part is the nothingness of doing nothing and the feeling not of going but of being taken.

All I could see after we went through the bridge was the sky and the bare floor and the sides of the gondola, and all I can remember about myself is how I wished that something would happen, because I definitely did not want to be going then, and I was lost even though I knew good and well that I was not even twelve miles from home yet. Because although we certainly had been many times farther away and stayed longer, this already seemed to be farther and longer than all the other times put together.

Then we could tell that it was beginning to slow down, and we stood up and started getting ready. And then it was stopping, and we were ready, and we climbed over and got down and started running for it. That was still in the bayou country and beyond the train smell there was the sour-sweet smell of the swamp. We were running on hard pounded slag then, and with the train quiet and waiting for Number Four, you could hear the double running of our feet echoing through the cypresses and the marshland.

The wide roadbed was almost half as high as the telegraph wires, and along the low right-of-way where the black creosote poles went along, you could see the blue and white lilies floating on the slimy green water. We came hustling hot to get to where we knew the empty car was, and then there we were.

And there old Luzana himself was.

He stood looking down at us from the door with an unlighted cigarette in his hand. We stopped dead in our tracks. I knew exactly what was going to happen then. It was suddenly so quiet that you could hear your heart pounding inside your head, and I was so embarrassed I didn't know what to do and I thought *now he's going to call us a name. Now he's never going to have anything to do with us any more.*

We were just standing there waiting and he just let us stand there and feel like two puppies with their tails tucked between their legs, and then he started talking.

"It ain't like that. It ain't like that. It just ain't like that, it just ain't."

And he was shaking his head not only as if we couldn't understand him but also as if we couldn't even hear him.

"It ain't. Oh, but it ain't."

We didn't move. Lil' Buddy didn't even dig his toe into the ground.

"So this is what y'all up to. Don't say a word, not a word. Don't open your mouth."

I could have sunk right on down into the ground.

"What the hell y'all think y'all doing? Tell me that. Tell me. Don't say a word. Don't say a goddam mumbling word to me."

We weren't even about to say anything.

"I got a good mind to whale the sawdust out of you both. That's just what I oughta do."

But he didn't move. He just stood looking down.

"Well, I'll be a son of a bitch."

That was all he said then, and then he jumped down, walked us back to where the switch frog was, and then there was nothing but just shamefaced waiting. Then Number Four came by and then finally we heard the next freight coming south and when it got there and slowed down for the switch he was standing waiting for a gondola and when it came he picked me up and put me on and then he picked Lil' Buddy up and put him on and then he caught the next car and came to where we were.

So we came slowpoking it right on back and got back in Gasoline Point before the whistles even started blowing for one o'clock. Imagine that. All of that had happened and it wasn't really afternoon yet. I could hardly believe it.

We came on until the train all but stopped for Three Mile Creek bridge and then he hopped down and took us off. He led us down the hill and went to a place the hobos used under the bridge. He sat down and lit another cigarette and flipped the match into the water and watched it float away and then he was looking at us and then he motioned for us to sit down too.

That was when he really told us what hitting the road was, and what blue steel was. He was talking evenly then, not scolding, just telling us man to boys, saying he was talking for our own good because doing what we were trying to do was more than a notion. He was talking quietly and evenly but you still couldn't face him, I know I couldn't and Lil' Buddy naturally couldn't because he never looked anybody straight in the eye anyway.

We were back and sitting under Three Mile Creek bridge and he was not really angry and then we were all eating our something-to-eat and then we could talk too, but we didn't have much to say that day. He was doing the talking and all we wanted to do was ask questions and listen.

That was when he told us all about the chain gang and the penitentiary and the white folks, and you could see everything he said and you were there too, but you were not really in it this time because it was happening to him, not you, and it was him and you were not him, you were you. You could be rawhide and you could be blue steel but you couldn't really be Luzana Cholly, because he himself was not going to let you.

Then he was talking about going to school and learning to use your head like the smart white folks. You had to be rawhide but you had to be patent leather too, then you would really be nimble, then you would really be not only a man but a big man. He said we had a lot of spunk and that was good but it wasn't good enough, it wasn't nearly enough.

And then he was talking about Negroes and white folks again, and he said the young generation of Negroes were supposed to be like Negroes and be like white folks too and still be Negroes. He sat looking out across the water then, and then we heard another freight coming and he got up and got ready and he said we could watch him but we'd better not try to follow him.

Then we were back up on the hill again and the train was coming and he stood looking at us with the guitar slung over his shoulder and then he put his hands on our shoulders and looked straight at us, and we had to look at him then, and we knew that we were not to be ashamed in front of him any more.

"Make old Luze proud of you," he said then, and he was almost pleading. "Make old Luze glad to take his hat off to you some of these days. You going further than old Luze ever even dreamed of. Old Luze ain't been nowhere. Old Luze don't know from nothing."

And then the train was there and we watched him snag it and then he was waving good-by.

The Senegalese

HOYT W. FULLER

Two spectacular additions had been made to the body of passengers aboard the Foch when I returned to the French ship after a day of wandering about Algiers. The first sight I beheld as I walked up the gangplank were several hundred African soldiers, all crowded together rather like cattle on the prow. They had been relieved of duty after two years in the Algerian War and were bound for French African ports. The soldiers wore winter-weight, olive-drab uniforms that desperately needed naphtha baths, and the uniforms were garishly garnished by shirts, socks, ties, and shoes of assorted colors and styles. Twenty-four hours earlier I had sailed from Mallorca after a year's residence, during which I had come to suspect that the omnipresent Spanish soldier was the world's least military. But, compared to these French African troops, the Spanish soldiers seemed in retrospect as martial as hand-picked hussars.

The second diverting sight aboard ship was the Senegalese.

I did not see him immediately. I stood awhile on deck watching the milling soldiers and wondering where and how so many men would eat and sleep. It was when I started below to my stateroom that I saw him. He came swaggering along the deck, looking like a defiant personification of an outrageous caricature of a Negro conjured up by an especially malicious Mississippi cartoonist.

He had the anthracite color of his race, with undertones of blue in the ebony skin, and his bulbous little eyes and nose might have been stuck as an afterthought on his apple-round face. He wore an orange-red turtleneck sweater and a tan plaid suit cut in the Italian style, featuring squared shoulders, brief jacket, and trousers that hugged his legs like ballet tights. His shoes were cinnamon suede, pointed and as immaculate as a mannequin's. He was short, but extraordinarily muscled, and the characteristic Senegalese imperiousness gave him the air of a particularly pugnacious gamecock.

He smiled as he approached. Thinking the smile was meant for someone behind me, I turned to see. There was no one. Only Europeans leaning over the railing, watching the activity on the pier. Then he was before me, holding out his hand, dazzling me with the healthiest-looking teeth on the breathing side of a toothpaste ad. The wide smile that almost never left the round face could be—I was to learn—as deceptive as it was compelling.

We shook hands vigorously.

"Hello," he said in English, his voice high-pitched and sing-songy. "You American boy, yes?"

He did not speak English well, and the few phrases and sentences he was able to construct were inordinately punctuated with the word "boy." Since I knew more French than he did English, we talked in French.

He asked the usual questions. Where was I going, and why, and had I ever been in Africa before? I told him I was en route to newly independent Guinea, that I simply wanted to meet Africans and see Africa and find out for myself what they were like, and this was my first time on the continent.

He was, he said, Louis Guèye, a chemical engineer working in Algiers, and was on his way to his native Senegal to attend a professional conference at the old city of St. Louis.

"I been in America," he said, trying his English again. He named three places which, de-Gallicized, turned out to be Alabama, New Orleans, and Kansas City. He said he had gone there with his father on business trips after World War II. He chose not to go into details, and I did not press him.

"My father is mayor of Dakar," he said.

That information impressed me. Lamine Guèye, the mayor, had been much in the French press in recent weeks. At this very moment he was playing host to eminent leaders from the French West African territories of Senegal, Sudan, Dahomey, and Niger, sitting in Constituent Assembly at Dakar. They were meeting to draw up a constitution creating the Federation of Mali, named after the ancient West African empire. Perhaps, I thought, through Louis I might be able to meet Guèye and possibly even Leopold Senghor, Senegal's celebrated poet-statesman and deputy in the Parliament at Paris, a man whose poetry I had long admired. This was January 10, 1959. The Foch would dock at Dakar the morning of January 16 and I could spend the day in the city. I said what I was thinking.

"Bon!" Louis nodded. "Later I will give you my father's address. He will be glad to do what he can do for you. I think Senghor will be in Dakar."

The gangplank was drawn and the anchor hoisted, and now the launch tugged the ship from the pier. It was cloudy, darkness had crept in from the land, and the evening breeze, unwarmed by sun, chilled the open deck. In the city, lights flickered on along the streets and in the buildings. Algiers, from the sea, is a giant hill with chains of buildings sliding down and spilling over on each flank. The Casbah, hung on one side, is a ravaged ruin in the daylight. At night all the city has the illusory glitter of a mound of brilliant jewels.

I asked Louis his opinion of Algiers, what his life was like there, and what he felt about the Algerian War still furiously raging in pockets in the mountains. He talked long, expressively, and a trifle loud, always smiling, the tiny eyes darting at passers-by. He did not like Algiers, not really. "I could never like any place ruled by the French dogs," he said. But his job was there, and his salary was good, and he would stay for a while. He said his wife was French but he did not love her, and perhaps he would divorce her on his return to Algiers and marry his Arab lover. "Sidi is traveling with me to St. Louis," he said. "She is a white girl too, you know. Beautiful. I will introduce you."

On the Algerian War he was passionately partisan. The French Army and the *colons* had committed unspeakable atrocities against the Algerian people, and the world did not know of it because the French Government suppressed all the facts. He had many friends among the Arabs who were secretly fighting the French in Algiers, and he helped them in any way he could. Even with all the rest of Europe and America aiding the French, the Algerians would win eventually. One way or another. There was no way now to permanently keep the Algerians from gaining control of their own country. "It is a thing you will live to see," he assured me, widening the smile an extra millimeter. "Not only in Algeria, but in all of Africa, the white man's days are numbered. In twenty years we will have all of them out, except the ones we want to work for us."

At length I interrupted Louis and made my excuses. I wanted to go to my cabin for awhile before dinner. Perhaps we could continue the discussion at another time. "Yes, I wish to talk with you about many things," he said. "Now I must find Sidi."

My cabinmates were a long-legged, sprightly white-haired Canadian bachelor named Johnson and a short, square, wry-humored Frenchman named Bouvet. Both men were lounging in their bunks when I entered the cabin, Mr. Johnson reading a Philip Wylie pocket-book and M. Bouvet thumbing through a copy of *Paris Match* purchased in Algiers. I had seen both men, each alone, in the city during the day, Mr. Johnson stalking along uncertainly, hands jammed in his pockets, an expression of grave concentration on his finely molded face, M. Bouvet strolling with amiable bulldog nonchalance in streets he knew very well. The Frenchman was, he said, a business representative of a firm with interests in all the French African port cities.

He was highly critical of both Americans and Africans and liked to malign them, but not, for some reason, in the presence of Mr. Johnson, although the Canadian spoke and understood virtually no French.

I had encountered M. Bouvet in Algiers in the morning while en route to the Casbah with two gentle young Africans from the ship. M. Bouvet had just come from the Casbah, he told us, and the gendarmes would allow no one to enter. Persuaded of this and characteristically wishing to infract no rules, the two Africans suggested turning back. To be agreeable, I consented. However, during the afternoon, when Ibra and Keita had returned to the ship for lunch, I entered the Casbah with no difficulty at all. I informed M. Bouvet of this.

"Ah," he grinned slyly. "The gendarmes could see you are an American. The Arabs will not harm Americans. Your country is giving them guns to kill the French."

The third-class dining room was a cheerless, claustrophobic room, small and low, with a ceiling of ivory-painted air and furnace pipes and two portholes for windows. It was furnished with eight oblong tables for eight affixed with benches, mess-hall style. A small, semicircular counter in the corner served as bar and store for both third-class passengers and crew, although most passengers preferred to use the second-class salon. The single door opened off a narrow passageway and was directly opposite the always untidy kitchen. The room's appearance, unfortunately, matched the food, an insult to the vaunted reputation of French cuisine. The room also suited the elaborately indifferent service provided by a droll French sailor and a wiry, gray-haired African with a talent for good-natured impertinence.

Third-class passengers were served in two shifts, and my cabinmates and I ate on the second one. Ours was a colorful assortment of humans. A table for two just inside the door was reserved for a flannel-robed Arab woman of tawny hue and late middle age and a sun-faced African pygmy the size of a ten-year-old at the calculated age of "around thirty." A third of the other diners were French soldiers, in and out of uniform, bound for Abidjan. There were three bearded priests in white flannel cassocks, two nuns, and several French families. Five of the people at my table were soldiers. Besides myself, the civilians were M. Bouvet and a grotesquely disfigured young Frenchman with a face that looked severely burned and twisted and only two normally developed fingers on each hand.

When I went in to dinner that evening, I saw that Louis and his Arab friend had been added to the motley assemblage. The girl, while perhaps less "beautiful" than Louis had proclaimed her, was undeniably attractive. She was petite and shapely, with hair almost as bright a red as Louis' sweater, and she had great, inscrutable black-rimmed eyes. They sat together at the table in front of the bar, facing the rear of the dining room, and were in the direct line of vision of fully half the diners, including me, every time we raised our eyes from our plates—which, I noted, was now considerably more frequent than before.

I was surprised to see Louis in the dining room. I had not really thought about it, but I suppose I had assumed he was traveling in more comfortable surroundings. After all, he was only going from Algiers to Dakar, and he was an engineer and the son of the mayor of one of Africa's principal cities. Apparently he too felt some explanation was necessary, for he raised the subject at his first opportunity. He called me to his table on my way out, introduced me to Sidi, and launched at once into his reasons for being in so plebeian a setting. "I'm traveling third-class because I'm taking along my car," he said. "It's in the hold. A Dauphine. Costs as much as a passenger, you know."

"I don't blame you at all," I said sympathetically. "It's only sensible to save money."

Louis invited me to have a beer, and I accepted. "What you think about this girl?" he asked in English, crushing Sidi against him. "She beautiful girl, yes, boy?" Sidi, understanding the import if not the words, blushed prettily, fluttering thick-lashed hazel eyes. I said she was indeed a bit of all right. "I got many such girls in Algiers, boy, in France also," Louis said. Then he thought of something he wanted to tell me and reverted to French.

"On many occasions I have passed as an American in France," he said. "My English is not very good, but people who don't speak English at all don't know that. These French people are stupid. In Marseilles and Toulon I often posed as an American."

He was rather pleased at this, so I asked what advantages the deception brought him.

"The women!" he beamed, hugging Sidi playfully. "They like American black men. I tell them I'm American and they swarm around like flies."

Louis did not look like any American Negro I had ever seen, but I recognized this meant nothing. I had often heard American whites say that all Negroes look alike to them. Possibly this was also true of the French.

"But being an American black man really comes in handy in the bars and nightclubs," Louis went on. "They do not want Africans in the places. I tell them in English, 'I not African, I American black boy, from Alabama,' and I get in everytime."

"You mean," I said, somewhat aghast, "that there's racial discrimination in bars and nightclubs in France? I saw Africans in such places all over Paris!"

Louis laughed. "Paris is not Marseilles and Toulon. It is a different story once you leave Paris."

This line of talk had little appeal for Sidi. She squirmed out of Louis' vise, smiled an apology, and left. As she undulated out of the room, Louis slapped me on the shoulder and winked. "Beautiful girl, boy. Beautiful girl."

Several African non-commisssioned officers came in to buy beers and, at Louis' invitation, joined us at the table. They all seemed interested in meeting an American Negro and asked where I was going. However, they proved rather unresponsive when I told them Conakry. One soldier, a Guinean, seemed actually embarrassed. I asked him to tell me about Conakry, but he apparently knew very little about it. "It is a nice city," he said. He had not been home since the country voted itself independent of France in September, 1958, he said. He was now being mustered out of the Army and had no idea what he would do. I asked if he could recommend a hotel in Conakry but he knew nothing about hotels. At the first opportunity he took his beer and quietly drifted to the bar, where another group of Africans had gathered.

"You work for the American Government?" asked a burly, jovial Dahomeyan.

I told him no.

"You got a job with Sékou Touré?"

"No," I laughed. "I'm simply going down to Guinea to see what it's like."

"Ah!" he grinned, rubbing his thumb and forefinger together significantly. "Then you are rich!"

Louis ordered another round of beers. When I tried to reciprocate, the Africans would not permit it. "No, you are our guest!" declared the good-humored one, throwing a heavy comradely arm about my shoulder. After hearing answers to a stream of biographical questions, however, he soon lost interest in me and joined the group at the bar. The remaining soldier, a serious, mustached Ivory Coast corporal, ordered another round of beers. He had been silent and watchful much of the time but now wanted to discuss what was on his mind.

"Do you know why the Guinean soldier did not know about the hotels?" he asked.

I confessed I didn't.

"He is an ordinary man. In Africa only Europeans and government people know about hotels and such things. Do you understand?"

"Yes," I said.

"Have you been in Paris?" he asked after a moment.

I said I had.

"There are many American black men in Paris," he said searchingly.

I agreed that there were many American Negroes in Paris.

"They are not friendly," he said. "They pass you on the street and pretend they do not see you. Why is that so?"

I said I did not know—if, indeed, it was true.

"It is true," he declared with quiet emphasis. "I lived in Paris two years, and my brother is now a student at the Sorbonne. The American black men never stop to shake hands and talk. Why? Don't they know we are brothers? It is necessary to be friends."

This was discomforting, and my French was not really up to a complex sociological reply which, in any case, would have been pulling straws. I had no answer for him. I simply looked embarrassed, as I was, and shrugged a disclaimer of personal guilt.

Louis ended the tension. He ordered more beer and plunged into a description of his apartment in Algiers. "Decorated in the smartest fashion," he said. "Everything direct from Paris. My wife selected the pieces. She is Parisian, you know, and has excellent taste."

Then he was struck with a great idea. "Look," he cried. "How

would you like to come to Algiers to visit me for a week or
two?"

I said I would like to visit Algiers but that the expense ruled
such a visit unlikely.

"No, I will send you the ticket!" he exclaimed. "I will send it
to Conakry when I get back to Algiers."

He brushed aside my protests, searching his pockets for paper
and something to write with. Finding neither, he appealed to
me. "I want your address in Conakry. I will send for you."

I loaned him my Parker ballpoint and gave him a calling
card. I told him I did not yet know where I would be staying and
that I could be reached through Poste Restante. He scribbled
that down and then asked for another card on which to write his
father's address. He also wrote a note on the card requesting
that I be received and assisted as a favor to him. I thanked him
and put the card in my wallet.

"Would you like my uncle's address in Conakry?" Louis asked
suddenly. "He can help you find out anything you want to know
there. He is head of the Post Office."

"Yes, of course," I said. "I don't really know anyone in
Conakry. I have only a couple of names from Paris. Perhaps
your uncle would be able to advise me."

He wrote another name and address on a new card I provided.

I swallowed the last of my beer, shook hands with Louis and
the corporal, and started to go. Then I realized my pen had not
been returned. I asked Louis for it and he said he had already
given it to me. We both looked in our pockets without producing
it. "Well, it certainly can't be lost," I said, as amiably as the
situation warranted. "You had it only a moment ago."

"It must be in your pockets someplace," Louis said. He then
got up from the table to speak to a soldier at the bar. The
matter, for him, was closed.

The corporal stared first at Louis, then at me. There was
neither surprise nor sympathy in his eyes.

I turned and left the room.

Among the passengers on board the Foch were an American
Negro political scientist, Clyde Williams, his French-born wife,
Lucie, and their baby, Carl. The Williamses were en route to
Kano, Northern Nigeria, where Clyde would remain for a year
observing the effects of self-government beginning in March in

that Moslem-dominated region, the largest in the Nigerian Federation. Lucie and Carl would return in the fall to Swarthmore
College, where Lucie was professor of French. They were second-
class passengers and spent some of their time in the salon. I
found them there after dinner. We were talking quietly when
Louis and Sidi entered, Sidi wearing hip-hugging green lounge
pants and black blouse. Louis waved in our direction and herded
Sidion toward the bar. I asked the Williamses if they had met
Louis. They had.

"Quite a character," Clyde said.

"He *is* a little spectacular," Lucie said discreetly.

I told them what had happened to my pen and they smiled
noncommittally. It was, after all, a serious implication. The
Williamses guided the conversation into safer channels.

While we talked I occasionally glanced across the room at
Louis. He was irrepressible, forever in motion, physically or
verbally, bouncing from one group to another, and dominating
the conversation wherever he alighted, often by plain shouting.
His voice stabbed the ears, his hands smote and carved the
air.

The Europeans in the salon also found Louis distracting.
However, there was little curiosity or humor in their regard.
Rather, they glared at him with an intense though impotent
loathing. It was as if the vain and ebullient Senegalese embodied all that white men hate and fear in black men.

And Louis, conscious of their muted hatred, drew it to him,
draped it about him like a cloak, warmed his frozen ego by its
heat and voltage. Here in essence was the dilemma of Africa:
that these white and black human beings, thrown together in
this space, their past, their present, and their future inextricably
joined by History, nevertheless found it impossible to negotiate
the simple acts of humanity that would have made them no
longer strangers. The roots of their mutual alienation reached so
deep and fastened so firm that not even the threat of doom
could shock them free. That colonialism was only a chapter in
the timeless saga of man's brutality to the human spirit was a
truth its heirs dared not teach and a truth its victims had no
desire to learn. The Europeans, blinded by an emotion com-
pounded of pride and guilt, would not recognize in Louis a
creature fashioned by their own greed and ruthlessness. And
Louis, embittered by rejection, tormented by the shame and

degradation of his blood, would go on dreaming of racial vengeance, oiling the gears that keep in motion the cycle of hate and
fear.

In the next two days I made it a point to avoid Louis. As the ship
plowed westward through the Straits of Gibraltar and on toward
Casablanca, I spent much of the time talking with Ibra Kassa,
one of the young Africans with whom I had gone into Algiers.
Ibra was returning from studying in Paris to take up a job in the
treasury department at Abidjan. Small and wiry, he was similar
in size to Louis but the Senegalese's opposite in almost every
other respect. He was soft-spoken and retiring, with alert, listening eyes and an amiable, reflective manner. He wore rimless
glasses and looked an African version of the mild-mannered
clerk. But the quiet façade shielded a quick, perceptive mind
and a formidable intellect. His information relative to the political and economic history of French-speaking Africa was ency-
clopedic, and he had in his possession a small library of
pertinent books and pamphlets. In studying world history, he
had been especially attentive to America's political and economic development, and his knowledge of American literature
was astounding. He discussed Faulkner and Wright with insight
and clarity worthy of an American literary historian.

Eventually I raised the subject of Louis. As with other African
subjects, Ibra approached it with great caution. And, as with
everyone he mentioned by name, Ibra made his reference as
positive as possible. "Louis is very young," he said of a man his
own age, "and perhaps he is enthusiastic."

Was Louis to be believed in all the things he said?

Ibra saw no reason to doubt Louis generally. "Perhaps he
exaggerates a little bit."

I did not mention the incident of the disappearing pen.

On the second morning after Algiers the Foch docked in
Casablanca harbor and I spent the day in the city. A friendly
Frenchman met at a sidewalk café drove me on a tour through
the villa-thick sector now largely inhabited by U.S. Air Force
personnel and along the white deserted beach. I walked through
the bustling medinah near the pier and tramped through the old
market quarter. In the heart of the city I saw M. Bouvet with
one of the French soldiers in civilian clothes. "What do you
think of this city?" M. Bouvet asked.

During one of his tirades against Africans, M. Bouvet had thrown in Moroccans for good measure. Like the Africans and the Algerians and the Tunisians, Moroccans were stupid and lazy and owed everything to the French. Prior to Morocco's independence, he and his family had lived in Casablanca. But, of course, they had to leave. French businesses could not remain with the government in the hands of barbarians. The city was dying since the French left, and I would see for myself when we got there.

It was obvious that many businesses were closed in Casablanca but, not having seen the city under French control, I still found it beautiful and exciting. I told M. Bouvet so.

"No, it is nothing now," M. Bouvet insisted. "I have just come from the Dragon d'Or, the best Oriental restaurant in all Africa. But *le patron* fears he will have to close. No customers. All the French have gone."

I gestured toward the flourishing shops. "But there are still businesses here," I said. "Look around you."

M. Bouvet shook his head, grinning slyly. "Ah, yes, the new businesses. They are all owned by Americans. Since the war the Americans have been coming here in droves. The Americans run Casablanca now."

A few moments later I saw Louis in the middle of the street, making inquiries of a Moroccan policeman, one of a brightly uniformed force who must be among the handsomest and most courteous police officers in the world. Louis saw me and waved. I nodded and continued on my way. On the curb I passed an Arab woman in white robe and veil, her dark eyes staring familiarly. It was with a start that I realized this was Sidi, waiting for Louis.

That evening after dinner, with the ship moving southward on the three-day voyage to Dakar, Clyde Williams approached me in the salon. "Here is your pen," he said. "Louis asked me to give it to you."

I asked what had been Louis' explanation.

"He said he had drunk too much beer and didn't remember putting it in his pocket." Clyde added: "Quite a character!"

With the return of the pen, Louis apparently assumed the rupture in our camaraderie to be automatically healed. The following morning he collared me on my way from the dining room and asked if I had received it. He briefly repeated the drunk excuse and then dismissed the whole incident. "I want you come listen hot discs, boy," he said. "I got pick-up in cabin. Fine music, boy. Belafonte. You like Belafonte?"

I said I did.

"I got many Belafonte discs," he said. "You come listen."

I said I had something else to do but that I would come and hear his music some other time.

Shortly after lunch he found me alone on the deck, leaning over the railing and trying to sight the African coast through the milky blue haze. I had seen neither land nor a passing ship since Casablanca, and only a school of porpoises cavorting around the ship had relieved the monotonous calm of the voyage and the sea. "You come listen music now?" Louis said. "I think you like, boy. Very fine music."

The simplest solution seemed to be to go along and spend a few minutes listening to records—and Louis. We descended to third-class and he led me to a cabin at the opposite end of the corridor from my own. He rapped on the door and a feminine voice inside said, in French, "Come in."

I had assumed the voice was Sidi's, but when we entered the stateroom I saw instead that it belonged to someone else. A thin African girl with whom I had seen Sidi on deck was sitting on the lower bunk. She looked surprised when she saw me and put aside the pencil and pad she had been using. She wore a bandana, a housecoat, and bedroom slippers. So, Louis and Sidi did not share a stateroom! Was this due to prudence or sensitivity to official regulations? Sidi was there also, lying in the upper bunk, a hand to her forehead. When she saw me she tried to raise up but, groaning, fell back on the bed. "Excuse me," she murmured. "I am a little bit sick."

I apologized for bursting in on them, silently cursed myself for having surrendered to Louis' entreaties, and turned to leave. Both girls protested, insisting they were put to no discomfort. Even the music would not bother them, they insisted. Meanwhile, Louis had already gone to the other end of the stateroom and was arranging the record player under the porthole.

I chatted for a few seconds with the African girl. Her name was Fanta, she was a secretary in Dakar and was returning from a vacation visit to Algiers. She had been practicing short-hand when Louis and I came in.

"Come see discs, boy," Louis called.

I went to his end of the stateroom as bidden. There was an expensive-looking leather record carrier packed with long-playing albums. The case matched that of the player itself, an attractive machine. Louis extracted several albums and displayed them on the table. Some were of French and South American popular singers and musicians with whom I was not familiar. There was a Sammy Davis Jr. album and one each by Louis Armstrong and Harry Belafonte. All albums were affixed with small stickers bearing the name, "Louis."

"What do you want to hear first?" he asked in French.

I said it didn't matter.

"Not Louis Armstrong!" he said in English, frowning in distaste. "He big clown-boy. I see him in Paris. No like clown-boy Louis."

He put the Sammy Davis Jr. album on the turntable. "He fine boy. I like."

He listened appreciatively through a few bars, cocking his head. Then he began talking, almost shouting, all but drowning the singing. He lifted the Belafonte album cover and examined the picture on it with an air that suggested he had done so many times before. "Nice boy, Belafonte," he said. "I know Belafonte in Paris." He asked if I had ever met the singer, and I said I had been introduced to him when he visited the office where I worked in Chicago. This interested Louis very much. He dug out several other Belafonte albums and studied the pictures on them. They all showed Belafonte as being a rose-tan color. Finally Louis asked if Belafonte was a Negro. He asked the question in French, with deliberate casualness, as if the answer —whatever it would be—could only confirm what he already knew.

I said that in America Belafonte was a Negro.

Louis was silent a moment. Then, with the same studied nonchalance, he asked if Clyde Williams was a Negro. Clyde is what Negroes in the South sometimes term "muddy-yellow," the color of sun-bleached clay. I said that Clyde was also a Negro. "And his wife?" I said that Lucie was white, a native of France. "*Ah, elle est francaise!*" he exclaimed, nodding his head, the fact of her French origins apparently explaining the phenomenon of her union with an American Negro.

At this point a knock sounded on the door. Fanta opened it to admit a nun. The Sister spoke to everyone, said something sympathetic to Sidi, and settled on the bed beside Fanta. They talked in low, confidential tones. It seemed a splendid opportunity to take my leave and I proceeded to do so. "Don't go," Louis whispered, winking toward the nun. "She is trying to convert Fanta to Catholicism. She has been annoying Fanta since Algiers. We are all Moslems. The stupid Frenchwoman is wasting her time."

I said good-by and went to my own cabin.

For the remainder of that day and most of the next I saw Louis only at meals. I spent much of the time in my cabin reading material loaned me by Ibra and Clyde and, unavoidably, chatting with my cabinmates. Mr. Johnson, especially, had to be contended with. He liked to talk, and since he knew only a few words of French, aimed much of his conversation at me. He had retired from a Toronto bank, had sailed on to England, and now was en route to Johannesburg by way of French West Africa, Nigeria, and the Central African Federation. He would debark at Dakar and travel overland to Nigeria. Time did not matter. It was only important that he be back in London at Christmas, 1959.

M. Bouvet slept more and talked less, but felt compelled to periodically air grievances against the villains of his life. "Why are Americans always boasting?" he asked, referring to American tourists observed at Bordeaux. I suggested, tauntingly, that it might be because they have so much to boast about. "Bah!" he growled. "We have automobiles, houses, and refrigerators in France also. The difference is that the French don't waste their money on frivolous things. They put it in the bank."

Like Mr. Johnson, M. Bouvet was leaving the ship at Dakar. Since he knew all the French port cities, I asked him about Conakry and its facilities. He gave a rundown on the city that, though unflattering, later proved rather exact. He recommended a hotel and a restaurant which I found adequate and reasonable, something none of the Guinean soldiers had been able to do. "But Conakry is a city without imagination, laid out like a box," he complained, abusing the French-planned city as if its ugliness was further proof of the inability of Africans. "Conakry is a terrible place. The worst in French Africa."

My next encounter with Louis occurred in the salon, where I

had joined the Williamses after dinner. The room was nearly filled, for the closer the ship sailed to Black Africa the freer the African soldiers moved about the salon and decks. They gathered in groups and at the bar, singing, arguing, horsing around. The civilian passengers remained aloof from the Africans, their exaggerated disregard testifying to their acute awareness. But their mask of indifference invariably dissolved whenever Louis appeared. He entered the salon now, with Sidi, wearing his fire-engine sweater.

Louis beamed a greeting at us as they passed, and a few minutes later returned to our table alone, having deposited Sidi with Fanta and a group of African soldiers. "Good evening," he greeted us in his inimitably happy way. "You are well, yes?"

We invited him to sit down. "For small time," he said in English. We talked at random, as the feeling was general that Louis had something on his mind. He became uncharacteristically quiet, the round little eyes darting from Clyde to me. Finally, with no sign of embarrassment, he said: "You two are very handsome. You are like Belafonte, only Belafonte looks more like a woman. Africans are not big and broad-shouldered like you. When the white men came to Africa they took away all the big strong men and left behind only the puny ones. That is why we are so small."

Lucie, concerned that Carl might awaken in the dark cabin, went to look in on him. When she had gone, Louis said he thought her a very fine woman. So unlike most whites. Then, drawing his provocation from private sources, he harangued the white race. "They have spread evil all over the world, everywhere they set their rotten feet."

"Are white people really so bad as all that?" Clyde asked reproachfully.

"Yes, yes, nearly all white people are dogs!" Louis nodded, keeping the wide smile on his face.

"Well, don't you think that racism is just as objectionable when indulged by black people as when practiced by whites?" Clyde asked.

Louis dismissed Clyde's reasoning with a chesty laugh. Abruptly, he decided it was time to rejoin his friends. He said good-by, got up, and strutted across the room.

The next day was the date of the traditional ship's gala, and the mood became festive toward evening. I had spent a rather grueling hour or so after lunch with an English-speaking Frenchman who had been to Norfolk and Mobile and who was intent upon sympathizing with me over racial oppression in the United States, and I headed for the salon and a cognac when the session was over. The Williamses were talking with a French administrator traveling to Cotonou, so I sat with Ibra and an African soldier. Africans were more numerous than ever in the room and those Europeans present seemed for the occasion more relaxed among them. Voices were raised a few octaves above normal, and Louis', unsurprisingly, was clearly distinguishable from time to time. It rose from the direction of the bar, where the crowd was several layers deep.

There came a sudden roar from the bar that softened the general din. Then Louis' sharp voice stung the near-silence like an angry wasp. "Shut up!" he shouted. And though the salon was soundless he repeated the words viciously. "Shut up!"

A bearded, middle-aged Swiss journalist charged through the ring around the bar, his face beety with rage and humiliation. He stalked across the room to where his friend the French administrator was sitting with the Williamses. At their invitation he sat down.

The soldier at our table went to find out what had happened at the bar. He reported that Louis simply had disagreed with the journalist's views on Africa, and the ensuing argument was climaxed by the commands we all heard.

The journalist was sailing to Conakry but, on the advice of his French friend, arranged at Dakar to by-pass Guinea. He was told that conditions were generally disorganized in the country since the departure of the French and that it would be safer to continue on to Abidjan. I wondered how much Louis' display of hostility had influenced the journalist's decision not to go to a territory governed entirely by Africans.

After dinner Louis appeared in the salon looking especially dapper in a gray suit, a girl on each arm. Sidi wore a white sheath and Fanta a gayly flowered print. Louis found a table and made a series of trips over the room—to speak to friends, to order drinks, to buy cigarettes. He stopped to ask if I was going to attend the gala and I told him I had planned to read. "Come, I buy champagne," he urged. "We have fine time, boy." I promised to seek him out if I changed my mind.

The following morning the Williamses reported that Louis was in top form during the festivities, culminating in his arresting performance on the ballroom floor with a spirited cha-cha-cha with an African soldier.

I did not talk with Louis again until the morning the Foch docked at Dakar. A considerable percentage of the European passengers were leaving the ship, my cabinmates among them, and the passageways and stairs were choked with luggage and traffic. To keep out of the way until the bustle had subsided, I sat on Mr. Johnson's now-deserted bunk and watched the activity on the pier through the porthole. M. Bouvet was out but Mr. Johnson was there, seated at the desk, fussing with the police landing card he had been given the night before. He had reached the question inquiring into his marital status and seemed stumped. He kept rubbing his forehead and tapping his pen on the desk. Finally he solicited my opinion. "What should I write here?" He asked. I suggested that he write simply, "Not married." He considered that a moment and apparently decided against it. "How do you say celibate in French?" he asked, with not a hint of a smile.

I said good-by to Mr. Johnson and mounted the steps to the deck. Several great ships were docked in berths of the mighty harbor, and the white modern skyline of the city loomed impressively beyond. Near the gangplank I saw Louis, giving instructions concerning his luggage to two African porters. Sidi stood beside him. She had changed again into her white robe and veil, and her dark eyes peered bewitchingly from their window.

When Louis saw me, he came forward, extending his hand. "Ah, I had been looking for you," he said in French. "You must call on my father today. I will not be at home, for I am leaving directly for St. Louis. But he will be at your service. You have my uncle's address in Conakry, and you will receive a letter from me within the week."

Louis paused a moment, his eyes fastened on mine, the broad grin on his face. He gestured his head toward the city. "You are really in Africa now, my friend," he said. "Someday soon perhaps you will return here. The white man will be gone, and it will be great."

He shook hands and returned to the top of the landing. Sidi, going before him, raised a pale arm and waved farewell. I waved back to her.

"She is nothing but a prostitute, you know," a familiar voice behind me said in French. I turned to find M. Bouvet, valise in hand, smiling roguishly.

"Oh," I made a sound of surprise. "Are you sure?"

"Of course," he replied. "They all are."

I spent most of the day in Dakar with the Williamses, walking over the exotic city, visiting the U.S. Information Service center, and trying to avoid the enervating heat. Much of the walking was done in a futile effort to locate Leopold Senghor, whom the Williamses also wanted to meet. The search led to the modernistic territorial assembly building where the Mali Federation meetings had been in progress and through the palm-bordered government center.

Louis would have seemed far less spectacular had I first seen him in this environment, I realized. The busy streets and teeming markets abounded with faces similar to his. Everywhere the blue-black men in shorts and robes and their proud, graceful, rainbow-costumed women ambulated along, self-assured and incontestably at home.

We failed to find Senghor, and I made no try at seeing the mayor. A phone call to his office determined that he was in conference. There was not, in any event, much time.

Weeks later, however, I spent several days in Dakar awaiting a plane connection to Lisbon, and time was not a problem. I decided to visit Lamine Guèye's home, intending only to pay my respects and depart. I took a taxi to the address Louis had written on my calling card. It was a four-story building in a crowded but clean neighborhood not far from the pier. On the third floor I found the door with the name "Guèye" engraved on a brass plate and rang the bell. I was surprised when a pretty, young blue-eyed blond Frenchwoman opened the door.

I introduced myself, explained how I came to call unexpected, and presented the card with Louis' message on it. The lady read the card and smiled. "You have the wrong address," she said.

"This is not the home of Lamine Guèye?" I asked, confounded.

She shook her head sympathetically. "Many people make that mistake because of the similarity in names," she said. "My husband is Louis Guèye, a lawyer."

She invited me to come inside while she wrote down the mayor's address and phone number, which she knew by heart. I waited in the cool and pleasant living room. A young African boy in white jacket was setting a table on the terrace under a mosquito net, and a little girl, blonde and blue-eyed like her mother, played alone on the floor. When Madame Guèye brought the paper with the mayor's address written on it, I thanked her and left.

Walking down the dark stairwell to the street I could only chuckle, recalling the image of the fantastic little Senegalese. I had no clue to the reason for the wrong address. Possibly he had at some previous time plucked it from a phone book expressly to use in a bizarre and deceptive game. I wondered anew just how much truth there was in all Louis' stories. Not much that was provable, in any case. That morning at the pier he had gone down the gangplank and climbed into a taxi, not bothering to collect the Dauphine supposedly in the ship's hold. The postmaster at Conakry did not answer to the name on my calling card, and the man had never heard of Louis Guèye. Chances were better than even that Lamine Guèye had never heard of him either. But I would make no effort to discover Louis' relationship with the mayor. It did not really seem so important. While finding that out might have revealed Louis as not what he claimed to be, it would not have changed in the least the meaning of what he was.

A Matter of Time

Frank London Brown

Handfuls of lemon-colored leaves clung to the blackening limbs and twigs of the boscage along the road near the house. A dull tuft smoked from the cabin's chimney. Fall. Willie Lee was getting restless. The mill was about due to reopen. And Mary Kate's maid-money from Mrs. Rice had stopped coming in. Mr. Rice himself was in a world of money troubles. He was a book-keeper at the mill and even he was laid off and broke. This meant that he and Mrs. Rice had to lay Mary Kate off. It was a mess all the way around.

Willie Lee walked to the steps in front of the porch. It careened like an overloaded skiff and Willie grabbed the banister to keep from falling. He decided to fix that thing this year for sure.

He turned around and went back out the yard, pulling his pants up and tucking in his shirt tails. He was very tall, and he wore a set of long, bushy sideburns. Once he'd seen a picture of Frederick Douglass and had thought about wearing a beard like Douglass', but he'd changed his mind and settled for sideburns. Abraham, his stub-tailed hound, got up when Willie walked back into the yard. He wagged his stub and followed Willie to the big persimmon tree. Willie sat on the ground and started to play with the dog's long, flappy ears. What to do, what to do.

The screen door slammed and a screaming little girl tumbled onto the porch. It slammed again and a little boy hurried after her. The girl, dark and very skinny, jumped off the porch and fled squealing to Willie. The boy stopped, tucked his plaid shirt in exactly the same way Willie did, and pursued the girl again, diving at her and crashing into Willie's chest.

Willie stood and slapped his thighs and started to cough in the brown fog that rose from his overalls.

"Now you little scounds just quit it! Make somebody break his nake."

The girl lifted a circle of dust around Willie, and the boy followed in her wake, making growling noises and screwing up his face. Abraham yapped into the battle and Willie slapped his thighs again.

"Dad-blast it! Stop that commotion! It's too hot. It's too hot, you-*heah!*"

"Florida hit me, daddy!"

"I did not!"

Abraham yapped, Willie walked away grumbling, and the children streaked into a path that bent through a plot of strong black trees and fallen leaves with orange edges. Willie watched them run:

"Don't you-all go too far. Your mother'll be after me if you go too far."

They zig-zagged through the shadows and branches, Abraham yelping and scrambling to keep up, and they did not answer.

Willie Lee got up. He started back into the house. He stopped.

Something very bad hit him in the chest. This was the second time. The first time was last spring, in the plant. He was unloading a bale of cotton for the mattress fillers. He'd thought at first that it was indigestion, but the pain went from bad to worse and before he knew anything, he had dropped the hand truck with the bale of cotton on it, and stood there heaving and gasping for breath, hurting in the chest like the devil.

The foreman noticed him and ran up and started hitting him on the back. It seemed to help and he caught his breath and sat down for a minute. The foreman was a signifying old something:

"You'd better take it easy with them young girls. Willie Lee. You look like you was goin' on away from here."

Willie Lee tried to smile, but he couldn't do it. The pain was still filling his chest, and he felt weak. Verlee, the foreman, watched him for a moment, then called:

"Luther! Sammy! Y'all come and do something with this cotton. I think Willie Lee's had too much of that young stuff. He can't get his breath."

Willie Lee started to reach for the cotton:

"I'm all right. I can make it okay."

Sammy and Luther hesitated. Willie Lee stooped to the cotton and started to lift it back to the hand truck. Sammy and Luther quickly put hands to the bale and Willie Lee grabbed the handles of the hand truck and took the cotton to the bat-head machine.

That was the first time.

Now it was happening again. Willie stood near the great tree, weaving and gasping for breath. The pounding in his chest beat against his ears and in the thick of his tongue. He called Bubba, but his voice was too weak to carry. He sat down. The pain was back again and it was getting bad. He called his daughter, Florida. Still no more than a croak from his throat. He lay on his back, but that hurt even more. He lay on his side. It was no good. He sat up, and another pain screamed out of the old one. This was worse than any of the others. He pulled his shirt open at the neck.

His stomach started doing something funny. It didn't feel so hot. He tried to scream, but this time nothing came.

The sky began to move. The trees turned baby blue, and the house wobbled and rippled and went gray.

He thought about Mary Kate. He heard the children's voices.

Abraham barked. Voices came near him. Then they washed away. The barking grew louder. He felt another pain, and the sky and the trees and the house went real light blue and melted into the voices and the barking.

He felt something rough and wet slide across his hand. Now a barking again. He heard some squeals, and somebody called his name. He tried to answer. When Mary Kate reached him, he was dead.

He was buried the next Friday. On the following Monday, the plant called the men back to work.

Cry for Me

WILLIAM MELVIN KELLEY

This is about my Uncle Wallace, who most of you know by his last name—Bedlow—because that's all they ever put on his records. I only got one of his albums myself. It has a picture of him on it, sitting, holding his two guitars, wearing his white dinner jacket, his mouth wide open and his eyes squinted shut. The name of the album is: *Bedlow—Big Voice Crying in the Wilderness* and I got it in particular because it has the only two songs he sang that I really like: *Cotton Field Blues* and *John Henry*. Besides that, I don't much like folk songs or folk singers. But I liked Uncle Wallace all right.

I guess I should tell you about the first time I met Uncle Wallace; this was even before he was folk singing, or maybe before any of us *knew* it. We just knew he was a relative, my old man's brother, come North from the South.

That was in June of 1957. We went to Pennsylvania Station to meet him. He sent us a telegram; there wasn't enough time for him to write a letter because, he told us later, he only decided to come two days before he showed up.

So we went to the station, and the loud-speaker called out his train from down South. A *whole* bunch of colored people got off

the train, all looking like somebody been keeping it a secret
from them they been free for a hundred years, all bulgy-eyed and
confused, carrying suitcases and shopping bags and boxes and
little kids.

My old man was craning his neck, looking to find Uncle
Wallace. None of us would-a recognized him because when my
old man come North twenty years ago he didn't bring but one
picture of Uncle Wallace and that was of him when he was
about seven. But my old man been back South once and saw
Uncle Wallace a man. He would recognize him all right.

But I heard my old man say to my mother, "Don't see him
yet."

And then we did see him; we could not-a missed him because
he come rumbling out the crowd—the size of a black Grant's
Tomb with a white dinner jacket draped over it (he had the
jacket even then, having won it in some kind-a contest driving
piles, or cutting wood)—and punched my old man square in the
chops so he flew back about twenty feet, knocking over this little
redcap, and springing all the locks on the four suitcases he was
carrying, scattering clothes in all directions like a flock of
pigeons in Central Park you tossed a rock at.

My old man is about six-five and two-fifty and works in heavy
construction and I ain't never seen anyone hit him, let alone
knock him off his feet, and I thought sure he'd go nuts and get
mad, but he didn't; he started to laugh, and Uncle Wallace stood
over him and said: "How you doing, Little Brother? I see you
ain't been keeping up your strength. Use to have more trouble
with you when I was six." And he reached out his hand to my
old man, who got up, and even though he was on his feet still
looked like he was lying down because Uncle Wallace was at
least a head taller.

My old man said, "Never could beat you, Wallace. Pa's the
only man could." And I remember figuring how to be able to do
that, my Grandpa Mance Bedlow must-a been close to eight feet
tall and made of some kind of fireproof metal.

Then my old man turned to us and said: "I'd like you to meet
my family. This is my wife, Irene." He pointed at my mother.
"And this is Mance; we call him Little Brother." He pointed at
my brother. "And this is my first-born, Carlyle junior." And he
pointed at me and I reached up my hand to Uncle Wallace
before I realized he'd probably crush it. He took it, but didn't

crush it at all, just squeezed it a little and smiled, looking down at me out tiny, red eyes in his black-moon face.

So we took Uncle Wallace home to the Bronx.

My old man got him a job with the same construction company he worked for, and the foreman, he'd send them both up on the girders and give them enough work for eight men and they'd get it done, and then they'd come home and Uncle Wallace'd watch television until one and then go to sleep. He never seen it before and it knocked him out.

He hadn't seen anything of New York but our house and the building he and my old man was practically putting up single-handed. That's why one Friday night, my old man said: "Carlyle, why don't you take old Wallace downtown and show him the city?"

I really didn't want to go; I mean, that's *nowhere*, getting stuck with a man could be your father, but I went.

First I took him to Harlem near where we used to live and we said hello to some of my old friends who was standing in front of a bar, watching the girls swishing by in dresses where you could see everything, either because the dresses was so tight over what they should-a been covering, or because there wasn't no dress covering the other parts. I guess Uncle Wallace liked that pretty much because everybody was colored and where we live in the Bronx, everybody is Italian. So in Harlem, he must-a felt at home.

Then we went to Times Square. I don't think he liked that too much, too big and noisy for him, him being right out of a cotton field. I was about to take him home, but then I said: "Hey, Uncle Wallace, you ever seen a queer?"

He looked down at me. "What's that, Carlyle?"

I was about to laugh because I figured maybe he ain't seen a queer, but I would-a thought *everybody* knew what they was. But then I decided just to explain—I knew how strong he was, but hadn't been knowing him long enough to know how fast he got mad. So I just told him what a queer was.

He looked down at me blank and sort of stupid. "No stuff?"

"I wouldn't lie to you, Uncle Wallace." I took him by the arm. "Come on, I'll show you some queers."

That's why we went to Greenwich Village.

It was comical to see him looking at his first queer, who was as queer as a giraffe sitting on a bird's nest. Uncle Wallace just gaped like he seen a farmer hitch a chipmunk to a plow, then turned to me. "Well, I'll be lynched, Carlyle!"

After that we walked around past the handbag and sandal shops and the coffee houses and dug the queers and some girls in sort of black underwear, and then all of a sudden, he wasn't with me no more. I turned all the way around, a little scared because if he would-a got his-self lost, I'd never see him again. He was halfway back up the block, his head way above everybody else's like he was standing on a box, and a look on his face like he been knocked up side his head with a cast-iron Cadillac. I ran back up to him, but by the time I got to where he been standing, he was most down some steps leading into a cellar coffee shop called *The Lantern*. I called to him but he must-a not heard me over the singing that was coming from inside. He was already at the door and a cross-eyed little blond girl was telling him to put a dollar in the basket she was tending. So I followed him down, paid my dollar, and caught up to him. "Hey, Uncle Wallace, what's the matter?"

He put his hand on my shoulder, grabbing it tight so I could hear the bones shift around. "Hush, boy." And then he turned to this little lit-up stage and there was this scrawny yellow Negro sitting on a stool playing the guitar and singing some folk song. He was wearing a green shirt open to his belly button, and a pair of tight black pants. What a queer!

The song he was singing was all about how life is tough—he looked like the toughest day he ever spent was when his boy friend didn't serve him breakfast in bed—and how when you're picking cotton, the sun seems to be as big as the whole sky. The last line was about how he'd pick all the cotton in the world and not plant no more and wouldn't have to work again and how he'd finally win out over the sun. When he finished, everybody snapped their fingers, which is what they do in the Village instead of clap.

Then he said: "And now, ladies and gentlemen, this next piece is another from the collection of Francis Mazer, a song he found during his 1948 trip through the South. A blues called *Wasn't That a Man.*" He struck a chord and started to sing: something about a Negro who swum a flooded, raging river with his two sons and his wife tied on his back. He sang it very fast so all the words ran together.

Uncle Wallace listened through one chorus, his eyes narrow-

ing all the time until they about disappeared, and then he was
moving, like a black battleship, and I grabbed his coat so he
wouldn't make a fool of his-self in front of all them white folks,
but then I just let him go. It was his business if he wanted to act
like a nigger, and I couldn't stop him anyway. So I just stood
there watching him walk in the dark between the little tables
and looming out in the spotlight, burying the yellow Negro in
his shadow.

Uncle Wallace reached out and put his hand around the neck
of the guitar and the notes choked off. His hand must-a gone
around the neck about three times.

The yellow Negro looked up at him, sort of shook. "I beg your
pardon?"

"Brother, you better start begging somebody's pardon for what
you doing to that song. You sings it all wrong."

Then a bald man in a shirt with the points of the collar all
twisted and bent come up and patted Uncle Wallace on the
back, hard. "Come on, buddy. Let's move out."

Uncle Wallace about-faced and looked way down at him.
"Brother, next time you come up behind me and touch me, you'll
find yourself peeping at me out of that guitar."

The bald man took a step back. Uncle Wallace looked at the
yellow Negro again. "Now, look-a-here, colored brother, you
can't sing my songs that way. You sing them like I made them
up or don't sing them at all. And if you *do* sing them your way,
then you may just never sing again, ever." He was still holding
the neck of the guitar.

"Your songs? You didn't write these songs," the yellow Negro
said. "They grew up out of the Rural Southern Negro Culture."

"Go on, nigger! They grew up out-a me. That song you was
just singing now, about the man and the river, I wrote that song
about my very own Daddy."

A couple people in the audience started to sit up and listen.
But that little yellow flit of a Negro didn't believe it. "I tell you,
these songs were collected in 1948 by Francis Mazer, and
there's no telling how long they've been sung. I heard the
original tapes myself."

Uncle Wallace's eyes went blank for a second. Then he said:
"What this Francis Mazer look like? He a little old gray-haired
man with a game leg?"

That stopped the yellow Negro for a while. "Yessss." He held onto the word like he didn't want to let it out.

"Sure enough, I remember him. He was a mighty sweet old gentleman, told me all he wanted to do was put my songs on a little strip of plastic. I asked him if he meant to write *all* my songs on that small space. He said I got him wrong, that the machine he had with him would make a record of them. And I said for him to go on. I was playing a dance and the folks was happy and I sang from Friday night until the next afternoon, and that little gentleman stood by just putting them spools in his machine and smiling. And when I got done he give me thirty dollars, U.S. currency, and I went out and bought me some new strings and a plow too." Uncle Wallace stopped and shook his head. "Mighty sweet old gentleman. And you say his name was Mazer?"

"This has gone far enough!" The yellow Negro was real ticked off now, sort of cross like a chick. "Arthur, get him out of here." He was talking to the bald man.

Uncle Wallace looked at the bald man too, sort of menacing. Then he looked at the yellow Negro. "I don't want you singing my songs *at all*." Then he just walked away, out of the lights and it was like the sun come up on the yellow Negro all at once.

But the bald man wouldn't let it stop there and said: "Hey, you, mister, wait!" He was talking to Uncle Wallace, who didn't stop because (he told me later) he never in his life got called *Mister* by no white man, so he thought the bald man was talking to someone else.

The bald man run after him and was about to put his hand on his shoulder, but remembered what Uncle Wallace said before and hot-footed it around in front of him and started to talk, backing up. "I'm Arthur Friedlander. I own this place. If you're what you say you are, then I'd like you to sing some songs."

That stopped Uncle Wallace, who told me once he'd sing for anybody, even a president of a White Citizen's Council, if he got asked. So he came to a halt like a coal truck at a sudden red light and looked down on Mister Friedlander and said: "You want me to sing?"

And Mister Friedlander said: "If you can. Sure, go on."

"But I ain't brung my guitars."

"He'll let you use his. Go on." He reached out sort of timid, like at a real mean dog, and took Uncle Wallace's arm and started to lead him back to the lights.

The yellow Negro, he didn't really want to give up his guitar, but I guess he figured Mister Friedlander would fire him if he didn't, so he left it resting against the stool and stormed off the stage.

Uncle Wallace and Mister Friedlander went up there and Uncle Wallace picked up the guitar and ran his fingers over the strings. It looked like he was holding a ukulele.

Mister Friedlander looked at the audience and said: *"The Lantern* takes pleasure in presenting a new folk singer." He realized he didn't know Uncle Wallace's name and turned around.

"Bedlow," Uncle Wallace said, sort-a shy.

"Bedlow," said Mister Friedlander to the audience.

A couple people giggled and a couple others snapped their fingers, but they was joking. Uncle Wallace whacked the guitar again, and all of a sudden music come out of it. I was surprised because way down deep I thought sure Uncle Wallace was just a fool. He didn't play right off, though, just hit it a couple times and started to talk:

"That song the other fellow was playing, I wrote that when my Daddy died, for his funeral. That was 1947. It's all about how when I was a boy we had a flood down home and where we was living got filled up with water. There was only one safe, high spot in that country—an island in mid-river. But none of us could swim but my Daddy, so he tied me and my brother on his back and my Mama, she hung on and he swum the whole parcel of us over. So everybody remembered that and when he was taken I made a song about it to sing over his trench . . ." He hit another chord, but still didn't sing yet, just stopped.

"Say," he said, "anybody got another guitar?"

Some folks started mumbling about him being a fake and stalling and a couple of them laughed. I was thinking maybe they was right.

A white boy with a beard come up with a guitar case and opened it and reached over a guitar to Uncle Wallace and so now he had two guitars. I thought he didn't like the yellow Negro's guitar, but he started to get them in the same tune— hitting one and then the other. And when he judged they was all right, he put one on his left knee, with his left hand around the neck like anybody would hold a guitar, and then put the other one on his right knee and grabbed the neck of that one with his right hand. His arms was way out and he looked like he was about to fly away. Then he clamped his fingers down on the strings of them both so hard and so fast they both sounded, not just a little noise, but a loud chord like an organ in church, or two men playing guitars. Then he started to stamp his feet and clamp his fingers and you could hear the blues get going and then he was singing . . .

Well, not really, because the most you could say about his voice was that it was on key, and it was sure loud! It wasn't deep and hollow, or high and sweet. It didn't even sound like singing. In fact, I don't think anybody ever heard him sing or really listened to him. It wasn't a voice you heard or listened to; it was a voice you swallowed, because it always seemed to upset your stomach. I heard him sing lots of times and it was always the same: not hearing anything, but feeling kind of sick, like you been drinking a gallon of wine, and the wine was fighting you inside, grabbing at your belly and twisting it around so you wanted to yell out, but didn't because you was scared the wine might take offense and tear you to pieces. And when he stopped and the grabbing stopped, you'd feel all weak and terrible, like maybe you would feel if you gotten a date with a girl you thought might give you some tail and you been thinking about it all day in school and then you went out with her and when you took her home, her folks was out, and so she took you inside and you *did* get some tail and now that it was all over, you wished she'd run inside and not given you anything because then it wouldn't be all over now and you'd still have it to look forward to. But pretty soon he'd start singing again and everything would be like it was before, feeling sick, and wishing you was *still* sick when you didn't feel sick no more.

So that's the way it was that Friday in the Village; that's the way it always was. And the people was always the same. When he got through grabbing at them, no one snapped their fingers; no one ordered anything. The cooks come out the kitchen and the waitresses sat down with the customers. People come down the steps and paid their money and managed to get into a seat before he reached out and caught them, and when the seats was all gone—because nobody left—people kept coming until they was standing and sitting in the aisles, packed right to the doors, and even on the stage with him, nobody moving or making a sound, just getting sick in the stomach and hating it and loving it all at the same time.

So Uncle Wallace sang right until Saturday morning at four. And then we went home and I slept all day.

That was how we found out what Uncle Wallace was, or did. But for a while after he sang that Friday, he didn't sing no more. It was like before: Uncle Wallace going to work, him and my old man building their building, coming home, and Uncle Wallace gassing himself on TV until one, then going to sleep.

But then the phone call came from Mister Friedlander and I answered it. He sounded real tired and said: "Hello? Is this the Bedlow residence? Do you have someone living with you or know of someone named Bedlow who sings folk songs?"

And when I answered the questions Yes, there was a silence and then I could hear sobbing on the other end of the line and through all the sobbing, him saying, "Thank God; Thank God," for about five minutes.

So at first I was about to hang up because I heard of guys calling up and cursing at women and all that mess, but then he said: "Who am I talking to?" I told him. "You were with that man who sang in my place four weeks ago? *The Lantern*? I'm Arthur Friedlander." So I said Hello, because I remembered him. He asked me what Uncle Wallace was to me and I told him.

"Carlyle," he said, "I've been trying to find your uncle for three weeks. I called Bedfords and Bradfords for the first two. It's like this, kid, every night a hundred people come into the place and ask for him and I have to say he isn't here and they get so mad they go away. He's ruining me! Where's your uncle now?"

I told him Uncle Wallace was at work.

"Listen, kid, there's a five in it for you if you can get him down here tonight by seven-thirty. And tell him I'll pay him thirty—no, make that fifty a week."

I said I could only *try* like I figured it might be hard to get Uncle Wallace to sing. Mister Friedlander give me his number and told me to call him back when I had an answer and hung up.

When Uncle Wallace come home, I said: "That man you sang for a month ago?—he wants you to come again . . . for money." I didn't have to add the money part because I could tell by his face, he was ready to go.

So I called back Mister Friedlander and told him we was coming. I said that to get Uncle Wallace to sing, which he hadn't wanted to do, I had to say Mister Friedlander was paying him seventy-five dollars a week.

Mister Friedlander didn't even seem surprised. He just said, "But you got him to come?"

"Yes, sir," I said.

"Good boy! I'm giving you ten dollars instead of five." Which is what I figured he'd do if I told him I had trouble.

When we turned the corner into *The Lantern*'s block there was a riot going on, with a hundred people, maybe even a thousand there, not all Village people neither. A whole bunch of them was in suits, and fur coats, and jewels. Man, if I been a pickpocket I could-a retired on what I could-a got there that night. And there was cops in their green cars with flashing lights going off and on, and on horses. Folks was pushing each other into the gutter and throwing punches. I looked up at Uncle Wallace and said: "Hey, we better split. We ain't got nothing to do with this, and you know how cops pick on colored folks."

"But I promised the man I'd sing, Carlyle," he said. But I could tell it wasn't that: he just wanted to sing, promise or no promise.

So we tried to sneak around behind all the rioting to get into *The Lantern*. And we most made it, but someone said: "Is that him?"

And someone answered: "Got to be."

I poked Uncle Wallace and said: "Now we really better get out-a here. These white folks think you done something."

"What?" he asked.

"I don't know, but we better get out-a here, *now*." And I grabbed his arm and started to pull him away, out-a there. I could tell he didn't want to go; he wanted to sing, but I figured I had to keep him out-a jail if I could.

Then someone started to yell at us to stop and I turned around to see how big they was and if there was more than we could handle, because either Uncle Wallace could flatten them

or we could outrun them. But it was Mister Friedlander, chugging up the stairs, yelling.

We stopped.

He got to us and said, "What's wrong'?'

"They think Uncle Wallace did something. He didn't do
nothing. We just got here. We don't know nothing about this
riot."

"Come inside. I'll explain," Mister Friedlander said. So we
went down the stairs and inside, and he locked the door.

The place was jammed! There was more people there than
that first Friday night.

Mister Friedlander said: "After you called, I put a sign in the
window saying: *Bedlow here tonight.* Those people, they're here
to see him. That's what the riot is." Then he asked me if I read
that New York Sunday paper which weighs so much and ain't
got no funnies. I told him No.

"Well, that Friday night your Uncle Wallace was here, there
was a guy here from that paper. And the next Sunday he wrote
an article—wait, I'll show you." So he ran behind the counter
and come out with this page of a newspaper that he got
magnified around forty times and pasted on cardboard. At the
top of the page was this title: *Big Voice Crying in the Wilderness.*

The article under it was about Uncle Wallace. It told all about
that other Friday night and said that Uncle Wallace was a voice
speaking for all the colored folks and that to hear him was to
understand the pain of discrimination and segregation and all
that kind of stuff, which seemed like a lot of B-S to me because I
didn't understand Uncle Wallace hardly myself; I didn't understand why he sang folk songs when he could sing rock-and-roll
or jazz. So how the hell could he be *my* voice or the voice of
anybody like me? But that's what this writer said anyway.

When I looked up from the story I must-a been frowning, or
maybe looked like I didn't get it, because Mister Friedlander
grabbed me by the shoulders and shook me. "Don't you see?
Your uncle is the hottest thing to hit New York since the
Chicago Fire. He's a fad!"

And all the time he was telling me this, Uncle Wallace was
standing by the window looking out at the people, not realizing
this was all about him. That was when I started to dig something about him I never had before, and when I started to really

like him and decided I'd have to look after him, even though he
was old enough and big enough and smart enough to look after
his-self: Uncle Wallace was innocent. To him you didn't sing
for money, or for people even, but because you wanted to. And I
guess the most important thing was that he wasn't some guy
singing about love who never loved, or hard work who never
worked hard, because he done all that, loved women and picked
cotton and plowed and chopped trees. And even though he was
in show business, he wasn't at all like anybody else in it. He was
more real somehow.

Anyway, I could say he was better that night than he was
before, but that wouldn't be really honest because I didn't dig
his music so I don't know if he was better or not. I think the
people liked him better, but I can't be sure of *that* either because
when he finished, they was in so much pain, they never snapped
their fingers for him, just sat staring, sad and hurting like
before.

After he sung three sets and was sitting back in the kitchen
drinking gin and fruit juice, this man come in with Mister
Friedlander. "Bedlow, this is A. V. Berger. He wants to speak to
you a minute."

This Mister Berger was five feet tall—tops—but weighed
close to three hundred pounds, with black hair, straight and
greasy. He was wearing a black wool suit—this was in mid-
summer now—with a vest and a scarf, which was black wool
too. And the English this man spoke was fantabulous! I can only
try to copy it. He hemmed and hawed a lot too so it sounded
like:

"Mister Bedlow, (hem) I'm a concert producer. And (hem) I
have been watching you perform. It seems quite likely that
(hem) I can use you in a concert (hem) I'm staging at Carnegie
Hall." He stopped there. I could see he was looking for Uncle
Wallace to jump in the air and clap his hands. I knew what
Carnegie Hall was, but I bet Uncle Wallace didn't. Mister Berger
thought Uncle Wallace was playing it cagey.

"Mister Bedlow, (hem) I'm prepared to offer you a good price
to appear in the show."

"What's it to be? A dance?" Uncle Wallace said. "Sure, I'll
play for a dance. That's what I done down home."

"No, Mister Bedlow. You (hem) misunderstand. This will be
a concert."

"Like what?" He turned to me. "Like what, Carlyle?"

"A concert, Uncle Wallace. That's when a whole lot of folks come and just sit and listen to you sing."

"You mean just like here?"

"No, Uncle Wallace. It's like a church." I was thinking about how the seats was arranged, but he didn't get me.

"But I don't sing church music, Carlyle. My songs is too dirty for church. They never let me sing in no church." He looked back at Mister Berger. "What kind-a church you running, mister, that they sing my kind-a songs in there?"

"(hem) I don't run a church, Mister Bedlow." Mister Berger looked sort-a bleak and confused.

"No, Uncle Wallace, it ain't in no church," I said. "It's in a big hall and they want you to sing for a couple thousand people."

"No stuff?"

"Yeah, sure," I said.

"That's (hem) right," said Mister Berger.

"Go on, Bedlow," chimed in Mister Friedlander.

So he did.

But that concert wasn't until October and Mister Berger asked him to appear in early July, so there was a lot of time in between, when Uncle Wallace was making all his records.

And there was that damn movie. It was about this plantation family and all their problems in the Civil War. It wasn't really such a bad movie, but Uncle Wallace made it worse. I mean, he was the best thing in it, but after he was on the screen you couldn't look at the movie no more.

The movie would be going on all right and then would come Uncle Wallace's scene. He be sitting on this log in raggedy clothes and they *even* had a bandana around his head. You know how they make movies about colored people in Hollywood; the slaves act like slavery was the best God-damn thing ever happened to them and all they did all day was sit around on logs and sing and love Old Master, instead of breaking their asses in his cotton field and waiting for the chance to run away or slit Old Master's throat wide open. But that wasn't the worst. Dig this! They made him sing *John Henry*. But it didn't matter. They didn't know Uncle Wallace. He started playing and singing, and when he got through, you had the feeling old John Henry wasn't no idiot after all. I mean, I heard some guy sing that song once and I said to myself: what an idiot this John Henry must-a

been, killing his-self to beat a machine when he could-a joined a
union, like my old man's, and made twice the money and kept
the machine out.

But when Uncle Wallace sang *John Henry* you didn't feel that
way. You felt like old John Henry was trapped and he had to do
what he did, like when a fellow says your Mama screws for
syphilitic blind men, you got to hit him; you don't think about it;
it don't even matter if he joking or not, you just got to hit him
even if he beats all hell out-a you. Well, that's what Uncle
Wallace did to you.

So when them white folks come back on the screen with their
dumb problems, and started kissing it up, you could see they
was cardboard; you could see they was acting, and you got up
and left out of there because you had to see real people again,
and even when you got out in the street you sort-a felt like the
people *out there* wasn't real neither, so what you did was go
back in and stand in the lobby until the next showing, when
Uncle Wallace come on again for his two minutes and you'd go
in and see him. Then you'd walk out again to the lobby. There
was always a whole lot of folks out there, waiting like you and
not looking at you because you was as cardboardy to them as
they was to you, and you'd wait for his two minutes again, and
like that all day until you got too hungry to see.

After he made the movie he come back East and it was
October and it was time for the concert at Carnegie Hall. And I
guess you know what happened at the concert, but I'll tell it
again and also some things I felt about it.

Mister Berger had-a told Uncle Wallace to play it cool and
save his best until last, which meant that Uncle Wallace was to
come out and sing a couple songs with only one guitar and
then—bingo!—lay the two guitars on them. So they fixed me up
in a tux and when the time come, I paraded out and give him
the other guitar.

Uncle Wallace was tuning the second guitar when a voice
come whispering up from the dark in the front row. "Hey,
nigger, you the same one, ain't you."

Uncle Wallace squinted down, and there in the front row with
all them rich white folks was this dark little Negro. There was a
woman with him and a whole bunch of little kids, all shabby-
looking, all their eyes shining like a row of white marbles.

"The same as what?" Uncle Wallace said.

And the voice come back. "The same fellow what played at a East Willson café in 1948."

"Yeah, I played there that year."

"There was one night in particular, when a cripple white man was taping you, and we all danced until the next day."

"Sure, it was!" Uncle Wallace snapped his fingers. "I remember you. You was with a *pretty* girl."

"You right, man. Here she is; my wife." He turned to the woman. "Honey, get up and meet Mister Bedlow." She did, and Uncle Wallace leaned over the edge of the stage and shook her hand. "Say, you know, I bought these big money seats because I wanted my kids to see you up close. Them is them." He pointed at the row of kids. "The oldest one, he's Bedlow. I named him after you because me and the wife wasn't getting on so good until that night." It was like they was all alone in that great big place, just those two down-home Negroes talking over old times. "And them others is Booker, Carver, Robeson, Robinson, and Bunche."

"Man, you do me proud. Pleased to meet you all. Say, you want to come up here and sit with me?"

"Now, you do *me* proud." So they all come up on stage like a row of ducks.

Then Uncle Wallace started to play and the littlest kid, that was Bunche—he was about three—he sat there for about one minute and then I saw him jump on his feet and start to do these wild little steps, just his feet moving like little pistons. Then the man got up and asked his wife to dance, and the next thing I knew, everybody was dancing—even me; I danced right out on stage—and all the rich white folks was on their feet in the aisles and their wives was hugging strangers, black and white, and taking off their jewelry and tossing it in the air and all the poor people was ignoring the jewelry, was dancing instead, and you could see everybody laughing like crazy and having the best old time ever. Colored folks was teaching white folks to dance, and white folks was dancing with colored folks, and all the seats was empty and people was coming on stage to dance. Then the other singers backstage come out and started to back up Uncle Wallace and we was all dancing, all of us, and over all the noise and laughing you could hear Uncle Wallace with his two guitars. You could hear him over the whole thing.

Then the air changed; you could feel it. It wasn't just air any more, it started to get sweet-tasting to breathe, like perfume, and the people started to run down the aisles toward the stage, and everybody on the stage started to dance in toward Uncle Wallace, and everybody, *everybody* in the whole place was sobbing and crying and tears was pouring down their cheeks and smearing their make-up and making their eyes red and big. I could hear Uncle Wallace singing louder than ever. The people was rushing toward him. They was all crying and smiling too like people busting into a trance in church and it seemed like everybody in the place was on stage, trying to get near enough to touch him, grab his hand and shake it and hug him and kiss him even. And then the singing stopped.

I pushed my way through the crowd up to his chair. The first thing I seen was his two guitars all tore up and smashed and the strings busted. Uncle Wallace was sitting in his chair, slumped over, his face in his lap. And this was real strange; he looked like an old, punctured black balloon, deflated and all. There wasn't a mark on him, but he was dead all right.

Mister Berger called in a whole bunch of doctors, but they just stood around shaking their heads. They couldn't figure out how he'd died. One of them said, "There isn't nothing wrong with him, except he's dead."

Now I know this'll sound lame to you, but I don't think anything killed him except maybe at that second, he'd done everything that he ever wanted to do; he'd taken all them people, and sung to them, and made them forget who they was, and what they come from, and remember only that they was people. So he'd seen all he wanted to see and there was no use going on with it. I mean, he'd made it. He got over.

It's kind of like that girl I was telling you about—the one who'd promised you some tail, and when you got it, you was sorry, because then you'd still have it to look forward to? Well, I think it's like that: getting tail and coming out of her house and there ain't nothing but pussycats and garbage cans in the street, and it's lonely and late and you wished you hadn't done it, but then you shrug and say to yourself: "Hell, man, you did, and that's it." And there ain't nothing to do but leave, because it's finished. But then there's something else. You're walking along and all at once you smile, and maybe even laugh, and you say: "Man, that was some *good* tail!" And it's a nice memory to walk home with.

Reena

PAULE MARSHALL

Like most people with unpleasant childhoods, I am on constant guard against the past—the past being for me the people and places associated with the years I served out my girlhood in Brooklyn. The places no longer matter that much since most of them have vanished. The old grammar school, for instance, P.S. 35 ("Dirty 5's" we called it and with justification) has been replaced by a low, coldly functional arrangement of glass and Permastone which bears its name but has none of the feel of a school about it. The small, grudgingly lighted stores along Fulton Street, the soda parlor that was like a church with its stained-glass panels in the door and marble floor have given way to those impersonal emporiums, the supermarkets. Our house even, a brownstone relic whose halls smelled comfortingly of dust and lemon oil, the somnolent street upon which it stood, the tall, muscular trees which shaded it were leveled years ago to make way for a city housing project—a stark, graceless warren for the poor. So that now whenever I revisit that old section of Brooklyn and see these new and ugly forms, I feel nothing. I might as well be in a strange city.

But it is another matter with the people of my past, the faces that in their darkness were myriad reflections of mine. Whenever I encounter them at the funeral or wake, the wedding or christening—those ceremonies by which the past reaffirms its hold—my guard drops and memories banished to the rear of the mind rush forward to rout the present. I almost become the child again—anxious and angry, disgracefully diffident.

Reena was one of the people from that time, and a main contributor to my sense of ineffectualness then. She had not done this deliberately. It was just that whenever she talked about herself (and this was not as often as most people) she seemed to be talking about me also. She ruthlessly analyzed herself, sparing herself nothing. Her honesty was so absolute it was a kind of cruelty.

She had not changed, I was to discover in meeting her again after a separation of twenty years. Nor had I really. For although the years had altered our positions (she was no longer the lord and I the lackey) and I could even afford to forgive her now, she still had the ability to disturb me profoundly by dredging to the surface those aspects of myself that I kept buried. This time, as I listened to her talk over the stretch of one long night, she made vivid without knowing it what is perhaps the most critical fact of my existence—that definition of me, of her and millions like us, formulated by others to serve out their fantasies, a definition we have to combat at an unconscionable cost to the self and even use, at times, in order to survive; the cause of so much shame and rage as well as, oddly enough, a source of pride: simply, what it has meant, what it means, to be a black woman in America.

We met—Reena and myself—at the funeral of her aunt who had been my godmother and whom I had also called aunt, Aunt Vi, and loved, for she and her house had been, respectively, a source of understanding and a place of calm for me as a child. Reena entered the church where the funeral service was being held as though she, not the minister, were coming to officiate, sat down among the immediate family up front, and turned to inspect those behind her. I saw her face then.

It was a good copy of the original. The familiar mold was there, that is, and the configuration of bone beneath the skin was the same despite the slight fleshiness I had never seen there before; her features had even retained their distinctive touches: the positive set to her mouth, the assertive lift to her nose, the same insistent, unsettling eyes which when she was angry became as black as her skin—and this was total, unnerving, and very beautiful. Yet something had happened to her face. It was different despite its sameness. Aging even while it remained enviably young. Time had sketched in, very lightly, the evidence of the twenty years.

As soon as the funeral service was over, I left, hurrying out of the church into the early November night. The wind, already at its winter strength, brought with it the smell of dead leaves and the image of Aunt Vi there in the church, as dead as the leaves—as well as the thought of Reena, whom I would see later at the wake.

Her real name had been Doreen, a standard for girls among West Indians (her mother, like my parents, was from Barbados), but she had changed it to Reena on her twelfth birthday—"As a present to myself"—and had enforced the change on her family by refusing to answer to the old name. "Reena. With two e's!" she would say and imprint those e's on your mind with the indelible black of her eyes and a thin threatening finger that was like a quill.

She and I had not been friends through our own choice. Rather, our mothers, who had known each other since childhood, had forced the relationship. And from the beginning, I had been at a disadvantage. For Reena, as early as the age of twelve, had had a quality that was unique, superior, and therefore dangerous. She seemed defined, even then, all of a piece, the raw edges of her adolescence smoothed over; indeed, she seemed to have escaped adolescence altogether and made one dazzling leap from childhood into the very arena of adult life. At thirteen, for instance, she was reading Zola, Hauptmann, Steinbeck, while I was still in the thrall of the Little Minister and Lorna Doone. When I could only barely conceive of the world beyond Brooklyn, she was talking of the Civil War in Spain, lynchings in the South, Hitler in Poland—and talking with the outrage and passion of a revolutionary. I would try, I remember, to console myself with the thought that she was really an adult masquerading as a child, which meant that I could not possibly be her match.

For her part, Reena put up with me and was, by turns, patronizing and impatient. I merely served as the audience before whom she rehearsed her ideas and the yardstick by which she measured her worldliness and knowledge.

"Do you realize that this stupid country supplied Japan with the scrap iron to make the weapons she's now using against it?" she had shouted at me once.

I had not known that.

Just as she overwhelmed me, she overwhelmed her family, with the result that despite a half-dozen brothers and sisters who consumed quantities of bread and jam whenever they visited us, she behaved like an only child and got away with it. Her father, a gentle man with skin the color of dried tobacco

and with the nose Reena had inherited jutting out like a crag
from his nondescript face, had come from Georgia and was
always making jokes about having married a foreigner—
Reena's mother being from the West Indies. When not joking,
he seemed slightly bewildered by his large family and so in awe
of Reena that he avoided her. Reena's mother, a small, dry,
formidably black woman, was less a person to me than the
abstract principle of force, power, energy, She was alternately
strict and indulgent with Reena and, despite the inconsistency,
surprisingly effective.

They lived when I knew them in a cold-water railroad flat
above a kosher butcher on Belmont Avenue in Brownsville,
some distance from us—and this in itself added to Reena's exotic
quality. For it was a place where Sunday became Saturday, with
all the stores open and pushcarts piled with vegetables and yard
goods lined up along the curb, a crowded place where people
hawked and spat freely in the streaming gutters and the men
looked as if they had just stepped from the pages of the Old
Testament with their profuse beards and long, black, satin
coats.

When Reena was fifteen her family moved to Jamaica in
Queens and since, in those days, Jamaica was considered too far
away for visiting, our families lost contact and I did not see
Reena again until we were both in college and then only once
and not to speak to . . .

I had walked some distance and by the time I got to the wake
which was being held at Aunt Vi's house it was well under way.
It was a good wake. Aunt Vi would have been pleased. There
was plenty to drink, and more than enough to eat, including
some Barbadian favorites: coconut bread, pone made with the
cassava root, and the little crisp codfish cakes that are so hot
with peppers they bring tears to the eyes as you bite into them.

I had missed the beginning, when everyone had probably sat
around talking about Aunt Vi and recalling the few events that
had distinguished her otherwise undistinguished life. (Someone, I'm sure, had told of the time she had missed the excursion
boat to Atlantic City and had held her own private picnic—
complete with pigeon peas and rice and fricassee chicken—on
the pier at 42nd Street.) By the time I arrived, though, it would
have been indiscreet to mention her name, for by then the wake

had become—and this would also have pleased her—a celebration of life.

I had had two drinks, one right after the other, and was well into my third when Reena, who must have been upstairs, entered the basement kitchen where I was. She saw me before I had quite seen her, and with a cry that alerted the entire room to her presence and charged the air with her special force, she rushed toward me.

"Hey, I'm the one who was supposed to be the writer, not you! Do you know, I still can't believe it," she said, stepping back, her blackness heightened by a white mocking smile. "I read both your books over and over again and I can't really believe it. My Little Paulie!"

I did not mind. For there was respect and even wonder behind the patronizing words and in her eyes. The old imbalance between us had ended and I was suddenly glad to see her.

I told her so and we both began talking at once, but Reena's voice overpowered mine, so that all I could do after a time was listen while she discussed my books, and dutifully answer her questions about my personal life.

"And what about you?" I said, almost brutally, at the first chance I got. "What've you been up to all this time?"

She got up abruptly. "Good Lord, in here's noisy as hell. Come on, let's go upstairs."

We got fresh drinks and went up to Aunt Vi's bedroom, where in the soft light from the lamps, the huge Victorian bed and the pink satin bedspread with roses of the same material strewn over its surface looked as if they had never been used. And, in a way, this was true. Aunt Vi had seldom slept in her bed or, for that matter, lived in her house, because in order to pay for it, she had had to work at a sleeping-in job which gave her only Thursdays and every other Sunday off.

Reena sat on the bed, crushing the roses, and I sat on one of the numerous trunks which crowded the room. They contained every dress, coat, hat, and shoe that Aunt Vi had worn since coming to the United States. I again asked Reena what she had been doing over the years.

"Do you want a blow by blow account?" she said. But despite the flippancy, she was suddenly serious. And when she began it was clear that she had written out the narrative in her mind many times. The words came too easily; the events, the incidents had been ordered in time, and the meaning of her behavior and of the people with whom she had been involved had been painstakingly analyzed. She talked willingly, with desperation almost. And the words by themselves weren't enough. She used her hands to give them form and urgency. I became totally involved with her and all that she said. So much so that as the night wore on I was not certain at times whether it was she or I speaking.

From the time her family moved to Jamaica until she was nineteen or so, Reena's life sounded, from what she told me in the beginning, as ordinary as mine and most of the girls we knew. After high school she had gone on to one of the free city colleges, where she had majored in journalism, worked part-time in the school library, and, surprisingly enough, joined a houseplan. (Even I hadn't gone that far.) It was an all-Negro club, since there was a tacit understanding that Negro and white girls did not join each other's houseplans. "Integration, Northern style," she said, shrugging.

It seems that Reena had had a purpose and a plan in joining the group. "I thought," she said with a wry smile, "I could get those girls up off their complacent rumps and out doing something about social issues. . . . I couldn't get them to budge. I remember after the war when a Negro ex-soldier had his eyes gouged out by a bus driver down South I tried getting them to demonstrate on campus. I talked until I was hoarse, but to no avail. They were too busy planning the annual autumn frolic."

Her laugh was bitter but forgiving and it ended in a long reflective silence. After which she said quietly, "It wasn't that they didn't give a damn. It was just, I suppose, that like most people they didn't want to get involved to the extent that they might have to stand up and be counted. If it ever came to that. Then another thing. They thought they were safe, special. After all, they had grown up in the North, most of them, and so had escaped the Southern-style prejudice; their parents, like mine, were struggling to put them through college; they could look forward to being tidy little schoolteachers, social workers, and lab technicians. Oh, they were safe!" The sarcasm scored her voice and then abruptly gave way to pity. "Poor things, they weren't safe, you see, and would never be as long as millions like themselves in Harlem, on Chicago's South Side, down South, all over the place, were unsafe. I tried to tell them this— and they accused me of being oversensitive. They tried not to listen. But I would have held out and, I'm sure, even brought some of them around eventually if this other business with a silly boy hadn't happened at the same time. . . ."

Reena told me then about her first, brief, and apparently innocent affair with a boy she had met at one of the houseplan parties. It had ended, she said, when the boys' parents had met her. "That was it," she said and the flat of her hand cut into the air. "He was forbidden to see me. The reason? He couldn't bring himself to tell me, but I knew. I was too black.

"Naturally, it wasn't the first time something like that had happened. In fact, you might say that was the theme of my childhood. Because I was dark I was always being plastered with Vaseline so I wouldn't look ashy. Whenever I had my picture taken they would pile a whitish powder on my face and make the lights so bright I always came out looking ghostly. My mother stopped speaking to any number of people because they said I would have been pretty if I hadn't been so dark. Like nearly every little black girl, I had my share of dreams of waking up to find myself with long blonde curls, blue eyes, and skin like milk. So I should have been prepared. Besides, that boy's parents were really rejecting themselves in rejecting me.

"Take us"—and her hands, opening in front of my face as she suddenly leaned forward, seemed to offer me the whole of black humanity. "We live surrounded by white images, and white in this world is synonymous with the good, light, beauty, success, so that, despite ourselves sometimes, we run after that white-ness and deny our darkness, which has been made into the symbol of all that is evil and inferior. I wasn't a person to that boy's parents, but a symbol of the darkness they were in flight from, so that just as they—that boy, his parents, those silly girls in the houseplan—were running from me, I started running from them . . ."

It must have been shortly after this happened when I saw Reena at a debate which was being held at my college. She did not see me, since she was one of the speakers and I was merely part of her audience in the crowded auditorium. The topic had some-thing to do with intellectual freedom in the colleges (McCarthy-

ism was coming into vogue then) and aside from a Jewish boy
from City College, Reena was the most effective—sharp, pro-
vocative, her position the most radical. The others on the panel
seemed intimidated not only by the strength and cogency of her
argument but by the sheer impact of her blackness in their
white midst.

Her color might have been a weapon she used to dazzle and
disarm her opponents. And she had highlighted it with the
clothes she was wearing: a white dress patterned with large
blocks of primary colors I remember (it looked Mexican) and a
pair of intricately wrought silver earrings—long and with many
little parts which clashed like muted cymbals over the micro-
phone each time she moved her head. She wore her hair cropped
short like a boy's and it was not straightened like mine and the
other Negro girls' in the audience, but left in its coarse natural
state: a small forest under which her face emerged in its
intense and startling handsomeness. I remember she left the
auditorium in triumph that day, surrounded by a noisy entour-
age from her college—all of them white.

"We were very serious," she said now, describing the left-wing
group she had belonged to then—and there was a defensiveness
in her voice which sought to protect them from all censure. "We
believed—because we were young, I suppose, and had nothing
as yet to risk—that we could do something about the injustices
which everyone around us seemed to take for granted. So we
picketed and demonstrated and bombarded Washington with
our protests, only to have our names added to the Attorney
General's list for all our trouble. We were always standing on
street corners handing out leaflets or getting people to sign
petitions. We always seemed to pick the coldest days to do that."
Her smile held long after the words had died.

"I, we all, had such a sense of purpose then." she said softly,
and a sadness lay aslant the smile now, darkening it. "We were
forever holding meetings, having endless discussions, arguing,
shouting, theorizing. And we had fun. Those parties! There was
always somebody with a guitar. We were always singing. . . ."
Suddenly, she began singing—and her voice was sure, militant,
and faintly self-mocking,

> *"But the banks are made of marble*
> *With a guard at every door*

And the vaults are stuffed with silver
That the workers sweated for . . ."

When she spoke again the words were a sad coda to the song.
"Well, as you probably know, things came to an ugly head with
McCarthy reigning in Washington, and I was one of the people
temporarily suspended from school."

She broke off and we both waited, the ice in our glasses
melted and the drinks gone flat.

"At first, I didn't mind," she said finally. "After all, we were
right. The fact that they suspended us proved it. Besides, I was
in the middle of an affair, a real one this time, and too busy
with that to care about anything else." She paused again,
frowning.

"He was white," she said quickly and glanced at me as though
to surprise either shock or disapproval in my face. "We were
very involved. At one point—I think just after we had been
suspended and he started working—we even thought of getting
married. Living in New York, moving in the crowd we did, we
might have been able to manage it. But I couldn't. There were
too many complex things going on beneath the surface," she
said, her voice strained by the hopelessness she must have felt
then, her hands shaping it in the air between us. "Neither one of
us could really escape what our color had come to mean in this
country. Let me explain. Bob was always, for some odd reason,
talking about how much the Negro suffered, and although I
would agree with him I would also try to get across that, you
know, like all people we also had fun once in a while, loved our
children, liked making love—that we were human beings, for
God's sake. But he only wanted to hear about the suffering. It
was as if this comforted him and eased his own suffering—and
he did suffer because of any number of things: his own uncertainty, for one, his difficulties with his family, for another . . .

"Once, I remember, when his father came into New York, Bob
insisted that I meet him. I don't know why I agreed to go with
him. . . ." She took a deep breath and raised her head very
high. "I'll never forget or forgive the look on that old man's face
when he opened his hotel-room door and saw me. The horror. I
might have been the personification of every evil in the world.
His inability to believe that it was his son standing there holding
my hand. His shock. I'm sure he never fully recovered. I know I

never did. Nor can I forget Bob's laugh in the elevator after-wards, the way he kept repeating: 'Did you see his face when he saw you? Did you . . .?' He had used me, you see. I had been the means, the instrument of his revenge.

"And I wasn't any better. I used him. I took every opportunity to treat him shabbily, trying, you see, through him, to get at that white world which had not only denied me, but had turned my own against me." Her eyes closed. "I went numb all over when I understood what we were doing to, and with, each other. I stayed numb for a long time."

As Reena described the events which followed—the break with Bob, her gradual withdrawal from the left-wing group ("I had had it with them too. I got tired of being 'their Negro,' their pet. Besides, they were just all talk, really. All theories and abstractions. I doubt that, with all their elaborate plans for the Negro and for the workers of the world, any of them had ever been near a factory or up to Harlem")—as she spoke about her reinstatement in school, her voice suggested the numbness she had felt then. It only stirred into life again when she talked of her graduation.

"You should have seen my parents. It was really their day. My mother was so proud she complained about everything: her seat, the heat, the speaker; and my father just sat there long after everybody had left, too awed to move. God, it meant so much to them. It was as if I had made up for the generations his people had picked cotton in Georgia and my mother's family had cut cane in the West Indies. It frightened me."

I asked her after a long wait what she had done after graduating.

"How do you mean, what I did. Looked for a job. Tell me, have you ever looked for work in this man's city?"

"I know," I said, holding up my hand. "Don't tell me."

We both looked at my raised hand which sought to waive the discussion, then at each other and suddenly we laughed, a laugh so loud and violent with pain and outrage it brought tears.

"Girl," Reena said, the tears silver against her blackness. "You could put me blindfolded right now at the Times Building on 42nd Street and I would be able to find my way to every news-paper office in town. But tell me, how come white folks is so *hard?*"

"Just bo'n hard."

We were laughing again and this time I nearly slid off the trunk and Reena fell back among the satin roses.

"I didn't know there were so many ways of saying 'no' without ever once using the word," she said, the laughter lodged in her throat, but her eyes had gone hard. "Sometimes I'd find myself in the elevator, on my way out, and smiling all over myself because I thought I had gotten the job, before it would hit me that they had really said no, not yes. Some of those people in personnel had so perfected their smiles they looked almost genuine. The ones who used to get me, though, were those who tried to make the interview into an intimate chat between friends. They'd put you in a comfortable chair, offer you a cigarette, and order coffee. How I hated that coffee. They didn't know it—or maybe they did—but it was like offering me hemlock. . . .

"You think Christ had it tough?" Her laughter rushed against the air which resisted it. "I was crucified five days a week and half-day on Saturday. I became almost paranoid. I began to think there might be something other than color wrong with me which everybody but me could see, some rare disease that had turned me into a monster.

"My parents suffered. And that bothered me most, because I felt I had failed them. My father didn't say anything but I knew because he avoided me more than usual. He was ashamed, I think, that he hadn't been able, as a man and as my father, to prevent this. My mother—well, you know her. In one breath she would try to comfort me by cursing them: 'But Gor blind them,' "—and Reena's voice captured her mother's aggressive accent—" 'if you had come looking for a job mopping down their floors they would o' hire you, the brutes. But mark my words, their time goin' come, 'cause God don't love ugly and he ain't stuck on pretty . . .' And in the next breath she would curse me, 'Journalism! Journalism! Whoever heard of colored people taking up journalism. You must feel you's white or something so. The people is right to chuck you out their office. . . .' Poor thing, to make up for saying all that she would wash my white gloves every night and cook cereal for me in the morning as if I were a little girl again. Once she went out and bought me a suit she couldn't afford from Lord and Taylor's. I looked like a Smith girl in blackface in it. . . . So guess where I ended up?"

"As a social investigator for the Welfare Department. Where else?"

We were helpless with laughter again.

"You too?"

"No," I said, "I taught, but that was just as bad."

"No," she said, sobering abruptly. "Nothing's as bad as working for Welfare. Do you know what they really mean by a social investigator? A spy. Someone whose dirty job it is to snoop into the corners of the lives of the poor and make their poverty more vivid by taking from them the last shred of privacy. 'Mrs. Jones, is that a new dress you're wearing?' 'Mrs. Brown, this kerosene heater is not listed in the household items. Did you get an authorization for it?' 'Mrs. Smith, is that a telephone I hear ringing under the sofa?' I was utterly demoralized within a month.

"And another thing. I thought I knew about poverty. I mean, I remember, as a child, having to eat soup made with those white beans the government used to give out free for days running, sometimes, because there was nothing else. I had lived in Brownsville, among all the poor Jews and Poles and Irish there. But what I saw in Harlem where I had my case load was different somehow. Perhaps because it seemed so final. There didn't seem to be any way to escape from those dark hallways and dingy furnished rooms . . . All that defeat." Closing her eyes, she finished the stale whiskey and soda in her glass.

"I remember a client of mine, a girl my age with three children already and no father for them and living in the expensive squalor of a rooming house. Her bewilderment. Her resignation. Her anger. She could have pulled herself out of the mess she was in? People say that, you know, including some Negroes. But this girl didn't have a chance. She had been trapped from the day she was born in some small town down South.

"She became my reference. From then on and even now, whenever I hear people and groups coming up with all kinds of solutions to the quote Negro problem, I ask one question. What are they really doing for that girl, to save her or to save the children? . . . The answer isn't very encouraging."

It was some time before she continued and then she told me that after Welfare she had gone to work for a private social-work agency, in their publicity department, and had started on her master's in journalism at Columbia. She also left home around this time.

"I had to. My mother started putting the pressure on me to get married. The hints, the remarks—and you know my mother was never the subtle type—her anxiety, which made me anxious about getting married after a while. Besides, it was time for me to be on my own."

In contrast to the unmistakably radical character of her late adolescence (her membership in the left-wing group, the affair with Bob, her suspension from college), Reena's life of this period sounded ordinary, standard—and she admitted it with a slightly self-deprecating, apologetic smile. It was similar to that of any number of unmarried professional Negro women in New York or Los Angeles or Washington: the job teaching or doing social work which brought in a fairly decent salary, the small apartment with kitchenette which they sometimes shared with a roommate; a car, some of them; membership in various political and social action organizations for the militant few like Reena; the vacations in Mexico, Europe, the West Indies, and now Africa; the occasional date. "The interesting men were invariably married," Reena said and then mentioned having had one affair during that time. She had found out he was married and had thought of her only as the perfect mistress. "The bastard," she said, but her smile forgave him.

"Women alone!" she cried, laughing sadly, and her raised opened arms, the empty glass she held in one hand made eloquent their aloneness. "Alone and lonely, and indulging themselves while they wait. The girls of the houseplan have reached their majority only to find that all those years they spent accumulating their degrees and finding the well-paying jobs in the hope that this would raise their stock have, instead, put them at a disadvantage. For the few eligible men around— those who are their intellectual and professional peers, whom they can respect (and there are very few of them)—don't necessarily marry them, but younger women without the degrees and the fat jobs, who are no threat, or they don't marry at all because they are either queer or mother-ridden. Or they marry white women. Now, intellectually I accept this. In fact, some of my best friends are white women . . ." And again our laughter —that loud, searing burst which we used to cauterize our hurt mounted into the unaccepting silence of the room. "After all, our goal is a fully integrated society. And perhaps, as some people believe, the only solution to the race problem is miscegenation. Besides, a man should be able to marry whomever he wishes. Emotionally, though, I am less kind and understanding, and I resent like hell the reasons some black men give for rejecting us for them."

"We're too middle-class-oriented," I said. "Conservative."

"Right. Even though, thank God, that doesn't apply to me."

"Too threatening . . . castrating . . ."

"Too independent and impatient with them for not being more ambitious . . . contemptuous . . ."

"Sexually inhibited and unimaginative . . ."

"And the old myth of the excessive sexuality of the black woman goes out the window," Reena cried.

"Not supportive, unwilling to submerge our interests for theirs . . ."

"Lacking in the subtle art of getting and keeping a man . . ."

We had recited the accusations in the form and tone of a litany, and in the silence which followed we shared a thin, hopeless smile.

"They condemn us," Reena said softly but with anger, "without taking history into account. We are still, most of us, the black woman who had to be almost frighteningly strong in order for us all to survive. For, after all, she was the one whom they left (and I don't hold this against them; I understand) with the children to raise, who had to *make* it somehow or the other. And we are still, so many of us, living that history.

"You would think that they would understand this, but few do. So it's up to us. We have got to understand them and save them for ourselves. How? By being, on one hand, persons in our own right and, on the other, fully the woman and the wife. . . . Christ, listen to who's talking! I had my chance. And I tried. Very hard. But it wasn't enough."

The festive sounds of the wake had died to a sober murmur beyond the bedroom. The crowd had gone, leaving only Reena and myself upstairs and the last of Aunt Vi's closest friends in the basement below. They were drinking coffee. I smelled it, felt its warmth and intimacy in the empty house, heard the distant tapping of the cups against the saucers and voices muted by grief. The wake had come full circle: they were again mourning Aunt Vi.

And Reena might have been mourning with them, sitting there amid the satin roses, framed by the massive headboard. Her hands lay as if they had been broken in her lap. Her eyes were like those of someone blind or dead. I got up to go and get some coffee for her.

"You met my husband." She said quickly, stopping me.

"Have I?" I said, sitting down again.

"Yes, before we were married even. At an autograph party for you. He was free-lancing—he's a photographer—and one of the Negro magazines had sent him to cover the party."

As she went on to describe him I remembered him vaguely, not his face, but his rather large body stretching and bending with a dancer's fluidity and grace as he took the pictures. I had heard him talking to a group of people about some issue on race relations very much in the news then and had been struck by his vehemence. For the moment I had found this almost odd, since he was so fair-skinned he could have passed for white.

They had met, Reena told me now, at a benefit show for a Harlem day nursery given by one of the progressive groups she belonged to, and had married a month afterwards. From all that she said they had had a full and exciting life for a long time. Her words were so vivid that I could almost see them: she with her startling blackness and extraordinary force and he with his near-white skin and a militancy which matched hers; both of them moving among the disaffected in New York, their stand on political and social issues equally uncompromising, the line of their allegiance reaching directly to all those trapped in Harlem. And they had lived the meaning of this allegiance, so that even when they could have afforded a life among the black bourgeoisie of St. Albans or Teaneck, they had chosen to live if not in Harlem so close that there was no difference.

"I—we—were so happy I was frightened at times. Not that anything would change between us, but that someone or something in the world outside us would invade our private place and destroy us out of envy. Perhaps this is what did happen. . . ." She shrugged and even tried to smile but she could not manage it. "Something slipped in while we weren't looking and began its deadly work.

"Maybe it started when Dave took a job with a Negro magazine. I'm not sure. Anyway, in no time, he hated it: the routine, unimaginative pictures he had to take and the magazine itself, which dealt only in unrealities: the high-society world of the black bourgeoisie and the spectacular strides Negroes were making in all fields—you know the type. Yet Dave wouldn't leave. It wasn't the money, but a kind of safety which he had never experienced before which kept him there. He would talk about free-lancing again, about storming the gates of the white magazines downtown, of opening his own studio—but he never acted on any one of these things. You see, despite his talent— and he was very talented—he had a diffidence that was fatal.

"When I understood this I literally forced him to open the studio—and perhaps I should have been more subtle and indirect, but that's not my nature. Besides, I was frightened and desperate to help. Nothing happened for a time. Dave's work was too experimental to be commercial. Gradually, though, his photographs started appearing in the prestige camera magazines and money from various awards and exhibits and an occasional assignment started coming in.

"This wasn't enough somehow. Dave also wanted the big, gaudy commercial success that would dazzle and confound that white world downtown and force it to *see* him. And yet, as I said before, he couldn't bring himself to try—and this contradiction began to get to him after awhile.

"It was then, I think, that I began to fail him. I didn't know how to help, you see. I had never felt so inadequate before. And this was very strange and disturbing for someone like me. I was being submerged in his problems—and I began fighting against this.

"I started working again (I had stopped after the second baby). And I was lucky because I got back my old job. And unlucky because Dave saw it as my way of pointing up his deficiencies. I couldn't convince him otherwise: that I had to do it for my own sanity. He would accuse me of wanting to see him fail, of trapping him in all kinds of responsibilities. . . . After a time we both got caught up in this thing, an ugliness came between us, and I began to answer his anger with anger and to trade him insult for insult.

"Things fell apart very quickly after that. I couldn't bear the pain of living with him—the insults, our mutual despair, his mocking, the silence. I couldn't subject the children to it any

longer. The divorce didn't take long. And thank God, because of
the children, we are pleasant when we have to see each other.
He's making out very well, I hear."

She said nothing more, but simply bowed her head as though
waiting for me to pass judgment on her. I don't know how long
we remained like this, but when Reena finally raised her head,
the darkness at the window had vanished and dawn was a still,
gray smoke against the pane.

"Do you know," she said, and her eyes were clear and a smile
had won out over pain, "I enjoy being alone. I don't tell people
this because they'll accuse me of either lying or deluding myself.
But I do. Perhaps, as my mother tells me, it's only temporary. I
don't think so, though. I feel I don't ever want to be involved
again. It's not that I've lost interest in men. I go out occasionally, but it's never anything serious. You see, I have all that I
want for now."

Her children first of all, she told me, and from her description
they sounded intelligent and capable. She was a friend as well
as a mother to them, it seemed. They were planning, the four of
them, to spend the summer touring Canada. "I will feel that I
have done well by them if I give them, if nothing more, a sense
of themselves and their worth and importance as black people.
Everything I do with them, for them, is to this end. I don't want
them ever to be confused about this. They must have their
identifications straight from the beginning. No white dolls for
them!"

Then her job. She was working now as a researcher for a
small progressive news magazine with the promise that once
she completed her master's in journalism (she was working on
the thesis now) she might get a chance to do some minor
reporting. And like most people she hoped to write someday. "If
I can ever stop talking away my substance," she said laughing.

And she was still active in any number of social action
groups. In another week or so she would be heading a delegation
of mothers down to City Hall "to give the Mayor a little hell
about conditions in the schools in Harlem." She had started an
organization that was carrying on an almost door-to-door cam-
paign in her neighborhood to expose, as she put it, "the blood
suckers: all those slum lords and storekeepers with their fixed
scales, the finance companies that never tell you the real price

of a thing, the petty salesmen that leech off the poor. . . ." In May she was taking her two older girls on a nationwide pilgrimage to Washington to urge for a more rapid implementation of the school-desegregation law.

"It's uncanny," she said and the laugh which accompanied the words was warm, soft with wonder at herself, girlish even and the air in the room which had refused her laughter before rushed to absorb this now. "Really uncanny. Here I am, practically middle-aged, with three children to raise by myself and with little or no money to do it and yet I feel, strangely enough, as though life is just beginning—that it's new and fresh with all kinds of possibilities. Maybe it's because I've been through my purgatory and I can't ever be overwhelmed again. I don't know. Anyway, you should see me on evenings after I put the children to bed. I sit alone in the living room (I've repainted it and changed all the furniture since Dave's gone, so that it would at least look different)—I sit there making plans and all of them seem possible. The most important plan right now is Africa. I've already started saving the fare."

I asked her whether she was planning to live there permanently and she said simply, "I want to live and work there. For how long, for a lifetime, I can't say. All I know is that I have to. For myself and for my children. It is important that they see black people who have truly a place and history of their own and who are building for a new and, hopefully, more sensible world. And I must see it, get close to it because I can never lose the sense of being a displaced person here in America because of my color. Oh, I know I should remain and fight not only for integration (even though, frankly, I question whether I want to be integrated into America as it stands now, with its complacency and materialism, its soullessness) but to help change the country into something better, sounder—if that is still possible. But I have to go to Africa. . . .

"Poor Aunt Vi," she said after a long silence and straightened one of the roses she had crushed. "She never really got to enjoy her bed of roses what with only Thursdays and every other Sunday off. All that hard work. All her life . . . Our lives have got to make more sense, if only for her."

We got up to leave shortly afterwards. Reena was staying on to attend the burial later in the morning, but I was taking the subway to Manhattan. We parted with the usual promise to get together and exchanged telephone numbers. And Reena did phone a week or so later. I don't remember what we talked about though.

Some months later I invited her to a party I was giving before leaving the country. But she did not come.

Attitude of blacks to white fighting pride

The Convert

LERONE BENNETT, JR.

A man don't know what he'll do, a man don't know what he is till he gets his back pressed up against a wall. Now you take Aaron Lott: there ain't no other way to explain the crazy thing he did. He was going alone fine, preaching the gospel, saving souls, and getting along with the white folks; and then, all of a sudden, he felt wood pressing against his back. The funny thing was that nobody knew he was hurting till he preached that Red Sea sermon where he got mixed up and seemed to think Mississippi was Egypt. As chairman of the deacons board, I felt it was my duty to reason with him. I appreciated his position and told him so, but I didn't think it was right for him to push us all in a hole. The old fool—he just laughed.

"Brother Booker," he said, "the Lord—He'll take care of me."

I knew then that that man was heading for trouble. And the very next thing he did confirmed it. The white folks called the old fool downtown to bear witness that the colored folks were happy. And you know what he did: he got down there amongst all them big white folks and he said: "Things ain't gonna change here overnight, but they gonna change. It's inevitable. The Lord wants it."

Well sir, you could have bought them white folks for a penny. Aaron Lott, pastor of the Rock of Zion Baptist Church, a man white folks had said was wise and sound and sensible, had come close—too close—to saying that the Supreme Court was coming to Melina, Mississippi. The surprising thing was that the white folks didn't do nothing. There was a lot of mumbling and whispering but nothing bad happened till the terrible morning when Aaron came a-knocking at the door of my funeral home. Now things had been tightening up—you could feel it in the air—and I didn't want no part of no crazy scheme and I told him so right off. He walked on past me and sat down on the couch. He had on his preaching clothes, a shiny blue suit, a fresh starched white shirt, a black tie, and his Sunday black shoes. I remember thinking at the time that Aaron was too black to be wearing all them dark clothes. The thought tickled me and I started to smile but then I noticed something about him that didn't seem quite right. I ran my eyes over him closely. He was kinda middle-sized and he had a big clean-shaven head, a big nose, and thin lips. I stood there looking at him for a long time but I couldn't figure out what it was till I looked at his eyes: they were burning bright, like light bulbs do just before they go out. And yet he looked contented, like his mind was resting somewheres else.

"I wanna talk with you, Booker," he said, glancing sideways at my wife. "If you don't mind, Sister Brown———"

Sarah got up and went into the living quarters. Aaron didn't say nothing for a long time; he just sat there looking out the window. Then he spoke so soft I had to strain my ears to hear.

"I'm leaving for the Baptist convention," he said. He pulled out his gold watch and looked at it. "Train leaves in 'bout two hours."

"I know *that,* Aaron."

"Yeah, but what I wanted to tell you was that I ain't going Jim Crow. I'm going first class, Booker, right through the white waiting room. That's the law."

A cold shiver ran through me.

"Aaron," I said, "don't you go talking crazy now."

The old fool laughed, a great big body-shaking laugh. He started talking 'bout God and Jesus and all that stuff. Now, I'm a God-fearing man myself, but I holds that God helps those who help themselves. I told him so.

"You can't mix God up with these white folks," I said. "When you start to messing around with segregation, they'll burn you up and the Bible, too."

He looked at me like I was Satan.

"I sweated over this thing," he said. "I prayed. I got down on my knees and I asked God not to give me this cup. But He said I was the one. I heard Him, Booker, right here—he tapped his chest—in my heart."

The old fool's been having visions, I thought. I sat down and tried to figure out a way to hold him, but he got up, without saying a word, and started for the door.

"Wait!" I shouted. "I'll get my coat."

"I don't need you," he said. "I just came by to tell you so you could tell the board in case something happened."

"You wait," I shouted, and ran out of the room to get my coat.

We got in his beat-up old Ford and went by the parsonage to get his suitcase. Rachel—that was his wife—and Jonah were sitting in the living room, wringing their hands. Aaron got his bag, shook Jonah's hand, and said, "Take care of your Mamma, boy." Jonah nodded. Aaron hugged Rachel and pecked at her cheek. Rachel broke down. She throwed her arms around his neck and carried on something awful. Aaron shoved her away.

"Don't go making no fuss over it, woman. I ain't gonna be gone forever. Can't a man go to a church meeting 'thout women screaming and crying."

He tried to make light of it, but you could see he was touched by the way his lips trembled. He held his hand out to me, but I wouldn't take it. I told him off good, told him it was a sin and a shame for a man of God to be carrying on like he was, worrying his wife and everything.

"I'm coming with you," I said. "Somebody's gotta see that you don't make a fool of yourself."

He shrugged, picked up his suitcase, and started for the door. Then he stopped and turned around and looked at his wife and his boy and from the way he looked I knew that there was still a chance. He looked at the one and then at the other. For a moment there, I thought he was going to cry, but he turned, quick-like, and walked out of the door.

I ran after him and tried to talk some sense in his head. But he shook me off, turned the corner, and went on up Adams Street. I caught up with him and we walked in silence, crossing the street in front of the First Baptist Church for whites, going on around the Confederate monument where, once, they hung a boy for fooling around with white women.

"Put it off, Aaron," I begged. "Sleep on it."

He didn't say nothing.

"What you need is a vacation. I'll get the board to approve, full pay and everything."

He smiled and shifted the suitcase over to his left hand. Big drops of sweat were running down his face and spotting up his shirt. His eyes were awful, all lit up and burning.

"Aaron, Aaron, can't you hear me?"

We passed the feed store, Bill Williams' grocery store, and the movie house.

"A man's gotta think about his family, Aaron. A man ain't free. Didn't you say that once, didn't you?"

He shaded his eyes with his hand and looked into the sun. He put the suitcase on the ground and checked his watch.

"Why don't you think about Jonah?" I asked. "Answer that. Why don't you think about your own son?"

"I am," he said. "That's exactly what I'm doing, thinking about Jonah. Matter of fact, he started *me* to thinking. I ain't never mentioned it before, but the boy's been worrying me. One day we was downtown here and he asked me something that hurt. 'Daddy,' he said, 'how come you ain't a man?' I got mad, I did, and told him: 'I am a man.' He said that wasn't what he meant. 'I mean,' he said, 'how come you ain't a man where white folks concerned.' I couldn't answer him, Booker. I'll never forget it till the day I die. I couldn't answer my own son, and I been preaching forty years."

"He don't know nothing 'bout it," I said. "He's hot-headed, like my boy. He'll find out when he grows up."

"I hopes not," Aaron said, shaking his head. "I hopes not."

Some white folks passed and we shut up till they were out of hearing. Aaron, who was acting real strange, looked up in the sky and moved his lips. He came back to himself, after a little bit, and he said: "This thing of being a man, Booker, is a big thing. The Supreme Court can't make you a man. The NAACP can't do it. God Almighty can do a lot, but even He can't do it. Ain't nobody can do it but you."

He said that like he was preaching and when he got through he was all filled up with emotion and he seemed kind of ashamed—he was a man who didn't like emotion outside the church. He looked at his watch, picked up his bag, and said, "Well, let's git it over with."

We turned into Elm and the first thing I saw at the end of the

Street was the train station. It was an old red building, flat like a slab. A group of white men were fooling around in front of the door. I couldn't make them out from that distance, but I could tell they weren't the kind of white folks to be fooling around with.

We walked on, passing the dry goods store, the barber shop, and the new building that was going up. Across the street from that was the sheriff's office. I looked in the window and saw Bull Sampson sitting at his desk, his feet propped up on a chair, a fat brown cigar sticking out of his mouth. A ball about the size of a sweet potato started burning in my stomach.

"Please Aaron," I said. "Please. You can't get away with it. I know how you feel. Sometimes I feel the same way myself, but I wouldn't risk my neck to do nothing for these niggers. They won't appreciate it; they'll laugh at you."

We were almost to the station and I could make out the faces of the men sitting on the benches. One of them must have been telling a joke. He finished and the group broke out laughing.

I whispered to Aaron: "I'm through with it. I wash my hands of the whole mess."

I don't know whether he heard me or not. He turned to the right without saying a word and went on in the front door. The string-beany man who told the joke was so shocked that his cigarette fell out of his mouth.

"Y'all see that," he said. "Why, I'll——"

"Shut up," another man said. "Go git Bull."

I kept walking, fast, turned at the corner, and ran around to the colored waiting room. When I got in there, I looked through the ticket window and saw Aaron standing in front of the clerk. Aaron stood there for a minute or more, but the clerk didn't see him. And that took some not seeing. In that room, Aaron Lott stood out like a pig in a chicken coop.

There were, I'd say, about ten or fifteen people in there, but didn't none of them move. They just sat there, with their eyes glued on Aaron's back. Aaron cleared his throat. The clerk didn't look up; he got real busy with some papers. Aaron cleared his throat again and opened his mouth to speak. The screen door of the waiting room opened and clattered shut.

It got real quiet in that room, hospital quiet. It got so quiet I could hear my own heart beating. Now Aaron knew who opened that door, but he didn't bat an eyelid. He turned around real slow and faced High Sheriff Sampson, the baddest man in South Mississippi.

Mr. Sampson stood there with his legs wide open, like the men you see on television. His beefy face was blood-red and his gray eyes were rattlesnake hard. He was mad; no doubt about it. I had never seen him so mad.

"Preacher," he said, "you done gone crazy?" He was talking low-like and mean.

"Nosir," Aaron said. "Nosir, Mr. Sampson."

"What you think you doing?"

"Going to St. Louis, Mr. Sampson."

"You must done lost yo' mind, boy."

Mr. Sampson started walking towards Aaron with his hand on his gun. Twenty or thirty men pushed through the front door and fanned out over the room. Mr. Sampson stopped about two paces from Aaron and looked him up and down. That look had paralyzed hundreds of niggers; but it didn't faze Aaron none— he stood his ground.

"I'm gonna give you a chance, preacher. Git on over to the nigger side and git quick."

"I ain't bothering nobody, Mr. Sampson."

Somebody in the crowd yelled: "Don't reason wit' the nigger, Bull. Hit 'em."

Mr. Sampson walked up to Aaron and grabbed him in the collar and throwed him up against the ticket counter. He pulled out his gun.

"Did you hear me, deacon. I said, 'Git.' "

"I'm going to St. Louis, Mr. Sampson. That's cross state lines. The court done said——"

Aaron didn't have a chance. The blow came from nowhere. Laying there on the floor with blood spurting from his mouth, Aaron looked up at Mr. Sampson and he did another crazy thing: he grinned. Bull Sampson jumped up in the air and came down on Aaron with all his two hundred pounds. It made a crunchy sound. He jumped again and the mob, maddened by the blood and heat, moved in to help him. They fell on Aaron like mad dogs. They beat him with chairs; they beat him with sticks; they beat him with guns.

Till this day, I don't know what come over me. The first thing I know I was running and then I was standing in the middle of the white waiting room. Mr. Sampson was the first to see me. He backed off, cocked his pistol, and said: "Booker, boy, you come one mo' step and I'll kill you. What's a matter with you niggers today? All y'all gone crazy?"

"Please don't kill him," I begged. "You ain't got no call to treat him like that."

"So you saw it all, did you? Well, then, Booker you musta saw the nigger preacher reach for my gun?"

"He didn't do that, Mr. Sampson," I said. "He didn't——"

Mr. Sampson put a big hairy hand on my tie and pulled me to him.

"Booker," he said sweetly. "You saw the nigger preacher reach for my gun, didn't you?"

I didn't open my mouth—I couldn't I was so scared—but I guess my eyes answered for me. Whatever Mr. Sampson saw there musta convinced him 'cause he throwed me on the floor besides Aaron.

"Git this nigger out of here," he said, "and be quick about it."

Dropping to my knees, I put my hand on Aaron's chest; I didn't feel nothing. I felt his wrist; I didn't feel nothing. I got up and looked at them white folks with tears in my eyes. I looked at the women, sitting crying on the benches. I looked at the men. I looked at Mr. Sampson. I said, "He was a good man."

Mr. Sampson said, "Move the nigger."

A big sigh came out of me and I wrung my hands.

Mr. Sampson said, "Move the nigger."

He grabbed my tie and twisted it, but I didn't feel nothing. My eyes were glued to his hands; there was blood under the finger-nails, and the fingers—they looked like fat little red sausages. I screamed and Mr. Sampson flung me down on the floor.

He said, *"Move the nigger."*

I picked Aaron up and fixed his body over my shoulder and carried him outside. I sent for one of my boys and we dressed him up and put him away real nice-like and Rachel and the boy came and they cried and carried on and yet, somehow, they seemed prouder of Aaron than ever before. And the colored folks—they seemed proud, too. Crazy niggers. Didn't they know? Couldn't they see? It hadn't done no good. In fact, things got worse. The Northern newspapers started kicking up a stink and Mr. Rivers, the solicitor, announced they were going to hold a hearing. All of a sudden, Booker Taliaferro Brown became the biggest man in that town. My phone rang day and night: I got threats, I got promises, and I was offered bribes. Everywhere I turned somebody was waiting to ask me: "Whatcha gonna do? Whatcha gonna say?" To tell the truth, I didn't know myself. One day I would decide one thing and the next day I would decide another.

It was Mr. Rivers and Mr. Sampson who called my attention to that. They came to my office one day and called me a shifty, no-good nigger. They said they expected me to stand by "my statement" in the train station that I saw Aaron reach for the gun. I hadn't said no such thing, but Mr. Sampson said I said it and he said he had witnesses who heard me say it. "And if you say anything else," he said, "I can't be responsible for your health. Now you know"—he put that bloody hand on my shoulder and he smiled his sweet death smile—"you *know* I wouldn't threaten you, but the boys"—he shook his head—"the boys are real worked up over this one."

It was long about then that I began to hate Aaron Lott. I'm ashamed to admit it now, but it's true: I hated him. He had lived his life; he had made his choice. Why should he live my life, too, and make me choose? It wasn't fair; it wasn't right; it wasn't Christian. What made me so mad was the fact that nothing I said would help Aaron. He was dead and it wouldn't help one whit for me to say that he didn't reach for that gun. I tried to explain that to Rachel when she came to my office, moaning and crying, the night before the hearing.

"Listen to me, woman," I said. "Listen. Aaron was a good man. He lived a good life. He did a lot of good things, but he's *dead, dead, dead!* Nothing I say will bring him back. Bull Sampson's got ten niggers who are going to swear on a stack of Bibles that they saw Aaron reach for that gun. It won't do me or you or Aaron no good for me to swear otherwise."

What did I say that for? That woman liked to had a fit. She got down on her knees and she begged me to go with Aaron.

"Go wit' him," she cried. "Booker. *Booker!* If you's a man, if you's a father, if you's a friend, go wit' Aaron."

That woman tore my heart up. I ain't never heard nobody beg like that.

"Tell the truth, Booker," she said. "That's all I'm asking. Tell the truth."

"Truth!" I said. "Hah! That's all you niggers talk about: truth.

What do you know about truth? Truth is eating good and
sleeping good. Truth is living, Rachel. Be loyal to the living."

Rachel backed off from me. You would have thought that I
had cursed her or something. She didn't say nothing; she just
stood there pressed against the door. She stood there saying
nothing for so long that my nerves snapped.

"Say something," I shouted. "Say something—anything!"

She shook her head, slowly at first, and then her head started
moving like it wasn't attached to her body. It went back and
forth, back and forth, back and forth. I started towards her, but
she jerked open the door and ran out into the night, screaming.

That did it. I ran across the room to the filing cabinet, opened
the bottom drawer, and took out a dusty bottle of Scotch. I
started drinking, but the more I drank the soberer I got. I guess
I fell asleep 'cause I dreamed I buried Rachel and that everything went along fine until she jumped out of the casket and
started screaming. I came awake with a start and knocked over
the bottle. I reached for a rag and my hand stopped in mid-
air.

"Of course," I said out loud and slammed my fist down on the
Scotch-soaked papers.

I didn't see nothing.

Why didn't I think of it before?

I didn't see nothing.

Jumping up, I walked to and fro in the office. Would it work?
I rehearsed it in my mind. All I could see was Aaron's back. I
don't know whether he reached for the gun or not. All I know is
that *for some reason* the men beat him to death.

Rehearsing the thing in my mind, I felt a great weight slip off
my shoulders. I did a little jig in the middle of the floor and
went upstairs to my bed, whistling. Sarah turned over and
looked me up and down.

"What you happy about?"

"Can't a man be happy?" I asked.

She sniffed the air, said, "Oh," turned over, and mumbled
something in her pillow. It came to me then for the first time
that she was 'bout the only person in town who hadn't asked me
what I was going to do. I thought about it for a little while,
shrugged, and fell into bed with all my clothes on.

When I woke up the next morning, I had a terrible headache
and my tongue was a piece of sandpaper. For a long while, I

couldn't figure out what I was doing laying there with all my clothes on. Then it came to me: this was the big day. I put on my black silk suit, the one I wore for big funerals, and went downstairs to breakfast. I walked into the dining room without looking and bumped into Russell, the last person in the world I wanted to see. He was my only child, but he didn't act like it. He was always finding fault. He didn't like the way I talked to Negroes; he didn't like the way I talked to white folks. He didn't like this; he didn't like that. And to top it off, the young whippersnapper wanted to be an artist. Undertaking wasn't good enough for him. He wanted to paint pictures.

I sat down and grunted.

"Good morning, Papa." He said it like he meant it. He wants something, I thought, looking him over closely, noticing that his right eye was swollen.

"You been fighting again, boy?"

"Yes, Papa."

"You younguns. Education—that's what it is. Education! It's ruining you."

He didn't say nothing. He just sat there, looking down when I looked up and looking up when I looked down. This went on through the grits and the eggs and the second cup of coffee.

"Whatcha looking at?" I asked.

"Nothing, Papa."

"Whatcha thinking?"

"Nothing, Papa."

"You lying, boy. It's written all over your face."

He didn't say nothing.

I dismissed him with a wave of my hand, picked up the paper, and turned to the sports page.

"What are you going to do, Papa?"

The question caught me unawares. I know now that I was expecting it, that I wanted him to ask it; but he put it so bluntly that I was flabbergasted. I pretended I didn't understand.

"Do 'bout what, boy? Speak up!"

"About the trial, Papa."

I didn't say nothing for a long time. There wasn't much, in fact, I could say; so I got mad.

"Questions, questions, questions," I shouted. "That's all I get in this house—questions. You never have a civil word for your pa. I go out of here and work my tail off and you keep yourself shut up in that room of yours looking at them fool books and now soon as your old man gets his back against the wall you join the pack. I expected better than that of you, boy. A son ought to back his pa."

That hurt him. He picked up the coffee pot and poured himself another cup of coffee and his hand trembled. He took a sip and watched me over the rim.

"They say you are going to chicken out, Papa."

"Chicken out? What that mean?"

"They're betting you'll 'Tom.' "

I leaned back in the chair and took a sip of coffee.

"So they're betting, huh?" The idea appealed to me. "Crazy niggers—they'd bet on a funeral."

I saw pain on his face. He sighed and said: "I bet, too, Papa."

The cup fell out of my hand and broke, spilling black water over the tablecloth.

"You did what?"

"I bet you wouldn't 'Tom.' "

"You little fool." I fell out laughing and then I stopped suddenly and looked at him closely. "How much you bet?"

"One hundred dollars."

I stood up.

"You're lying," I said. "Where'd you get that kind of money?"

"From Mamma."

"Sarah!" I shouted. "Sarah! You get in here. What kind of house you running, sneaking behind my back, giving this boy money to gamble with?"

Sarah leaned against the door jamb. She was in her hot iron mood. There was no expression on her face. And her eyes were hard.

"I gave it to him, Booker," she said. "They called you an Uncle Tom. He got in a fight about it. He wanted to bet on you, Booker. *He* believes in you."

Suddenly I felt old and used up. I pulled a chair to me and sat down.

"Please," I said, waving my hand. "Please. Go away. Leave me alone. Please."

I sat there for maybe ten or fifteen minutes, thinking, praying. The phone rang. It was Mr. Withers, the president of the bank. I had put in for a loan and it had been turned down, but Mr. Withers said there'd been a mistake. "New fellow, you know," he said, clucking his tongue. He said he knew that it was my lifelong dream to build a modern funeral home and to buy a Cadillac hearse. He said he sympathized with that dream, supported it, thought the town needed it, and thought I deserved it. "The loan will go through," he said. "Drop by and see me this morning after the hearing."

When I put that phone down, it was wet with sweat. I couldn't turn that new funeral home down and Mr. Withers knew it. My father had raised me on that dream and before he died he made me swear on a Bible that I would make it good. And here it was on a platter, just for a word, a word that wouldn't hurt nobody.

I put on my hat and hurried to the courthouse. When they called my name, I walked in with my head held high. The courtroom was packed. The white folks had all the seats and the colored folks were standing in the rear. Whoever arranged the seating had set aside the first two rows for white men. They were sitting almost on top of each other, looking mean and uncomfortable in their best white shirts.

I walked up to the bench and swore on the Bible and took a seat. Mr. Rivers gave me a little smile and waited for me to get myself set.

"State your name," he said.

"Booker Taliaferro Brown." I took a quick look at the first two rows and recognized at least ten of the men who killed Aaron.

"And your age?"

"Fifty-seven."

"You're an undertaker?"

"Yessir."

"You been living in this town all your life?"

"Yessir."

"You like it here, don't you, Booker?"

Was this a threat? I looked Mr. Rivers in the face for the first time. He smiled.

I told the truth. I said, "Yessir."

"Now, calling your attention to the day of May 17th, did anything unusual happen on that day?"

The question threw me. I shook my head. Then it dawned on me. He was talking about——

"Yessir," I said. "That's the day Aaron got——" Something in

Mr. Rivers' face warned me and I pulled up— "that's the day of the trouble at the train station."

Mr. Rivers smiled. He looked like a trainer who'd just put a monkey through a new trick. You could feel the confidence and the contempt oozing out of him. I looked at his prissy little mustache and his smiling lips and I got mad. Lifting my head a little bit, I looked him full in the eyes; I held the eyes for a moment and I tried to tell the man behind the eyes that I was a man like him and that he didn't have no right to be using me and laughing about it. But he didn't get the message. The bastard—he chuckled softly, turned his back to me, and faced the audience.

"I believe you were with the preacher that day."

The water was getting deep. I scroonched down in my seat, closed the lids of my eyes, and looked dense.

"Yessir, Mr. Rivers," I drawled. "Ah was, Ah was."

"Now, Booker—" he turned around— "I believe you tried to keep the nigger preacher from getting out of line."

I hesitated. It wasn't a fair question. Finally, I said: "Yessir."

"You begged him not to go in the white side?"

"Yessir."

"And when that failed, you went over to *your* side—the *colored* side—and looked through the window?"

"Yessir."

He put his hand in his coat pocket and studied my face.

"You saw *everything,* didn't you?"

"Just about." A muscle on the inside of my thigh started tingling.

Mr. Rivers shuffled some papers he had in his hand. He seemed to be thinking real hard. I pushed myself against the back of the chair. Mr. Rivers moved close, quick, and stabbed his finger into my chest.

"Booker, did you see the nigger preacher reach for Mr. Sampson's gun?"

He backed away, smiling. I looked away from him and I felt my heart trying to tear out of my skin. I looked out over the courtroom. It was still; wasn't even a fly moving. I looked at the white folks in front and the colored folks in back and I turned the question over in my mind. While I was doing that, waiting, taking my time, I noticed, out of the corner of my eye, that the smile on Mr. Rivers' face was dying away. Suddenly, I had a terrible itch to know what that smile would turn into.

I said, "Nosir."

Mr. Rivers stumbled backwards like he had been shot. Old Judge Sloan took off his glasses and pushed his head out over the bench. The whole courtroom seemed to be leaning in to me and I saw Aaron's widow leaning back with her eyes closed and it seemed to me at that distance that her lips were moving in prayer.

Mr. Rivers was the first to recover. He put his smile back on and he acted like my answer was in the script.

"You mean," he said, "that you didn't see it. It happened so quickly that you missed it?"

I looked at the bait and I ain't gonna lie: I was tempted. He knew as well as I did what I meant, but he was gambling on my weakness. I had thrown away my funeral home, my hearse, everything I owned, and he was standing there like a magician, pulling them out of a hat, one at a time, dangling them, saying: "Looka here, looka here, don't they look pretty?" I was on top of a house and he was betting that if he gave me a ladder I would come down. He was wrong, but you can't fault him for trying. He hadn't never met no nigger who would go all the way. I looked him in the eye and went the last mile.

"Aaron didn't reach for that gun," I said. "Them people, they just fell on——"

"Hold it," he shouted. "I want to remind you that there are laws in this state against perjury. You can go to jail for five years for what you just said. Now I know you've been conferring with those NAACP fellows, but I want to remind you of the statements you made to Sheriff Sampson and me. Judge—" he dismissed me with a wave of his hand—"Judge, this *man*—" he caught himself and it was my turn to smile—"this *boy* is lying. Ten niggers have testified that they saw the preacher reach for the gun. Twenty white people saw it. You've heard their testimony. I want to withdraw this witness and I want to reserve the right to file perjury charges against him."

Judge Sloan nodded. He pushed his bottom lip over his top one.

"You can step down," he said. "I want to warn you that perjury is a very grave offense. You——"

"Judge, I didn't——"

"Nigger!" He banged his gavel. "Don't you interrupt me. Now git out of here."

Two guards pushed me outside and waved away the reporters. Billy Giles, Mr. Sampson's assistant, came out and told me Mr. Sampson wanted me out of town before sundown. "And he says you'd better get out before the Northern reporters leave. He won't be responsible for your safety after that."

I nodded and went on down the stairs and started out the door.

"Booker!"

Rachel and a whole line of Negroes were running down the stairs. I stepped outside and waited for them. Rachel ran up and throwed her arms around me. "It don't take but one, Booker," she said. "It don't take but one." Somebody else said: "They whitewashed it, they whitewashed it, but you spoiled it for 'em."

Russell came out then and stood over to the side while the others crowded around to shake my hands. Then the others sensed that he was waiting and they made a little aisle. He walked up to me kind of slow-like and he said, "Thank you, sir." That was the first time in his whole seventeen years that that boy had said "sir" to me. I cleared my throat and when I opened my eyes Sarah was standing beside me. She didn't say nothing; she just put her hand in mine and stood there. It was long about then, I guess, when I realized that I wasn't seeing so good. They say I cried, but I don't believe a word of it. It was such a hot day and the sun was shining so bright that the sweat rolling down my face blinded me. I wiped the sweat out of my eyes and some more people came up and said a lot of foolish things about me showing the white folks and following in Aaron's footsteps. I wasn't doing no such fool thing. Ol' Man Rivers just put the thing to me in a way it hadn't been put before—man to man. It was simple, really. Any man would have done it.

The Winds of Change

LOYLE HAIRSTON

It was my big day and I was so hopped up I woke up before the alarm went off. Geez. The house was quiet except for Sis hummin' out in the kitchen. I set my watch by the clock and gauged my time; then laid out my vine, a clean shirt and things on the bed. After I brushed my kicks, I looked my wig over in the mirror. My stockin' cap slipped off my head when I was sleepin' and the waves in my hair done unstrung and was all tangled up.

"Damn!"

I mean I wouldn't make my *own* funeral without my *wig* bein' in shape. So I went into the livin' room and called Sonny for an appointment; I *had* to have a marcel! He said he could take me on round ten o'clock. Whew! Glancin' at my watch I seen I had plenty of time; so I went back in my room and took out my bongos and worked out a while.

And just when the licks was comin' good, she opens up on me again. I mean if she wasn't my sister——

"Waddell."

At eight o'clock in the *a.m.!* And pa's tryin' to cop a snooze in the next room.

"Waddell!"

I locked my door, bolted it. She's way out in the kitchen but her voice it busts t'rough the walls like a truck. I didn't say nothin'; the name I had for her was burnin' the tip of my tongue—but I didn't say nothin'. I just kept on workin' out on my bongos, tryin' to think about that audition gig I had to make at one o'clock. My big chance to cop a show, a off-Broadway show; my chance to make enough long bread to put her down— and she wanta heat me up and make me blow it——

"Waddell Wilkins!"

"Goddam it, Sis, leave me alone—*please!*"

"Don't you know papa's tryin' to sleep . . . !"

Don't *I* know it; she's blastin' like a H-bomb and askin' me don't *I* know pa's tryin' to sleep. Geez! I mean I couldn't bear it no longer; so I t'rowed my bongos on the bed and went and run some water in the bathtub.

"You takin' a *bath?*" She said as I went in the kitchen where she was washin' dishes. Her hair was undone, curlin' over her forehead from under her 'kerchief; and her slip was showin' t'rough her loose robe.

"I'm gon wash my head."

She dropped her towel in the dishwater and gaped at me like I just said I was gon commit a murder.

"Aw naw! Don't tell me that wavy-wigged-Waddell's gonna wash out his beauty tresses!"

"Lay off me, Sis; goddam it, lay off!"

" 'Lay off me, Sis; . . . lay off!' " She mocked back at me. "You slick-headed ditty-bop, if you spent half as much time tryin' to put something *inside* that worthless hat-rack as you did havin' your brains fried——"

"Goddam it, Sis . . . Aw go to hell."

I took a cake of soap from the cabinet and went back to the bathroom.

I mean what'd she know. She think I'm gon make a audition lookin' like a creep. You think they're lookin' for talent in the raw; appearance is half the game. A block-head knows that. If you ain't pressed and got the right spiel, you ain't sayin' *nothin'* to the silks; it's the only language they can dig.

". . . If you had any backbone you'd be outlookin' for a job . . ."

A job! What she think I'm knockin' myself out to make this audition gig for—my old-age pension; I asked her that!

"Hah! You'll never have to worry about old-age pension; at the rate you're goin', you'll starve to death before you're twenty-one."

Dig her; I mean just dig *her*. Like them Nationalists always say: black folks is like crabs in a barrel—try to climb out and they'll snatch you right back ever' time.

"You know what you are, Sis; you're a creep—that's what you are!"

Then she really exploded. I wrapped my towel round my ears and went on in my room and put my old clothes back on, then hung my *vine* on a hanger, figurin' I'd dress when I got finished at the barbershop. Sis was hammerin' away through the walls like she was in a stone fit; until I couldn't take no more.

I blasted her, "Shut your trap a minute and take a look at this dump you're livin' in. The walls is cracked; the ceilin's busted; the pipes leak; there ain't no heat; no hot water mosta the time; no fresh air. The only thing expensive here is your goddam rent. Geez.

"You want me to grow up a sap like pa—knockin' hisself out on a mail-handler gig at the Post Office where the pay is so lousy he's gotta work a part-time gig to keep the finance company from bustin' the door down . . . I mean are you a damn fool, Sis?"

Sometimes I have to ask myself how come ma had to die and leave me saddled with *her*. Geez . . .

I copped a hack to Ray's Barbershoppe. The joint was already hummin' with cats talkin' about "broads," the numbers they *missed,* integration, the silks, and the figure they was gon play *today*. Half of the chairs was full; there was a few squares *actual'* takin' regular haircuts. Five cats was settin' under the dryers in back diggin' the NEWS. I set down and tried to think about the audition; I mean what them gigs was really like and how many cats I had to compete with, and wonderin' how good I really was on the bongos. My man, Sonny, dug me.

"You ready, Baby."

"Yeah," I winked and took the resumé scratch-sheet he mapped out for me: background; how long I been studyin'; where at; workin' experience; and such particulars. It was boss, the way he faked it. After goin' over it I put it back in my pocket, checked the time, and watched Sonny put the finish on the cat he was workin' on. His wig was shinin' like black satin; and Sonny was layin' in the waves with his hands, rollin' a big one in front and workin' the others in, soft and delicate like they growed natural. It was a swingin' job.

When my turn come I told him I wanted one just like he laid on that cat. Sonny rubbed the process in so thick with his rubber gloves, it started stingin' a little t'rough the heavy layer of grease he packed in my scalp.

"Damn, Baby!"

"Cool it, Mamma," Sonny said, combin' the process into my

hair. "The secret to this business is to burn it so close to the scale, it'll look natural all the way to the roots.

When he finished I dug my wig in the mirror.

"That's boss, Baby—the best I ever seen."

"Wow!" The cat in the next chair said. "You been transformed, daddy-o; if you was a shade lighter, you could pass for a silk!"

"The only way you'll ever get your mop to grow natural again, Mamma," Sonny boasted, "is to have your head *shaved!*"

"Shee-it," I said, t'rowed my man a five-spot, and told him to bank the change.

After I put on my vine and they all wished me good luck, I went over to St. Nick's and took the A-train down to Fifty-ninth Street. It was only twelve o'clock, so I set in a Brass Rail on Eighth Avenue and tightened my nerves with a few slugs of Imperial. Then I boated it down to Forty-sixth' where the joint was, took a deep breath, and went inside.

They was runnin' off a dance number on the stage; only some cat in shirt sleeves and a cigar stump stuck in his teeth kept interruptin' 'em ever'time they got started. They was all in a sweat and I was tryin' to dig what was happenin' when this little blade-nosed cat switched over and told me to wait outside.

There was a settin' room on the left, full of silk broads settin' round a old table, smokin' and yackin' away about nothin'; so I set on a chair against the wall in the corridor. From another part of the building I heard all sorts of drums beatin' and feet stompin' and a sad chorus that couldn't find the beat. They must be *silks*, I thought; and just to ease my nerves I tried to pick up the beat on my bongos. That huddle of old silk broads stopped yackin' and *dug* me, their eyes slidin' over me and stoppin' on my hair, where they lit up and they whispered somethin' to one another. I played it cool.

Then this tall one, with green eyes and faded blond hair, eased out of the door with a cigarette in her mouth, lookin' round like she was pickin' out somebody to cop a light from. She asked one of the greys in the settin' room, lit up, then leaned against the wall by the dressin' room door. And daddy she was *built!* Without lookin' at her face, I knowed she was buzzin' me with her pearls. Not bad at all—for a silk.

And you could tell she thought I was a big-shot entertainer like Harry Belafonte or somebody from the way she was diggin'

me. Geez! I mean, soon's they think you're famous and pullin'
down that long bread they're ready to integrate the hell outa
you——

"Hi."

I played a freeze; like my thoughts had me up-tight. But she
was standin' right in front of me now; and I'm diggin' the way
them leotogs was spellin' the truth out to me the way they was
huggin' her. I mean I ain't no stone.

"Hello," I said, playin' it straight; silks think you can't talk
nothin' but slang.

"Excuse me, but aren't you Doug Ward?"

See what I mean. Like I'm psychic, I dig silks.

"No," I said and t'rowed her a sympathetic smile. Then three
more, one of 'em a member, bolted out of the dressin' room and
sailed over to where we was. Miss Fine said she was sorry and
introduced herself to me, then the three others. I nodded to 'em
and told 'em my name and dug 'em where they was sayin' the
most. I mean they all was stacked; and they was friendly as
hell. But this member—daddy, she was a real fox! Her big nut-
shaped eyes was so bright it made you squint when you looked
straight at 'em; and she musta been playin' the part of a African
in the play because she wore her hair short and natural, like
Miriam Makeba. But the way her big gold-looped earrings
gleamed against her long satin-smooth neck, she looked like a
African *Princess!* Without comin' outa my freeze, I dug her the
most.

We struck up a conversation, and Colleen—the bold one—
was tellin' me that they was all students with the American
Ballet outfit when I was called for my gig. I rushed off, hopin' I'd
get back before they left so I could put the sound on the
princess.

When I got inside and seen five cats in the middle of the
floor, stripped down to tights, squattin' behind them long-bellied
African drums, I got a feelin' in my gut that I didn't like. In
nothin' flat, the cat in charge let me know what the feelin' was.
They done changed the "locale" to a African settin' and when I
told him that I never done no primitive dancin', he told me, with
a lotta friggin' double-talk—to blow! I could see Sis's face,
mockin' and laughin' at me, so clear, I walked into the door.

I was gettin' on the elevator when I heard this Colleen's voice.
I turned and she gave *me* a sympathetic smile like she knowed

straight off what happened. She was dressed and said she was waitin' for the others; then she asked me where I was goin'. I shrugged my shoulders, tryin' to pull myself together.

"Want to come with us?"

". . . Ah . . . I mean—where?"

"To the UN. We're——"

"The UN . . .?"

"Oh, come on. It'll take your mind off this. Okay?"

And before I give her an answer, she told me to wait for the girls while she took her car outa the parkin' lot. After I seen the princess, I forgot ever'thing—but *her!* All the way across town I'm tryin' to figure how I'm gon get her alone so I can sound her, and they're busy yackin' about the UN. It floored 'em when I told 'em I ain't never been there. So I remembered what the NEWS always said about the joint and told 'em I didn't go because I thought the place was run by the commies. They bust laughin' on me. And that's when I learnt that Oleta, the princess, was a *pure* African; and that her brother was a member of her country's UN delegation. Geez! I mean I coulda hid in the ash tray on the armrest.

Colleen parked the car and we all strolled up the boulevard to the UN. Out in front a long row of flags was wavin' in the bright breeze, showin' off dazzlin' colors in all sorts of patterns; and I couldn't take my eye off that tall buildin' juttin' against the pale blue as we climbed the steps and went across the stone court to the "General Assembly Building."

Inside it was a boss lay-out; streamlined down to the carpets, with a soft bluish light streamin' in from the glass walls openin' on a side garden-court splashed with green and bright-colored flowers. But when I got upstairs and seen all them African cats settin' round the tables on the main floor, I damn near flipped! Some of 'em wore reg'lar blue-serge; some showed off their native styles. Papers was stacked neat on their desks alongside pitchers of water. And they kept leanin' over to one another, talkin' confidential—puttin' the *ig'* on the silks scattered amongs' 'em.

The gallery was buzzin' about "Lumumba" and "Tshombe" and the "Belgium mercenaries" and "Kasavuba" and some "resolution" the "Afro-Asian" delegations done put to the floor. Oleta pointed her brother out to me, settin' with a lotta young cats with smooth black round faces and woolly hair cropped even all

over. They all was beamin' like they had Charley's number; and
Charley was settin' there fussin' with his notes like he *knowed*
it. I mean it was all I could do to keep from jumpin' up on my
seat and bust out clappin'. No wonder the NEWS say the joint's
run by Reds!

If Sis could see this, she'd flip—for certain, I thought, sittin'
there between princess Oleta and Colleen, with my earphones
on, and listenin' to this African talkin' in *French*. And it's comin"
t'rough my earphones in *English!* Geez. I mean—*damn!*

By the time they got done hasslin' over that resolution and
blastin' the silks until they buckled, me and Oleta was hittin' it
off fine. And she was lookin' foxier by the minute. I copped her
address when we got downstairs. Colleen had to pick her ol' lady
up downtown and said that she didn't have time to drive us back
across town. We walked her to her car, where she said she was
very glad to meet me, shook my hand, wished me luck in show
business, and give me the nicest smile you could get from a "silk
broad." I mean it moved me.

"Now don't forget my party Friday night." She said to her gal
friends, while I was makin' some sounds to Oleta. "You too,
Oleta."

"Colleen, you know I have a class Friday night."

"Oh, posh with your class—I insist that you be there!"

"Oh, alright, we'll see," Oleta give in with a smile bright as a
rose. Colleen got in her car, then called me:

". . . Why don't *you* come too, Mr. Wilkins?"

"Well——"

"Here, I'll give you my address. We'd love to have you," she
said, winkin' at Oleta as she scribbled her address on the back
of a card.

All the way uptown, Princess Oleta and makin' that party
Friday night was the only thing on my mind. It was only
Monday and by Friday my process'd need retouchin'; so I went
by Ray's and made an appointment with Sonny for Friday. I was
hongry, but after blowin' my audition, I wasn't in no mood for
Sis's abuse; so I copped a sandwich and took in a flick.

Marilyn Monroe was playin' at the Loew's; only soon's I got
comfortable I went to sleep and dreamt I was with Oleta by the
lake in Central Park, playin' my bongos, and she was dancin' for
me; and I was watchin' her Fine Brown reflectin' in the water
shinin' with golden moonlight.Then she'd come over and stroke

my hair; and in the gleamin' pools of her eyes I seen myself holdin' her close; only I was stripped down like a African warrior and my hair was woolly like them cats at the UN. I woke up then. I mean the dream was gettin' outa hand!

All week long there was something about them Africans that was buggin' me. I mean without even tryin'—they was *sayin'* something. I told Sis about 'em before I left for the barbershop.

"You mean they ain't brown-nosin' to the white folks like some of our 'leaders.' "

I cut out then and there. Geez. You ask her a question and she gotta make a speech. After gettin' my kicks shined and my fingernails honed and polished, I set down in the barber chair, rubbin' the fuzz on my chin and thinkin' about Oleta and how fine she was in a way I ain't never seen in a girl, member or silk. Sonny stopped gassin' with some guys in the back and put the cloth round my neck. I told him to give me a shave. And he started crankin' the chair back.

"Not my face, daddy—my *head!*"

It shook the cat so, he dropped his clippers. I just grinned and laid back and shut my eyes, wonderin' where I could cop myself a deuce of African drums . . .

language ·

The Screamers

LeRoi Jones

Lynn Hope adjusts his turban under the swishing red green yellow shadow lights. Dots. Suede heaven raining, windows yawning cool summer air, and his musicians watch him grinning, quietly, or high with wine blotches on four dollar shirts. A yellow girl will not dance with me, nor will Teddy's people, in line to the left of the stage, readying their *Routines.* Haroldeen, the most beautiful, in her pitiful dead sweater. Make it yellow, wish it whole. Lights. Teddy, Sonny Boy, Kenney & Calvin, Scram, a few of Nat's boys jamming long washed handkerchiefs in breast pockets, pushing shirts into homemade cummerbunds, shuffling lightly for any audience.

"The Cross-Over," Deen laughing at us all. And they perform in solemn unison a social tract of love. (With no music till Lynn finishes "macking" with any big-lipped Esther screws across the stage.) White and green plaid jackets his men wear, and that twisted badge, black turban/on red string conked hair. (OPPRESSORS!) A greasy hipness, down-ness, nobody in our camp believed (having social worker mothers and postman fathers; or living squeezed in light skinned projects with adulterers and proud skinny ladies with soft voices). The theory, the spectrum, this sound baked inside their heads, and still rub sweaty against those lesser lights. Those niggers. Laundromat workers, beauticians, pregnant short haired jail bait separated all ways from "us," but in this vat we sweated gladly for each other. And rubbed. And Lynn could be a common hero, from whatever side we saw him. Knowing that energy, and its response. That drained silence we had to make with our hands, leaving actual love to Nat or Al or Scram.

He stomped his foot, and waved one hand. The other hung loosely on his horn. And their turbans wove in among those shadows. Lynn's tighter, neater, and bright gorgeous yellow stuck with a green stone. Also, those green sparkling cubes dancing off his pinkies. A-boomp bahba bahba, A-boomp bahba bahba, A-boomp bahba bahba, A-boomp bahba bahba, the turbans sway behind him. And he grins before he lifts the horn, at deen or drunk becky, and we search the dark for girls.

Who would I get? (Not anyone who would understand this.) Some light girl who had fallen into bad times and ill-repute for dating Bubbles. And he fixed her later with his child, now she walks Orange St. wiping chocolate from its face. A disgraced white girl who learned to calypso in vocational school. Hence, behind halting speech, a humanity as paltry as her cotton dress. (And the big hats made a line behind her, stroking their erections, hoping for photographs to take down south.) Lynn would oblige. He would make the most perverted hopes sensual and possible. Chanting at that dark crowd. Or some girl, a wino's daughter, with carefully vaselined bow legs would drape her filthy angora against the cardboard corinthian, eyeing past any greediness a white man knows, my soft tyrolean hat, pressed corduroy suit, and "B" sweater. Whatever they meant, finally to her, valuable shadows barely visible. Some stuck-up boy with "good" hair. And as a naked display of America, for I meant to her that same oppression. A stunted head of greased glass feathers, orange lips, brown pasted edge to the collar of her dying blouse. The secret perfume of poverty and ignorant desire. Arrogant too, at my disorder, which calls her smile mysterious. Turning to be eaten by the crowd. That mingled foliage of sweat and shadows: *Night Train* was what they swayed to. And smelled each other in The Grind, The Rub, The Slow Drag. From side to side, slow or jerked staccato as their wedding dictated. Big hats bent tight skirts, and some light girls' hair swept the resin on the floor. Respectable ladies put stiff arms on your waist to keep some light between, looking nervously at an ugly friend forever at the music's edge.

I wanted girls like Erselle, whose father sang on television, but my hair was not straight enough, and my father never learned how to drink. Our house sat lonely and large on a half-Italian street, filled with important Negroes. (Though it is rumored they had a son, thin with big eyes, they killed because he was crazy.) Surrounded by the haughty daughters of depressed economic groups. They plotted in their projects for mediocrity, and the neighborhood smelled of their despair. And only the wild or the very poor thrived in Graham's or could be roused by Lynn's histories and rhythms. America had choked the rest, who could sit still for hours under popular songs, or be readied for citizenship by slightly bohemian social workers. They rivaled pure emotion with wind-up record players that pumped Jo Stafford into Home Economics rooms. And these carefully scrubbed children of my parents' friends fattened on their rhythms until they could join the Urban League or Household Finance and hound the poor for their honesty.

I was too quiet to become a murderer, and too used to extravagance for their skinny lyrics. They mentioned neither cocaine nor Bach, which was my reading, and the flaw of that society. I disappeared into the slums, and fell in love with violence, and invented for myself a mysterious economy of need. Hence, I shambled anonymously thru Lloyd's, The Nitecap, The Hi-Spot, and Graham's desiring everything I felt. In a new English overcoat and green hat, scouring that town for my peers. And they were old pinch faced whores full of snuff and weak dope, celebrity fags with radio programs, mute bass players who loved me, and built the myth of my intelligence. You see, I left America on the first fast boat.

This was Sunday night, and the Baptists were still praying in their "faboulous" churches. Though my father sat listening to the radio, or reading pulp cowboy magazines, which I take in part to be the truest legacy of my spirit. God never had a chance. And I would be walking slowly towards The Graham, not even knowing how to smoke. Willing for any experience, any image, any further separation from where my good grades were sure to lead. Frightened of post offices, lawyer's offices, doctor's cars, the deaths of clean politicians. Or of the imaginary fat man, advertising cemeteries to his "good colored friends." Lynn's screams erased them all, and I thought myself intrepid white commando from the West. Plunged into noise and flesh, and their form become an ethic.

Now Lynn wheeled and hunched himself for another tune. Fast dancers fanned themselves. Couples who practiced during the week talked over their steps. Deen and her dancing clubs readied avant-garde routines. Now it was *Harlem Nocturne,* which I whistled loudly one Saturday in a laundromat, and the girl who stuffed in my khakis and stiff underwear asked was I a musician. I met her at Graham's that night and we waved, and I suppose she knew I loved her.

Nocturne was slow and heavy and the serious dancers loosened their ties. The slowly twisting lights made specks of human shadows, the darkness seemed to float around the hall. Any meat you clung to was yours those few minutes without interruption. The length of the music was the only form. And the idea was to press against each other hard, to rub, to shove the hips tight, and gasp at whatever passion. Professionals wore jocks against embarrassment. Amateurs, like myself, after the music stopped, put our hands quickly into our pockets, and retreated into the shadows. It was as meaningful as anything else we knew.

All extremes were popular with that crowd. The singers shouted, the musicians stomped and howled. The dancers ground each other past passion or moved so fast it blurred intelligence. We hated the popular song, and any freedman could tell you if you asked that white people danced jerkily, and were slower than our champions. One style, which developed as Italians showed up with pegs, and our own grace moved towards bellbottom pants to further complicate the cipher, was the honk. The repeated rhythmic figure, a screamed riff, pushed in its insistence past music. It was hatred and frustration, secrecy and despair. It spurted out of the diphthong culture, and reinforced the black cults of emotion. There was no compromise, no dreary sophistication, only the elegance of something that is too ugly to be described, and is diluted only at the agent's peril. All the saxophonists of that world were honkers, Illinois, Gator, Big Jay, Jug, the great sounds of our day. Ethnic historians, actors, priests of the unconscious. That stance spread like fire thru the cabarets and joints of the black cities, so that the sound itself became a basis for thought, and the innovators searched for uglier modes. Illinois would leap and twist his head, scream when he wasn't playing. Gator would strut up and down the stage, dancing for emphasis, shaking his long gassed hair in his face and coolly mopping it back. Jug, the beautiful horn, would wave back and forth so high we all envied him his connection, or he'd stomp softly to the edge of the stage whispering those raucous threats. Jay first turned the mark around, opened the way further for the completely nihilistic act. McNeeley, the first Dada coon of the age, jumped and stomped and yowled and finally sensed the only other space that form allowed. He fell first on his knees, never releasing the horn, and walked that way across the stage. We hunched together drowning any sound, relying on Jay's contorted face for evidence that there was still music, though none of us needed it now. And then he fell backwards, flat on his back, with both feet stuck up high in the air, and he kicked and thrashed and the horn spat enraged sociologies.

That was the night Hip Charlie, the Baxter Terrace Romeo, got wasted right in front of the place. Snake and four friends mashed him up and left him for the ofays to identify. Also the night I had the grey bells and sat in the Chinese restaurant all night to show them off. Jay had set a social form for the poor, just as Bird and Dizzy proposed it for the middle class. On his back screaming was the Mona Lisa with the mustache, as crude and simple. Jo Stafford could not do it. Bird took the language, and we woke up one Saturday whispering Ornithology. Blank verse.

And Newark always had a bad reputation, I mean, everybody could pop their fingers. Was hip. Had walks. Knew all about The Apple. So I suppose when the word got to Lynn what Big Jay had done, he knew all the little down cats were waiting to see him in this town. He knew he had to cook. And he blasted all night, crawled and leaped, then stood at the side of the stand, and watched us while he fixed his sky, wiped his face. Watched us to see how far he'd gone, but he was tired and we weren't, which was not where it was. The girls rocked slowly against the silence of the horns, and big hats pushed each other or made plans for murder. We had not completely come. All sufficiently eaten by Jay's memory, "on his back, kicking his feet in the air, Ga-ud Dam!" So he moved cautiously to the edge of the stage, and the gritty muslims he played with gathered close. It was some mean honking blues, and he made no attempt to hide his intentions. He was breaking bad. "Okay, baby," we all thought, "Go for yourself." I was standing at the back of the hall with one arm behind my back, so the overcoat could hang over in that casual gesture of fashion. Lynn was moving, and the camel walkers were moving in the corners. The fast dancers and practicers making the whole hall dangerous. "Off my suedes, motherfucker." Lynn was trying to move us, and even I did the one step I knew, safe at the back of the hall. The hippies ran for girls. Ugly girls danced with each other. Skippy, who ran the lights, made them move faster in that circle on the ceiling, and darkness raced around the hall. Then Lynn got his riff, that rhythmic figure we knew he would repeat, the honked note that would be his personal evaluation of the world. And he screamed it so the veins in his face stood out like neon. "Uhh, yeh, Uhh, yeh, Uhh, yeh," we all screamed to push him further. So he opened his eyes for a second, and really made his move. He looked over his shoulder at the other turbans, then marched in time with his riff, on his toes across the stage. They followed; he marched across to the other side, repeated, then finally he descended, still screaming, into the crowd, and as the sidemen followed, we made a path for them around the hall. They were strutting, and all their horns held very high, and they were only playing that one scary note. They moved near the back of the hall, chanting and swaying, and passed right in front of me. I had a little cup full of wine a murderer friend of mine made me drink, so I drank it and tossed the cup in the air, then fell in line behind the last wild horn man, strutting like the rest of them. Bubbles and Rogie followed me, and four eyed Moselle Boyd. And we strutted back and forth pumping our arms, repeating with Lynn Hope, "Yeh, Uhh, Yeh, Uhh." Then everybody fell in behind us, yelling still. There was confusion and stumbling, but there were no real fights. The thing they wanted was right there and easily accessible. No one could stop you from getting in that line. "It's too crowded. It's too many people on the line!" some people yelled. So Lynn thought further, and made to destroy the ghetto. We went out into the lobby and in perfect rhythm down the marble steps. Some musicians laughed, but Lynn and some others kept the note, till the others fell back in. Five or six hundred hopped up woogies tumbled out into Belmont Avenue. Lynn marched right in the center of the street. Sunday night traffic stopped, and honked. Big Red yelled at a bus driver, "Hey, baby, honk that horn in time or shut it off!" The bus driver cooled it. We screamed and screamed at the clear image of ourselves as we should always be. Ecstatic, completed, involved in a secret communal expression. It would be the form of the sweetest revolution, to hucklebuck into the fallen capitol, and let the oppressors lindy hop out. We marched all the way to Spruce, weaving among the stalled cars, laughing at the dazed white men who sat behind the wheels. Then Lynn turned and we strutted back towards the hall. The late show at the National was turning out, and all the big hats there jumped right in our line.

Then the Nabs came, and with them, the fire engines. What was it, a labor riot? Anarchists? A nigger strike? The paddy wagons and cruisers pulled in from both sides, and sticks and billies started flying, heavy streams of water splattering the marchers up and down the street. America's responsible immigrants were doing her light work again. The knives came out, the razors, all the Biggers who would not be bent counterattacked or came up behind the civil servants, smashing at them with coke bottles and aerials. Belmont writhed under the dead economy and splivs floated in the gutters, disappearing under cars. But for awhile, before the war had reached its peak, Lynn and his musicians, a few other fools, and I, still marched, screaming thru the maddened crowd. Onto the sidewalk, into the lobby, half-way up the stairs, then we all broke our different ways, to save whatever it was each of us thought we loved.

Language.

Sarah

Martin J. Hamer

It snowed on Thanksgiving Day. With the wonder of all the preparations and the knowledge that a man was coming to visit, the snow was more than Clyde could bear. "It's snowing!" he screamed. "Mama, it's snowing!" In a frenzy he ran into the kitchen to tell his mother the news. He was in the way; he was sent back into the living room. He came sneaking back, frightening his Aunt Bea with a loud "Boo!" He ran out again and opened the window. The snow was falling in great silver flakes. He took what he could catch in his hands and blew it across the room. "Snow! Snow!" he cried. He was placed in a chair and given a magazine.

Bea Boyce had come early to help out. She was a rotund woman, forty-six years of age, with a romantic air and quick brown eyes. As she moved around and around, setting the open-leafed table, her taffeta dress swished and swirled about her and she hummed in a very high key. She placed the silverware with elaborate care and folded the linen napkins into white fluffed caps. When she remembered that the shoes she wore were open at the toes, she said aloud to no one in particular that she hoped Mr. Boyce would think to bring her rubbers. Then she began to whistle "The Twelve Days of Christmas," the wobbly sound coming from between her large, pursed lips, the effort hollowing her cheeks and arching her penciled-in eyebrows. Sarah called from the kitchen that house whistling was bad luck.

"It's not Christmas, anyway," Clyde said. "It's Thanksgiving!" His aunt rolled her eyes at him, and he pushed himself into the farthest corner of the chair and tried to roll his eyes at her.

"You're getting too cute," she said. "Mr. George will fix you, though. He's going to fix your wagon, but good!"

"Don't frighten the boy," said Sarah. She came from the

kitchen with the water glasses tinkling in her slender hands, and after placing them on the table she viewed herself solemnly in the mirror. Her hair was drawn straight back from her oval face, and her pierced ears showed tiny pearl earrings to match the necklace hanging in the fullness of her breast. Unlike her sister's, her brown pupils moved slowly. Her expression was apprehensive, and there was the suggestion of a clown's sorrow about her mouth where the lipstick had been drawn boldly onto the dark facial skin of her upper lip. Turning her body from side to side, she smoothed her purple dress about her hips and asked Bea, "How do I look?"

"Like a belle of the ball," said Bea.

Sarah frowned. "A belle of the ball at forty. A real belle of the ball." She placed one leg out in front of her and pressed a hand to its knee. "I think this dress is too short."

"What do you mean, too short? Look at mine!"

"Yours is too short too," Sarah said.

"Well, honey, that's the style these days."

"Dress like this will only put ideas in his head."

"And that ain't what you want?"

"I most certainly do *not*. Getting a man means about as much to me as getting an ice-cream cone."

"Which is why," said Bea, "you're making all this fuss about dinner." She went back to the table and fluffed a fallen napkin. "You just better pray that Ann's not in one of her moods. 'Cause, child, she'll sure mess things up for you."

"She'd better not," said Sarah angrily. "She'd just better be on her *p*'s and *q*'s if she knows what's good for her."

"I can't see why you even invited her. You know how she is."

"I invited her for the same reason I invited you—you're family."

"Well," said Bea, "remember what Papa used to say: Ain't nothing worse—Ain't nothing worse than family."

"I just wish you'd shut up," said Sarah, "for once!"

The doorbell rang, and Clyde scrambled into the hallway calling, "Who is it? Who is it?"

"It's me!"

"It's me!"

"It is I," shouted the final and strongest voice from far below, and his Aunt Ann's three boys came thundering up the four flights to the landing. They swept past him, shaking snow, fists, and tongues in his face. When Ann appeared on the landing, she took his small bewildered form in her arms and pressed him deep into the damp fur collar of her coat. Before they were inside, the bell rang again and Mr. Boyce came up the stairs puffing. A great wool muffler swathed his neck, and his mustache sparkled with melting snow. Bea Boyce made it clear to everyone that he had not thought enough to bring her rubbers.

Ann sat near the oilstove and warmed her bony frame in its shimmering heat. She was dressed in black, and the huge iron cross that hung about her neck made her corner of the room solemnly remote. Mr. Boyce sprawled on the couch, hung one hand on his vest pocket in the manner of a train conductor, and caressed his bushy mustache with the other. His wife fluttered among the children like a bird. "The boys have grown," she said. "They give no trouble," replied Ann. In less than ten minutes, thought Sarah, they've used Clyde's caps, broken his gun, crushed a plastic soldier, and rolled most of his marbles under the piano. "Well," she said loudly, "you all just make yourselves comfortable." "Gimme that!" said Ann's oldest. Without looking up, Ann said, "Now, now." Then she reached into her purse and took out her Bible. Sarah picked up a cigarette from the table and started to light it. Mr. Boyce brought out a fat cigar. "I hope you're not going to light that thing before dinner," said Bea. He glowered at her, rolling the fat cigar between his jaundiced-looking fingers. He harrumphed and placed it back in his pocket. Sarah's match popped loudly, and Mr. Boyce watched as a cloud of smoke obscured her. "Blow a smoke ring. Aunt Sarah! Blow a smoke ring!" Bea frowned, the doorbell rang, and everyone became silent. When a light rap sounded at the door, Bea crossed her legs and whispered to Mr. Boyce to sit straight. Ann took one hand from her Bible and began to finger her cross. Her boys gaped stupidly at the door, and Clyde moved cautiously toward his mother. Sarah closed her eyes and prayed: Please, Lord, don't let anything go wrong. "Come in!" she called. "Come in!"

A huge man entered, his black coat glistening with melted snow, and immediately a chilled air, heavy with the pungent odor of stale tobacco, spread about the room. "Come in, Mr. George," said Sarah. "Come in and meet the folks." He removed his coat and stood before them in a neat but tattered blue suit, a bright new white shirt, and a faded maroon-colored tie. His gaze moved easily from face to face; his slightly graying hair and soft features made him appear calm, but there was the indication of surprise in his manner, and his brow was drawn and deeply furrowed. Sarah introduced him to Mr. Boyce. "How do you do, sir," said Mr. George. Mr. Boyce was flattered. He pumped the tall man's arm, mumbling that it was a pleasure to meet a gentleman. Bea was squirming on the couch all the while, and by the time she was introduced her skirts were so high you could see where her stockings ended. When Sarah saw that Mr. George had noticed, she said, "Now, you wouldn't think she was the oldest, would you?" Everyone was silent. "And," Sarah went on loudly, "over here's my other sister, Ann."

Ann extended her left hand, holding on to her cross with her right. "I've heard a lot about you," she said.

"Thank you," said Mr. George warmly.

"I wouldn't be so quick to say thank you if I were you. You're not at all what I expected."

Mr. George stopped smiling. Sarah quickly said, "These are all her boys, except one. This one." She pushed Clyde forward. "This is Clyde. Well," she said to the boy, "what do you say?" Clyde stared at Mr. George and then retreated back behind Sarah.

"Boy sure needs to be taught," said Ann. "I've never seen a child so backward."

The fire could be heard burning in the oilstove, and Sarah closed her eyes to pray to God. "I brought you these," said Mr. George awkwardly. When Sarah turned, he was handing her two brown-paper-wrapped packages. Embarrassed, she mumbled "Thank you" and looked toward the floor. He was standing in a small puddle of dark water. "One of you boys fetch a piece of newspaper," she said loudly. "And one of you come take the gentleman's coat." Ann's boys moved furiously about the room. "The paper's in there," she screamed. "Take the coat in there, and the rest of you go get washed! Bea! Come help me in the kitchen." Bea rose like a princess, the swishing sound of her dress adding to the confusion. "Hurry up now, you boys," Sarah screamed. "Put those things up! Get washed! Dinner's almost ready." She turned to leave the room: she turned back. "Oh, have a seat, Mr. George. Do have a seat."

"And, dear Lord," droned Ann, asking the blessing, "help those of us who have erred from your path of righteousness and who are even now sittin' in your house, at your table, eatin' your food without your grace." One of her boys snickered. A loud pop echoed in the silence, and as Ann continued the boy whimpered softly, the short, gurgling wheeze of his breath punctuating his sobs. "God, we thank you for this food which we are about to receive, for the nourishin' of the body, and for Christ's sake"— she looked up—"Amen."

"Amen," they all chorused.

"Leg or breast?" asked Sarah. "Just let me know." She carved the turkey, and the plates were passed in silence, filled with turnips, rice, and bread stuffing. Clyde poured the gravy on his plate for so long that Mr. Boyce quipped, "That bird can't swim, son." Everyone laughed; Bea frowned; then she went out of her way to pass Mr. George the bread. Struggling to cut her share of the bird, Sarah took time to make note. I'm going to have to speak to her before this day is over.

"How many churches, Mr. George," Ann began slowly, "do they have out there in Queens?" She rested her fork on her plate, the effort of the question distracting her from eating.

"What kind of churches?" asked Mr. George.

"Baptist," came the reply.

"Wouldn't know," he said curtly. "I'm Episcopalian."

Mr. Boyce grinned. Ann stiffened her bony frame until it loomed like a cattail over her boys. "How many of those do you have, then?"

Mr. George hesitated and looked toward the ceiling. In the interim Mr. Boyce belched. Sarah waited for him to excuse himself; then she asked Mr. George, "Did you know that the Boyces are business people? They own that candy store at the corner, one of the nicest in the neighborhood."

"Is that so?" said Mr. George.

"You in business too?" asked Mr. Boyce.

"No, not me," he said. "Don't you know I work with Sarah?"

"I thought you met in a dance hall," said Ann.

"I just read in the paper," said Mr. Boyce, "about two people who got married."

"What's that got to do with anything?" asked Bea.

"If you'd let me finish." He wiped his mouth. "I was going to say they got married in a dance hall."

"Couldn't be no worse sin," said Ann. She placed a finger in her mouth, and to Clyde's wonder and Sarah's chagrin removed a small bone covered with masticated food.

"Is that the wishbone?" Clyde asked.

"If it is," chimed Mr. Boyce, "better give it to his mama." He chuckled; Sarah banged her fork onto her plate, rose, and announced that she was going for dessert. In the kitchen she leaned against the cupboard and cried. They were all against her, and Bea was even trying to make time with him. Nothing's worse than family. Nothing's worse. Oh, Papa! Why'd you have to be right? She moved to get the dessert plates and saw the packages on the table. Unwrapping them carefully, she found the first was a bottle of Scotch; the second, a fuzz-covered monkey in a red velvet suit. It played a blue metal drum and raised a plastic bowler while marching to the sound of an unsteady, tinny beat. I don't know what he sees in me. Lord! I sure don't know what he sees in me. But if You let him go on seeing it, I'll treat him well, I swear it. I'll treat him well.

She re-entered the room and was pleased to see that Mr. George had become the center of attention. He had grown up not far from them on St. Nicholas Avenue, and he was telling them how nice Harlem was in those days. "Curtains at all the foyer windows," he said. "And I used to make my money by going around polishing the mailboxes."

"Yeah," said Mr. Boyce, "those were really the days. Really the days——"

"Now, out in Queens, where I am now——" he went on.

Sarah thought of Queens. Beautiful Queens. That's where she'd like to live. Throw out all this junk and move to Queens. Only thing I'd keep—she looked about the room—is the piano; Clyde will have to learn to play someday. And maybe the couch. It needs a new cover. With a new cover it won't look so bad. She straightened her shoulders, walked to the table, and handed Clyde the monkey. "Say thank you to Mr. George," she prompted.

"Is that his father?" asked Ann's youngest.

"Hush!" said Ann.

"That's all right," Mr. George said. "Children don't know any better."

"You sure have a fine sense for the pumps in life," said Bea.

"Bumps!" corrected Mr. Boyce.

"Bumps, pumps!" screamed Bea. "No matter what you call it, you ain't got it!"

Mr. Boyce harrumphed and looked down at the tablecloth.

"Can't get together, get apart," said Ann sweetly. "Man's a worse worry than hell."

"Is that why you ain't got one?"

"Okay, now, you all," said Sarah.

"Okay yourself," screamed Bea. "You ain't much better. Different one every time you turn around!"

"Why don't you shut up!"

"Look to God," said Ann. "You all better learn to look to God for your happiness. Better put your faith in the Lord——"

Tears blurred Sarah's vision. I'm going to move to Queens, she thought. Beautiful Queens. And I'm not going to see any of them again.

The dessert was eaten in silence. Afterward, Bea announced that she would do the dishes, and Ann offered to help. Sarah sat with Mr. George on the couch while Ann's boys, who had overeaten, moved more or less circuitously about the room. They stumbled into furniture and relatives like doped flies until finally the two younger ones crashed into one another and fell to the floor and to sleep. The oldest one continued to traverse the route for about five more minutes, and then, on receiving a sudden call from nature, he departed for the bathroom. He was found some time later, asleep on the stool. Clyde, no longer finding it necessary to protect his monkey, fell asleep near the stove, and in the big chair nearby, Mr. Boyce, his belt and shoes undone, began to snore. Soft shadows moved across the cracked plaster walls of the green room. Only an occasional clatter of a dish or piece of silverware from the kitchen interrupted the silence. Mr. George yawned, stretched, and let his big hand fall lightly on Sarah's thigh. She jumped. "What do you think I am?" she said.

"We're finished," said Ann, entering the room. "Well, will you look at this." She motioned toward her boys and Bea's husband. "Child, what did you put in that food? All right now, c'mon"— she clapped her hands. "Everybody up and out! Dinner's over, day's over, time to go home and to bed!"

The confusion began again. Mr. Boyce wanted Mr. George's

address; Sarah could not find a pencil. Bea came back from the window with the news that so much snow had fallen none of them would be able to get home. "Then you all better hurry now," said Sarah, "before it gets worse." She could not find a pencil, so Mr. Boyce stood in the middle of the room and repeated Mr. George's phone number over and over again until all of the boys were shouting it at the top of their lungs. Finally Sarah got them all to the door. "Good-by." "Good-by." "Gimme that!" "So long." "You must come by the store sometime." "Mama! He took my——" "Whenever you stop here, stop there." "Fine dinner, Sarah," said Mr. Boyce. "Why don't you come to church sometime?" "Gimme!" "Will you two behave! Give him back his monkey!" "So long, Mr. George," said Mr. Boyce. "Don't come crying to me," said Ann. "Stop it! You're pulling my clothes off." "Good-by." "Good-by." "So long." They left. Sarah watched them from the window, a huddled group of people in the cold night and the snow. "The world is a beautiful place," she said softly.

"What'd you say?" asked Mr. George.

"I said the world is a beautiful place."

"Only sometimes," he said. "Only sometimes."

Sarah sighed, discouraged that he could not feel what she felt, and began to tidy the room. She cleaned around Clyde, who had fallen asleep in a chair. She emptied the ashtrays and picked up bits of paper from the floor. Then she put the lights out, leaving the oilstove to light the room, and sat down on the couch next to Mr. George. "There's something I'd like to tell you," she said.

"What beats me," he interrupted, "is why you invited your whole family. I thought it was just going to be me, you, and the boy."

"You had to meet them sometime," she said, annoyed. "Anyway, I love my family——"

"Do they always act like that?" he asked.

"Like what?"

"Never mind," he said, and was silent.

She leaned back on the couch. "There's something I have to tell you. Mr. George, I have to know how you feel about something I have to tell you."

He drew in his mouth reflectively and slapped a hand to his knee. "OK," he said, "I'm listening."

"Once I made a mistake," she went on slowly, "of not telling a fellow all about me. When people come to find out things about you later, they sometimes come to hate you. I want to tell you the worst things about me. That way, if you can't understand, we can quit and neither of us will be the worse off for it. If we stay together, I don't want to have any secrets from you."

"Sort of like a test, huh?" said Mr. George.

"Sort of," said Sarah. "I just hope I pass."

"Well, listen now, Sarah, I don't care about——"

"Hush! I've got to tell you this! Just like I had to have you meet my family—no matter how they treat me. You'll just have to understand. I want to tell you about Clyde's father." She paused, and when he remained quiet, she went on. "I met him in a museum five years ago when I was doing daywork on Fifty-seventh Street. I used to walk past that museum every day. They had this fence made out of wooden slats, and inside was a garden, a beautiful garden with a black stone pool and statues and everything. After a while I got to thinking that one day I was going to go there. Can you imagine that? Me, going to that museum. Well, one day I did." She stopped and listened. It was the wind gently rattling the sashes and tapping the snow lightly against the panes. "I'll never forget that day. It was a Sunday in August, and I had on my blue cotton dress, the one with the paisley print, and my white heels and white gloves. I was really dressed to kill. Really dressed to kill. I left my madam at two that afternoon, went straight there, and when I got inside I went to the lunchroom, ordered myself a glass of iced tea, and took it straight to the patio. I can't begin to tell you how I felt. There I was inside, sitting down, and I could see the place where I used to look through. Do you understand what I'm trying to say? Do you?"

"Sort of," said Mr. George. He stared steadily into the fire, rubbing the tips of his thumbs together.

"Well," Sarah said, "after a while I felt like I'd been there all my life. In fact, I was even getting a little bored, and then this fellow came up. He came over to my table and sat down. Just like that. He came over, sat down, and started to talk. We went together that same afternoon, and we stayed together after, for a year. I was really a fool." She shook her head sadly. "Some fool. But I loved him. I loved him because I could respect him. But I guess I respected him too much. I started being honest with him, and he started to hate me."

"What were you honest about?" asked Mr. George.

"I told him about the men I'd known. I never loved any of them, but I was hurt plenty, and even though it was in the past I had to tell him."

"Why?"

"I don't know. I guess it made me feel better. I don't know. The important thing is that he couldn't stand knowing I'd been with other men. And when I got pregnant, we broke up." She paused. "Ain't you going to say nothing?"

"What's there to say?" said Mr. George. He rested his head on the back of the couch and touched her shoulder with his hand. She stood up. "I'd better get Clyde to bed, and I think I'm getting a little sleepy too."

"You're——"

"Clyde! Get up and go to bed." He rose, half asleep, leaving his monkey balanced precariously in the chair, and left the room.

"You're sure making it hard for me," said Mr. George.

"Not if you're a man, I ain't making it hard. A man is supposed to understand a woman's weakness."

"That's not what I'm——"

"He's supposed to understand anything."

"OK!" shouted Mr. George. "I understand. Now, for the love of God, let's talk about something else."

"I wish I could! I wish I could meet somebody who could make me forget about him. Somebody with just a little of his good side. You know, he took me to more places in that one year than I've ever been before—or since! And please, don't get the idea that I'm saying we don't go out. I just mean he took me downtown, to places we can't afford to go to."

Mr. George stood. "Sarah, what do you want?"

She was silent for a while, and then she answered, "I don't know."

"Well," he said, "since you had your say tonight, maybe I'd better have mine." He paused while she sat down on the couch. "I like you." He turned from her and watched the shadows on the wall. "As far as anything else goes, I guess I ain't happy and I ain't sad. I'm sure not rich—but I ain't poor either. I ain't ugly and I ain't good-looking, and I don't like going downtown among white folks. They make me nervous."

The fire in the stove had burned low. The room was almost dark, and he could barely see her face in the remaining light. "Will you look see how much oil's left in the stove?" she asked. He stooped and then kneeled, peering about the hot metal carefully. "Not much," he finally said. "Looks like it's on *E.*"

"Well then, you'd better turn it out." He fumbled about for the knob while she went on talking in a low voice. "I've been on pins and needles all day," she said. "I wanted everything to go right. I even prayed to God." She went over to him. He was still fumbling about the stove, and when she touched him he tried to rise, almost knocking it over. "Damn it! I've never known a man to be so clumsy." His slap sent her crashing into the chair. "Oh, God," she cried, "aren't there any men left anywhere in this world!"

"*Chica, chica, chica, chi—ca, chi—ca, chi—ca.*" The fuzz-covered monkey in his red velvet suit stopped drumming when he bumped into her leg. She reached down, picked it up, and hurled it at him in the darkness.

The Sky Is Gray

Ernest J. Gaines

Go'n be coming in a few minutes. Coming 'round that bend down there full speed. And I'm go'n get out my hankercher and I'm go'n wave it down, and us go'n get on it and go.

I keep on looking for it, but Mama don't look that way no more. She looking down the road where us jest come from. It's a long old road, and far's you can see you don't see nothing but gravel. You got dry weeds on both sides, and you got trees on both sides, and fences on both sides, too. And you got cows in the pastures and they standing close together. And when us was coming out yer to catch the bus I seen the smoke coming out o' the cow's nose.

I look at my mama and I know what she thinking. I been with Mama so much, jest me and her, I know what she thinking all the time. Right now it's home—Auntie and them. She thinking if they got 'nough wood—if she left 'nough there to keep 'em warm till us get back. She thinking if it go'n rain and if any of 'em go'n have to go out in the rain. She thinking 'bout the hog—if he go'n get out, and if Ty and Val be able to get him back in. She always worry like that when she leave the house. She don't worry too much if she leave me there with the smaller ones 'cause she know I'm go'n look after 'em and look after Auntie and everything else. I'm the oldest and she say I'm the man.

I look at my mama and I love my mama. She wearing that black coat and that black hat and she looking sad. I love my mama and I want put my arm 'round her and tell her. But I'm not s'pose to do that. She say that's weakness and that's cry-baby stuff, and she don't want no cry-baby 'round her. She don't want you to be scared neither. 'Cause Ty scared of ghosts and she always whipping him. I'm scared of the dark, too. But I make 'tend I ain't. I make 'tend I ain't 'cause I'm the oldest, and I got to set a good sample for the rest. I can't ever be scared and I can't ever cry. And that's the reason I didn't never say nothing 'bout my teef. It been hurting me and hurting me close to a month now. But I didn't say it. I didn't say it 'cause I didn't want act like no cry-baby, and 'cause I know us didn't have 'nough money to have it pulled. But, Lord, it been hurting me. And look like it won't start till at night when you trying to get little sleep. Then soon's you shet your eyes—umm-umm, Lord, Look like it go right down to your heart string.

"Hurting, hanh?" Ty'd say.

I'd shake my head, but I wouldn't open my mouth for nothing. You open your mouth and let that wind in, and it almost kill you.

I'd just lay there and listen to 'em snore. Ty, there, right 'side me, and Auntie and Val over by the fireplace. Val younger 'an me and Ty, and he sleep with Auntie. Mama sleep 'round the other side with Louis and Walker.

I'd just lay there and listen to 'em, and listen to that wind out there, and listen to that fire in the fireplace. Sometime it'd stop long enough to let me get little rest. Sometime it just hurt, hurt, hurt. Lord, have mercy.

II

Auntie knowed it was hurting me. I didn't tell nobody but Ty, 'cause us buddies and he ain't go'n tell nobody. But some kind o' way Auntie found out. When she asked me, I told her no, nothing was wrong. But she knowed it all the time. She told me to mash up a piece o' aspirin and wrap it in some cotton and jugg it down in that hole. I did it, but it didn't do no good. It stopped for a little while, and started right back again. She wanted to tell Mama, but I told her Uh-uh. 'Cause I knowed it didn't have no money, and it jest was go'n make her mad again. So she told Monsieur Bayonne, and Monsieur Bayonne came to the house and told me to kneel down 'side him on the fireplace. He put his finger in his mouth and made the Sign of the Cross on my jaw. The tip of Monsieur Bayonne finger is some hard, 'cause he always playing on that guitar. If us sit outside at night us can always hear Monsieur Bayonne playing on his guitar. Sometime us leave him out there playing on the guitar.

He made the Sign of the Cross over and over on my jaw, but that didn't do no good. Even when he prayed and told me to pray some, too, that teef still hurt.

"How you feeling?" he say.

"Same," I say.

He kept on praying and making the Sign of the Cross and I kept on praying, too.

"Still hurting?" he say.

"Yes, sir."

Monsieur Bayonne mashed harder and harder on my jaw. He mashed so hard he almost pushed me on Ty. But then he stopped.

"What kind o' prayers you praying, boy?" he say.

"Baptist," I say.

"Well, I'll be—no wonder that teef still killing him. I'm going one way and he going the other. Boy, don't you know any Catholic prayers?"

"Hail Mary," I say.

"Then you better start saying it."

"Yes, sir."

He started mashing again, and I could hear him praying at the same time. And, sure 'nough, afterwhile it stopped.

Me and Ty went outside where Monsieur Bayonne two hounds was, and us started playing with 'em. "Let's go hunting," Ty say. "All right," I say; and us went on back in the pasture. Soon the hounds got on a trail, and me and Ty followed 'em all cross the pasture and then back in the woods, too. And then they cornered this little old rabbit and killed him, and me and Ty made 'em get back, and us picked up the rabbit and started on back home. But it had started hurting me again. It was hurting me plenty now, but I wouldn't tell Monsieur Bayonne. That night I didn't sleep a bit, and first thing in the morning Auntie told me go back and let Monsieur Bayonne pray over me some more. Monsieur Bayonne was in his kitchen making coffee when I got there. Soon's he seen me, he knowed what was wrong.

"All right, kneel down there 'side that stove," he say. "And this time pray Catholic. I don't know nothing 'bout Baptist, and don't want know nothing 'bout him."

III

Last night Mama say: "Tomorrow us going to town."

"It ain't hurting me no more," I say. "I can eat anything on it."

"Tomorrow us going to town," she say.

And after she finished eating, she got up and went to bed. She always go to bed early now. 'Fore Daddy went in the Army, she used to stay up late. All o' us sitting out on the gallery or 'round the fire. But now, look like soon's she finish eating she go to bed.

This morning when I woke up, her and Auntie was standing 'fore the fireplace. She say: " 'Nough to get there and back. Dollar and a half to have it pulled. Twenty-five for me to go, twenty-five for him. Twenty-five for me to come back, twenty-five for him. Fifty cents left. Guess I get a little piece o' salt meat with that."

"Sure can use a piece," Auntie say. "White beans and no salt meat ain't white beans."

"I do the best I can," Mama say.

They was quiet after that, and I made 'tend I was still sleep.

"James, hit the floor," Auntie say.

I still made 'tend I was sleep. I didn't want 'em to know I was listening.

"All right," Auntie say, shaking me by the shoulder. "Come on. Today's the day."

I pushed the cover down to get out, and Ty grabbed it and pulled it back.

"You, too, Ty," Auntie say.

"I ain't getting no teef pulled," Ty say.

"Don't mean it ain't time to get up," Auntie say. "Hit it, Ty."

Ty got up grumbling.

"James, you hurry up and get in your clothes and eat your food," Auntie say. "What time y'all coming back?" she say to Mama.

"That 'leven o'clock bus," Mama say. "Got to get back in that field this evening."

"Get a move on you, James," Auntie say.

I went in the kitchen and washed my face, then I ate my breakfast. I was having bread and syrup. The bread was warm and hard and tasted good. And I tried to make it last a long time.

Ty came back there, grumbling and mad at me.

"Got to get up," he say. "I ain't having no teef pulled. What I got to be getting up for."

Ty poured some syrup in his pan and got a piece of bread. He didn't wash his hands, neither his face, and I could see that white stuff in his eyes.

"You the one getting a teef pulled," he say. "What I got to get up for. I bet you if I was getting a teef pulled, you wouldn't be getting up. Shucks; syrup again. I'm getting tired of this old syrup. Syrup, syrup, syrup. I want me some bacon sometime."

"Go out in the field and work and you can have bacon," Auntie say. She stood in the middle door looking at Ty. "You better be glad you got syrup. Some people ain't got that—hard's time is."

"Shucks," Ty say. "How can I be strong."

"I don't know too much 'bout your strength," Auntie say; "but I know where you go'n be hot, you keep that grumbling up. James, get a move on you; your mama waiting."

I ate my last piece of bread and went in the front room. Mama was standing 'fore the fireplace warming her hands. I put on my coat and my cap, and us left the house.

IV

I look down there again, but it still ain't coming. I almost say, "It ain't coming, yet," but I keep my mouth shet. 'Cause that's something else she don't like. She don't like for you to say something just for nothing. She can see it ain't coming, I can see it ain't coming, so why say it ain't coming. I don't say it, and I turn and look at the river that's back o' us. It so cold the smoke just raising up from the water. I see a bunch of pull-doos not too far out—jest on the other side the lilies. I'm wondering if you can eat pull-doos. I ain't too sure, 'cause I ain't never ate none. But I done ate owls and black birds, and I done ate red birds, too. I didn't want kill the red birds, but she made me kill 'em. They had two of 'em back there. One in my trap, one in Ty trap. Me and Ty was go'n play with 'em and let 'em go. But she made me kill 'em 'cause us needed the food.

"I can't," I say. "I can't."

"Here," she say. "Take it."

"I can't," I say. "I can't. I can't kill him, Mama. Please."

"Here," she say. "Take this fork, James."

"Please, Mama, I can't kill him," I say.

I could tell she was go'n hit me. And I jecked back, but I didn't jeck back soon enough.

"Take it," she say.

I took it and reached in for him, but he kept hopping to the back.

"I can't, Mama," I say. The water just kept running down my face. "I can't."

"Get him out o' there," she say.

I reached in for him and he kept hopping to the back. Then I reached in farther, and he pecked me on the hand.

"I can't, Mama," I say.

She slapped me again.

I reached in again, but he kept hopping out my way. Then he hopped to one side, and I reached there. The fork got him on the leg and I heard his leg pop. I pulled my hand out 'cause I had hurt him.

"Give it here," she say, and jecked the fork out my hand.

She reached and got the little bird right in the neck. I heard the fork go in his neck, and I heard it go in the ground. She brought him out and helt him right in front o' me.

"That's one," she say. She shook him off and gived me the fork. "Get the other one."

"I can't, Mama. I do anything. But I can't do that."

She went to the corner o' the fence and broke the biggest switch over there. I knelt 'side the trap crying.

"Get him out o' there," she say.

"I can't, Mama."

She started hitting me cross the back. I went down on the ground crying.

"Get him," she say.

"Octavia," Auntie say.

'Cause she had come out o' the house and she was standing by the tree looking at us.

"Get him out o' there," Mama say.

"Octavia," Auntie say; "explain to him. Explain to him. Jest don't beat him. Explain to him."

But she hit me and hit me and hit me.

I'm still young. I ain't no more'an eight. But I know now. I know why I had to. (They was so little, though. They was so little. I 'member how I picked the feathers off 'em and cleaned 'em and helt 'em over the fire. Then us all ate 'em. Ain't had but little bitty piece, but us all had little bitty piece, and ever'body jest looked at me, 'cause they was so proud.) S'pose she had to go away? That's why I had to do it. S'pose she had to go away like Daddy went away? Then who was go'n look after us? They had to be somebody left to carry on. I didn't know it then, but I know it now. Auntie and Monsieur Bayonne talked to me and made me see.

V

Time I see it, I get out my hankercher and start waving. It still 'way down there, but I keep waving anyhow. Then it come closer and stop and me and Mama get on. Mama tell me go sit in the back while she pay. I do like she say, and the people look at me. When I pass the little sign that say White and Colored, I start looking for a seat. I jest see one of 'em back there, but I don't take it, 'cause I want my mama to sit down herself. She come in the back and sit down, and I lean on the seat. They got seats in the front, but I know I can't sit there, 'cause I have to sit back o' the sign. Anyhow, I don't want sit there if my mama go'n sit back here.

They got a lady sitting 'side my mama and she look at me and grin little bit. I grin back, but I don't open my mouth, 'cause the wind'll get in and make that teef hurt. The lady take out a pack o' gum and reach me a slice, but I shake my head. She reach Mama a slice, and Mama shake her head. The lady jest can't understand why a little boy'll turn down gum, and she reached me a slice again. This time I point to my jaw. The lady understand and grin little bit, and I grin little bit, but I don't open my mouth, though.

They got a girl sitting 'cross from me. She got on a red overcoat, and her hair plaited in one big plait. First, I make 'tend I don't even see her. But then I start looking at her little bit. She make 'tend she don't see me neither, but I catch her looking that way. She got a cold, and ever' now and then she hist that little hankercher to her nose. She ought to blow it, but she don't. Must think she too much a lady or something.

Ever' time she hist that little hankercher, the lady 'side her say something in her yer. She shake her head and lay her hands in her lap again. Then I catch her kind o' looking where I'm at. I grin at her. But think she'll grin back? No. She turn up her little old nose like I got some snot on my face or something. Well, I show her both o' us can turn us head. I turn mine, too, and look out at the river.

The river is gray. The sky is gray. They have pull-doos on the water. The water is wavey, and the pull-doos go up and down. The bus go 'round a turn, and you got plenty trees hiding the river. Then the bus go 'round another turn, and I can see the river again.

I look to the front where all the white people sitting. Then I look at that little old gal again. I don't look right at her, 'cause I don't want all them people to know I love her. I jest look at her little bit, like I'm looking out that window over there. But she know I'm looking that way, and she kind o' look at me, too. The lady sitting 'side her catch her this time, and she lean over and say something in her yer.

"I don't love him nothing," that little old gal say out loud.

Ever'body back there yer her mouth, and all of 'em look at us and laugh.

"I don't love you, neither," I say. "So you don't have to turn up your nose, Miss."

"You the one looking," she say.

"I wasn't looking at you," I say. "I was looking out that window, there."

"Out that window, my foot," she say. "I seen you. Ever' time I turn 'round you look at me."

"You must o' been looking yourself if you seen me all them times," I say.

"Shucks," she say. "I got me all kind o' boyfriends."

"I got girlfriends, too," I say.

"Well, I just don't want you to get your hopes up," she say.

I don't say no more to that little old gal, 'cause I don't want have to bust her in the mouth. I lean on the seat where Mama sitting, and I don't even look that way no more. When us get to Bayonne, she jugg her little old tongue out at me. I make 'tend I'm go'n hit her, and she duck down side her mama. And all the people laugh at us again.

VI

Me and Mama get off and start walking in town. Bayonne is a little bitty town. Baton Rouge is a hundred times bigger 'an Bayonne. I went to Baton Rouge once—me, Ty, Mama, and Daddy. But that was 'way back yonder—'fore he went in the Army. I wonder when us go'n see him again. I wonder when. Look like he ain't ever coming home. . . . Even the pavement all cracked in Bayonne. Got grass shooting right out the sidewalk. Got weeds in the ditch, too; jest like they got home.

It some cold in Bayonne. Look like it colder 'an it is home. The wind blow in my face, and I feel that stuff running down my nose. I sniff. Mama say use that hankercher. I blow my nose and put it back.

Us pass a school and I see them white children playing in the yard. Big old red school, and them children jest running and playing. Then us pass a café, and I see a bunch of 'em in there eating. I wish I was in there 'cause I'm cold. Mama tell me keep my eyes in front where they blonks.

Us pass stores that got dummies, and us pass another café, and then us pass a shoe shop, and that baldhead man in there fixing on a shoe. I look at him and I butt into that white lady, and Mama jeck me in front and tell me stay there.

Us come to the courthouse, and I see the flag waving there. This one yer ain't like the one us got at school. This one yer ain't got but a handful of stars. One at school got a big pile of stars— one for ever' state. Us pass it and us turn and there it is—the dentist office. Me and Mama go in, and they got people sitting ever' where you look. They even got a little boy in there younger 'an me.

Me and Mama sit on that bench, and a white lady come in there and ask me what my name. Mama tell her, and the white lady go back. Then I yer somebody hollering in there. And soon's that little boy hear him hollering, he start hollering, too. His mama pat him and pat him, trying to make him hush up, but he ain't thinking 'bout her.

The man that was hollering in there come out holding his jaw.

"Got it, hanh?" another man say.

The man shake his head.

"Man, I thought they was killing you in there," the other man say. "Hollering like a pig under a gate."

The man don't say nothing. He jest head for the door, and the other man follow him.

"John Lee," the white lady say. "John Lee Williams."

The little boy jugg his head down in his mama lap and holler more now. His mama tell him go with the nurse, but he ain't thinking 'bout her. His mama tell him again, but he don't even yer. His mama pick him up and take him in there, and even when the white lady shet the door I can still hear him hollering.

"I often wonder why the Lord let a child like that suffer," a lady say to my mama. The lady's sitting right in front o' us on another bench. She got on a white dress and a black sweater. She must be a nurse or something herself, I reckoned.

"Not us to question," a man say.

"Sometimes I don't know if we shouldn't," the lady say.

"I know definitely we shouldn't," the man say. The man look like a preacher. He big and fat and he got on a black suit. He got a gold chain, too.

"Why?" the lady say.

"Why anything?" the preacher say.

"Yes," the lady say. "Why anything?"

"Not us to question," the preacher say.

The lady look at the preacher a little while and look at Mama again.

"And look like it's the poor who do most the suffering," she say. "I don't understand it."

"Best not to even try," the preacher say. "He works in mysterious ways. Wonders to perform."

Right then Little John Lee bust out hollering, and ever'body turn they head.

"He's not a good dentist," the lady say. "Dr. Robillard is much better. But more expensive. That's why most of the colored people come here. The white people go to Dr. Robillard. Y'all from Bayonne?"

"Down the river," my mama say. And that's all she go'n say, 'cause she don't talk much. But the lady keep on looking at her, and so she say: "Near Morgan."

"I see," the lady say.

VII

"That's the trouble with the black people in this country today," somebody else say. This one yer sitting on the same side me and Mama sitting, and he kind o'sitting in front of that preacher. He look like a teacher or somebody that go to college. He got on a suit, and he got a book that he been reading. "We don't question is exactly the trouble," he say. "We should question and question and question. Question everything."

The preacher jest look at him a long time. He done put a toothpick or something in his mouth, and he jest keep turning it and turning it. You can see he don't like that boy with that book.

"Maybe you can explain what you mean," he say.

"I said what I meant," the boy say. "Question everything. Every stripe, every star, every word spoken. Everything."

"It 'pears to me this young lady and I was talking 'bout God, young man," the preacher say.

"Question Him, too," the boy say.

"Wait," the preacher say. "Wait now."

"You heard me right," the boy say. "His existence as well as everything else. Everything."

The preacher jest look cross the room at the boy. You can see he getting madder and madder. But mad or no mad, the boy ain't thinking 'bout him. He look at the preacher jest's hard's the preacher look at him.

"Is this what they coming to?" the preacher say. "Is this what we educating them for?"

"You're not educating me," the boy say. "I wash dishes at night to go to school in the day. So even the words you spoke need questioning."

The preacher jest look at him and shake his head.

"When I come in this room and seen you there with your book, I said to myself, There's an intelligent man. How wrong a person can be."

"Show me one reason to believe in the existence of a God," the boy say.

"My heart tell me," the preacher say.

"My heart tells me," the boy say. "My heart tells me. Sure, my heart tells me. And as long as you listen to what your heart tells you, you will have only what the white man gives you and nothing more. Me, I don't listen to my heart. The purpose of the heart is to pump blood throughout the body, and nothing else."

"Who's your paw, boy?" the preacher say.

"Why?"

"Who is he?"

"He's dead."

"And your mom?"

"She's in Charity Hospital with pneumonia. Half killed herself working for nothing."

"And 'cause he's dead and she sick, you mad at the world?"

"I'm not mad at the world. I'm questioning the world. I'm questioning it with cold logic, sir. What do words like Freedom, Liberty, God, White, Colored mean? I want to know. That's why *you* are sending us to school, to read and to ask questions. And because we ask these questions, you call us mad. No, sir, it is not us who are mad."

"You keep saying 'us'?"

" 'Us' . . . why not? I'm not alone."

The preacher jest shake his head. Then he look at ever'body in the room—ever'body. Some of the people look down at the floor, keep from looking at him. I kind o' look 'way myself, but soon's I know he done turn his head, I look that way again.

"I'm sorry for you," he say.

"Why?" the boy say. "Why not be sorry for yourself? Why are you so much better off than I am? Why aren't you sorry for these other people in here? Why not be sorry for the lady who had to drag her child into the dentist office? Why not be sorry for the lady sitting on that bench over there? Be sorry for them. Not for me. Some way or other I'm going to make it."

"No, I'm sorry for you," the preacher say.

"Of course. Of course," the boy say, shaking his head. "You're sorry for me because I rock that pillar you're leaning on."

"You can't ever rock the pillar I'm leaning on, young man. It's stronger than anything man can ever do."

"You believe in God because a man told you to believe in God. A white man told you to believe in God. And why? To keep you ignorant, so he can keep you under his feet."

"So now, we the ignorant?"

"Yes," the boy say. "Yes." And he open his book again.

The preacher jest look at him there. The boy done forgot all about him. Ever'body else make 'tend they done forgot 'bout the squabble, too.

Then I see that preacher getting up real slow. Preacher a great big old man, and he got to brace hisself to get up. He come 'cross the room where the boy is. He jest stand there looking at him, but the boy don't raise his head.

"Stand up, boy," preacher say.

The boy look up at him, then he shet his book real slow and stand up. Preacher jest draw back and hit him in the face. The boy fall 'gainst the wall, but he straighten hisself up and look right back at that preacher.

"You forgot the other cheek," he say.

The preacher hit him again on the other side. But this time the boy don't fall.

"That hasn't changed a thing," he say.

The preacher jest look at the boy. The preacher breathing real hard like he jest run up a hill. The boy sit down and open his book again.

"I feel sorry for you," the preacher say. "I never felt so sorry for a man before."

The boy make 'tend he don't even hear that preacher. He keep on reading his book. The preacher go back and get his hat off the chair.

"Excuse me," he say to us. "I'll come back some other time. Y'all, please excuse me."

And he look at the boy and go out the room. The boy hist his hand up to his mouth one time, to wipe 'way some blood. All the rest o' the time he keep on reading.

VIII

The lady and her little boy come out the dentist, and the nurse call somebody else in. Then little bit later they come out, and the nurse call another name. But fast's she call somebody in there, somebody else come in the place where we at, and the room stay full.

The people coming in now, all of 'em wearing big coats. One of 'em say something 'bout sleeting, and another one say he hope not. Another one say he think it ain't nothing but rain. 'Cause, he say, rain can get awful cold this time o' year.

All 'cross the room they talking. Some of 'em talking to people right by 'em, some of 'em talking to people clare 'cross the room, some of 'em talking to anybody'll listen. It's a little bitty room, no bigger 'an us kitchen, and I can see ever'body in there. The little old room 's full of smoke, 'cause you got two old men smoking pipes. I think I feel my teef thumping me some, and I hold my breath and wait. I wait and wait, but it don't thump me no more. Thank God for that.

I feel like going to sleep, and I lean back 'gainst the wall. But I'm scared to go to sleep: Scared 'cause the nurse might call my name and I won't hear her. And Mama might go to sleep, too, and she be mad if neither us heard the nurse.

I look up at Mama. I love my mama. I love my mama. And when cotton come I'm go'n get her a newer coat. And I ain't go'n get a black one neither. I think I'm go'n get her a red one.

"They got some books over there," I say. "Want read one of 'em?"

Mama look at the books, but she don't answer me.

"You got yourself a little man there," the lady say.

Mama don't say nothing to the lady, but she must 'a' grin a little bit, 'cause I seen the lady grinning back. The lady look at me a little while, like she feeling sorry for me.

"You sure got that preacher out here in a hurry," she say to that other boy.

The boy look up at her and look in his book again. When I grow up I want be jest like him. I want clothes like that and I want keep a book with me, too.

"You really don't believe in God?" the lady say.

"No," he say.

"But why?" the lady say.

"Because the wind is pink," he say.

"What?" the lady say.

The boy don't answer her no more. He jest read in his book.

"Talking 'bout the wind is pink," that old lady say. She sitting on the same bench with the boy, and she trying to look in his face. The boy make 'tend the old lady ain't even there. He jest keep reading. "Wind is pink," she say again. "Eh, Lord, what children go'n be saying next?"

The lady 'cross from us bust out laughing.

"That's a good one," she say. "The wind is pink. Yes, sir, that's a good one."

"Don't you believe the wind is pink?" the boy say. He keep his head down in the book.

"Course I believe it, Honey," the lady say. "Course I do." She look at us and wink her eye. "And what color is grass, Honey?"

"Grass? Grass is black."

She bust out laughing again. The boy look at her.

"Don't you believe grass is black?" he say.

The lady quit laughing and look at him. Ever'body else look at him now. The place quiet, quiet.

"Grass is green, Honey," the lady say. "It was green yesterday, it's green today, and it's go'n be green tomorrow."

"How do you know it's green?"

"I know because I know."

"You don't know it's green. You believe it's green because someone told you it was green. If someone had told you it was black you'd believe it was black."

"It's green," the lady say. "I know green when I see green."

"Prove it's green."

"Surely, now," the lady say. "Don't tell me it's coming to that?"

"It's coming to just that," the boy say. "Words mean nothing. One means no more than the other."

"That's what it all coming to?" that old lady say. That old lady got on a turban and she got on two sweaters. She got a green sweater under a black sweater. I can see the green sweater 'cause some of the buttons on the other sweater missing.

"Yes, ma'am," the boy say. "Words mean nothing. Action is the only thing. Doing. That's the only thing."

"Other words, you want the Lord to come down here and show Hisself to you?" she say.

"Exactly, ma'am."

"You don't mean that, I'm sure?"

"I do, ma'am."

"Done, Jesus," the old lady say, shaking her head.

"I didn't go 'long with that preacher at first," the other lady say; "but now—I don't know. When a person say the grass is black, he's either a lunatic or something wrong."

"Prove to me that it's green."

"It's green because the people say it's green."

"Those same people say we're citizens of the United States."

"I think I'm a citizen."

"Citizens have certain rights. Name me one right that you have. One right, granted by the Constitution, that you can exercise in Bayonne."

The lady don't answer him. She jest look at him like she don't know what he talking 'bout. I know I don't.

"Things changing," she say.

"Things are changing because some black men have begun to follow their brains instead of their hearts."

"You trying to say these people don't believe in God?"

"I'm sure some of them do. Maybe most of them do. But they don't believe that God is going to touch these white people's hearts and change them tomorrow. Things change through action. By no other way."

Ever'body sit quiet and look at the boy. Nobody say a thing. Then the lady 'cross from me and Mama jest shake her head.

"Let's hope that not all your generation feel the same way you do," she say.

"Think what you please, it doesn't matter," the boy say. "But it will be men who listen to their heads and not their hearts who will see that your children have a better chance than you had."

"Let's hope they ain't all like you, though," the old lady say. "Done forgot the heart absolutely."

"Yes, ma'am, I hope they aren't all like me," the boy say.

"Unfortunately I was born too late to believe in your God. Let's hope that the ones who come after will have your faith—if not in your God, then in something else, something definitely that they can lean on. I haven't anything. For me, the wind is pink; the grass is black."

IX

The nurse come in the room where us all sitting and waiting and say the doctor won't take no more patients till one o'clock this evening. My mama jump up off the bench and go up to the white lady.

"Nurse, I have to go back in the field this evening," she say.

"The doctor is treating his last patient now," the nurse say. "One o'clock this evening."

"Can I at least speak to the doctor?" my mama say.

"I'm his nurse," the lady say.

"My little boy sick," my mama say. "Right now his teef almost killing him."

The nurse look at me. She trying to make up her mind if to let me come in. I look at her real pitiful. The teef ain't hurting me a tall, but Mama say it is, so I make 'tend for her sake.

"This evening," the nurse say, and go back in the office.

"Don't feel 'jected, Honey," the lady say to Mama. "I been 'round 'em a long time—they take you when they want to. If you was white, that's something else; but you the wrong shade."

Mama don't say nothing to the lady, and me and her go outside and stand 'gainst the wall. It's cold out there. I can feel that wind going through my coat. Some of the other people come out of the room and go up the street. Me and Mama stand there a little while and start to walking. I don't know where us going. When us come to the other street us jest stand there.

"You don't have to make water, do you?" Mama say.

"No, ma'am," I say.

Us go up the street. Walking real slow. I can tell Mama don't know where she going. When us come to a store us stand there and look at the dummies. I look at a little boy with a brown overcoat. He got on brown shoes, too. I look at my old shoes and look at his'n again. You wait till summer, I say.

Me and Mama walk away. Us come up to another store and us stop and look at them dummies, too. Then us go again. Us pass a café where the white people in there eating. Mama tell me keep my eyes in front where they blonks, but I can't help from seeing them people eat. My stomach start to growling 'cause I'm hungry. When I see people eating, I get hungry; when I see a coat, I get cold.

A man whistle at my mama when us go by a filling station. She make 'tend she don't even see him. I look back and I feel like hitting him in the mouth. If I was bigger, I say. If I was bigger, you see.

Us keep on going. I'm getting colder and colder, but I don't say nothing. I feel that stuff running down my nose and I sniff.

"That rag," she say.

I git it out and wipe my nose. I'm getting cold all over now— my face, my hands, my feet, ever'thing. Us pass another little café, but this'n for white people, too, and us can't go in there neither. So us jest walk. I'm so cold now, I'm 'bout ready to say it. If I knowed where us was going, I wouldn't be so cold, but I don't know where us going. Us go, us go, us go. Us walk clean out o' Bayonne. Then us cross the street and us come back. Same thing I seen when I got off the bus. Same old trees, same old walk, same old weeds, same old cracked pave—same old ever'thing.

I sniff again.

"That rag," she say.

I wipe my nose real fast and jugg that hankercher back in my pocket 'fore my hand get too cold. I raise my head and I can see David hardware store. When us come up to it, us go in. I don't know why, but I'm glad.

It warm in there. It so warm in there you don't want ever leave. I look for the heater, and I see it over by them ba'ls. Three white men standing 'round the heater talking in Creole. One of 'em come to see what Mama want.

"Got any ax handle?" she say.

Me, Mama, and the white man start to the back, but Mama stop me when us come to the heater. Her and the white man go on. I hold my hand over the heater and look at 'em. They go all the way in the back, and I see the white man point to the ax handle 'gainst the wall. Mama take one of 'em and shake it like she trying to figure how much it weigh. Then she rub her hand over it from one end to the other end. She turn it over and look at the other side, then she shake it again, and shake her head and put it back. She get another one and she do it jest like she did the first one, then she shake her head. Then she get a brown one and do it that, too. But she don't like this one neither. Then she get another one, but 'fore she shake it or anything, she look at me. Look like she trying to say something to me, but I don't know what it is. All I know is I done got warm now and I'm feeling right smart better. Mama shake this ax handle jest like she done the others, and shake her head and say something to the white man. The white man jest look at his pile of ax handle, and when Mama pass by him to come to the front, the white man jest scratch his head and follow her. She tell me come on, and us go on out and start walking again.

Us walk and walk, and no time at all I'm cold again. Look like I'm colder now 'cause I can still remember how good it was back there. My stomach growl and I suck it in to keep Mama from yering it. She walking right 'side me, and it growl so loud you can yer it a mile. But Mama don't say a word.

X

When us come up to the courthouse, I look at the clock. It got quarter to twelve. Mean us got another hour and a quarter to be out yer in the cold. Us go and stand side a building. Something hit my cap and I look up at the sky. Sleet falling.

I look at Mama standing there. I want stand close 'side her, but she don't like that. She say that's cry-baby stuff. She say you got to stand for yourself, by yourself.

"Let's go back to that office," she say.

Us cross the street. When us get to the dentist I try to open the door, but I can't. Mama push me on the side and she twist the knob. But she can't open it neither. She twist it some more, harder, but she can't open it. She turn 'way from the door. I look at her, but I don't move and I don't say nothing. I done seen her like this before and I'm scared.

"You hungry?" she say. She say it like she mad at me, like I'm the one cause of ever'thing.

"No, ma'am," I say.

"You want eat and walk back, or you rather don't eat and ride?"

"I ain't hungry," I say.

I ain't jest hungry, but I'm cold, too. I'm so hungry and I'm so cold I want cry. And look like I'm getting colder and colder. My feet done got numb. I try to work my toes, but I can't. Look like I'm go'n die. Look like I'm go'n stand right here and freeze to death. I think about home. I think about Val and Auntie and Ty and Louis and Walker. It 'bout twelve o'clock and I know they eating dinner. I can hear Ty making jokes. That's Ty. Always trying to make some kind o' joke. I wish I was right there listening to him. Give anything in the world if I was home 'round the fire.

"Come on," Mama say.

Us start walking again. My feet so numb I can't hardly feel 'em. Us turn the corner and go back up the street. The clock start hitting for twelve.

The sleet's coming down plenty now. They hit the pave and bounce like rice. Oh, Lord; oh, Lord, I pray. Don't let me die. Don't let me die. Don't let me die, Lord.

XI

Now I know where us going. Us going back o' town where the colored people eat. I don't care if I don't eat. I been hungry before. I can stand it. But I can't stand the cold.

I can see us go'n have a long walk. It 'bout a mile down there. But I don't mind. I know when I get there I'm go'n warm myself. I think I can hold out. My hands numb in my pockets and my feet numb, too, but if I keep moving I can hold out. Jest don't stop no more, that's all.

The sky's gray. The sleet keep falling. Falling like rain now— plenty, plenty. You can hear it hitting the pave. You can see it bouncing. Sometime it bounce two times 'fore it settle.

Us keep going. Us don't say nothing. Us jest keep going, keep going.

I wonder what Mama thinking. I hope she ain't mad with me. When summer come I'm go'n pick plenty cotton and get her a coat. I'm go'n get her a red one.

I hope they make it summer all the time. I be glad if it was summer all the time—but it ain't. Us got to have winter, too. Lord, I hate the winer. I guess ever'body hate the winter.

I don't sniff this time. I get out my hankercher and wipe my nose. My hand so cold I can hardly hold the hankercher.

I think us getting close, but us ain't there yet. I wonder where ever'body is. Can't see nobody but us. Look like us the only two people moving 'round today. Must be too cold for the rest of the people to move 'round.

I can hear my teefes. I hope they don't knock together too hard and make that bad one hurt. Lord, that's all I need, for that bad one to start off.

I hear a church bell somewhere. But today ain't Sunday. They must be ringing for a funeral or something.

I wonder what they doing at home. They must be eating. Monsieur Bayonne might be there with his guitar. One day Ty played with Monsieur Bayonne guitar and broke one o' the string. Monsieur Bayonne got some mad with Ty. He say Ty ain't go'n never 'mount to nothing. Ty can go jest like him when he ain't there. Ty can make ever'body laugh mocking Monsieur Bayonne.

I used to like to be with Mama and Daddy. Us used to be happy. But they took him in the Army. Now, nobody happy no more. . . . I be glad when he come back.

Monsieur Bayonne say it wasn't fair for 'em to take Daddy and give Mama nothing and give us nothing. Auntie say, Shhh, Etienne. Don't let 'em yer you talk like that. Monsieur Bayonne say, It's God truth. What they giving his children? They have to walk three and a half mile to school hot or cold. That's anything to give for a paw? She got to work in the field rain or shine jest to make ends meet. That's anything to give for a husband? Auntie say, Shhh, Etienne, shhh. Yes, you right, Monsieur Bayonne say. Best don't say it in front of 'em now. But one day they go'n find out. One day. Yes, s'pose so, Auntie say. Then what, Rose Mary? Monsieur Bayonne say. I don't know, Etienne, Auntie say. All us can do is us job, and leave ever'thing else in His hand. . . .

Us getting closer, now. Us getting closer. I can see the railroad tracks.

Us cross the tracks, and now I see the café. Jest to get in there, I say. Jest to get in there. Already I'm starting to feel little better.

XII

Us go in. Ahh, it good. I look for the heater; there 'gainst the wall. One of them little brown ones. I jest stand there and hold my hand over it. I can't open my hands too wide 'cause they almost froze.

Mama standing right 'side me. She done unbuttoned her coat. Smoke rise out the coat, and the coat smell like a wet dog.

I move to the side so Mama can have more room. She open out her hands and rub 'em together. I rub mine together, too, 'cause this keep 'em from hurting. If you let 'em warm too fast, they hurt you sure. But if you let 'em warm jest little bit at a time, and you keep rubbing 'em, they be all right ever' time.

They got jest two more people in the café. A lady back o' the counter, and a man on this side the counter. They been watching us ever since us come in.

Mama get out the hankercher and count the money. Both o' us know how much money she got there. Three dollars. No, she ain't got three dollars. 'Cause she had to pay us way up here. She ain't got but two dollars and a half left. Dollar and a half to get my teef pulled, and fifty cents for us to go back on, and fifty cents worse o' salt meat.

She stir the money 'round with her finger. Most o' the money is change 'cause I can hear it rubbing together. She stir it and stir it. Then she look at the door. It still sleeting. I can yer it hitting 'gainst the wall like rice.

"I ain't hungry, Mama," I say.

"Got to pay 'em something for they heat," she say.

She take a quarter out the hankercher and tie the hankercher up again. She look over her shoulder at the people, but she still don't move. I hope she don't spend the money. I don't want her spend it on me. I'm hungry, I'm almost starving I'm so hungry, but I don't want her spending the money on me.

She flip the quarter over like she thinking. She must be thinking 'bout us walking back home. Lord, I sure don't want walk home. If I thought it done any good to say something, I say it. But my mama make up her own mind.

She turn way from the heater right fast, like she better hurry up and do it 'fore she change her mind. I turn to look at her go to the counter. The man and the lady look at her, too. She tell the lady something and the lady walk away. The man keep on looking at her. Her back turn to the man, and Mama don't even know he standing there.

The lady put some cakes and a glass o' milk on the counter. Then she pour up a cup o' coffee and set it side the other stuff.

Mama pay her for the things and come back where I'm at. She tell me sit down at that table 'gainst the wall.

The milk and the cakes for me. The coffee for my mama. I eat slow, and I look at her. She looking outside at the sleet. She looking real sad. I say to myself, I'm go'n make all this up one day. You see, one day, I'm go'n make all this up. I want to say it now. I want to tell how I feel right now. But Mama don't like for us to talk like that.

"I can't eat all this," I say.

They got just three little cakes there. And I'm so hungry right now, the Lord know I can eat a hundred times three. But I want her to have one.

She don't even look my way. She know I'm hungry. She know I want it. I let it stay there a while, then I get it and eat it. I eat jest on my front teefes, 'cause if it tech that back teef I know what'll happen. Thank God it ain't hurt me a tall today.

After I finish eating I see the man go to the juke box. He drop a nickel in it, then he jest stand there looking at the record. Mama tell me keep my eyes in front where they blonks. I turn my head like she say, but then I yer the man coming towards us.

"Dance, Pretty?" he say.

Mama get up to dance with him. But 'fore you know it, she done grabbed the little man and done throwed him 'side the wall. He hit the wall so hard he stop the juke box from playing.

"Some pimp," the lady back o' the counter say. "Some pimp."

The little man jump up off the floor and start towards my mama. 'Fore you know it, Mama done sprung open her knife and she waiting for him.

"Come on," she say. "Come on. I'll cut you from your neighbo to your throat. Come on."

I go up to the little man to hit him, but Mama make me come and stand 'side her. The little man look at me and Mama and go back to the counter.

"Some pimp," the lady back o' the counter say. "Some pimp." She start laughing and pointing at the little man. "Yes, sir, you a pimp, all right. Yes, sir."

XIII

"Fasten that coat. Let's go," Mama say.

"You don't have to leave," the lady say.

Mama don't answer the lady, and us right out in the cold
again. I'm warm right now—my hands, my yers, my feet—but I
know this ain't go'n last too long. It done sleet so much now you
got ice ever'where.

Us cross the railroad tracks, and soon's us do, I get cold. That
wind go through this little old coat like it ain't nothing. I got a
shirt and a sweater under it, but that wind don't pay 'em no
mind. I look up and I can see us got a long way to go. I wonder
if us go'n make it 'fore I get too cold.

Us cross over to walk on the sidewalk. They got jest one
sidewalk back here. It's over there.

After us go jest a little piece, I smell bread cooking. I look,
then I see a baker shop. When us get closer, I can smell it more
better. I shet my eyes and make 'tend I'm eating. But I keep 'em
shet too long and I butt up 'gainst a telephone post. Mama grab
me and see if I'm hurt. I ain't bleeding or nothing and she turn
me loose.

I can feel I'm getting colder and colder, and I look up to see
how far us still got to go. Uptown is 'way up yonder. A half mile,
I reckoned. I try to think of something. They say think and you
won't get cold. I think of that poem, *Annabel Lee*. I ain't been to
school in so long—this bad weather—I reckoned they done
passed *Annabel Lee*. But passed it or not, I'm sure Miss Walker
go'n make me recite it when I get there. That woman don't
never forget nothing. I ain't never seen nobody like that.

I'm still getting cold. *Annabel Lee* or no *Annabel Lee*, I'm still
getting cold. But I can see us getting closer. Us getting there
gradually.

Soon's us turn the corner, I see a little old white lady up in
front o' us. She the only lady on the street. She all in black and
she got a long black rag over her head.

"Stop," she say.

Me and Mama stop and look at her. She must be crazy to be
out in all this sleet. Ain't got but a few other people out there,
and all of 'em men.

"Yall done ate?" she say.

"Jest finished," Mama say.

"Yall must be cold then?" she say.

"Us headed for the dentist," Mama say. "Us'll warm up when
us get there."

"What dentist?" the old lady say. "Mr. Bassett?"

"Yes, ma'am," Mama say.

"Come on in," the old lady say. "I'll telephone him and tell him yall coming."

Me and Mama follow the old lady in the store. It's a little bitty store, and it don't have much in there. The old lady take off her head piece and fold it up.

"Helena?" somebody call from the back.

"Yes, Alnest?" the old lady say.

"Did you see them?"

"They're here. Standing beside me."

"Good. Now you can stay inside."

The old lady look at Mama. Mama waiting to hear what she brought us in here for. I'm waiting for that, too.

"I saw yall each time you went by," she say. "I came out to catch you, but you were gone."

"Us went back o' town," Mama say.

"Did you eat?"

"Yes, ma'am."

The old lady look at Mama a long time, like she thinking Mama might be jest saying that. Mama look right back at her. The old lady look at me to see what I got to say. I don't say nothing. I sure ain't going 'gainst my mama.

"There's food in the kitchen," she say to Mama. "I've been keeping it warm."

Mama turn right around and start for the door.

"Just a minute," the old lady say. Mama stop. "The boy'll have to work for it. It isn't free."

"Us don't take no handout," Mama say.

"I'm not handing out anything," the old lady say. "I need my garbage moved to the front. Ernest has a bad cold and can't go out there."

"James'll move it for you," Mama say.

"Not unless you eat," the old lady say. "I'm old, but I have my pride, too, you know."

Mama can see she ain't go'n beat this old lady down, so she jest shake her head.

"All right," the old lady say. "Come into the kitchen."

She lead the way with that rag in her hand. The kitchen is a little bitty little thing, too. The table and the stove jest about fill it up. They got a little room to the side. Somebody in there laying cross the bed. Must be the person she was talking with:

Alnest or Ernest—I forget what she call him.

"Sit down," the old lady say to Mama. "Not you," she say to me. "You have to move the cans."

"Helena?" somebody say in the other room.

"Yes, Alnest?" the old lady say.

"Are you going out there again?"

"I must show the boy where the garbage is," the old lady say.

"Keep that shawl over your head," the old man say.

"You don't have to remind me. Come, boy," the old lady say.

Us go out in the yard. Little old back yard ain't no bigger 'an the store or the kitchen. But it can sleet here jest like it can sleet in any big back yard. And 'fore you know it I'm trembling.

"There," the old lady say, pointing to the cans. I pick up one of the cans. The can so light I put it back down to look inside o' it.

"Here," the old lady say. "Leave that cap alone."

I look at her in the door. She got that black rag wrapped 'round her shoulders, and she pointing one of her fingers at me.

"Pick it up and carry it to the front," she say. I go by her with the can. I'm sure the thing 's empty. She could 'a' carried the thing by herself, I'm sure. "Set it on the sidewalk by the door and come back for the other one," she say.

I go and come back, Mama look at me when I pass her. I get the other can and take it to the front. It don't feel no heavier 'an the other one. I tell myself to look inside and see just what I been hauling. First, I look up and down the street. Nobody coming. Then I look over my shoulder. Little old lady done slipped there jest 's quiet 's mouse, watching me. Look like she knowed I was go'n try that.

"Ehh, Lord," she say. "Children, children. Come in here, boy, and go wash your hands."

I follow her into the kitchen, and she point, and I go to the bathroom. When I come out, the old lady done dished up the food. Rice, gravy, meat, and she even got some lettuce and tomato in a saucer. She even got a glass o' milk and a piece o' cake there, too. It look so good. I almost start eating 'fore I say my blessing.

"Helena?" the old man say.

"Yes, Alnest?" she say.

"Are they eating?"

"Yes," she say.

"Good," he say. "Now you'll stay inside."

The old lady go in there where he is and I can hear 'em talking. I look at Mama. She eating slow like she thinking. I wonder what 's the matter now. I reckoned she think 'bout home.

The old lady come back in the kitchen.

"I talked to Dr. Bassett's nurse," she say. "Dr. Bassett will take you as soon as you get there."

"Thank you, ma'am," Mama say.

"Perfectly all right," the old lady say. "Which one is it?"

Mama nod towards me. The old lady look at me real sad. I look sad, too.

"You're not afraid, are you?" she say.

"No'm," I say.

"That's a good boy," the old lady say. "Nothing to be afraid of."

When me and Mama get through eating, us thank the old lady again.

"Helena, are they leaving?" the old man say.

"Yes, Alnest."

"Tell them I say good-by."

"They can hear you, Alnest."

"Good-by both mother and son," the old man say. "And may God be with you."

Me and Mama tell the old man good-by, and us follow the old lady in the front. Mama open the door to go out, but she stop and come back in the store.

"You sell salt meat?" she say.

"Yes."

"Give me two bits worse."

"That isn't very much salt meat," the old lady say.

"That's all I have," Mama say.

The old lady go back o' the counter and cut a big piece off the chunk. Then she wrap it and put it in a paper bag.

"Two bits," she say.

"That look like awful lot of meat for a quarter," Mama say.

"Two bits," the old lady say. "I've been selling salt meat behind this counter twenty-five years. I think I know what I'm doing."

"You got a scale there," Mama say.

"What?" the old lady say.

"Weigh it," Mama say.

"What?" the old lady say. "Are you telling me how to run my business?"

"Thanks very much for the food," Mama say.

"Just a minute," the old lady say.

"James," Mama say to me. I move towards the door.

"Just one minute, I said," the old lady say.

Me and Mama stop again and look at her. The old lady take the meat out the bag and unwrap it and cut 'bout half o' it off. Then she wrap it up again and jugg it back in the bag and give it to Mama. Mama lay the quarter on the counter.

"Your kindness will never be forgotten," she say. "James," she say to me.

Us go out, and the old lady come to the door to look at us. After us go a little piece I look back, and she still there watching us.

The sleet 's coming down heavy, heavy now, and I turn up my collar to keep my neck warm. My mama tell me turn it right back down.

"You not a bum," she say. "You a man."

BIOGRAPHICAL NOTES

JAMES BALDWIN was born in New York in 1924. His career as a writer began while he was a student of Public School 24 in Harlem —he wrote the school song. His first novel, *Go Tell It on the Mountain* (1952), was acclaimed by the critics. His stories and essays have since appeared in *Harper's, Esquire, Atlantic Monthly, The Reporter,* and many other publications here and abroad. Among his other books are *Notes of a Native Son* (1955), *Giovanni's Room* (1956), *Nobody Knows My Name* (1961), *Another Country* (1962), and *Going To Meet the Man* (1965). Two of his plays, *Blues for Mr. Charlie* (1964) and *Amen Corner* (1965), have been successfully produced.

LERONE BENNETT, JR., was born in Clarksdale, Mississippi, in 1928. After graduating from Morehouse College in Atlanta, he became general assignment reporter and later city editor for the *Atlanta World*. In 1960 he became the first senior editor of *Ebony* magazine. His poems, short stories, and articles have appeared in many publications. His published books are *Before the Mayflower* (1962), *The Negro Mood* (1964), *What Manner of Man* (1964), and *Confrontation, Black and White* (1965).

ARNA BONTEMPS was born in Louisiana in 1902. He was brought up and educated in California. He first arrived in New York during the early twenties, just in time to participate in the upsurge of creativity known as the Negro Renaissance. He has written novels, some poetry and essays, and more than a dozen books for children and young adults. With Langston Hughes he compiled and edited *The Poetry of the Negro* (1949) and *The Book of Negro Folklore* (1958). Among his other books are *100 Years of Negro Freedom* (1961), *American Negro Poetry* (1964), and *Anyplace But Here*

(1966), written with Jack Conroy. For more than two decades he has been Librarian at Fisk University.

FRANK LONDON BROWN was born in Kansas City, Missouri, in 1927 and attended Wilberforce University, Roosevelt University, and Chicago Kent College of Law. His novel *Trumbull Park* was published in 1959. His articles and short stories have appeared in *Downbeat, Ebony, Chicago Review,* and other publications. He was formerly an associate editor of *Ebony.* At the time of his death in 1962 he was director of the Union Leadership Program of the University of Chicago.

STERLING A. BROWN is the dean of American Negro poets, and an occasional short story writer. He was born in Washington, D.C., in 1901 and attended the public schools of that city. He later attended Williams College. For more than thirty years he has had a distinguished career as a professor of English, mainly at Howard University. He served as adviser in Negro studies for the Federal Writer's Project. His books are *Southern Road* (1932), *The Negro in American Fiction* (1938), and *Negro Poetry and Drama* (1938). With Arthur P. Davis and Ulysses Lee he edited the major anthology of American Negro literature, *The Negro Caravan* (1941).

CHARLES W. CHESNUTT was the first Negro master of the short story form. He was born in Cleveland, Ohio, on June 20, 1858. At the age of sixteen he began to teach in the public schools of North Carolina and was appointed a principal at the age of twenty-three. From his experiences in North Carolina he found the ingredients for some of his best short stories and a number of novels. His first stories appeared in the *Atlantic Monthly* in 1887. In 1928 Chesnutt was awarded the Springarn Gold Medal, for his "pioneer work as a literary artist depicting the life and struggle of Americans of African descent." He died on November 15, 1932.

JOHN HENRIK CLARKE was born in Union Springs, Alabama, and grew up in Columbus, Georgia. He came to New York City in 1933 to pursue a career as a writer. He has been a staff member of five different publications and was cofounder of the *Harlem Quarterly* and one of the original members of the Harlem Writers' Guild. He has a life-long interest in African history and his articles on that subject have been published in journals throughout the world. Since 1962 he has been associate editor of *Freedomways* magazine. His first book, *Rebellion in Rhyme* (poetry), was published in 1948. He has recently edited two anthologies on Harlem—*Harlem, A Community in Transition* and *Harlem, U.S.A.* In addition to his other assignments he is director of the Heritage Teaching Program for HARYOU–ACT, the antipoverty agency in Harlem.

ARTHUR P. DAVIS is an essayist, scholar, and journalist. He was born in 1904 in Hampton, Virginia. He was educated at Hampton Institute, Howard University, and Columbia University, where he received his doctorate in 1942. Since 1944 he has been professor of English at Howard University. With Sterling A. Brown and Ulysses Lee he edited the anthology *The Negro Caravan* (1941).

JOHN P. DAVIS was educated at Bates College and later received his master's degree at Harvard Law School. He has been publicity director for Fisk University, head of the Washington bureau of the *Pittsburgh Courier*, and for a number of years he was editor and publisher of *Our World* magazine. Presently he is director-editor of Special Publications of the Phelps–Stokes Fund in New York. He also edited *The American Negro Reference Book* (1966).

W. E. B. DU BOIS has been called, and rightly so, the intellectual father of the black Americans. He was born in Great Barrington, Massachusetts, 1868. He was educated at Fisk University, Harvard University and the University of Berlin. During his long life he held many positions: professor of economics and history at Atlanta University from 1896 to 1910; editor of *The Atlanta Studies* until 1911; one of the founders of the National Association for the Advancement of Colored People; founder and editor of *The Crisis;* founder of the Pan-African Congresses; and first director of the Secretariat for *Encyclopaedia Africana*, which he also conceived. Among his many books are these works of fiction: *The Quest of the Silver Fleece* (1911), *Dark Princess* (1928), and *Black Flame: A Trilogy* (1958–1962). He died in Ghana, West Africa, in 1963, on the eve of the Great March on Washington.

PAUL LAURENCE DUNBAR was the first Negro writer to reach a large American reading audience. He was born in Dayton, Ohio, in 1872 and educated in the public schools of that city. His formal education ended with graduation from high school. Unable to go to college, he worked as an elevator operator and continued to write poetry. His first book of poetry, *Oak and Ivy* (1893), attracted little attention. However, his second book of poetry, *Majors and Minors* (1895), caught the eye of William Dean Howells, who wrote a commendatory preface to his third book, *Lyrics of a Lowly Life* (1896). The sponsorship of Howells helped make Dunbar a national literary figure. Other volumes of his poetry followed in quick succession. Four collections of his short stories and four novels appeared later. He died at the age of thirty-four at the height of his popularity.

RUDOLPH FISHER was born in 1897 in Washington, D.C. He prepared himself to be both a doctor and a writer—in fact, Fisher's first short story was published in the *Atlantic Monthly* as he completed his medical studies at Columbia University. Most of Rudolph Fisher's short stories were published between 1925 and 1934. Several of his short stories were published in the annual anthology of *Best Short Stories*. Fisher died in December, 1934, just as his writing began to receive national attention.

HOYT W. FULLER was born in Atlanta, Georgia, in 1927 and studied at Wayne State University and the University of Florence. He has worked for many newspapers and magazines, including *Ebony, Michigan Chronicle,* and *Detroit Tribune.* In 1965–1966 he held a John Hay Whitney Opportunity Fellowship. He has had articles published in *The New Yorker, Southwest Review, The Nation, North American Review,* and other publications. He is presently the managing editor of the *Negro Digest.*

ERNEST J. GAINES was born on a plantation in Louisiana in 1933. When he was fifteen he moved to Vallejo, California, where he attended school until he was drafted into the army in 1953. In 1955 he resumed his studies at San Francisco State College and was graduated two years later. In 1958 he received a Wallace Stegner Creative Writing Fellowship to study at Stanford University and in 1959 the Joseph Henry Jackson Literary Award. His first novel, *Catherine Carmier,* was published in 1964. His short stories have been published in *Negro Digest* and other publications.

LOYLE HAIRSTON was born in Mississippi in 1926. He served in the navy during the Second World War and afterward moved to New York City. His articles and book reviews have been published in *Freedomways* and other magazines. He recently completed his first novel, *Honeysuckle Across the Tracks.*

MARTIN HAMER grew up in Harlem and has since lived in every borough in New York City except Staten Island. He worked as an electromechanical designer while attending City College, where he majored in psychology. His short stories have been published in the *Atlantic Monthly, Negro Digest,* and *The Best Short Stories of 1965.*

CHESTER HIMES was born in Jefferson City, Missouri, in 1909 and attended the public schools of that city. After a short stay at Ohio State University he held a variety of jobs while attempting to start his career as a writer. His first short story was published in *Esquire* in 1934. Among his most notable books are *If He Hollers Let Him Go* (1945), *Lonely Crusade* (1947), *Cast the First Stone* (1953), *The*

Third Generation (1954), and *Cotton Comes to Harlem* (1965), which is one of a group of novels that he calls "Harlem domestic stories." For over ten years Himes has lived in Paris.

LANGSTON HUGHES was born in Joplin, Missouri, in 1902. He attended Central High School in Cleveland and after graduation spent two years in Mexico with his father. In 1925 he received his first poetry award in a contest conducted by *Opportunity* magazine. He is the best-known and the most versatile writer produced by the Harlem literary renaissance. His literary career extends over a period of more than forty years. Among his books are *The Weary Blues* (1926), *Not Without Laughter* (1930), *The Big Sea* (1940), and the books about the urban folk hero Jess B. Semple.

ZORA NEALE HURSTON was born in 1903 in a small all-Negro town in Florida. She was educated at Morgan Academy of Morgan College, Howard University, and Barnard College, where, with the help of Dr. Franz Boas, she obtained a fellowship in anthropology to do research in folklore. She received fellowships from the Rosenwald Foundation in 1935 and the Guggenheim Foundation in 1936 and 1938. Among her best-known works are *Jonah's Gourd Vine* (1934), *Mules and Men* (1935), *Their Eyes Were Watching God* (1937), and *Dust Tracks on the Road* (1942). Miss Hurston died in Florida in 1960.

LEROI JONES was born in Newark, New Jersey, in 1934. He attended high school in Newark and graduated from Howard University at the age of nineteen. A John Hay Whitney Fellowship in 1961 helped him continue his writing. He has produced two volumes of poetry and a book on jazz, *The Blues People*. His first novel, *The System of Dante's Hell*, was published in 1965. *The Dutchman, The Slave*, and *The Toilet*, among his one-act plays, have enjoyed successful off-Broadway runs.

WILLIAM MELVIN KELLEY was born in New York City in 1937. From the Fieldston School he went to Harvard University, where he studied under Archibald MacLeish and John Hawkes. For his first novel, *A Different Drummer* (1963), he received the Richard and Hinda Rosenthal Foundation Award of the National Institute of Arts and Letters. His other books are *Dancers on the Shore* (1964) and *A Drop of Patience* (1965).

JOHN OLIVER KILLENS was born in Macon, Georgia, in 1916 and educated in schools on both sides of the Mason–Dixon line. He served with the National Labor Relations Board before and after the Second World War. His career was launched in 1954 with his highly successful novel *Youngblood*. His second novel, *And Then*

We Heard the Thunder (1963), was drawn in part from his experiences as a soldier in the amphibian forces in the South Pacific. Besides his two novels he has contributed a number of articles to various publications and has written for television and motion pictures. His first nonfiction book, *Black Man's Burden,* was published in 1965. Killens has served as chairman of the Harlem Writers' Guild.

PAULE MARSHALL was born of Barbadian parents in Brooklyn, New York, in 1929. Her parents immigrated to America after the First World War. After graduating from Brooklyn College she worked in libraries and was a feature writer for the magazine *Our World,* traveling on assignments to Brazil and the West Indies. Her first novel, *Brown Girl, Brownstones,* was published in 1959. She is also the author of a book of short novels, *Soul Clap Hands and Sing* (1961).

CLAUDE MCKAY was born in Jamaica, West Indies, in 1890. In 1912 he came to the United States and studied at the University of Kansas for two years. He was first known for his poems, particularly for the volume *Harlem Shadows* (1922). His novel *Home to Harlem* (1928), is still the most famous book ever written about the world's best known ethnic ghetto. He was the first Negro writer to receive the medal of the Institute of Arts and Sciences. Claude McKay died in 1948.

ALBERT MURRAY was born in Nokomis, Alabama, in 1916 and spent his early youth in Mobile. He was educated at Tuskegee Institute and at New York University. A retired Army Air Force Major, he was associate professor of air science in the Air Force ROTC. Murray's essays, criticism, and short stories have appeared in *New World Writing, Life, The New Leader,* and other publications. He also contributed to the anthology, *Anger and Beyond* (1966).

CARL RUTHVEN OFFORD was born in Trinidad. After coming to the United States he wrote poetry, articles, and short stories. His first novel, *The White Face,* was published in 1941, and his second, *The Naked Fear,* in 1951. Presently, he is a part-time publisher and a full-time insurance salesman.

ANN PETRY was born in Old Saybrook, Connecticut. She studied pharmacy at the University of Connecticut and later worked in her family's drugstore. After moving to Harlem she worked for several social agencies and was later a reporter for *The People's Voice.* Her first novel, *The Street* (1946), was written on a Houghton Mifflin Literary Fellowship. Her other books are *The Country Place* (1947), *The Drugstore Cat* (1949), *The Narrows* (1953), *Harriet Tubman:*

Conductor on the Underground Railroad (1955), and *Tituba of Salem Village* (1965).

JOHN CASWELL SMITH was formerly the executive secretary of the Urban League of Greater Boston. Before coming to the Urban League as the Boston executive in 1932, he was boys worker with the Northampton, Massachusetts, Y.M.C.A. and dean of men at Virginia State College. His first short stories, articles, and book reviews were published in *Opportunity*. His story, "Fighter," published as an *Atlantic Monthly* "first," was also included in the O'Henry Memorial Collection *Best Short Stories of the Year*.

MARY ELIZABETH VROMAN was born in Buffalo, New York, in 1923 and was raised in the British West Indies. She returned to the United States and attended Alabama State College. Two of her short stories, "See How They Run" and "And Have Not Charity," were published in *Ladies Home Journal*. "See How They Run" was purchased by Metro-Goldwyn-Mayer and released in 1953 as the movie *Bright Road*. Her first novel, *Esther*, was published in 1963. She was the first Negro woman to be granted membership in the Screen Writers Guild. In 1952 she received a Christopher Award for inspirational magazine writing.

RICHARD WRIGHT was born in 1908 in Natchez, Mississippi. He had little formal education. At the age of nineteen he went to Chicago, where he worked on several jobs, mostly menial, while learning the craft of writing. In 1938 he won a five-hundred-dollar *Story* magazine prize for the best short story written by a Writers' Project worker. His book of short stories, *Uncle Tom's Children*, was published the same year. After the publication of his first novel, *Native Son*, in 1940, he became internationally famous. In addition to a Guggenheim Fellowship, he received the Spingarn Medal for achievement in the field of Negro interest. *Native Son, Twelve Million Black Voices* (1941), and *Black Boy* (1945) are the most notable of his nine published books. Richard Wright died in Paris on November 28, 1960.

FRANK YERBY was born in Augusta, Georgia, in 1916. By the time he was seventeen years old he had published several poems in small magazines. In 1944 *Harper's* accepted his story "Health Card," which won a special O'Henry Award for that year. He is the author of eighteen best-selling novels, whose sales have totaled over 21,000,000 copies. His books have been translated into nearly a dozen languages and a number of his novels have been made into highly successful movies. His nineteenth novel, *The Odor of Sanctity*, was published in 1965.

AMERICAN CENTURY SERIES

WHEN ORDERING, please use the Standard Book Number consisting of the publisher's prefix, 8090-, plus the five digits following each title. (Note that the numbers given in this list are for paperback editions only. Many of the books are also available in cloth.)

I Wonder As I Wander by Langston Hughes (0068-7)
Science in Nineteenth-Century America ed. by Nathan Reingold (0069-5)
The Course of the South to Secession by Ulrich Bonnell Phillips (0070-9)
American Negro Poetry ed. by Arna Bontemps (0071-7)
Horace Greeley by Glyndon G. Van Deusen (0072-5)
David Walker's Appeal ed. by Charles M. Wiltse (0073-3)
The Sentimental Years by E. Douglas Branch (0074-1)
Henry James and the Jacobites by Maxwell Geismar (0075-X)
The Reins of Power by Bernard Schwartz (0076-8)
American Writers in Rebellion by H. Wayne Morgan (0077-6)
Policy and Power by Ruhl Bartlett (0078-4)
Wendell Phillips on Civil Rights and Freedom ed. by Louis Filler (0079-2)
American Negro Short Stories ed. by John Henrik Clarke (0080-6)
The Radical Novel in the United States: 1900–1954 by Walter B. Rideout (0081-4)
A History of Agriculture in the State of New York by Ulysses Prentiss Hedrick (0082-2)
Criticism and Fiction by William Dean Howells and *The Responsibilities of the Novelist* by Frank Norris (0083-0)
John F. Kennedy and the New Frontier ed. by Aïda DiPace Donald (0084-9)
Anyplace But Here by Arna Bontemps and Jack Conroy (0085-7)
Mark Van Doren: 100 Poems (0086-5)
Simple's Uncle Sam by Langston Hughes (0087-3)
Stranger at the Gates by Tracy Sugarman (0088-1)
Waiting for Nothing by Tom Kromer (0089-X)
31 New American Poets ed. by Ron Schreiber (0090-3)
From Plantation to Ghetto: An Interpretive History of American Negroes by August Meier and Elliott M. Rudwick (0091-1)
Documents of Upheaval ed. by Truman Nelson (0092-X)

THE MAKING OF AMERICA
Fabric of Freedom: 1763–1800 by Esmond Wright (0101-2)
The New Nation: 1800–1845 by Charles M. Wiltse (0102-0)
The Stakes of Power: 1845–1877 by Roy F. Nichols (0103-9)
The Search for Order: 1877–1920 by Robert H. Wiebe (0104-7)
The Urban Nation: 1920–1960 by George E. Mowry (0105-5)

AMERICAN PROFILES
Thomas Jefferson: A Profile ed. by Merrill D. Peterson (0200-0)
Franklin D. Roosevelt: A Profile ed. by William E. Leuchtenburg (0201-9)
Alexander Hamilton: A Profile ed. by Jacob E. Cooke (0202-7)
Mark Twain: A Profile ed. by Justin Kaplan (0203-5)
Theodore Roosevelt: A Profile ed. by Morton Keller (0204-3)
Woodrow Wilson: A Profile ed. by Arthur S. Link (0205-1)
John C. Calhoun: A Profile ed. by John L. Thomas (0206-X)